You Bring Me Home

You Bring Me Home

NAKIA CRAMER

SENNEBEC SHORES PRESS

Published by: Sennebec Shores Press, Appleton, Maine, in the United States of America. SennebecShoresPress@gmail.com

ISBN (Paperback): 979-8-218-43859-3

ISBN (eBook): 979-8-218-43860-9

Cover Art and Imprint Design: Sennebec Shores Press and Cynthia Pace for Elevate Media

Editors: Kristen Breanne of Your Editing Lounge, Heather LaneMcCants

OTHER BOOKS BY THE AUTHOR

Alice's dreams are a stark contrast to her mundane life as a bored New England housewife and over the years, her disengaged husband James has lost sight of the vibrant and attractive woman she is. So, Alice escapes her lonesome reality through the freedom of her dreams, and finds Harrison, a wildly successful British actor with a charming demeanor, captivating green eyes, and the body of a chiseled god. The two embark on a road trip headed for New Orleans, where together they make life-altering memories that give Alice hope for a new, adventure-filled life. When she awakens to find herself back in her monotonous reality, Alice spontaneously sets off on a vacation to London alone, fueled by frustration and a desire to live a life that's as good as her daydreams. Sparks fly and flames ignite as Alice throws caution to the wind and follows her heart.

She lives in daydreams…wouldn't you?

PRAISE FOR NAKIA CRAMER

★ ★ ★ ★ ★

"Absolutely 110% recommend! She Lives in Daydreams is a 5 ★ novel that you can't put down and leaves you wanting more!" – Amazon Customer

★ ★ ★ ★ ★

"This book was deliciously written. I could not put this book down!!! Saved it for my holiday read and it did not disappoint. Loved Harrison!!! Personally related to Alice's journey of self discovery as many of us women would. I really truly felt for James's character and that story line was an excellent reminder of how important it is to communicate your needs to your partner.
Did not expect the ending and would love to see a continuation of the story!!!!!" – Kindle Customer

★ ★ ★ ★ ★

"This book was a literal dream come true! You don't have to be a Harry Styles fan to enjoy it! But if you are a fan…. You're in for a real treat!! May we all be as brave in our pursuit of happiness as Alice is in this book! I loved it!!!!" – Amazon Customer

Reviews mean more to indie authors than you might think.
If you have a few moments, please consider leaving your review
wherever you purchased any of Nakia's books.

Author's Warning

This book is a work of fiction but does contain content that some
readers may deem emotionally distressing or triggering.
For a list of potential triggers please refer to the back of the
Acknowledgements page.

Playlist

SIDE A
She - Harry Styles
I Can Dream About You - Dan Hartman
I Love Your Smile - Shanice
Escapade - Janet Jackson
Lovin', Touchin', Squeezin' - Journey
Damn I Wish I Was Your Lover - Sophie B. Hawkins
Daydreaming - Harry Styles
Crazy For You - Madonna
Make You Feel My Love - Adele
Heartbreak Weather - Niall Horan
Any Time, Any Place - Janet Jackson (Seven Minute Version)
Love Touch - Rod Stewart
You & I (Piano Version) - One Direction
I've Had The Time of My Life - Bill Medley and Jennifer Warnes
I Wanna Dance with Somebody (Who Loves Me) - Whitney Houston
Adorn - Miguel
Paper Rings - Taylor Swift
My Heart Can't Tell Me No - Rod Stewart
I'll Be Alright Without You - Journey
Don't Let it Break Your Heart - Louis Tomlinson
Love Bites - Def Leppard
I Found Someone - Cher
Let It Go - James Bay
Freedom - Wham!
Kiwi - Harry Styles

Playlist

SIDE B
Sweet Creature - Harry Styles
Steal My Girl - One Direction
Birds of a Feather - Billie Eilish
Lose Control - Teddy Swims
This Town - Niall Horan
The Way Love Goes - Janet Jackson
We've Got Tonight - Bob Seger
Lover - Taylor Swift
Gorilla - Bruno Mars
High On You - Survivor
Put a Little Love on Me - Niall Horan
Wildest Dreams - Taylor Swift
Let's Dance - David Bowie
Take Me Home Tonight - Eddie Money
Closer - Nine Inch Nails
Human - Rag'n'Bone Man
No Judgement - Niall Horan
When You Love Someone - Bryan Adams
Landslide - Stevie Nicks & Harry Styles (Live at the Troubadour)
I'm Your Man - Wham!
Goodbye for Now (Piano) - Harry Styles

A Note from Alice

Welcome! If you're new here, allow me to get you caught up on what happened in *She Lives in Daydreams,* although, if I'm being honest, the best way for you to understand it is to go read it. Nakia did an excellent job telling my story, and it would be a shame for you to miss out on the details. That girl can really paint a picture.

Anyhow, I spent decades in a marriage that left me feeling empty, ignored, and alone. My (soon-to-be) ex-husband, James, disregarded me entirely after we lost a child early in our marriage, and over time it made me feel undesirable and angry. As if all I was good for was to be his live-in maid. To escape that reality, I found myself whisked away in daydreams with a gorgeous British movie star named Harrison Edwards. I couldn't help myself. The man was sculpted, sexy, and easily managed to infiltrate my subconscious. One night I had a dream about finding him swimming in a stranger's pool, and then he asked me to drive him to New Orleans. Who'd pass up that opportunity? Not me. So off we went. Little did we know we'd fall in love on the way. Ultimately, that dream made me realize living in a marriage that made me miserable every single day was for the birds, so I left on a trip to London to try to clear my head and find some happiness for myself, even if it was only a short-term solution. But, let me tell you, what *happened* in London certainly didn't *stay* in London...

I met the actual Harrison Edwards while I was there, only it wasn't a dream. We spent time together, got to know one another, and became inseparable. In a very short time with him, I realized what my life could be if I was bold enough to step into the light that he brought to my world. I deserved that happiness, and I grabbed ahold of it with both hands. I left London with the intention of telling James it was over. Shortly after I got back home, I did just that. Then, plot twist, I found out I was pregnant. I was in my 40s, carrying the child of a movie star who was more than ten years younger than me. Crazy, right?

Then Nakia left you dangling on a cliffhanger, and here we are. Some folks missed the irony of a story about Harrison Edwards ending the way it did. But if you know Nakia's muse and you know how that muse ends a performance, you'll understand.

Check out her social media for more info on that, and please, while you're there, enjoy the view. There's a QR Code you can scan on the back cover, and her handles for her socials are listed in the back of this book as well.

If you're one of the many people who read *She Lives in Daydreams*, thank you, first of all. The story resonated with so many people all over the world, and many reached out to share how it made them feel seen, heard, and understood. It made a lot of people feel like they weren't alone, and that was the intention. That, plus you know...a little spice, a few good laughs, and all the details you could ever want about Harr...ison Edwards.

You know Nakia wasn't going to leave you hanging for too long though, right? She knows how you feel about Harrison; she knew you wanted more. So strap in, 'cause the rest of my story is gonna be fun.

Love,

Alice

For the incomparable Oscar,

the sweetest creature I have ever known.

You will forever be the greatest love of my life.

CHAPTER

1

"It's none of your business!" The familiar sound of Harrison's voice burst through my front door, his accent lost amongst his urgency.

"Listen, buddy, I don't know who you think you are," I heard James' voice boom as I rushed toward the sound of their argument.

"Respectfully, that's *also* none of your business," Harrison spat back.

"It is when it involves *my wife*." James stood a bit taller as he said the word *wife*, cocky and pointed as if trying to exert some sort of ownership over me. His forearm rested against the door frame, further blocking the entry when I rounded the corner and Harrison's face came into view.

"I'm certain she's about to be your *ex-wife*, mate." The words *ex* and *wife* punctuated by a smug momentary pause, Harrison's stance and expression resolute.

"Alright," I said calmly, "let's not." My eyebrows raised, I slid past James and leaned against the door frame, separating them, trying to hide the excitement that Harrison's presence provoked.

"Alice, who the hell is this chump?" James asked, his face flushed with anger, an air of bravado surrounding him. "He thinks he can just knock on *my* door and claim to *know* you, then demand to speak to you? Nah, not happening." He shook his head defiantly.

"James…" I paused, nervous to divulge too much too quickly as a flashback tore through my mind of my glass door shattering when he'd slammed it in a fit of rage. But he deserved to know, didn't he? I continued hesitantly, "This is Harrison, and he *does* know me. I met him while I was in London. And I'll remind you that this is also *my* door, and I am *my own* person. You don't speak for me." I shook my head, frustrated. I could see the vein in James' temple appear as his face bloomed redder with growing embarrassment. The Brit was right and he was wrong, and as he came to realize that, it infuriated him even more. His nostrils flared as his eyes narrowed in my direction.

"Oh, I see what this is now. Fucking great…" The corners of his mouth turned down as he nodded, soured at the thought of me even having a conversation with another man. "Your new man's come to claim you, has he?" His voice heavy with contempt.

"I don't think now is the time for—" I started to say, but was cut off.

"I think now is a perfect time for me to leave before your little *friend*," his fingers formed air quotes as he said it, "ends up being sent back home in a body bag." James snatched his jacket from the hook on the wall and shoved Harrison out of the way as he stormed across the porch and down the steps toward his truck.

I wasn't going to chase after him or shout for him to stay. I shook my head and sighed as Harrison reached out to hug me, but my anxiety about James turning around and inflicting physical harm only allowed me to let Harrison's hands rest awkwardly on my shoulders.

"Darling, are you okay?" Harrison asked, unfazed by James' verbal and physical assault, looking down at my belly that had yet to show any indication of new life, before looking back up at my face.

Still cautious not to embrace Harrison until James was out of sight, my eyes remained fixed on his truck. I watched as he violently backed it out of its usual spot, nearly colliding with Harrison's rental, spinning up gravel and churning dust into the sky as he took his anger out on the road. As soon as his taillights were out of view, I threw my arms around Harrison and pulled him against me.

"God, I'm so glad to see you." My words were muffled against his shoulder. "Thank you for coming so quickly."

"That's the first time a woman's ever said *that* to me." The thickness of his accent had returned, and I giggled as I rubbed my cheek softly against his neck while he laughed at his own joke. I paused to fill my lungs with the familiar scent of his spicy vanilla cologne, then cupped his perfect jaw in my hands and kissed him on the mouth, and again just below his ear on his neck, then the dimple of his left cheek. The beard he was required to grow for the film was gone, and only day-old scruff remained. My lips once again met his and I lingered there, eyes closed, savoring the feeling.

His kiss was just as I remembered, so soft against mine, intentional. My pulse raced as I tried to decide what I wanted more, to kiss him again with every bit of longing I'd felt since I saw him last, or to open the gates of my soul and just stare into his beautiful eyes.

"I've missed you so much, Alice." It was almost as if he could hear me thinking the same thing. With his forehead against mine, he looked into my eyes and one of his gorgeous chestnut curls dropped against my cheek. He raked his right hand through the tousled curls, twisting them into place while he smiled at me, his dimples a reminder that everything was going to be just fine.

"I've missed you too, babe." I embraced him; the feeling of his arms around me again was euphoric.

He took a step back, looked me up and down, and then shook his head as if in disbelief. "Such a pretty face, on a pretty neck," he whispered before leaning in to kiss my neck. Then his lips found mine again, longer this time than last. He held my body firmly against his with one arm while his fingertips traced gently behind my ear, drawing goosebumps as they trailed toward my collarbone.

"Come inside," I offered quietly against his kiss, wrapping my arms around him and pulling him in through the doorway with me.

Parts of my body pulsed with the knowledge I could have him right here, right now. His hands were on my hips and then slid up to my ribs, his mouth on mine. It felt like we'd never been apart. Granted, it had only been a few weeks, but the days felt like months as they passed, and every ounce of my being had craved him to feel complete again. I'd be lying if I said I didn't want to strip him naked right there in my kitchen and show him just how much I'd missed him...but this wasn't the place and now wasn't the time.

"Okay, we gotta stop or I'm going to lose control of myself." I laughed as I pulled away from him.

"What's the worst that could happen? You get pregnant?" He chuckled, proud of himself for being clever.

"You got jokes today, funny man?" I teased.

"I've got anything you need right here, love." He gestured with his hand along the height of his body, comically trying to be suave.

"Moving swiftly on..." I jokingly raised my eyebrows into an exaggerated look of concern before continuing. "Now that you're here, you must have a plan?" I pulled out a chair at the kitchen table for him, then pulled one out for myself and sat down.

"Well, darling, I've come to take you home. The car's outside, the jet's ready when we are," he explained as he rested his elbows against the table beside me. *I love it when he calls me darling.*

"You know I can't just pack a bag and vanish? You understand twenty-plus years of marriage, despite a pending divorce, deserves a decent goodbye, right?"

"Of course, and I've got a room booked around here somewhere so that you can do whatever properly needs doing. And then once it's done, we can vanish together."

I stared at him as he spoke and attempted to suppress my eagerness. How had I ever gotten this lucky? Harrison was wise beyond his years and more understanding than any man I'd ever known. He gave me the space to do whatever I needed to feel okay with my actions and never doubted me. He trusted my judgment implicitly and I was so thankful for him, for the humble person he was, and that celebrity hadn't turned him into something he wasn't. Harrison Edwards was everything I'd ever dreamed of, hoped for, and needed, but never had with James.

"I love you," I said sincerely. "Do you have any idea how much?"

"I do in fact because, darling, I feel the same for you. I can't wait to get you out of here, honestly. I know this has been your home, and it's beautiful, Alice, but I can't wait to get you back to London." His masculine hands lay against my kitchen table. Hands that in my dreams wore chunky jewelry, rings on every finger. Hands that in my dreams did wildly erotic things to my body...but sitting here in my home with me, in reality, international movie star Harrison Edwards was just a regular guy who somehow loved me.

CHAPTER
2

As the New England sky shifted from blue to pink and the crisp fall afternoon slipped into golden hour, I showed Harrison around the farmhouse that I'd been calling home. We wandered the grounds and I shared stories with him from the last twenty years of living here, snapping the occasional selfie with him and the sunset, and taking photos of my favorite perennial gardens in hopes I could replicate them when I got settled in London. The sky morphed from pink to orange and then into a cool glittering black as I helped Harrison load everything I planned to take with me into his car. I'd already shipped all my boxes to London last week, and aside from my overnight bag and a few lingering clothes in my dresser, the only parts left of me here were memories.

With my back against the driver's side door of his rental car, he leaned in and kissed me. I didn't want him to leave but knew he couldn't stay. He kissed me softly, again and again, each one followed by a whispered, "I love you," then climbed into the car and set off down the long dirt driveway in search of the only B&B in town. I could have gone with him; nothing was stopping me from being with him, from leaving home for the night, for the rest of my life even, but a nagging sense of responsibility and obligation had me hoping James would reappear so we could talk without an audience and hopefully clear the air before I disappeared into it.

But James was nowhere to be found. Hours had passed since he stormed off and he had yet to return. I reminded myself that texting him would only give him false hope. *Let him come back on his own terms, in his own time, Alice. If he doesn't, he'll have to live with that, not you.* While I sat staring at a muted television screen, waiting to hear his truck in the driveway like I had so many nights before, I hoped he hadn't spent the evening drowning his sorrows with his buddies, and that he'd show up here sober and calmer than when he left. Something in my gut told me the chances of that were slim to none.

James didn't handle conflict or loss well, and his response was always the same; retreat to silence, find comfort in alcohol, and refuse to acknowledge his role in it. If you just brushed it under the rug, eventually it would disappear or be forgotten. That was evident in the fact that we'd been amicably living in the same house since the divorce papers were served to him, still sleeping in the same bed though never touching one another, and cohabitating just like nothing had ever happened. He still had no idea I was pregnant despite the sickness that came and went whenever it wanted. And I wasn't about to offer up that information. I knew better than to throw gasoline on a blazing inferno, after all. So, why would I do anything to upset the balance we'd found? Keeping that secret had been a tough decision, but one I felt was necessary to get through my last few weeks here unscathed.

The irony of it all was how helpful he'd become since I first started showing signs of "illness" which was actually morning sickness. He'd look after me, do dishes, sweep, and help with laundry while I sat by, thoroughly astonished. Where the hell was that guy for twenty-two years of marriage? Why'd he show up last minute after the curtains had been drawn and the lights shut off on any possibility of saving a marriage he'd never really been a part of? I'd felt alone and abandoned emotionally, left to fend for myself with no one to keep me afloat for decades, and *now* he wanted to be the guy I'd longed for? The husband he'd become in the last few weeks was everything I'd ever wanted from him. Well, that and to feel desired by him...but that ship had now sailed and those days of feeling invisible and inadequate were gone.

Too little, much too late, James.

I grabbed a sleeve of saltines from the cabinet and a bottle of water from the fridge and made my way upstairs to bed thinking to myself, *James will show up when James shows up, I guess,* and in the meantime, I settled into what might be my last night in this old farmhouse.

It was pitch black when I heard him stumble into the kitchen downstairs, slam the door, and then fall into the table. I chuckled to myself as I heard him murmur, "Fuck," and keep moving through the house, probably bouncing off the cabinets and walls in the process. The clock across the room with its familiar blue glow said it was 3:45 a.m. *So much for sober...*

I lay there, still, wondering if I should pretend to be asleep. Wondering if he would even speak to me when he got into the bedroom. Would he even come upstairs? Moments later, the sound of the toilet flushing and then him dragging his feet across the living room floor and his clumsy footsteps on the stairs indicated he would. I listened as his alcohol-laden breathing entered the room before his clothes began hitting the bedroom floor, piece by piece. James had always been a creature of habit, so when the change left in the pocket of his jeans jingled against the floor, I braced myself for what was coming next. Then, like a corpse, he dropped himself onto the bed beside me.

Even, slow breathing, Alice. Pretend you're asleep. Nothing will be resolved if he's drunk.

Soon, I heard his labored snoring beside me, and as the volume escalated, I glanced again at the neon lights of the clock. 3:58 a.m. I closed my eyes, thankful that no conversation would have to be had tonight, and that this life was about to be replaced with a new one.

I'd done all the usual housework, cut back and weeded what was left behind after a few cold New England nights in two of my favorite garden beds, spent almost an hour on the phone with Harrison, then cleaned up and fixed myself lunch before James finally came downstairs the next day. When he did, he found me sitting at the kitchen table, sandwich in hand.

"Alice, I need to apologize." He rubbed at his tired, stubbly face with both hands.

His remorseful expression was shrouded by his hangover, and for the first time, I noticed how he'd aged. His salt-and-pepper hair had transitioned to bright silver at his temples, while the rest was in desperate need of a trim. The crow's feet and laugh lines he'd developed over the years were punctuated by his fading summer tan. There were bags under his eyes, and his face was swollen, the kind of puffiness that hangs around after a good cry. I wondered if that was what kept him upstairs so long.

"Apologize? For what? You don't owe me any apologies, James."

It's too late for that now.

"Well, I don't apologize for shoving that guy, that's for damn sure." He sat down in the chair across from me. "And I don't apologize for the way I left, but I do apologize for not coming back at a decent time, and I apologize for coming home wasted. I'm sorry." He looked me in the eye while he spoke, then rested his forehead against his folded forearms in front of him when he finished, a signature James move.

He looks pathetic, I thought and took a bite of my sandwich.

"Thank you, but it's alright. You're going to have to learn to rein yourself in, James. I'm not always going to be here. You already know that," I said calmly as I set my lunch back on my plate.

He looked up at me, his hungover eyes squinted, adjusting to the light. "I assume that's gonna kick me in the dick sooner than later if your boy's in town, right?"

"He's not a boy, James. Harrison's a grown man."

"Is he? Because he looks like a child, Alice," he said pointedly, the bass back in his voice.

I stared at him, eyes narrowed but otherwise expressionless, waiting for his attitude to adjust itself.

"Sorry," he said dejectedly.

"He's not a bad person, James. I don't expect you to be friends with him, but I do expect you to either support me in my decisions and wish me well or keep quiet altogether. It's as simple as that. Remember we agreed to support one another?"

"I know, I know. I'm sorry. It just sucks. I fucked everything up and now I'm paying for it, watching you find a new life right in front of my eyes with some young guy and bringing him to our house? That seems a bit much, doesn't it?" His emotions circled back to sadness.

I chose to ignore his question. "James, we've spent what feels like a lifetime together. Do you realize that? We've been together since, well, since I was barely old enough to know better." I chuckled. "We've seen some *shit* together, been *through* some shit. You know you'll always matter to me, and I'm always going to care for you and want what's best for you. I'll always be a phone call away if you choose to remain friends, but if you can't accept the choices I'm making about my life, us being friends can just as easily be taken off the table."

"I know." He rubbed the side of his face again with his hand. "Christ! Alice, I don't know what I'm going to do without you! You're gonna leave with him, aren't you? He's here to take you back with him, isn't he?" He dropped his head back down to his forearms.

Cue the theatrics, I thought. *Tears! Bring on the tears!*

"I'm going to be leaving this afternoon, and tomorrow morning I'll be on a flight to London, yes." My voice was matter-of-fact because any other way would lead him to believe he could change my mind.

His head shot back up, a shocked scowl on his face. "You're staying with him tonight?!"

It was obvious he'd moved his head too quickly and his hangover was showing him who was in control. He gave me a long slow blink as his eyebrows furrowed and he swallowed hard.

"James," I said blankly, ready to caution him again.

"I think I'm going to be sick." His hand rose to cover his mouth as he shot from the table and ran toward the bathroom.

When he returned he looked haggard, despondent.

"You okay?" I asked.

"Physically, I'm fine. Mentally...I'm, I don't know, sad? Heartbroken? Add a little self-loathing in there, I guess. I understand your feelings and your want for the divorce, even though I'd rather we fix it. And I get why you're leaving…as much as I hate it. I guess I'm just terrified for what my life is going to look like without you here all the time. I'm so used to leaning on you for all these little things, and even the big things. For everything, really. You've been my rock, Alice. I just wish I could go back and be yours again. I wish I'd known last night would be our last night together. I wouldn't have spent those hours in a bar..." His voice trailed off as he realized he'd squandered the time he'd had left with me.

Wish in one hand, James, and shit in the other, and see which one fills up faster. It's always what you want, what you'll be missing, not having your needs met. Selfish, all of it, I thought as I sighed.

"We can talk about this until we're both blue in the face, James. All we're doing is chasing our tails." I got up and took my empty plate to the sink, and as I set it against the stainless steel, I stood with my back to my soon-to-be ex-husband and thought about the number of times I'd been in this very spot feeling enraged, depressed, hopeless. There were days I wanted to throw a plate like this against the wall just to hear it shatter. I thought of the years I spent washing dishes and vacuuming, doing laundry, and being miserable to please someone else, to make their life easier for them, and how all I got in return was loneliness and the expectation of me giving even more. And then I thought of the man across town waiting for me, and I smiled. Maybe leaving wasn't going to be as hard as I thought.

CHAPTER 3

James showered while I packed what was left of my existence in this house into my suitcase upstairs. I went from room to room, making sure there was nothing of importance being forgotten, and stopped to stare from each of the windows, trying to burn the view into my memory, knowing I'd never be back here again. My own blood, sweat, and tears had turned this dilapidated farmhouse into a sanctuary for us, and my heart would miss the dreams I once had of this place. It had been my comfort for a long time despite it also feeling like a prison. My marriage had mimicked that concept. It's strange how the two could coexist with such similarity and still be so wildly opposite.

Downstairs, my eyes swept across the last room from outside its doorway. Soft white curtains hung silent against wavy old glass windows, that one creaky floorboard whose voice was always stifled by an antique braided farmhouse rug. My wooden bookcases vacant, their occupants somewhere over the Atlantic caged in newspaper and cardboard, and the comfiest chair in the house staring back at me from the corner, empty arms outstretched like an old friend I'd never hug again. I sighed as I turned my back on the den that had always wrapped its arms around me, and headed toward the kitchen.

With nothing left of me or for me here, I took my suitcase out to the porch where I found James leaning against one of the columns, staring out across the frost-battered fields.

"I'm going soon," I said.

"I know." He didn't turn around.

I stood there unmoving, watching him from behind. Part of me hoped he'd give me one last apology for the ways he'd made me feel over the years so I could leave this place feeling validated, but instead, he said nothing at all. We stood in silence until James spotted Harrison's car coming up the driveway in the distance.

"Alice." He turned to me, his eyes bloodshot, his cheeks glazed in tears. "I've loved you every single day since I've known you—"

"James," I cut him off, my voice cautionary.

"Alice, I need to say this before he takes you away from me forever. I need to get it out of my head or my heart will explode every time I think of you for the rest of my life. I've loved you, Alice, every moment of my life since I met you, in the best ways I knew how. I fell short most of the time, short of what you deserved, short of what you needed. I fell short of being the man you deserved, who would turn himself inside out to keep you happy, to make you feel wanted. I thought I was giving you all you needed. I thought I was making you happy. I thought you knew I've always wanted you. You've always been the only woman I ever looked at, the only one I wanted. I should have told you more often, showed you. I should have been here and listened more. And I'm so sorry for that. For letting you down. And I'll regret being the downfall of this marriage for the rest of my life, Alice. You're so beautiful and you were so devoted to me. And I wasted it all. You were everything I ever wanted. Everything I'll always want...and everything I never ever wanted to lose." New tears melted into the sheen on his cheeks as he looked at me, his eyes begging me to stay.

Harrison's car pulled up and parked just beyond the porch as I stepped toward James and hugged him for the last time. "I've loved you just as long, James. Always will, but I've got to go now," I whispered in his ear and then gave him one last fleeting kiss behind his ear as I pulled away from him. James wiped at his eyes with the backs of his sleeves, snuffed his nose, and cleared his throat to try to collect himself as the sound of Harrison's footsteps in the gravel grew closer.

"Do you need another minute? I can wait by the car?" Harrison said hesitantly from the bottom step. *God, he was a sight for sore eyes.*

I started to speak but James' voice overtook mine. "You take *care* of her, you understand? You won't find a more beautiful gift on this earth than this woman." James' right hand shot out toward Harrison who quickly climbed the stairs and respectfully, but reluctantly, shook his hand.

"Absolutely. You have my word," Harrison responded, standing straight-backed, looking James in the eye, an unspoken battle of testosterone raging between them as they stared at each other.

Eager to get this interaction over with, I rolled my suitcase toward Harrison, who softened at my glance and smiled so sweetly at me, those dimples reminding me that what was about to be would be infinitely better than what had been. I couldn't wait to get back to him.

As Harrison walked back toward the car, I heard James mutter under his breath, "Prick."

"You'll be fine," I said reassuringly.

"Right." His tone was indifferent.

"Feels like it right now, but this isn't the end of the world, James. I promise."

"Can I text you?" he asked.

"If you need to, yes, but not if you want to." I shot him a look of warning.

He drew in a deep breath through his mouth and sighed heavily, his emotions overtaking him again. His voice barely a whisper he said, "Alice, I'm so sorry. I love you."

I smiled at him, one of those strained smiles where your bottom lip rolls into your top lip, and lands somewhere between being polite and fighting back tears. Just because I was the one who chose to leave didn't mean this didn't feel like failure. It didn't mean this wasn't breaking my heart too. Tears filled my eyes and I softly whispered through staggered breaths, "Love you too." I turned my eyes away from him and headed down the steps.

I stood at the door of the car, my fingertips on the handle, and looked at the land I'd so lovingly tended, at the house I'd cared for, and then at James. A man I had poured so much love into, a man I turned myself into someone else for, a man that I had suffered loss with, and a man that had made me feel so incredibly unworthy and empty for far too long. In one quick movement, I opened the door and threw myself into the passenger seat, teetering on the edge of sobbing.

"Darling, are you okay?" Harrison questioned.

"Please just drive. I just need a moment. I'm so sorry." I wiped at my face with the collar of my t-shirt.

Harrison put the car in gear and in an instant we were driving away from my little New England farmhouse in the beautiful rolling fields. I focused my blurred gaze on James as he watched me drive out of his life, and just before he was out of sight I saw him collapse into a chair on the porch, his head in his hands.

I glanced over at Harrison, who was visibly concerned about me, my worried face red now, swollen and slick with tears, and apologized again.

"It's going to be okay, darling. I promise we'll be alright."

CHAPTER
4

We drove for a while, giving me time to get my emotions sorted and my messy face back in order, and for us to decide where to grab an early dinner. We traveled into the next city over, passing the pharmacy where I'd purchased the pregnancy test that would forever bond me to Harrison. I couldn't help but smile as we passed by and reactively squeezed his hand in mine. It's funny, looking back, how I was so terrified that day and in the days that followed, but now I was so at ease with the outcome. Harrison was as attentive and devoted as he could be from afar, eager to be a father. He'd told me as much many times on the phone in the last few weeks.

We ended up at a small truck stop diner just off the highway. Its neon "Open" sign flickered red, the N burnt out and vacant, much like the parking lot. One pickup truck and two big rigs were the only patrons there before we walked in. When we entered, all three of the men inside looked up at us, none of them seeming to realize or care who was now in their presence, then returned their focus to the meatloaf or chicken pot pie in front of them. You could hear the scraping of silverware against plates and the intermittent buzzing of that neon sign in the window but nothing more. *The food must be good if no one's talking*, I thought. We chose a booth in the back corner and I opted to let Harrison face the back wall, leaving his back toward the door and the rest of the patrons in an effort to preserve his privacy. In no time, our waitress arrived.

"Alright, what can I get for ya?" She pulled at a pen that was tucked atop her ear, one of her mousey brown curls coming loose with it, and stared at her server's notepad, her gum popping as she spoke.

"Alice, you go ahead, darling." Harrison nodded to me.

Her eyes shot to him as soon as he spoke, then narrowed as she looked him over.

That accented voice drew more attention sometimes than his appearance.

"I'm going to have the turkey club please, light on the mayo." I looked up at her and held out my menu in her direction, desperate to divert her attention. But she didn't reach for it. She stared at Harrison, eyes even more narrowed now, trying to work out in her mind exactly who she was looking at.

"Darling, can you have turkey?" he asked in a low voice.

"The turkey isn't deli meat, is it? It's real turkey, oven-roasted?" I asked her, but she was still focused on Harrison.

"Do I know you?" Her question to him was almost accusatory.

"Uh, no, I don't think we've met." Harrison shook his head and tried to shield himself by looking back at his menu, his accent deliberately more Americanized than the last time he spoke.

My arm still held my menu at her, my eyes fixed on her reactions to him.

"You seem...familiar." Her head remained cocked to the side, her lips poking out as she stared at him.

"I'm not sure where from. I've never been here before."

"Mm-hmm." Her wheels were still turning, trying to work out who he was. "Turkey's real, honey," she said to me but never took her eyes off of him.

"I'd like to have the same as my lady then, the turkey club but with *extra* mayo, please." Harrison took my outstretched menu along with his and set them down on the table in front of the waitress before returning his focus to me.

"Hmph...okay then. Strange..." Her voice trailed off as she began to write out our orders on her notepad. "Drinks?" she asked without looking up and popped her gum again.

"I'll just have water, please," I said and looked toward Harrison.

"The same for me as well. Thank you."

"Mm-hmm." She picked up our menus and looked at him again, then at me, before her eyes landed on him once more.

"You look like that British fella, the one from the movies. You sure you're not him?" she asked.

"Indeed, I am British, but that's about as far as it goes." He raised his hands as if to say, *sorry, don't know what else to tell you*, before dropping them to his lap beneath the table.

She sucked her teeth as she curled her lip and eyed him a final time, then spun around and headed for the kitchen.

"Can you hardly wait to get back to *this*?" he asked, rolling his eyes at the situation.

"We'll get through it. I've got a tough skin, babe. Don't underestimate me."

"I can certainly appreciate our unspoken understanding of when to avoid the conversation and how we play off of one another when we have to mask who I am. You're good, Alice, very clever." He winked at me and I felt his ankle land against mine under the table.

The waitress came back with our water and silverware and laid them in front of us as we sat in silence, all the while giving Harrison the most obvious side-eye. When she walked away, Harrison and I talked quietly about his filming schedule in Brazil and how he'd had to be fitted for a prosthetic beard because he'd tried, and failed, to grow one to the extent they wanted. Poor guy, his facial hair was always so patchy, but I loved the scruff when he grew it. He explained how much more time he had to spend in hair and makeup because of it and how his days were longer for it. Wake up, work out, hair and makeup for hours, filming for full ten to twelve-hour days sometimes, then back to makeup for removal, and finally back to his temporary home. It was grueling, but he said he loved it nonetheless.

We fell silent again when our food arrived in an attempt to keep our nosey waitress from putting any more pieces of Harrison's persona together, and when the coast was clear again, we chatted as we ate. I asked about Shelby and Lawrence and got up to speed on what to expect when I got to London. Sadly, Harrison would be leaving almost as soon as my feet were inside his door to head back to Brazil, but I understood. The sooner filming was over, the sooner he would be back with me.

I watched him as he ate, studying him and his striking features. The volume in his messy chestnut curls and the way the shorter hair around his temples feathered against his tan skin. The perfect symmetry of his nose and the cute way the tip moved ever so slightly whenever his lips did. His strong brow, and the endless depth of his green eyes. The rise and fall of the curvature of his lips, the sharp chisel of his jaw clenching as he chewed his food, and his beauty mark that punctuated one of his delicious dimples. His features would soon be our child's features, and I smiled at the thought. I was so taken by this man and all the littlest details that made him who he was. The aforementioned dimples appeared when he noticed me watching him.

"You okay, darling?"

"I'm okay, just lost in thought is all," I said wistfully.

"Must have been something wonderful to make you smile at me like that, even your cheeks are pink."

"I was just watching you. Admiring you. Thinking that...I'd love if our baby was a boy."

His eyes lit up. "Oh, Alice." He was beaming. "All this time I've been secretly hoping for a girl. I mean, I'll be happy either way, but hearing you say it..."

"I can see him now; a precocious, wide-eyed little miniature version of you. A holy terror with a heart of gold, a toothy grin, and endless energy. I imagine he'll be full of stories and wonder and laughter, imaginative and artistic and silly. Just like his daddy." I smiled again, feeling bashful at my admission, and looked down at my plate, then out the window beside us.

Harrison's hand was at my chin, pulling my attention back to him. "We're going to be the best parents any kid has ever had." His ocean-green eyes stared back at me, genuine and heartfelt.

"I'm thankful it's you I get to share this journey with." I leaned over the table and kissed him.

"I've wanted to be a father for as long as I can remember, so it's me who's thankful, Alice. You've given me everything I've ever wanted. Unconditional love, a true feeling of security, hope for the future, and now, a child. I've never loved anyone the way I love you, darling, so it's me who's thankful, trust me."

He leaned in and kissed me again across the table, then repositioned himself back on the bench seat. "You sure you don't want to come to Brazil with me?"

"I mean, yes, I'd love to be there with you, obviously."

"Obviously," he mimicked, acting full of himself, knowing I love the way he says the word; his accent always diluting it into something more like *ovrishly*.

I shook my head at him, dismissing his silliness. "But if I'm being honest with myself, I think my time would be better spent at the house, settling in. That way, when you get back, I'll already have all the boxes unpacked and I'll have integrated myself into the usual swing of things. And it will give me some time to get to know Shelby and catch up with Nigel, maybe see some sights I didn't see last time I was there because some handsome stranger completely distracted me and took up all my time." I scrunched half my face at him and stuck out the tip of my tongue.

"What an arrogant son of a bitch he must be. The audacity," he joked.

"Oh, you have no idea. Turns out, he made me fall in love with him and everything. Isn't that some shit?" I rolled my eyes, looking completely put out.

"The world is a cruel, cruel place, Alice." He tried so hard to look serious until I threw a piece of turkey at him.

"Heey!" He scowled and threw it back at me.

"Okay, okay! Truce!" I threw both my hands up, laughing, and noticed everyone in the diner was looking at us.

"You need to stop that, right now." His face stern as the corners of his mouth quivered, resisting laughter. "You need to calm down."

I shook my head as if I were erasing my expression and looked at him as seriously as I could. "You're one to talk," I joked as he raked his curls away from his face with his right hand and laughed even louder than the last time. "Let's get outta here, want to?" I leaned in and asked him quietly. "I'm ready to go."

He scrunched his nose up and nodded, pulled his wallet from his pocket, dropped a hundred-dollar bill onto the table, then stood and reached for my hand.

Back in the car and headed for the B&B, I asked him about his stay last night. I mentioned how I had always admired the building's exterior but had never been inside, and how even after living in town for as long as I had, I'd never met the owners. I babbled on about the architecture and surmised what historic treasures and fun stories it must hold, and with each new crazy idea I shared, Harrison's eyebrows raised a little higher and he laughed a little more.

"Just you wait 'til we get there, love," he'd said. "It is a treasure, indeed."

CHAPTER 5

The Pink Thistle Bed & Breakfast stood watch on the edge of town. Its hulking Greek revival structure was indicative of its centuries-old history, but in this era, it felt strikingly out of place. Small cookie-cutter ranch-style homes lined the street to the north, and on the south side, a dilapidated mobile home park stretched out for innumerable acres. Across the street lay a massive cemetery, many of its plots overgrown and unkempt, its lichen-dotted headstones decorated with veteran flags and forgotten flowers. We saw a lot of tourists pass through this town, but rarely did they stop for an overnight, as larger cities with modern accommodations were only an hour's drive away, leaving The Pink Thistle frequently vacant.

With no foot traffic, and only the most random reservation, the B&B was long overdue for updates and repairs. The porch was a mess of peeling paint and scattered cobwebs. Tiny flies trapped to their deaths hung stoic against the yellow glow of the porch light while stained wicker furniture was scattered around the porch, their cushions removed, one seat bottom completely missing, leaving the furniture to look like discarded trash ready for pickup.

Inside, the smell of lingering mildew and grease from tonight's dinner greeted us before any host might have thought to, along with a faded floral air freshener to try to mask the bouquet of stench and decay. I looked around. Everything was so dark. Dark wood, dark carpets, dark wallpaper. Multiple lamps were turned on but cast no usable light, and there was no one in sight, not a soul here to greet us, only the sound of Pat Sajak's voice blaring from a room somewhere in the depths of the house after someone opted to buy a vowel.

With a look of disgust on my face, I glanced around confused. "This is crazy. Does anyone work here?"

Harrison shifted my suitcase handle to his left hand. "It took a phone call last night as I stood in this very spot to get anyone's attention, but yeah. They're older, and I guess they forgot I was coming and didn't hear me arrive." He shrugged, then his right hand reached for mine.

"Do they even care that you're here now?" I laughed. "This is bizarre." I looked around. "And are they deaf?" Pat Sajak sent us to a commercial and it felt like the studio audience was right there applauding in the room with us.

Door after closed door flanked the open foyer. The only open one led to what I assumed was the kitchen in the back left corner, a harsh white flickering light shone across a visibly dirty linoleum floor where scattered crumbs cast shadows. The corners of my mouth shifted downward in disappointment.

"I think we're on our own until breakfast," he laughed. "We're in room number six. C'mon." He squeezed my hand a little tighter, leading me toward the stairs.

I felt compelled to grab a broom and go sweep the spider webs from the front porch, or turn on every light in the place until I could actually see my surroundings. It was as if I was intruding on some senior citizens' evening by sneaking into their vacant bedroom for the night; like I was some sort of squatter and Harrison was my accomplice.

I'd driven by this place my entire life and somehow never been inside.

The floorplan my imagination had created was bright, airy, and welcoming with large windows and alabaster walls. But this was...not that. I was embarrassed that he'd stayed here last night, knowing he did it just to be as close to me as he could, instead of choosing one of the fancier chain hotels in the next town over. The thought of him sleeping here, trying to find rest and recharge in this gloomy place when I know he lives for sunshine, made me grimace and sigh, the taste of air freshener and apprehension now on my tongue.

Each squeaky step was muffled by a tattered floral mosaic carpet, and each rise in elevation showed me a little more of the dark second floor. I stopped on the landing and looked around. It was simple, two rooms on each side, a lone sconce between their doors, and a shared bathroom tucked straight ahead underneath another set of carpeted stairs. The lavatory door was left ajar and I could see some of the decor from where I stood. An obvious addition when the house became a B&B, its 1970s aesthetic stood out like a sore thumb against the rest of the house.

I looked nervously at Harrison, who was a step ahead of me, still holding my hand.

"What's wrong?" he asked, biting at the inside of his lip, a playfulness in his eyes.

Eyebrows raised with a smirk on my face, I responded, "You serious?"

"What do you mean *am I serious*?" He was trying not to laugh, but I could see the telltale crinkles forming at the corners of his eyes, his dimples on the verge of making themselves known.

"Okay." I nodded. I licked my lips and swallowed before I let loose my fake excitement. "Show me where we're sleeping tonight. I can't wait to meet the ghosts in the closet. Or will they be sleeping in the bed with us?"

"Oh, they're lovely. We got along swimmingly last night. They even told me a bedtime story." He laughed, reminding me that I could be sleeping in the morgue and I'd be okay with it as long as he was beside me.

Wait, was this place ever a morgue? I ran the history of the mansion through my head, trying to remember. *I'll do some research while I lay awake tonight,* I thought.

"So, wait. There's more than one?" I asked playfully.

"Oh yes, two ghosts for every room I think." He winked at me before gently pulling me toward the stairs in front of us. *Thank God he was being a good sport about this.*

On the third-floor landing, there was once again one lone sconce on either wall, barely illuminating an antique velvet settee and ottoman straight ahead of us that sat in front of two large cloudy windows. The dingy white curtains on one side were torn, leaving the ruffled hem dangling toward the floor.

When my hand left the stair rail, I curled my fingertips across my palm and felt the grime I'd collected as I climbed the stairs. *This definitely feels like a funeral home*, I thought.

"Two rooms on this level, with private loos," Harrison advised.

To my left was room number 5, the sign on the door indicating its name "Lilac Lair," and to my right, room number 6, the "Sunflower Suite."

"A suite?" I feigned excitement, my eyes wide. "Say it isn't so!" My dirty hand landed on my chest.

"Oh, you think it's dark in here, you just wait." Harrison turned the knob and swung the door open. "Welcome to the Sunflower Suite, my love." He held his arm out in a grand gesture, ushering me in.

Inside, bright yellow wallpaper covered in thousands of vibrant orange sunflowers and dried drippy brown water spots assaulted my eyes. It was so vivid I could almost hear it buzzing, a wild contrast to the darkness that was the rest of the house.

"Wow." I stood in amazement, blinking, trying to understand why anyone would make these decor choices. I glanced around, my eyes bouncing from matching bedside sunflower lamps on top of sunflower crocheted doilies, to sun-faded sunflower curtains and a sunflower bedspread. "This is insanity," I said, realizing my still filthy hand was on my cheek before I pulled it away quickly.

Harrison plopped himself down on the bed and kicked his shoes off on the lemon-yellow shag carpet that spread out from beneath it.

"It's like a bad acid trip. I don't know how I got any sleep last night at all. Between this, and well, the ghosts," he joked.

At least he can laugh about this catastrophe, I thought to myself before setting off across the room to find the bathroom sink.

I called out to him from inside the bathroom. "Did they tell you a good story?"

I pulled back the shower curtain to reveal iron stains lining the tub under the spout, the curtain discolored with soap scum along the bottom edge. I stepped back to the sink and found the mirror in front of me speckled with age, and the hot and cold water handles squeaked when turned on from years of caked-on turquoise-colored mineral deposits.

I winced at the thought of him walking in here last night and seeing this place so dirty and run down after hours and hours of travel. *This is not what he's used to and he never once complained about it*, I thought, completely forgetting to listen to Harrison's response to my question.

"You know, once upon a time someone loved this home," I said, hoping he could still hear me with the water running. "They probably spent a fortune to build it and make it the showpiece of the town. The columns across the front porch would have shown off how stately it is, and all the windows would have given a nod to the wealth of the owner." I dried my hands and walked back into the bedroom, stopping to look out one of the windows.

"Weird, isn't it? Wealth was once defined by how many windows your house had." Without thinking, I ran my fingertips along the cracked yellow paint of the window sill, collecting dust as I went. I quickly pulled my hand away when I noticed the collection of dead houseflies that lay trapped between the window panes.

"What? Seriously? Americans are an odd lot." He shook his head as he said it.

Wiping my hands on my jeans, I walked back toward him and explained, "There were window taxes way back when, so if you had a lot of windows in your house, it showed the neighbors you could afford to not only buy them but to be taxed on them as well. I'm surprised you don't know this; it was quite prevalent in England. It's sad that this ancient, massive house ended up draped, literally, in violently floral wallpaper, and it's filthy and falling apart as we speak. It's always reminded me of New Orleans." My eyes fell to the floor as one of the worn boards squeaked under the weight of my foot.

Harrison knew how much I loved architecture, that it had been my dream long ago to become an architect, and how I found houses like these thrilling to explore. He also knew how much I adored New Orleans. One night in London we relaxed in his hot tub while I'd rattled on in full detail about the dream I'd had of him, where he and I fell in love on a whirlwind road trip as we meandered from New England to New Orleans.

His voice pulled me from my thoughts. "It's just for tonight, and it could be worse, right? I mean, imagine if we were in the Cactus Room?" He faked a shiver. "So many needles." He closed his eyes and shook his head.

I chuckled to myself. "You're such a weirdo," I said as I sat down on the bed beside him.

"But I'm your weirdo, and you're stuck with me forever now." He took my hand in his, lacing his fingers between mine sweetly before he fluttered his eyelashes at me, then crossed his eyes, and stuck out his tongue.

Of course, I appreciated his attempt to make me laugh. I'd missed him and his goofy antics so much. The terrible jokes we'd shared, the way he could effortlessly make me laugh. He understood me without me having to explain myself. Just the way he made me feel when I was in his presence was so calming.

"It was weird seeing you at the house, ya know? I felt like I couldn't properly welcome you like I wanted to."

"I think you did just fine."

"I mean, I wanted to throw myself into your arms and kiss you when I saw you, but with James there, it felt…inappropriate."

"Well, there are no more obstacles, darling, you can kiss me all you like."

"I've missed your physical being so much, Harrison." I laid my head on his shoulder. "I'm just so glad to see you again, even if it is in this haunted mansion."

"Have you been feeling better lately?" he asked as if we hadn't talked at length on the phone about it in the last few weeks, and again when he saw me yesterday.

"I'm leveling out, I think. I have more good days than bad now. Maybe it's my age that caused the sickness so early. I really don't know, but I can confidently say that I'm exhausted, mentally, emotionally, and physically. The last twenty-four hours have been a lot." I sighed.

"I'm sure it has, love, but you're here with me now, and the hard part is over."

"I'm not sure it is," I joked. "This place is kinda gross and I'm embarrassed that you had to stay here last night on account of me. I know this isn't what you're used to."

"I managed just fine, darling. The bed was comfortable, the shower had good pressure, and the company at breakfast was charming."

"Oh really? Do tell," I said.

"Well, Claire, our host, is a lovely woman and makes a fine breakfast. This morning when I got to the dining room, she'd made delicious hash browns, eggs in various forms, coffee, pancakes. There was juice and all sorts of fruit. Granted I think she forgot that I was here alone because she made enough food for an army, but I was hungry and we sat and chatted for a long time. She's a sweetheart." He seemed happy as he spoke of her. "She's actually running this place alone. Her husband died about five years ago, I think she said, and since his passing, she's been unable to handle the physical upkeep of the place. She has no children or family to help her."

"Well, now I feel terrible. I didn't realize all that. I wish I'd known her sooner, before I was leaving town. I would have loved to help her around here."

"I think I'll leave a little gift for her on our way out tomorrow after breakfast. She's doing the best she can under the circumstances, but I'd love to help her out a bit." He had a mischievous look in his eye.

"You're awful sweet, you know that?" I rolled my head from side to side, stretching my neck.

"You look tired, love. Let's settle in for the night, okay?" He walked across the room to his suitcase and snatched out one of his t-shirts. "Here, this should work." He held it out to me before returning to sit on the bed.

"You know I've got my own clothes, right?" I laughed.

"I know, I just like to see you in my stuff. But, and I can't stress this enough, I also like to see you *out* of my stuff." He grinned bashfully.

I took the shirt from him and drew it up to my face, taking a deep breath. "I can't even put into words how much I've missed you." I exhaled, and took a step toward the bathroom to change my clothes.

"Now hold on a moment. Don't go yet." He reached out and grabbed my hand, turning me back to face him.

I watched his hands as he gently placed one on each of my hips and drew me closer, stopping only when I was standing directly in front of him, both my legs between his knees as he sat at the edge of the bed.

"Alice?" His voice was quieter, more serious.

"Hmm?" My eyes remained focused on his hands against my body.

"It feels like it's been ages since I've touched you." His hands slid upward and found the warmth of my bare skin. Lifting the hem of my shirt slowly, he waited until I made eye contact with him then leaned in and kissed the front of my exposed stomach, soft slow kisses at first, his lips lingering gently against my body before moving closer to my waist, the fleeting presence of his tongue warm against my flesh. The t-shirt he'd handed me moments ago slipped from my hand and landed at my feet.

His right hand reached further up beneath my shirt and unclasped my bra while the other landed on my ass, helping to lift me onto his lap. His eyes never left mine as I sat there straddling him. Silence. His nostrils flared and a crooked smile spread across his face as he pulled the corner of his bottom lip into his mouth, letting it fall back into place slowly. He was pacing himself. His eyes fixed on mine caused my breathing to deepen, my chest rising and falling closer to his face. The palm of his right hand moved further up my back, the strength of his forearm against my spine, his thumb and fingertips lightly gripping the back of my neck. With a lift of his elbow, the length of his forearm flipped my shirt up and over my head, leaving it pooled against my chest between us.

He gently brushed the stray strands of hair away from my face. "All I want to do tonight is kiss you, Alice. Every inch of you." The tip of his index finger trailed softly from the bridge of my nose to the tip, then dropped to my lips, parting them softly, his mesmerizing eyes remaining locked on mine. He kissed my bottom lip, sucking it gently into his mouth, his tongue grazing it before I felt his teeth playfully bite at it. He took his time, his fingertip slipping down my chin, tracing the front of my throat slowly, raising goosebumps on my skin. He continued to kiss me, the warmth of his breath landing against my top lip as his breathing deepened. Lower still, his fingers traced the rise of my cleavage before pulling the shirt and bra from between us and dropping them to the floor without ever breaking eye contact. His chin and then his cheek nuzzled against my breast before his mouth worked its way back up to meet mine.

I'd missed the way his hands felt against my skin, his impressive, soft hands that were now against my ribcage, large enough to make me feel small against them, strong enough to make me feel fragile, and gentle enough to make me feel incredibly feminine. They cupped my breasts as he kissed my earlobe, my face lifting to the ceiling, exposing more of my neck and granting him permission. His index finger traced the H. tattoo I'd gotten in London when I was with him last and he smiled, then caressed my back up to my shoulders and stopped when he felt the tension in them.

"You carry your emotions here." His fingertips pressed harder against the tightness, circling, trying to release the knots beneath my skin. "Let me take care of you, Alice." He stood, holding me tight against his torso, and turned to set me down on the edge of the bed.

He knelt and removed my shoes for me, rubbing each foot in succession, then picked up the t-shirt I was meant to put on earlier and motioned for me to lift my arms. The cool cotton was soft against my skin. He took me by the hands, silently asking me to stand. He unbuttoned my jeans and slid them down over my hips, and when I repositioned myself at the edge of the bed, he proceeded to pull them from my legs and toss them into a chair in the corner.

"Lay back, rest." He kissed me softly on the mouth, then pulled back the covers and fluffed the pillows behind me.

All I wanted was to give myself to this man, knowing our time together was limited, but I was exhausted from everything the day had thrown at me.

"I'm sorry," I offered.

"Never a need to be sorry, love."

"Will you keep me safe from the ghosts?" I asked quietly, pulling my legs up onto the bed and snuggling under the hideous quilt.

"I'll never let anything happen to you," he said softly, peeling his clothes off down to his boxer briefs before crawling onto the bed and spooning me from behind. "Either one of you." The warmth of his palm landed gently against the lower part of my belly, his fingertips moving back and forth, rhythmically caressing me toward sleep.

How on earth did I ever get this lucky?

CHAPTER

6

The morning was chillier than I expected when we left the B&B, and a haze of fog hovered close to the ground as Harrison and I tucked our luggage into the trunk of the rental. Claire watched us from the front porch, pulling her cardigan around her tightly to keep the damp cold from her frail frame. She waited for us to pull away, waving lovingly like a grandmother sending her grandkids back home after a long weekend. She'd yet to see what Harrison left for her in our room, and I secretly wished I could have seen her reaction when she found the check. Claire's struggles would soon be a thing of the past.

With Harrison at the wheel, we began our journey to the small airstrip where his private jet was waiting for us, about a thirty-minute drive beyond the outskirts of the opposite side of town. Once upon a time, our little town had been frequented by the wealthy on their way to their summer homes on small outlying islands, and this airstrip had served as their means to get to said islands, but those days were long gone since the airport in Boston had swallowed up their business. It had been months since I'd driven past "the strip," but even then, the grass had grown so tall you could barely see through the chain-link fence. It looked abandoned and had for years, the main building looking rundown by anyone's standards and rarely used. There were a handful of people who still came in when someone needed them; this morning I was thankful for them and for the fact that we didn't have to travel all the way to Boston. The sooner we could get on the jet and back to London, the happier I'd be, even though it meant Harrison would be leaving again. I was ready to start my new life and leave this one behind.

"No ghosts last night, huh?" I asked, breaking the silence.

"I think you intimidated them," he joked. "Maybe they only haunt the people who are sleeping alone."

"I gotta say, I'm a little disappointed. I guess they...*ghosted* me." I winced, jokingly.

"Maybe they went on vacation." He shot me a smirk.

"Oh? And where do you think they went? The Boo-hamas?"

"I was thinking more like Mali-boo," he teased.

"Well, either way, I bet they're having an un-boo-lievable time." I flipped my hair with my hand, acting fancy.

"Oh, I'm sure they're feeling fab-boo-lous!" His chin poked out back and forth with each syllable.

"Oh my God, you're a nut."

"Do you have any idea how much fun we're going to have with a tiny version of us to share these jokes with? I can't wait, Alice. Honestly." I watched as his happiness made his dimples and the tiny lines around his eyes appear.

Truth is, I couldn't wait to see him as a father. He was built for it. Whimsical in his approach to life, happy and carefree. Silly jokes and always wanting to take care of people and bring them joy. He was a natural caregiver and knew how to give those in need the comfort they were seeking, myself included. He'd shown up for me at the exact right moment, and knowing I had the rest of my life to look forward to with him was all I needed to make me happy these days.

"I love you." I smiled and then turned to look out the passenger side window, familiar places whizzing past.

"Well, I love you, darling."

After a brief pause, I said, "I think I'm actually going to miss this place."

I felt his hand land on my left knee as he continued to drive. "We can come back any time you like, love."

We slowed to a stop at the only light in town. My eyes scanned the buildings of Main Street one last time. To my left, the old café where the older gentlemen would sit at the counter and have their morning coffee and the teenagers spent their afternoons. The shuttered pet store beside it that had been void of activity for years, and the ladies' clothing boutique that was barely still in business. Beyond them sat the library that I'd loved, and the fire station abuzz with trucks returning from a call. My town was small and antiquated, struggling to keep air in its lungs, but it had been home. I'd loved it here.

None of the sleepy little shops were open yet; it was too early still. From the corner of my eye, a familiar plaid flannel shirt and battered blue jeans stood with their back to me, and as I turned to get a better look at the figure, I saw the palms of his hands raised, holding him and his downturned forehead firmly against the large panes of glass in front of him. It was James, and those panes of glass housed the hardware store where we first met twenty-two years ago. The foliage on the daisies at his feet were stiff and brown from the frost we'd had, but one small blossom hung vigilant, mimicking James' posture, clinging to life despite the cold it had endured.

Just as the light turned green, James turned and his eyes met mine. His forehead and cheek were smeared with black marks, his hair disheveled, and he carried a look of absolute exhaustion. The front of his clothes were dirtier than his face, the sleeve of his shirt ripped, and half of the bottom of his flannel shirt was untucked against his relaxed jeans. *Had he been in some sort of accident? Why would he be down in town this early looking like this?* I couldn't understand what I was looking at beyond the tearful, downtrodden expression on his face spelling out just how lost this man already seemed to be without me.

Oblivious, Harrison's foot found the gas pedal and as the car accelerated, I was carried away from James for the last time, our eyes still locked on one another; mine alive with concern and James' void of any life at all, yet somehow pleading with me to run from the car and help him. I couldn't turn away from him. Internally I was screaming, desperate to make sure he was okay. It had been my purpose for so long to take care of him that to just shut it off didn't come easily. I sat silent, internally panicking, stifling a sob, strapped to my seat, staring. The look on James' face as he slipped further into the distance gave me no answers as to what had happened, and only left more ache in my chest that something was terribly wrong.

I watched him in the side mirror until he faded entirely from my sight, and tried to shield Harrison from realizing the sadness that was now pouring from me by keeping my face turned tightly toward the passenger window. The shops whirled past, nothing but a teary blur, fewer and fewer until Main Street turned into guard rails and then to weather-beaten fields. Beige ground, gray fog, white sky.

"Darling, what can I do to help?" Harrison asked quietly, shifting his hand higher to my thigh after noticing me wipe at my face with the sleeve of my shirt.

"I'm sorry," I apologized again. I felt like all I'd done was apologize to him lately. "I just need a little time is all. I hope you understand, this isn't easy for me." I still couldn't look at him and watched out the window as the fields turned into a forest of leafless trees.

"I know. Take your time. Let it all out. You can't heal unless you purge out the emotion. I'm right here though, and you don't have to feel awkward if you need to talk about it."

Before I could form a response, my eyes caught sight of angry black smoke plumes lying like a crumpled blanket in the sky. It wasn't new. It looked like it had been hanging in the air a while, barely moving, only its outer-most edges beginning to dissipate. Could this smoke have come from flames knocked down by those fire trucks I saw pulling back into the station as we came through town earlier? I rubbed at my eyes, trying to wipe the blur of the tears away, my mind trying to calculate what I was seeing.

"Jesus Christ," I whispered against my hand that was now covering my mouth.

"What's wrong?"

"I think..." My other hand landed on my chest as I struggled to find the words. "Oh my God."

"Love, what is it?" Harrison's voice was more pointed this time.

As the pavement we were traveling met the edge of my old gravel driveway, I saw another fire truck crest the hill and descend toward us. No lights, no sirens, no urgency. Only more black smoke rose from behind it, billowing from the hollow space where my house once stood.

"Harrison, I think he..." I paused, blinking hard, trying to will myself to make it all make sense. "Jesus Christ! I think he burned my house to the ground." I was mystified.

"Do you want me to turn around and go back?" he asked as he slowed the car to a stop on the side of the road.

I just sat there, looking back in the direction of where the farmhouse used to sit, the fire truck pulling out of the driveway and heading back toward town.

"I...I don't know." I turned to look at him slowly, my eyes vacant with disbelief.

"Let's go back. You'll feel better if you do," he offered again. His hand enveloped the gearshift, but the car remained still.

I scowled to myself, picturing the soot smeared on James' face. *Had he done this intentionally? He looked like he'd been in a struggle. Maybe it was an accident? He wouldn't do that, after all the time and money and all the love we had poured into that house. It had to be an accident. It had to be, right?*

"No." I shook my head in defiance. "I don't need to see it. I don't *want* to see it." I faced forward, eyes on the road ahead of us, my disbelief turning to anger.

"Are you sure? We're right here, Alice. It's no problem."

"NO! Harrison! I said I don't want to!" I barked back at him and began to cry, instantly remorseful for shouting at him. "I'm so sorry. I know you're just trying to help." Both my palms covered my cheeks, fingers over my eyes, trying to hide my emotions.

"It's fine, darling. I promise you it is. We can go see, or if you're sure you don't want to, then we'll continue on."

When I moved my hands and glanced at him, he had such a sweet look on his face. His eyes bright and reassuring, his closed-mouth smile still enough to bring out his dimples. I wiped my palms on my pants, then reached out with both hands and held his face before kissing him slowly.

"I'm so sorry. I love you." My eyes still closed from our kiss, I exhaled as I spoke.

"I love you, darling. Always, through everything, no matter what." He stared at me a moment, hesitant to leave. "If you're sure you want to go, we'll go." His eyes continued to question me.

I wiped at my cheeks with the backs of my hands and cleared my throat. "Yes, I'm sure. It's not my problem anymore. I've said my goodbyes. I'm done here." My indifference was surprising, even to me.

Harrison put the rental back into drive and we pulled away, literally and figuratively, from the life previously known as mine.

CHAPTER 7

Two days ago, when I'd called to share our news, Harrison left Brazil in such a panic to get to me that he only waited long enough for the pilot to arrive. There were no crew on board, and thus we were left alone for our seven-hour flight back to London. Most of that time was spent cuddled together on the couch swapping stories or watching movies under the same soft blanket where he'd first explored my body with his hands, the first time he'd noticed the birthmark on my thigh, and the first time I'd ever really let myself get lost in my attraction to him. It was a surreal experience to close my eyes and rest my body against a man who used to live purely in my daydreams. To know those daydreams became my reality and not only had I survived the hardest days of my life, leaving my husband, divorce pending, but that I was carrying the child of the man in those daydreams, on a flight to share the rest of my life with him in London. Even my wildest imagination hadn't given me this kind of happily ever after.

But I'd be lying if I said I wasn't still thinking about the look on James' face when he turned around this morning and found me looking back at him, and the black smoke billowing up into the sky from what remained of the house I loved so much. All the while Harrison sat beside me oblivious, watching films to pass the time while my mind spiraled. Surely James hadn't done it on purpose; it was all he had left of us. Wouldn't he be clinging to it? I really couldn't picture him holding a match to a gasoline-soaked house, but I definitely *could* imagine him feeling so lost in life that he'd left the stove on trying to cook for himself for the first time in years or walking away after lighting the fireplace and forgetting to put the screen in front of it. Accident or not, the look on his face this morning was one of complete and irreparable devastation, and now he really had nothing left. There was a part of me that wanted to call him, to reach out and make sure he was okay, but any contact initiated by me would only give him false hope. And, if he'd done this on purpose, I'd be falling right into the trap he'd set out in front of me.

There's a reason why the windshield is so much bigger than the rearview mirror. Remember what's ahead of you, not what you just walked away from. I kept reminding myself, *it's not my problem anymore. It's time to be happy, Alice. I need to stand in my truth. Nobody can drag me down.* Eventually, between Harrison's warm chest against my cheek, his rhythmic breathing, and the sound of his heartbeat coupled with the movie in the background, I fell asleep, finally free from the swirling chaos inside my head.

When we landed, there was Lawrence in his svelte black suit, waiting for us on the tarmac, the back door of the SUV open, inviting us in. He stood regal at the vehicle's door, ever the professional. I waved excitedly in his direction as I approached, prompting his features to soften.

"Lawrence! I've missed you!" I threw my arms around him and leaned in when he hugged me back.

"It's good to have you back, ma'am." He dipped his chin, acknowledging Harrison. "Boss." In the background, men loaded our bags into the back of the SUV.

"We're headed to the house, Lawrence. No stops between here and there."

Lawrence acknowledged Harrison's request and then smiled in my direction. "I've a surprise for you in the car." He looked pleased with himself as he spoke.

I poked my head into the vehicle and much to my surprise, there was Nigel sitting up front in the passenger seat.

"NIGEL! Oh my gosh, get out here so I can hug you!" I excitedly pulled at the door handle and reached for him, then swaying back and forth, I hugged my friend. "I missed you!"

"I missed you too." He stepped back and held me at arm's length to look me over. Lowering his voice and narrowing his eyes he said, "Something's different..."

I leaned back in for another hug and whispered in his ear, "I'm pregnant, shhh."

He held me away from him once more. "STOP IT!" His hands rose and covered his entire face, then slid down so his fingertips landed against his cheeks, his eyes wide.

I shrugged, a jokingly cocky look on my face.

"Well then, we have a lot to discuss, don't we?"

"And we'll have plenty of time to do it. I'm here now, for good."

One eyebrow lifted, he asked, "But what about you-know-who?" His head wobbled in exaggeration.

"I left him. Paperwork's been served." I dusted my hands together and made a check mark motion in the air.

"Girl." His eyes widened again and his hand lay spread across his chest dramatically.

The sounds of the back hatch slamming closed interrupted us followed by a quick, "We all set?" from Lawrence.

"I know I am," I said, taking Harrison's hand as he helped me into the backseat of the car.

"Let's go," Nigel said as he jumped back into the passenger seat.

Lawrence has always been Harrison's driver. A strong, quiet man, thoughtful and devoted to his job, and devoted to Harrison's safety, he straddled the line of driver, bodyguard, and also a long-term friend. We'd barely scratched the surface of getting to know one another when I was here before because I'd been so swept up in Harrison, but with him going back to Brazil and Lawrence staying here, it would allow me to dive a little deeper with him.

Nigel on the other hand, had been my Uber driver the last time I was in London, and we'd become fast friends. He's sassy and hilarious and incredibly knowledgeable about the ins and outs of the city. Nigel was also the person I'd requested as my own personal driver if the opportunity ever arose, and that was the topic of discussion for our entire ride back to the house.

"Nigel, how are you getting on under Lawrence's tutelage?" Harrison asked through the open partition.

I looked at him, confused. Last I knew they hadn't even interacted yet. *What have I missed? I haven't been gone that long, have I?*

Nigel shifted in his seat to face us. "Quite well. He's an excellent teacher, and I want to thank you again, sir, for the opportunity."

"Please, none of that sir stuff; just Harrison. And welcome to the family. What my Alice wants, she'll get, and you came highly recommended." He squeezed my hand in his.

"She's a doll, isn't she?" Nigel winked at me.

"She is indeed." Harrison looked over at me, pausing a moment before smiling and then kissing me on the cheek.

I'll never get over the dimples, I thought.

"I've been doing ride-alongs to get used to the way Lawrence does things, and while you're away in Brazil, that will continue."

"Yes, I should be wrapping up filming in about six weeks. That should be sufficient time for you to learn what Lawrence has in store for you, then you'll be on your own with Alice. You'll be in a vehicle identical to this one, that way we can utilize both of you to create diversions if need be. Has Lawrence taken you for defensive driving lessons yet?"

"Not yet, I think that's..." He hesitated and looked to Lawrence for guidance.

"Next week, boss. We'll be sure to get him up on two wheels." Lawrence smirked.

I pictured the large SUV rounding an orange traffic cone at high speed, both passenger tires lifting off the ground, the SUV teetering. My eyes shot to Harrison, worried for Nigel.

He shrugged in response. "It's a part of the job. You've got to be ready for anything. Your safety is my priority." He leaned in, his mouth barely against my earlobe, and whispered, "You and our little one." He then pressed his parted lips against the space just behind my ear.

"We're almost home, aren't we?" I wanted this man all to myself in the privacy of our own home.

Harrison looked at me, his eyes sentimental. "Yes, darling, we're almost home."

CHAPTER
8

Lawrence and Nigel left together once our bags were unloaded. Shelby had long since completed her daily tasks and gone home, and Harrison and I were alone together, finally. The time change hadn't affected me yet, but it was late here in England. Harrison was leaving in a few hours to return to Brazil, and I sensed his thoughts were in the same place mine were. He dropped our bags on the entry rug and closed the front door, the sound of the automatic locks confirming there would be no more interruptions.

"It's been a long day; are you tired?" The words fell from his mouth quietly.

I looked up at him and shook my head slightly. Then without a word, Harrison turned to face me, his green eyes finding mine, shattering every window that ever existed to my soul, infiltrating every single one of my indecent thoughts. His nostrils flared, and I knew exactly what he wanted. His fingertips against the underside of my chin, he lifted it toward his, his hands shifting to cradle my face before moving to press against the back of my neck. He paused, licked his lips, and smiled.

I watched him as he studied my face, his dark eyelashes against his tan skin, the curve of his lips, and the stubble emerging after a few days of neglect. My breathing deepened just thinking about feeling his bare body against mine again. He stepped toward me, and pressing my back against the front door, he lightly kissed my bottom lip, teasing, his mouth barely touching mine. Then he stopped and looked into my eyes before kissing me again, this time hungry. The way he'd missed me while we were away from one another was obvious now. The sound of fervent breathing was broken by the tumbling of one of my shoes falling down the entry steps as I kicked them off.

The strength of his biceps, the softness of his skin, and the feeling of his mouth against mine drove me crazy as I lifted one of my legs to wrap it around his. His fingertips slipped down my back, lower and lower still, until the palms of his hands cupped my ass, lifting me against him. With my mouth against the side of his neck and my hands in the curls of his tousled hair, he carried me down the entry stairs and across the living room while my tongue grazed his bottom lip, pulling it into my mouth, playfully biting at it. I kissed across his cheek, his hair spilling out between my fingers, and my mouth landed on his earlobe, drawing it into my mouth and sucking gently before my tongue ran along its edge. My hands gripped the bulge of his biceps as he ascended the steps, carrying me toward the bedroom.

Like déjà vu, my mind slipped back to the first time he carried me into his bathroom with its black marble floors, the hammered copper bathtub, the teak benches, and lush plants beneath copper showerheads. That night we'd danced in the kitchen, cooked dinner together, and then he'd carried me to this shower and made love to me in the shadows that danced around us from the bedroom lights.

Harrison held me against him as he bypassed his bedroom and we found ourselves once again in his bathroom, the heated marble warm against my bare feet when he set me down. He pulled his t-shirt up and over his head and threw it backward, his eyes fixed on mine. I stood watching him, craving him. The defined muscles at his ribs moved with every breath he took and his abs, tanned to a golden bronze from the Brazilian sunshine, flexed as he moved while parts of me began to pulsate.

"Alice." His voice was low as my name rolled from his tongue.

I held his gaze and said nothing. *I love the way he says my name and he knows it.*

He unbuttoned his jeans and lowered the zipper without ever breaking eye contact with me. The muscles of his upper body tightened and relaxed with each movement causing the gold cross that lay nestled between his pecs to catch and reflect light. I watched his every move; the muscles in his hands, his forearms, his chest; veins swollen and ever present from strenuous daily workouts as a means to keep him film-ready. I pulled my bottom lip into my mouth slowly as I looked up and my eyes met his.

"I've missed you." His eyes said it as much as his mouth did. His thumbs slipped slowly under the black band of his boxer briefs and pushed them and his jeans down ever so slightly, exposing the deep v-cut of his hips. The trail of wispy dark hair that began below his belly button teased my eyes lower until it disappeared out of my view, inviting my imagination to find the trail's end. He smiled knowing where my mind was, his eyes lustful, the sight of his left dimple emerging just enough to further quicken my pulse.

"I've missed you too." I swallowed hard and held my gaze upward, focusing on his eyes nearly eight inches higher than mine, trying to avoid looking at his sculpted chest only inches away from my mouth.

He took a step closer to me; I could feel the heat from his body against my face.

"Yeah?" He leaned in, his baritone whisper landing just in front of my ear as he grazed his cheek against mine. The softness of his lips against my neck made me inhale sharply.

"Yeah..." I whispered to the ceiling, my head falling to the side as his mouth explored my neck. His hands made quick work of unfastening my jeans and dropping them to the floor.

My fingers were in his hair again as I inhaled deeply, filling my lungs with the smell of his skin, his hair, his cologne. I savored every moment because I knew in a few hours it would be six long weeks before I would have this opportunity again. Gently, Harrison moved my hair, exposing the top of my shoulder, then pulled the neck of my shirt to the side, dragging my bra strap with it, and traced his tongue across my collarbone, slowing to concentrate as his other hand reached back to turn on the showerhead above us.

Warm water fell like rain from the ceiling, and I laid my head back, allowing it to wash down over my body as Harrison pulled my shirt off and slung it against the glass wall. His mouth landed on my chin and kissed down the front of my throat, his tongue warm against my skin as my fingertips reacquainted themselves with the contours of his back. My mind flashed back to the way I'd taken control of him the last time we were in here, straddling him on the bench, the curls of his hair collecting water droplets against his forehead, the way he'd jokingly called me a tease before I used my body to drive him crazy and then prove him wrong.

I unhooked my bra, and Harrison's fingers delicately slipped the straps from my shoulders, letting it fall to the floor, the warmth of his hands replacing the garment against my body. He caressed my bare skin with his hands and his mouth, focusing his attention on my breasts before dropping to his knees and kissing my belly, nuzzling his cheek against it, reminding me what we'd created together the last time I was here. I pushed his dark curls away from his face and held his head as he continued to kiss my abdomen, his hands lingering at my hips, fingertips teasing the skin at the edges of my panties until my legs started to tremble. I wanted to feel him inside me, right now, but I also wanted to leave him with a memory that would keep him anxious to get back home.

I lifted his chin, our eyes meeting again. "I love you," I whispered as I pulled him back to his feet.

"I love you, so much, Alice." His words muffled as his mouth met my neck again.

I pushed his jeans down over his hips and ran my hands backward over his boxer briefs, my palms landing against his ass cheeks. "This is nice." I squeezed with both hands, then trailed my fingertips back up to the top of the band in the front, letting my ring fingers linger at the indentations above his hips, my thumbs teasing toward the dark trail of hair that was now within reach. The impurity of my thoughts was beyond my control as I slowly slipped both hands beneath the band of his underwear and reached for his ass again. But this time, I pulled them to the floor and pushed them away before kissing up the insides of both of his legs, stopping to dedicate attention to each of the tattoos I encountered on the way, the lion on his thigh just as wet as I was when I reached it. My hands had covered the majority of his body, with one exception, and as I gently ran my tongue upwards along the length of his shaft, I heard him moan when I reached the tip.

When I looked up, his head was laid back, water from the shower had diverted itself into tiny channels from his neck to his chest, and down past his abdominal muscles, glistening as it snaked its way toward his feet. This man was perfection. From the beautiful messy curls on top of his head, to the cerulean green eyes that could ignite fires within me, to the way his perfect toes lay against the marble floor, I was captivated by him.

Harrison's eyes remained closed until he realized I was fully standing in front of him. Then he watched me as I admired his body, tall and firm, my eyes falling from his gaze to his dimples, down to his tattooed collarbone, his pecs to his abs. My eyebrow rose when I saw just how ready he was to make love to me, and I looked up at him again.

"Bloody hell, Alice, you're the most beautiful creature I've ever known..." He drew in a deep breath as he took me by the hand and sat himself on the bench against the wall, leaving me standing, facing him, the showerhead above me sending water cascading down my back.

"You okay?" Smirking, I tipped my chin down, then shifted my eyes up at him.

"I think we've had this conversation before, in this same place," he said, his expression teasing my memory.

"And how'd that work out for you?" I stepped closer to him.

"Wonderful." His dimples were showing.

"Yeah?" I placed his hands on my breasts. "I'm pretty sure you called me a *tease*." My gaze lustful, locked on his eyes.

"Mmph. That doesn't sound like something I'd say…" His brows furrowed and his expression became intense as he focused on the movement of his own hands. Delicately concentrating strength and softness around my nipples, he licked his lips and looked up at me, his eyes asking permission for more.

"You still think I'm a tease, Mr. Edwards?" I bit my bottom lip, knowing it drove him wild, my knees landing against the front of the soft teak between his spread legs.

He shook his head slightly, his eyes still fixed on what his hands were doing to my breasts. I watched him, his eyes becoming more intense, his touch alternating between barely there and rough pinching, trying to elicit a reaction from me.

"What do you want, Harrison?" I moved his hair away from his temple and laid my arms around his neck.

He scooched forward and looked up at me. "I want you, Alice, all of you."

His hands dropped to grip my hips, pulling my belly against his mouth; he kissed below my navel, pressing into my soft flesh. His hands explored me, my ribcage, my back, tracing again along the H. tattoo, and he grinned, proud of himself. The warm suction of his mouth against the underside of my breast made my knees weak, and when his fingertips fell to my hips again, he stared into my eyes and peeled the wet panties down over my legs.

My own wet hair clung to my body as I lifted one knee onto the bench, then the other, and held my body in front of him, dropping down slightly, teasing the tip of his erection with everything he longed for. I watched him lustfully as I moved, kissed his forehead, then the bridge of his nose. And as I slowly lowered myself down onto him, allowing him to penetrate me, I kissed him deeply on the mouth. I'd missed him and the way he loved my body so much. His arms wrapped around me tightly and held me down on top of him as he leaned back against the cold tiles on the wall, his hips lifting slightly, pushing himself deeper into me.

I couldn't stop myself from moaning. I didn't want to. The way he made love to me was worth screaming about. It was attentive and unselfish and unrelenting. The sounds we made echoed off the shower glass and reverberated from the tiles. Harrison didn't care that I wasn't in perfect shape. He didn't care that my belly wasn't flat. He loved me for the person I was, not for the way my body looked, though he loved that too. He celebrated every inch of me that night, in the shower where we'd climaxed together, and again in his bed where our wet bodies left damp outlines on the sheets.

Afterward, we lay together, caressing one another, sharing kisses with the knowledge that it would be more than a month before we could touch each other again, before we could really look into each other's eyes and confess our love for one another. Despite Lawrence waiting in the driveway and Harrison's jet waiting for him at the airport, he took his time, and whispered repeatedly in my ear, "I love you"—"I love you"—"I love you"—"You're my whole world, Alice," and I never felt more adored in my life as I did that night, in my new home, with the love of my life.

CHAPTER 9

I woke alone the next morning to the smell of bacon and French toast wafting up from the kitchen. Glancing at the pillow beside me, I thought about how Harrison had been here just hours ago. The indentation he'd left behind was proof, but he'd left for Brazil while I was asleep, whispering, "I love you" before disappearing down the stairs. I rolled over and buried my face against the softness of his pillowcase, wishing he was still here. A long, slow inhale filled my lungs with the scent of his hair, reminding me of the way his right hand would rake his curls away from his face, twisting them on top of his head to secure them. His hands were magic, and I sighed longingly as the night before replayed in my head. I understood his work obligations and knew it wasn't forever, but that didn't stop me from wanting him here with me.

Today would be full of unpacking, getting settled, and acquainting myself with my new home. As I sat up to greet the day, I noticed a box sitting on my nightstand, a royal blue ribbon tied neatly in a bow holding its contents captive with a small tag on top that simply stated *My Love*. I pulled gently on the end of the ribbon and let it fall away before lifting the top. Inside, a small card, and another box, but this time, Tiffany blue with a white ribbon.

What has he done? I thought as I pulled out the tiny envelope.

My dearest Alice, wear this as a sign of my love until I can present you with something proper. I love you, XX H.

I opened the box to find a diamond solitaire necklace, emerald cut just like the engagement ring he'd given me in the dream I'd had of us in New Orleans.

He remembers the tiniest details, I thought as I pulled it from the box and clasped it around my neck. It was stunning, and I immediately felt undeserving of such a beautiful gift.

While I sat at the edge of the bed, I let my changing body tell me how I felt. Thankfully the morning sickness didn't seem to be rearing its ugly head, and I was looking forward to the breakfast I knew Shelby had ready for me downstairs. I glanced out across the balcony, then went in to use the bathroom, washed my hands and brushed my teeth, then paused when I passed the closet door. Harrison had made sure an entire closet was available to me last time I was here, and today I found that not only had he carried my luggage upstairs before he'd left, but all the boxes I'd shipped were stacked neatly against the closet walls, and a white cashmere robe hung waiting for me to put it on, above a pair of matching slippers.

This man thinks of everything! I smiled to myself as I slipped it on, tying the belt at the waist. The same *A.* that he'd tattooed on his ribcage was embroidered on the left chest of the robe in metallic gold thread.

I twirled myself around in front of the mirror, laughing at how giddy I felt, then grabbed my phone from the nightstand and snapped a quick photo of myself. With the diamond center stage, nestled among bare cleavage, edged by cashmere and gold embroidery, I sent it to Harrison with a, *Thank you for loving me, I adore you.* Moments passed and no response came. *He must be on set*, I thought as I slipped my phone into the pocket of my robe and set off to the kitchen to find Shelby.

She was wiping down the stove when I got there, humming a tune to herself I didn't recognize as she worked. Plates of food lined the counter;

bacon, hard-boiled eggs still in their shell, French toast, a bowl of fresh fruit, and a small pitcher of maple syrup. A carafe of apple juice sat in an ice bucket and a pitcher of water filled with ice rounded out the options.

"Good morning. Something smells heavenly down here." I leaned against the counter and curiously looked down my nose toward the plates of food she'd laid out.

"Well good morning to you, sleepy head. I'm so glad you're back!" She came around the counter and hugged me, holding on a smidge longer than normal.

"How have you been?" I broke from her hug and began opening cupboards to look for a glass.

"Oh, I'm just fine but..." She waited until I turned to face her to finish. "I think I'd rather know how *you've* been." She raised an eyebrow at me, arms folded across her chest.

I turned away from her again. "What do you mean?" I tried to hide my expression as I filled a glass with apple juice.

"He called me and was absolutely elated. I believe the first words out of his mouth were, *Shelby, I'm going to be a dad!* And trust me when I tell you, I could hear how wide that smile of his was and feel his excitement through the phone. He was absolutely buzzing. He told me I needed to make sure I didn't buy or feed you anything you can't have and how he was so excited for you to be coming home sooner than planned and that we should work together to get the house set up to make you feel as comfortable as possible."

I bowed my head, no longer in control of my own smile. "He was *that* excited?"

"I'm pretty sure I heard him do a cartwheel," she joked.

"He's such a sweetheart. Gosh, I love him." I started fixing myself a plate of food. "C'mon, eat with me. I hate to eat alone."

"Oh, I had my breakfast hours ago."

"And what was it? A cup of coffee? Don't let this go to waste. Get some food and sit with me, Shelby. Let's make a habit of this while it's just us."

"Oh fine, you don't have to twist my arm." She grabbed another plate from the cupboard and reached for a piece of French toast.

I sat down at the table and looked out over the backyard. This wasn't going to be hard to get used to. The landscape here wasn't that different from the grounds at the farmhouse, and I could spend hours in the gardens Harrison had already started. I glanced at Shelby as she poured syrup over her French toast.

"Do you have other jobs that you attend to for other families or is Harrison your only employer?" I asked.

"This is it. When I'm done here for the day, I just do my own thing, but I stick close by on the off chance he calls for me. When he's out of town, I try to get caught up on things I don't get to every day, like baseboards and windows, that kind of thing."

"I'm looking forward to getting to know you, and honestly, not being alone all the time. I felt deserted every day in my marriage and I hated it. I spent all my time by myself, and I'm grateful you'll be around when Harrison isn't." I nodded appreciatively, hoping she wouldn't feel pity for me.

"That must have been hard. How long were you married?" she asked.

"Too long. Over twenty years. That sounds crazy, doesn't it? We were young. I mean, don't get me wrong, James isn't some horrible person; he's just completely unaware of anything and everything beyond his own needs and feelings. And I always felt like nothing more than the maid." As soon as I said it, I felt awkward. "I'm sorry, I didn't mean…"

"Alice, it's fine. I am in fact, the maid. Though I prefer my actual title, which is *House Manager,* because trust me, I do much more than just clean the house."

"Oh, I like that. And you're right, women take on so many of the fine details, things men never even think about."

"Harrison is far more advanced in thought and initiative than any man I've ever met, but he's also busier than any man I've met, so I don't mind handling the details for him. He really is a genuinely caring and considerate person, but that's not news to you by now, I'm sure. And a job like this doesn't cross one's path often, so I value it, and him. His needs are always going to be my first priority, and now yours as well."

"Well, that's sweet of you, but I hope I can handle my own needs; no need for you to take on any of my stuff. I can definitely see why Harrison always speaks so highly of you. He's said more than once that you're like family to him."

"Well, he's like family to me, like a big brother who actually cares." She swiped the last bite of her French toast through the remaining puddle of syrup, then stood and carried her plate to the sink.

"You know, this food is delicious, and I appreciate you so much for going to all this trouble, but you don't need to do this all the time. There's no way I can eat all this," I laughed.

"I wasn't sure what you liked, so I made a little of each, and who can resist the smell of bacon? No one I know."

"I'm okay with black coffee, toast, and scrambled eggs. And for the record, I'm also perfectly okay with making them myself. You don't have to do all this for me, but I do appreciate it."

"Oh, it's no trouble at all. I'm here early. I don't mind, really."

"Well, if you insist on making my breakfast, then I insist you sit and eat with me each morning. Deal?"

Shelby nodded. "I can handle that. It's a deal." She reached for my plate. "You all finished?"

"I can take care of this," I protested.

"Stop it, I'm already up and headed to the sink."

"Thank you. Everything was delicious." As Shelby carried my dishes to the sink, I thought of the boxes upstairs in the closet and began contemplating the rest of my day. "I've got a closet full of things to sort through and try to find room for today. It feels a bit weird to be sprinkling my life in amongst Harrison's without him here to give his input. Will you be sticking around, or do you have somewhere else to be?"

"I'm going to load the dishwasher, set it running, then run to the shops. Is there anything you'd like to have that isn't already here? He had me bring in a bunch of things for you yesterday."

I got up and perused the cabinets, then the fridge and freezer. Everything I could want was already stocked. "No, I think I'm okay with what's here actually."

"Well, if you won't be needing anything, I'll skip the shopping and probably start a deep clean on the gym equipment upstairs, but I'll keep out of your way."

"You'll never be in my way, Shelby. If anything, I'll be looking forward to the conversation. Whenever you need a break, come find me."

My pocket buzzed, and I opened my phone to find a text from Harrison.

Good morning beautiful. I hope you slept well. Glad you like your gift. xx

I responded immediately.

It's absolutely stunning. I miss you so much already. Just had breakfast with Shelby. How's filming?

As I waited for his response, I quietly stared out the windows to the backyard while Shelby finished the dishes, then headed up the stairs toward the home gym, when my phone vibrated again.

Going well. How do I look? Another vibration then and a photo popped up. An out-of-focus selfie showed Harrison with his full prosthetic beard and a painful-looking black eye with a bloody cut above his eyebrow, his cheeks smeared with a mixture of fake dirt and painted-on bruises.

Handsome but scary. I like you better without bruises. Sending kisses to those fake wounds, babe. Gonna unpack some stuff today, but I won't move anything of yours.

I watched a bird poke around a shrub for berries in the backyard while I waited for his response. It was an adorable creature, a dusky gray-green until it turned to face me, its blaze-orange chest holding my attention. *Must be a robin*, I thought and noted how much smaller they were in England, their vibrant orange the only commonality with their American cohort. Giving up on his hunt for fruit, he'd begun to scratch at the earth in what seemed a search for insects, when another vibration diverted my attention back to my phone.

Sending those kisses right back to you, love. Wish I was there to cover you in them myself. As for the house, it's home for you now, do whatever you like, whatever makes you feel comfortable and whatever you think looks good. I trust you. Gotta run, love. I'll be in touch when the day is done. xxx

I replied simply, *xxx* and hit send.

I realized then that I hadn't talked to Emma since I'd arrived in my new home. She'd been such a good friend to me, despite the fact we'd never met. Emma's a West Coast girl while I'd always been in New England, and with everything that was going on in our everyday lives, we just hadn't managed to meet up yet. She'd sweetly offered to fly across the country just to be with me when I learned of my pregnancy, but I'd told her it was something I was going to have to navigate alone. She'd always been willing to drop what she was doing to be a loyal friend to me, and I adored her for it.

Landed in London last night late. Permanently. Harrison is back in Brazil working for 6 weeks while I settle in. All is well. Oh, and I think James burned my house to the ground on my way out of town, but that's a whole other story. How's things? I hit send and smirked, knowing her response would be one of surprise.

In no time my phone buzzed.

Wait, he did WHAT? Are you serious?

I laughed as I responded.

I'm serious, I don't have proof, but apparently the house is now a pile of charred remains, and I saw him on the way out of town with black smears on his face and ripped clothes. I don't know what happened, but I guess he's not only single but homeless as well. When can you get some time off? I'm here alone for the next 6 weeks. Come see me.

Her response was almost immediate. *I'll put in a request if you're serious. I've never been to London.*

I quickly typed in, *I'm serious. Let me know,* and hit send.

I dropped my phone back into my pocket and let out a deep sigh, rubbing my face with the palms of my hands. I shuffled upstairs toward the bedroom, and passing the gym waved at Shelby as she wiped down the equipment. I daydreamed of Harrison while I showered, then got dressed and stood looking at myself in the mirror. I had been in the UK for less than twenty-four hours and I already felt like a different woman. I smoothed my t-shirt against my body, down over the fullness of my belly and the curves of my hips, and noticed that instead of my eyes falling to my waist and its circumference or where my breasts landed on my chest, I was looking back at my own eyes. There was a brightness in them I hadn't seen for as far back as I could remember, a light I thought had been extinguished. James' lack of interest had killed any self-confidence I'd had and made me feel like there was nothing about me that was attractive enough to make a man want me. But now I stood taller, straighter, the weight of a thousand disappointments finally off my shoulders. My skin looked clearer, even the natural curls in my auburn hair looked more relaxed. I leaned in closer to the mirror, examining my details. A new gray hair had sprouted along my hairline, my under eyes showed the faintest look of crepey skin, and the skin along my jaw wasn't as tight as it used to be, but the fine lines that were starting to appear actually made me smile to myself. *Harrison loves me just as I am,* I thought. *He can't keep his hands off of me. Why would I ever want to wish that away?* And frankly, I'd earned every crease, every line, every barely-there silver accent. I'd persevered through loss, weathered what felt like a million shit storms in my marriage, and yet, the sun had risen again and brought warmth back into my life. I stepped back and looked myself up and down one more time and nodded to my reflection, smoothing that singular gray hair back instead of pulling it out. *I look damn good for being in the midst of a divorce and pregnant at forty*, I thought, and no one was going to tell me otherwise.

"Well, these boxes aren't going to unpack themselves," I said to my reflection, then set off to tackle the closet.

CHAPTER
10

The day had been busy from the beginning, and I'd been consumed with thoughts of home in addition to a missed work call that reminded me I needed to get in touch with Arlo. He had no idea what my life had become in the last few days, and when I dropped the, "This is my two-week notice," on him, he was understandably pretty shocked. Then his shock turned to annoyance when I tried to explain what happened. *I dropped everything and moved to London. Things happened so fast...* From his perspective, it probably sounded like I was making up a bullshit excuse not to work for him anymore. And truthfully, with everything happening, I'd never even given him a second thought until now.

I offered to stay on until the long-distance became an issue, or just to get him through until he hired someone else, but in a somewhat snarky tone he said, "Thanks, but no thanks," and he'd "do just fine" without me. *Way to make me feel insignificant.* After that, I really didn't care anymore. I threw him a fake, "No hard feelings?" and wished him well.

In the afternoon, I'd sifted through photos and clothing and knick-knacks, placing chosen items throughout the house in places that wouldn't look too cluttered and could be simple reminders of who I used to be, the happier times in the life that I previously lived. When I got to the boxes that held my favorite books, I worried the library wouldn't have room. The last time I was here, it seemed like there was enough space for Harrison's collection, but none to spare. So, I moved all my favorites to a stack on my side of our bed. *Our bed.* I smiled to myself just thinking about it. Then moved some of the remaining books into their own box and went downstairs to make space for them.

Harrison's library was gorgeous; rich in color, and lush in design, it was easily one of my favorite rooms in the house. A beautiful view of the yard rolled out from behind gold velvet curtains, and an inviting chair was situated in the corner, draped in a cashmere blanket I remembered was as soft as butter. The decanter on the side table now held two etched glasses instead of one, and upon further inspection, an A was etched into the additional glass. He'd done so many things in such a short amount of time to make sure I felt like this was my home too.

I set my box down and pictured him sitting here conducting business calls when I was here before, his chestnut curls framing his face, his glasses perched on his perfect nose, his eyebrows drawn tightly together in concentration. *He's even sexier when he's in work mode*, I thought. I ran my fingers along the edge of his desk wondering what he was doing at this very moment. Probably delivering lines as he jumps from a fake airplane somewhere over a jungle, his handsome face painted to look battered and bruised as he lands in a CGI-concocted snake pit, knife drawn, ready to fight the bad guy and save the beautiful bombshell.

Looking around I thought, *this truly is a perfect space to relax into a good book,* and that's when I noticed the same small bird flitting around outside the library window. It landed briefly on the outside sill, then flitted again before landing once more. As I approached the window, I could see its face, neck, and chest ablaze in the same burnt orange I was so captivated by earlier, but up close now, I could see how it faded to a blueish-gray, his cape an olive brown and his pantaloons white against tiny toothpick-sized legs. His adorable little toes clung to the sill as I stood there watching, and it too peered back at me, its small black eyes round and alert, its head tilting and craning as it watched me. I reached my index finger toward the glass, expecting him to take flight once again, but instead, he gently tapped his thin black beak against the glass that separated us. He'd have had me by the finger if not for the clear glass divider.

"Inquisitive little fella, aren't you?" I asked him and watched again as his head cocked to one side. I moved my finger up the glass and tapped again, and watched as he took flight to rise and tap the glass with his beak, just where my finger lay.

Back on the sill, he watched me, as if asking me my name.

"I'm Alice. I hope you don't mind, I'm new here."

His tiny black orbs blinked in response.

"I hope we can be friends. I'll have to look you up and see what you like for treats."

He flitted away toward a sunny patch of grass and nosed around until he found whatever it was that tickled his fancy, carrying it up into a nearby shrub. I turned my back to the window, content in the fact my new friend had found something to fill his belly, and my eyes landed on an empty space among the shelves where a yellow sticky note clung to the frame.

'I can't wait to see what brilliant adventures you fill this space with. I love you. H.'

His handwriting an instant comfort, he was always thinking of me, anticipating when I'd need to feel him near me, ready to make me feel loved, even when he was miles away in another country, and I was still trying to wrap my head around it. I'd never had a man in my life that thought of me before he thought of himself. James was the only long-term relationship I'd ever had, and over the last twenty-two years, he'd somehow managed to make me believe love like this, like I share with Harrison, was the stuff of fairytales. That it wasn't for real people, and it certainly wasn't for someone like me.

I wondered then what James was doing. The house had been burned to the ground, leaving him homeless and now entirely on his own for the first time in decades. I pictured him standing there in smoldering rubble, his tan skin visible by the tear streaks on his soot-smeared face, smoke still billowing up around him. *I bet he's losing his mind. He's probably been at the bar since I left. Oh well, not my problem anymore.* Then I wondered if James would have reacted any differently if he'd known the actual level of who Harrison really was when he came to the house. I shook my head. *It doesn't matter, Alice. That was then. None of it matters anymore.*

I plucked the sticky note from the shelf and stuck it to the desktop, intending to keep all of his little notes as reminders of how thoughtful my new love could be, his handwriting a reminder that until he returns home to me, I'll be alright.

Tap tap. My friend was back at the window. *Tap tap tap.* I approached him again, and just like before, he looked up at me, seemingly happy to have regained my attention.

"Hello again, friend. I think you're a robin, but let me make sure, so I can give you a proper name. There's no reason we should be strangers." I pulled my phone from my back pocket and snapped a quick photo. The bird never flinched and seemed unfazed by my movements. I dropped his photo into my phone's search bar. The immediate result told me this was a European Robin, a small bird, typically unafraid of human activity and a fan of nuts, insects, berries, and earthworms. Often found near gardeners for that very reason; a patch of overturned soil was basically an invitation to be besties. The result also said males were aggressive and would fiercely defend their territory and could sometimes be seen arguing with their own reflection. I wondered if this was what was happening with my little robin.

"Sit tight, let me see if I can find something for you," I said, half expecting this intelligent little gent to smile up at me with gratitude.

Within minutes I was in the backyard, barefoot in October, with a handful of mixed snacks I thought might entice him.

"Robin? Where are you, friend?" I held out my hand, offering up blueberries, raisins, a few raspberries, and some unsalted peanuts. I looked around the yard and couldn't find him. "Robin? C'mon, buddy. I have snacks."

He'd vanished. I kicked myself for having left the library window at all. *I should have stayed and let him get used to me*, I thought. I'd done this back at the farmhouse, tempted birds with off-season treats to befriend them, but it had been a while. Maybe these UK birds were going to be harder to convince. I looked around again and found the yard still.

"Okay, Robin, I'm going back inside, and taking these delicious snacks with me." I turned to head back inside when he plopped down beside me on the arm of a patio chair.

"Hi there. Aren't you handsome," I quietly cooed as his head once again cocked from side to side, taking me in, evaluating if I was a lunatic or a friendly food source.

"I'll do better next time, but for now I brought you these." I slowly opened my palm and let him observe. He blinked back at me, but gave no indication of his thoughts. He popped up into the air when I attempted to sit in the chair he was on, finding comfort on the gutter above the door a safe distance away, but still happy to keenly observe my every move. He watched as I settled in, and I lowered my hand to rest, palm open, offering snacks free for the taking in the same spot he'd been just moments ago.

"I'm not sure you heard me through the window earlier but I'm Alice, your new neighbor. I'm very pleased to meet you and hope we can be friends. Don't you like blueberries, Robin? I hope it's okay I call you Robin. Sorry, it's not very clever—" In the split second it took me to look down at my hand, Robin landed atop a blueberry, gripped his toes in, and was gone again, back above the gutter to feast from a distance. His watchful eyes fixed on me as he pecked at and devoured the tart little berry.

"You don't have to be afraid of me. I'll keep your belly full, I promise." I wiggled my fingers, causing a raspberry to teeter against two raisins. Robin dropped what remained of his blueberry down onto the patio stone and cocked his head again. I imagined he was weighing his options, sticky raisins or a plump little raspberry. Little did he know, he could have it all.

He swooped down again, this time landing with one foot on the raspberry and one foot firmly on me, his tiny nail curving in tune with the shape of my finger. A cock of the head, his black eye an endless void as he stared at me. "You don't have to be afraid, Robin. I'm your friend." I gave him a soft half-smile and expected him to flit away again. But he didn't. He stood firm in the spot where he'd landed and began ripping at bits of the raspberry with his tiny beak, his foot still gripping my finger.

"That must be a pretty good treat this time of year, huh?" I asked him softly. He shook his head, dislodging the gathered bits from the sides of his beak, sending fruit fragments scattering. "I should have brought you a bowl of water. Next time I'll be better prepared. There's always the stream. You must know where to find it." I sat there watching him, wondering what he could be thinking of me.

It's a strange thing, to have a wild bird land on you. They barely weigh anything, light as a feather you might say, but at the same time, their fragility is heavy. Your body stiffens at first, afraid to rattle them from their perch, but then the longer they stay, the more those stiff muscles need oxygen, and the heavier a weightless bird becomes. Ultimately, it's not the bird's fault, but a wild bird is like loneliness I suppose. Drops in unexpectedly, gets comfortable, and then feels like the weight of the world is upon you.

I watched as Robin made a mess of his raspberry, then moved on to another blueberry. He wasn't interested in peanuts or raisins it seemed. I'd do more research and keep some food close by for him, maybe set up a little water dish where he could sip or splash, whatever made him happiest. I'd been kidding myself thinking I wouldn't feel alone here. Shelby couldn't be here all the time and I shouldn't expect Nigel to be either. Maybe if Robin came back to visit from time to time, the weight of the loneliness I had already started to feel without Harrison here might transform itself back into oxygen and feel weightless again.

I sat with Robin for a while. He'd had his fill of snacks and moved on to preening and stretching his wings while sitting happily on my wrist as ribbons of random sunlight broke through low-slung clouds and landed against his body. When finally, he left, flying off towards the edge of the woods, presumably in search of a drink from the stream, I returned to the library. I unpacked my books, positioning them all on the open shelves. Over the next few hours, I reloaded then unloaded the box several times, making our books one cohesive lot, before shifting my focus to hanging and organizing all the clothes I'd shipped over.

When I finally collapsed onto the couch with a sandwich and some chips—excuse me, *crisps*—I was exhausted. Shelby had long since gone home and what felt like a normal dinner time was, in reality, pushing 10:30 p.m. local time. Getting used to the time change was a feat of its own. I picked up my cell phone for the first time since this morning and realized I had multiple unread messages. The first one I opened was from Harrison:

Hello, love, filming has wrapped for the day. I just wanted to tell you how much I love you and hope you are settling in without any trouble. Finding everything ok? I miss you. XX

I responded:

All is well here. Unpacking all day, missing you, wishing you were here. Thank you again for this beautiful necklace, and thank you for loving me the way you do. Finding your notes makes me feel like you aren't so far away. Wanted to ask, would it be okay if Emma came for a visit? Just to keep me company? xx

While I waited for his response, I opened a message from Nigel.

Hey hey, let's get together for a bit in the coming days and chat? We need to catch up and you can tell me all about this little one you've got marinating.

I tapped in my reply as I made quick work of my sandwich.

Absolutely. Give me a few days to get settled and we'll make a plan. I'll text you tomorrow. Can't wait to see you!

And then, I opened Emma's text.

All clear, when do you want me? I'm so excited to finally meet you, and hug you, and we can both see the sights of London together!

I waited to hear from Harrison again before I responded to Emma. I needed to know he was okay with me inviting her before I just opened the doors of our home to someone that technically neither of us had actually met. He was so private about his life, and I didn't want to infringe on his trust. I finished my dinner as my mind drifted to the places I wanted to show Emma in London; I still hadn't seen Hampton Court Palace, Strawberry Hill House, and I know we would both love Borough Market, and of course, Notting Hill. Maybe I'd take her to the zoo, and I'm sure she'd want to see Buckingham Palace. Then my phone buzzed again.

Absolutely, Emma is always welcome. Darling, it's your home now too, there's never a need to ask. xx

You're the sweetest. I'll see when she can come visit, but for now, I'm gonna take a shower and daydream you're there with me, just like I did this morning ;) It's been a tiring day and the time change is messing with me. I love you so much! xoxo

Love you too, darling, both of you ;) Sleep well love xx

I sent a message back to Emma.

Whenever you can. Use Heathrow, and just let me know the details. We have so much to see and do. I hope you can stay longer than a week. I'm so excited to see you!

I hit send then took my dishes to the sink. I washed them by hand and laid them to dry on the counter, no longer enraged by the task of washing dishes like I had been for so many years, all the while thinking of the night Harrison and I met. I'd been sitting in the garden of The Spaniards Inn most of the afternoon, sipping Shirley Temples and losing myself in books until the sun went down, and then, like magic, there he was. The way he looked at me, propped up by his toned arm draped in tattoos, his eyes a brilliant cerulean green reflecting the golden twinkle lights that hung above the table, the way he'd smiled at me nearly stopped my heart from beating. I'd seen him in my daydreams, and I'd even run off on a road trip with him in my dreams, but having him standing there in front of me for the first time had taken my breath away.

Harrison Edwards wasn't your run-of-the-mill man, not in the least, and any dream I could conjure in my mind, couldn't hold a candle to the reality of him. Everything about him is a nuanced paradox in the best ways possible. Fiercely strong and still gentle, wildly intelligent but fun and child-like in his silliness. He's masculine and feminine and sensitive, and steadfast in his convictions. He loves art and music and literature, football and muscle cars and motorcycles. He's just, everything all at once, in one very structurally sound, muscular sweetheart of a package.

Dishes and daydreaming done, I made sure the doors were all locked. Despite the sound of their automation, making sure they were secure was a habit I'd probably never shake. Then one by one I turned off the lights and made my way upstairs. Each step reminding me of the way he'd carried me to the bedroom last night and made me yearn for him. I'd finally found a man who could make me feel irresistible, craved, beautiful just the way I was without conditions. Harrison never made me feel like I needed to change myself to deserve his love or that I needed to lose myself completely to sustain a relationship with him, and now, work had whisked him away.

It's just temporary, Alice. You've lived through worse; you'll get through this too.

I showered, got ready for bed, and checked my phone one last time after I snuggled down under the covers. Emma had sent another text.

I booked my flight. I'll be there in two weeks! TWO WEEKS! Can you even believe it?! I emailed you the flight info. Can't wait to see you! Is it cold there? I'll just pack for all the weather. Oh, I need plug converters, don't I? This is so exciting! OMG love you!

I giggled as I read it; Emma was going to be a welcome distraction from

Harrison's absence.

CHAPTER
11

The next few days were more of the same, breakfast with Shelby, unpacking, settling into my new home, finding a new routine, stolen moments with Robin whenever no one else was around. I'd see him out in the yard, but unless I was alone, he acted like a stranger. Shelby and I had started going for afternoon walks before she left for the day, which I really enjoyed, and it allowed me time to get to know her better.

I learned about her childhood and the family she referred to as "adoptive" using air quotes when she first mentioned it. Her natural parents, who had never been married, separated when she was a toddler. She remembered her father still coming to see her a few times, but when he lost his job and times got tough, he vanished, and her mother ultimately became a drug addict as a result of his abandonment. Shelby had been taken in by an aunt and uncle she barely knew just before she started school. Immediately overwhelmed by the five biological children they already had, she felt intimidated, and kept to herself, rarely speaking unless spoken to.

She relived the day she learned her mother had died of an overdose. Recalling sitting at the kitchen table, hungry, her aunt taking a call in the other room while Shelby tried to stop her belly from growling, desperate not to look needy but knowing there was nothing in the cabinets to eat. Moments later, her aunt came into the kitchen and put the kettle on. With her back turned to Shelby she said, "Well, your mum's dead. She took too much medicine, and it killed her, so now I'm stuck with you." Shelby was only seven at the time. She wept as she told me how she could still hear that woman's voice in her head saying those words all these years later. She didn't really remember much about her mother, but she couldn't seem to forget her aunt no matter how hard she'd tried.

Shortly after that, Shelby met Harrison in primary school. She told me about how she used to get bullied nearly every day by the other children because her family was poor and she rarely had new clothes; she was stuck with all the stained or ripped hand-me-downs from the older kids. Her aunt was so busy with her other children that Shelby would often go to school with her hair still knotted from the previous night's sleep, or without any lunch. She said she felt forgotten amongst a sea of children at home, and like a spectacle at school because all her classmates would mock her, and pick at her about her appearance.

Then one day when an older girl at school was berating her for taking too long at the drinking fountain—Shelby said she remembered it as if it were yesterday—Harrison had appeared out of nowhere, stepped in, and protected her. He took the time to talk with her and get to know her. He even gave her his lunch that day. From then on, they'd been inseparable. She said there were times when he would bring her some of his clean clothes to put on before class and how he would help her brush the tangles from the back of her hair, never caring what the other kids said about them. He always brought extra food for her to eat and never once looked at her like she was less of a person than he was. With tears in her eyes, she told me Harrison was more of a brother to her than any of those kids she had lived with at her aunt's, and that ultimately, she felt he had saved her life.

When school was done and they'd become adults, time let them drift away from daily interaction and Shelby struggled again to find work that would sustain her. Her aunt had eventually forced her out of the house, leaving her to sleep in public parks, but Harrison always found a way to keep a roof over her head. As soon as he began his career and started making real money, he'd called to offer her a position on staff, whatever she felt comfortable doing; he just wanted to make sure she was taken care of and that she would never be made to feel unseen, or unsafe ever again.

From that moment on she'd dedicated her life to taking care of the person that had spent so much time taking care of her. Harrison had taken her in, made her a space of her own, and given her freedom. Freedom from fear, freedom from ridicule, and freedom to find confidence in herself. She felt she could never fully repay him for all he'd done for her, but would always handle whatever she could to make his life easier for him, just as he had done for her.

Their friendship was enviable. Harrison never divulged that kind of information to me or went into all that Shelby had gone through in her life. Granted, it wasn't his story to tell, but I felt so much closer to her now that she trusted me with her feelings and her history. I cringed thinking back to our first meeting that morning in the kitchen when she and Harrison had made me a surprise breakfast. I'd been territorial and behaved as if she were the enemy, my competition. Hindsight told me she would never be that.

Our daily breakfast dates and walks brought forth new stories, and new insight into who Shelby was, and our friendship blossomed, unfurling over the days we shared, connecting us like sisters. I told her about my marriage and James, the baby we'd lost, what I'd endured. I told her how lonesome I'd felt for the last two decades and how much I appreciated her company while Harrison was away. I shared my road trip dream with her, and how it ultimately brought me to London, allowing Harrison to cross my path at just the right time, exactly when I needed him. I even shared with her how nervous I really was about carrying this child, Harrison's child. In my mind, I was a failure when it came to pregnancy, no matter how long ago it had been. And I thought about the loss of that baby every single time this child crossed my mind, every time I touched my abdomen, every time I thought of Harrison. I allowed Shelby access to my innermost thoughts and fears, and I trusted her with them all, just as she had done with me.

Of course, there were days when the subjects didn't run so deep. We talked about Emma and how she would be here to visit soon, and the preparations I wanted to make before her arrival. I told Shelby about how I met Nigel and that I had recommended him to Harrison, not realizing she was present the day after I left London when Harrison brought Nigel in for his first interview. She said she loved him instantly. So, when he came over later in the week for tea, it was easy for the three of us to fall into conversation like long-lost friends.

CHAPTER
12

Tea with Nigel was about to be anything but ordinary. It was clear he was ready to rummage through all the sordid details of my last few weeks, based solely on the pep in his step and the cheeky grin on his face as I watched him through the window approaching the front door.

Maybe it was because he'd recently been welcomed into the Harrison Edwards entourage, or maybe he was just more comfortable with me now than my last visit, but as soon as he was through the front door he was quick with a hug, rubbing my nearly non-existent belly with a wide toothy grin, then smattering me with air kisses before he blew past me toward the living room, bellowing a bright and cheerful, "Shelby, daaarling!" when he saw her prepping tea in the kitchen. His aura full of energy and enthusiasm, he certainly was a breath of fresh air against the gray London afternoon.

"Are you just completely over the moon? Look at you, you're glowing. Bloody hell, I would be too, baby or not." His hands spoke as much as his mouth as we settled onto the couch.

"It certainly wasn't in the short-term plan, that's for sure, but it's a welcome gift, and Harrison is so excited." My hand instinctively landed on my stomach as I spoke.

"I can imagine he is! You landed an absolute god of a man. You know that right? I know you know. I mean, is there anything he can't do to sheer perfection? I could barely hold eye contact with him during my interview. I don't know how you managed to find the nerve to actually fall in love with him."

I could hardly keep up. I didn't remember Nigel being this high-strung last time I was here, but maybe that's just because I was a client then and he wasn't sure he could be himself with me. Today, though, his energy was twice that of mine, or maybe I was just exhausted from all the unpacking.

"He's certainly special. Unlike anyone I've ever known. And he just makes me feel so lucky." I couldn't contain my smile.

"Speaking of, does the ex know about all this? What did he say? How did that play out? Harrison came to get you, right? Did he just show up, unannounced? Did you ask him to come? And was James there? Did anyone get walloped in the face during a row? Tell me everything." When he finally stopped talking his expression was blank, yet somehow sharp and focused as he sat there blinking at me awaiting my response. Overwhelmed, I wasn't sure where to begin.

"Well, James has been served the papers, and while he's remorseful and wanted to try to fix it, I, of course, already had a foot out the door. But that's not entirely because of Harrison. I'd been unhappy for a really long time. Unhappy and complacent. I mean, you know that. We talked a little bit about it before. But when I met Harrison and fell so deeply in love with him, it certainly helped me clear the clouds from my head and shake away the fact that I'd gotten so used to just being miserable. It helped me make an informed decision, but no, I didn't tell James about Harrison initially, and I don't think he knows who Harrison actually is." Nigel nodded as I continued. "Then, yes, Harrison showed up at my door unannounced the morning after I told him I was pregnant, and James was the one who answered the door. Talk about awkward." I rolled my eyes. "But James had already accepted that the divorce was happening at that point, and he recognized his role in the breakdown and ultimate demise of our marriage. So, I mean really, what was he going to say? There was no resurrecting it from the grave. And…" I paused for effect, looking at Nigel as if completely shocked, "he actually shook Harrison's hand. And that was the day *after* he'd shoved him. That was the part that surprised me the most I think, the handshake. Then again," I looked away at the ceiling, my index finger tapping my lips. "I think I witnessed the aftermath of him burning the farmhouse to the ground, so there's that too." I sat and pondered what I'd just said, still wondering if that was actually what happened.

Nigel's eyes were wide when I stopped speaking. "Darling, you've left me with so many more questions."

Shelby set the tray of tea on the coffee table, positioning the single cup of black coffee in front of me, then settled onto the couch with us, a welcome interruption from the inquisition.

"Decaf," she said as she shot me a look and I grimaced thinking about the lack of caffeine. In the time it took for us to share that glance, it was clear she'd been listening from the kitchen, and I was thankful when she diverted the conversation away from James.

"Nigel, how's it going with Lawrence? Have you pissed yourself in training yet?" Shelby laughed as she fixed herself a cup of tea.

"Haven't done that yet, but I think we could be coming up on a day where I might, just this week I believe. Defensive driving is it? More like *bring an extra set of trousers with you to work.* We're having a go of it though, and Lawrence is a likable gent."

"Well, that's good. It will be nice for him to have some backup now that there are more of us in this growing entourage." Shelby stirred her tea as she spoke. "And especially good for you to train under him so you'll share habits."

"Darling, I'd train under that man any day." Nigel's expression as he stirred milk into his tea made Shelby nearly spit hers out.

"I don't think Lawrence is of that persuasion, my dear, but good luck to you." She cleared her throat and then giggled.

"Now, Shelby, I've got to know, have you ever been married?" Nigel asked.

"Oh no, that life's not for me." Shelby shook her head. "I'm happy just as I am. Responsible only for myself. No one to answer to. No one to give me any grief about anything."

"But don't you get lonely?" I asked.

"Sometimes, but I've gotten used to the ebb and flow of it. It comes and goes. And my work here keeps me plenty busy."

"We need to find you a man, my darling," Nigel mumbled before sipping his tea, his eyes wide as he glanced up at Shelby.

"It will happen if it's supposed to." She shrugged. "Besides, Nigel, maybe you're the one that needs a man." Shelby was half joking as she lifted her cup to her mouth, but Nigel's response wasn't jovial.

"I've kept a lover for so many years, I've lost track of the time he's been in my life. Some days it feels like only yesterday, and others it feels like lifetimes." There was a sadness in his eyes as he spoke.

"Oh? It never became anything serious then?" Shelby asked.

"We kept things casual for so long that it just never evolved. And now, looking back, I wish I'd been more persistent for his attention. I don't know if he would have given it to me if I'd asked, but..." His voice trailed off and he glanced toward a window, his mind obviously taking him somewhere else.

Moments passed in silence, and Shelby and I shared questioning glances with one another before I took him by the hand and asked, "Nigel, you okay?"

"Oh," he motioned with his hand as if pushing the thought aside, "I know he's kept other lovers over the years. He's told me as much. But I never did. He was it for me, all I needed or could ever want. I just didn't want to let myself be too vulnerable. I don't know why I was afraid to show him that part of myself. I mean we were shagging for Christ's sake; how much more vulnerable can one be? Wanting him was one thing, but I guess I didn't want him to know I *needed* him." Nigel's energy from earlier had turned completely around, and now he seemed like a shell of himself.

Shelby and I looked at one another, concern for our friend written all over both our faces. Nigel had never shown me this side of himself; it was obviously something he kept very private. While I appreciated him being candid with me, with both of us, I was worried for him.

"Do you think he took the other lovers because he didn't know how you felt? Him knowing you needed him and truly loved him may have made all the difference." Shelby gave him a soft reassuring smile as she delivered the gut-wrenching question.

"I don't know. I live with the regret of not telling him every day, but things between us lately have fallen by the wayside. So sometimes I feel like maybe I did the right thing. We never lived together, just met up at each other's places here and there, from time to time. My God, those trysts were so full of passion we could have lit the bed on fire. It was as if our bodies were designed to fit perfectly with one another." Nigel leaned back into the couch, his face to the ceiling, his hand on his chest. "Of course, we would seek each other out when we needed the familiar comfort of one another's arms as well, or the comfortable silence we could bask in together, the afterglow of temporary love. Even in hard times, in times of sadness or grief, we would be each other's landing place, the safe haven in all of life's storms. We were like an addiction for one another. We'd seek a fix, and let it burn through us, a habit neither of us could break. And I never tried to. I'd have done anything for him, anytime without question. But I guess I don't know if he felt quite like that for me." Nigel turned again toward the window and let out a despondent sigh. "I haven't seen him in over a month, and it's been two weeks now without so much as a text. That's not normal. Maybe he's found someone younger, someone new that's quelled the need for a fix." He shrugged. "Maybe it's run its course. I don't know."

"Unsolicited advice, but maybe tell him how you really feel. If you show him even half of the emotion you just showed us, things might change. See what happens. All is not lost yet. There's still time," I offered and gave him a knowing look.

Nigel shot me a tight-lipped half-smile of acknowledgment followed by a heavy sigh.

"And, if all else fails, use the excuse of the new job keeping you busy and exhausted. I'm sure you'll set things right." Shelby patted him on the knee and reached for her tea again.

Then, just as if someone flipped a light switch, Nigel changed the subject. His face bright with renewed enthusiasm, as if nothing had ever been discussed, he pivoted back to questioning me about James. A coping mechanism I'd used many times over the years myself, I recognized the desperation for self-preservation, a means of hiding the tears that were surely on the verge of being noticeable. And so, I obliged. Despite being sick of talking about James, I wanted to spare Nigel any further discomfort.

The afternoon crept on, and streaks of sunlight illuminated the faces of my friends and the room around them as it slipped below the clouds before dipping out of sight. What was a foggy day in London had turned to a crisp cool night, and after all the gossip and laughter and tea had been consumed, and everyone had gone home, I was exhausted.

I showered, taking my time to let the pressure of the hot water work at the tension I was carrying in my shoulders. As the water washed over me, I closed my eyes and thought of Harrison somewhere in Brazil. I could see his face in my mind, smiling at me, laughing, his eyes full of life, excited for the future we would share together. I could hear his voice telling me he loved me. Memories replayed in my mind. The Dales, the first time he'd kissed me. The look on his face when I found him on my front porch ready to whisk me away like some knight in shining armor. The dream sequence on the balcony in New Orleans. The way his mouth felt against my thighs...and then, for a fleeting moment, the memory of his hands on my body in this very shower actually felt real. God, I missed him.

Fifteen minutes later I threw on my robe and ran a comb through my hair before grabbing my phone from the bathroom counter, slipping it into my pocket, and setting off in search of pajamas. I paused in front of Harrison's closet door, my hand resting on the handle for a moment, debating whether or not I should even be thinking about going into his personal space. *"It's your home now too, there's never a need to ask."* His words echoed in my head. One small movement and the door carefully swung open in front of me. Before I knew it, the light was on, and I was running my fingertips along the edges of his suits. Sequins and embellished sleeves reminded me of his celebrity before finding the well-worn t-shirts hanging on the opposite wall. I pulled a familiar white shirt from its hanger, LIVE AID written across the front with a rainbow-striped graphic. I untied the belt of my robe and let it fall to the floor. The t-shirt was soft and smelled like Harrison as I pulled it down over my head. The weight of it nowhere close to the strength of one of his hugs. Without thought I pulled a pair of his boxer briefs from the drawer and put them on as well before picking up a bottle of his cologne from the dresser. I lifted the cap and let one pump of fine mist land on my wrist. It was like he was here in the room with me. I replaced the cap on the bottle and repositioned it carefully back into its spot beneath the blue bandana that hung on the wall, then grabbed my phone from the pocket of my robe.

I dialed his number and sat down, my back against his dresser. Suddenly, there he was, smiling back at me. *Thank God for video calls, even if the quality is garbage.*

"Hi, love." His voice was soothing and calm.

"Hi, babe, I miss you," I greeted him.

"Darling, how was your day? Where are you?"

I panned the camera around to show my surroundings and then down to show his t-shirt, flashing him my bare legs in the process. "I'm sitting in your closet. I just wanted to feel close to you."

He laughed. "You've got my pants on as well I see." Shaking his head, he continued, "That's pretty close." His dimples made me miss him even more. "You alright?" he asked, half-joking.

"Yeah, I'm okay." I sighed. "Your cologne doesn't smell as good on me as it does on you." I wrinkled my nose and scowled, disappointed.

"Sorry to hear that, but that shirt certainly looks better on you than me. Wish I was there to see you in it."

"I'd rather you were here to see me out of it, if I'm being honest." I faked a smile.

"Soon, darling. I'll be back just as soon as I can be. In the meantime, I know you're a bit out of sorts there alone, feeling turned around and unsure of what to do next. So, I went ahead and made you an appointment with a doctor just to be sure everything is as it should be."

"Oh? Okay, thank you. That's probably for the best, I wouldn't know where to begin." I trusted his judgment implicitly, and I knew he wouldn't have me seeing just anyone in regard to carrying his first child, but still, I was curious.

"Alice, I want you to know that I wish I could go to this first appointment with you. It's only going to be a quick introductory meeting, so you'll feel comfortable with her, and I think they'll draw your blood, but truly, I feel like such a bastard not being there."

"Stop it. Don't lose any sleep over that. I appreciate you taking the time to set it up and it's probably good to start early given the experience I had in the past. And, you know, my advanced age." I rolled my eyes.

"Darling, you're perfect, and I'm certain this time will be different. We must keep positive outlooks, okay?" His eyes through the screen were blurred along with the rest of his face, choppy with a not-so-great signal, but they were a comfort nonetheless.

"I know. I'm just tired. It's been a long day. Nigel came over and we sat and had a good long visit. Shelby made us tea, joined in with us, and gosh, we really had a great time."

"I'm glad to hear that, love. I'm missing out on all the good stuff at home, huh?"

"All you're missing is me being exhausted." Ironically, I yawned as I said it.

"I don't want to miss a second of any of this with you," Harrison yawned, triggered by mine, "and our ever-changing little one." He blinked hard trying to focus. Our signal was terrible. "No matter how regular or unexciting you think the days are there, I miss you, Alice, with everything in me. I've never had the chance to follow along with the progress of a pregnancy, to track the day that my baby grows from the size of a peanut to a walnut."

He was so serious, but I couldn't help but giggle at how fascinated he was.

"Right now, I don't think it's any bigger than a fleck of black pepper. So, don't get ahead of yourself." I laughed. "By the time you're home again, we might be at the walnut stage, who even knows?" I shrugged.

I could faintly make out his smile through the pixelated screen. "I've scheduled that appointment for next week. And this midwife comes noted as the best in the profession. She's called Della and I'm sure she'll take wonderful care of you. So, fear not, love. I've set it all up. Lawrence will take you. He's been given all the info he needs."

"Thank you for loving me."

Gosh, I wish he was here with me.

"Oh darling, you make it easy. So, tell me, is Emma coming to see you?"

"Yes, she'll be here in about..." I had to stop and think about it. "In about nine days, so after my appointment, I guess. I might ask Shelby to come with me."

"Oh, that's a wonderful idea. I'm glad you two are getting on so well."

"Shelby and I are thick as thieves. I'm so thankful for her, truly. I know if I called her, she'd be here in a heartbeat. She's really become a good friend and I've found such comfort in her."

"I'm so glad to hear that. It's a huge relief to me as well to know you're surrounded by people we can trust while I'm away. But next time, come with me?"

"Is next time already in the works?" I asked hesitantly.

"No, not for now. I'll finish this film, and be home with you until well after the little one comes. I've got a few fun things I'm planning for us before we become three, but nothing is solidified yet. Speaking of, did you hear anything further about the divorce and when things will actually be final?"

"I think the paperwork has all been submitted and the last thing my lawyer said was, it would likely be final in mid-November." My hand mindlessly fondled the necklace he'd given me and I watched his eyes as they fell to the diamond between my fingers.

"That necklace looks beautiful on you, Alice. I can't wait to put something just as magnificent on your left hand. Do you have any reservations about that? Is it too quick?"

"You want me to be honest?" I asked.

"Brutally. Always." His eyebrows tightened together as if he were bracing himself for bad news.

"I'd marry you right now, no ring required, if I could. We could get married the day the divorce is final, I don't care. I just want to be with you and for you to never doubt that I'm going to be beside you for the rest of our days."

"I feel the same way, darling. I can't wait to scream from the rooftops that you're my girl. And though it might be controversial these days, there are things that I'm quite old-fashioned about. I really want you to share my last name before we bring a child into this world, Alice."

"Well, we're in agreement on all of it. It's not too soon. Once you get home, we can talk about it more in-depth. These are things I'd rather talk about in person. You know?"

"I do. And it's late there, darling. You should go get some rest before you fall asleep in the closet." He laughed as he pointed a warning finger toward me.

I yawned again. "I love you. I'll chat with you tomorrow." I kissed my fingertips and touched the phone's camera.

"I love you more than you'll ever know, darling." He brought the phone to his face and kissed the screen.

"G'night."

"Goodnight, my love."

I stood from my resting spot, grabbed my robe from the floor, turned off the light, and shut the door on my way back to our bedroom. I put my phone on the nightstand and slid my tired body between the weight of the covers, grabbed Harrison's pillow, and snuggled into it. The scent of his cologne wafted from my nearby wrist, and closing my eyes, I inhaled deeply.

One day closer to having you back home with me, I thought as I pictured him dropping a suitcase and running toward me to wrap his arms around me again.

CHAPTER
13

The days passed quickly as I fully settled into *our* house. I found routine in my mornings with Shelby, working together to tend to things around the house and determine who would be responsible for what tasks moving forward. Often if the days were warm, we would work in the gardens together and then share lemonade on the patio. Robin would pop in and snag a worm from the freshly turned soil, then be off again until the next one laid itself bare against the fall air. Robin seemed to always be around and would now come when I called his name as long as I was alone. He didn't seem to want to share his friendship with anyone else but me, and truth be told, I liked it just fine that way.

Shelby helped me gather local favorites to create a welcome basket for Emma, which I was excited to share with her when she arrived in just a few days. And after early dinners, Shelby and I would walk the grounds. I hadn't decided yet if I would go through the process to get a driver's license as I had Nigel, Lawrence, and even Harrison to take me anywhere I wanted to go. But changing my address had been another story.

I'd filled out a change of address card online, but still ended up calling my old post office to forward any of my mail that had accumulated to our post office box. Harrison kept one for privacy reasons and usually Shelby would bring us yesterday's mail each morning along with the paper. There was no longer a house connected to my old mailbox, so I assumed they'd been holding my mail. I'd gone to high school with the gentleman who ran the post office, Ted, and while I wouldn't say we were friends, we were certainly acquaintances and spoke often when I had to go in for various reasons. He was shocked when I said I'd crossed the pond for good and that James and I were divorcing after all this time. He tried to be polite and asked about the weather and what it was like having to drive on the other side of the road, but I didn't divulge anything more than he needed to know, brushing his question off with a simple, "So far I haven't driven." Before we hung up, he asked me if I'd moved because of what had happened to the farmhouse, and I'd said matter-of-factly, "No, we separated before that."

"What happened to the house itself?" He'd pushed further.

I knew he wasn't being malicious, but talk spreads like wildfire in a town that size, and I kept my answers short. "I'm not sure; you'd have to ask James."

To which he replied, "No one's seen James in a while."

Odd, I thought, but didn't ask anything further on the topic. James and Ted knew one another in passing, also not what I'd consider friends, but me asking about James or even acting like I cared would absolutely get back to him, and that was the last thing I wanted. I'd changed the subject back to mail, reconfirmed he had my proper forwarding address, and hung up the phone.

That didn't mean I didn't stew on it though. For days I'd been wondering what actually happened to my house. I'd scoured the internet for any kind of report or news story and had come up empty-handed. Nothing, not a word. And after talking to Ted, I was wondering what the hell happened to James.

James was always one for theatrics. He was a happy-go-lucky man's man until someone wronged him or he wanted to present like he wasn't the bad guy. He'd put on a great show and convince the biggest skeptics of how pitiful and downtrodden he was. Knowing James, he collected the insurance money on the house and just vanished so people would think he died in that fire. He didn't have the sense to realize people would have seen him in town the next day, myself included. Maybe that's why he looked so pathetic when we'd locked eyes. But they couldn't cut him a check that fast, could they? Wouldn't I still have to sign off on that? And he'd obviously need to be alive to cash it. Maybe he'd gone off on another camping trip, taken to the woods to sort out his emotions. It was pretty chilly this time of year to be camping though.

The more I thought about it, the more my head spiraled. And the more I spiraled, the more I wondered who actually knew what happened. Would he have confided in someone? Was someone keeping this secret for him? Who would he have contacted? Who would he trust with whatever shenanigans he'd conjured up in his head? There was no one I was willing to contact back there to find out, that's for sure. In true middle-aged friend fashion, none of the women I knew from back home had reached out to me since I'd left town. They were probably all throwing themselves at poor, sad, lonely James. I rolled my eyes at the thought of it. *Good luck to 'em*, I thought, though now I'd taught him all the lessons he'd ever need to keep someone happy. I bet once the world learned about Harrison and me, my phone would be ringing off the hook. They'd all want to say they knew me and brag about how we were friends. They'd all have something to say about who I was back then. Back when they thought they knew me. I could see the exclusives now just coming out of the woodwork. I was better off without them, all of them. Every part of my life had improved since I left.

Either way, those so-called "friends" and James and his bullshit were no longer my concern. *Put it out of your head, Alice. Fuck him and fuck them too.*

I'd heard from all my "internet friends" as James had dismissively referred to them, as if they were nothing more than figments of my imagination. *Asshole.* Every single one had reached out to me in the last two weeks to ask how things were going. They knew about me going on vacation and returning home to leave my husband. They knew I packed everything and moved to London, and although I trusted them, they still didn't know anything about Harrison. They probably thought I was having some sort of mid-life crisis, but in my eyes, it was a full-blown life overhaul to rid myself of wasted time, wasted energy on things that no longer served me, and to walk away from all things unfulfilling. The new me was done with all of the unhappiness I'd wallowed through for the last two decades. Not to mention, their heads would probably spin when they found out what I'd really been up to.

Little did James know, those "strangers" were the life raft that kept me afloat while I drowned in his idiocy. Before I dropped everything and went to London on a whim, they were the ones that encouraged me to find my voice. They supported me and my feelings and listened when I needed to talk. They were my cheerleaders in my pursuit of happiness when no one else was. James had no clue how valuable they had been and would always be to me.

No one in my life knew about Harrison aside from Shelby, Nigel, Emma, and Lawrence. I assumed Harrison had briefed Victor and Hank, his security detail. They'd gone to Brazil with him to keep him safe while he was away, and I'm sure he'd confided in them. But other than that, we were still a secret to the outside world, and for now at least, no one in London had any reason to suspect who I was. Those blurred paparazzi images from the magazine cover had never shown my face, so with my anonymity still intact, I drank in what was left of fall in London as I awaited Emma's arrival.

CHAPTER 14

A week later, everything was done. I was moved in. I was settled. There was nothing more to unpack or rearrange or get used to. My body had adjusted to the time change, I was rested, and feeling less morning sickness. My new normal was comfortable and I was blissful about it. Shelby and I could go out wandering through the local shops and no one gave us a second look. I'd indulged in warm October afternoons in the garden of The Spaniards Inn for a change of scenery, to have lunch or dinner, or even just to sit and read in their beautiful garden to pass the time. Being there allowed me to lose myself in thoughts of the night I met Harrison. The night he'd approached me, where he'd turned my world completely upside down and transformed my life into everything I'd ever dreamed of and never thought truly possible. He was five thousand miles away, but being at The Spaniards Inn made me feel close to him even when I wasn't at home.

The morning of my first midwife appointment was just like any other. As soon as I opened my eyes, I reached for my phone. It was a rarity to wake up and not have a text from Harrison, and this morning was no different.

Good morning darling. You're beautiful and I love you. I hope today is filled with joy and laughter, and all the best things. xx

I responded, *I love you too. I'll be glad to get this first appointment out of the way. And, it's one day closer to you being home with me. I miss you.*

Almost immediately my phone buzzed again, and his message read, *I can't wait to hold you again. Let me know when you arrive at your appointment. xx*

I tapped in, *I will. Love you most. xx* and hit send.

I lay there for a bit thinking about how badly I wanted him here with me, to be able to go to these appointments together so he wouldn't miss a single step of this pregnancy. I wanted to be able to look back on these days together for years to come and share how we were feeling. But no matter what thoughts went through my head, I just kept coming back to how badly I wanted to feel the strength of his arms around me. I'd lived so long without physical touch from James, that getting it from Harrison had become my primary love language.

Finally, I pulled myself from the comfort of our bed and showered, then had breakfast and a walk with Shelby. When the time came to leave, she and I found Nigel standing at the open back door of the SUV, a wide grin on his face.

I stopped and gave him a quick hug as Shelby climbed into the backseat. "Well, good morning. I didn't expect to see you here."

"I'm full of surprises, love." He pulled back and gave me air kisses on either side of my face before taking me by the hand and helping me into the vehicle. He then made his way to the driver's seat.

Once he was settled, I made eye contact in the rearview mirror and touched his shoulder through the lowered partition. "I expected to see Lawrence driving. Congrats on finishing your training, Nigel!"

"Oh, thank you. Now I'm all yours. Only pissed myself once riding with Lawrence last week during defensive driving, so I guess that means I'm tougher than I look? Who knows!" he joked and brushed at the air with his hands, swatting it as if the question was an annoyance. "Are we excited for this appointment today?"

I couldn't help but smile as he spoke. Nigel truly was a light in my life. "I'm excited to meet Della and see what kind of person she is, and confirm what I think we all already know." I shot Shelby a knowing look.

"Well then ladies, we're off! We don't want to be late." The partition started to rise, and Nigel blurted out, "I'm putting this up so you two don't distract me. BABY ON BOARD!" he screamed out of nowhere, and I burst out laughing, then Shelby and I were left once again to ourselves.

"So, what do you think she'll be like?" I asked, feeling the vehicle hug the curves of the paved driveway and slow when it reached the gate.

"I haven't a clue. I've never been in this position, but I feel special you've asked me to tag along."

I took her by the hand. "I'm so glad you're here, Shelby. I've always hated going to the doctor, and this one is even more nerve-wracking because I don't like having my blood drawn." I squeezed her hand as I said it. "I don't know how I'm ever going to push an entire human being out of me." My eyes widened in alarm, accentuating how nervous I was.

Shelby shrugged. "You'll be just fine today. I'm sure the whole thing will be quick. You aren't that far along yet to have too much to discuss. I can't help you with the rest though, sorry." She chuckled and then picked up her cell phone to answer a text. "Sorry, I've got to handle this," she said as her fingers quickly typed a response.

"No worries," I said and turned my face toward the window.

My mind began to wander as I watched the fields and trees turn to stone buildings, the city of London coming into view. I thought about my eighteen-year-old self in this same predicament and how twenty-two years hadn't changed how nervous I was to be in this position. I thought about waking up on that Thanksgiving morning, terrified and in pain. Pain that had been completely foreign to me, but I somehow still recognized it as loss. I could see it all playing through my mind as if it were just yesterday. I remembered what it felt like being told that I had lost that child. James' child. Losing that baby set the tone for the last two decades of my life. *What if it happens again?* I thought. I laid my hand against my stomach. I wasn't far enough along to show, but the instinct to keep my abdomen safe must have come along automatically with the change in hormones. *What if I devastate Harrison the same way I devastated James?* I couldn't live with myself if it happened again.

Twenty-two years, one month, and an entirely different man were the only differences between that pregnancy and this one. Oddly enough, Harrison and I were almost on par with the same dates that James and I had been. *Maybe I'm only fertile in the fall*, I thought and smiled, catching sight of my reflection in the window. *Or maybe I'm only fertile when I'm happy*. I watched as my eyebrow shot up in response.

Nigel slowed the vehicle nearly to a stop then turned a corner and pulled into a small, very full parking lot. Shelby put her phone into her purse, smiling.

"Everything okay?" I asked her.

"Oh yes, just fine. You ready?" She switched the subject almost to an obvious extent and smiled as if she had some secret she was keeping.

"Why are you smiling like that?" I looked at her, puzzled.

Nigel opened the back door and held out his hand for me.

"No reason," she responded.

I cocked my head as I locked eyes with her. My eyebrows drew together tightly, distrustful of her response. Something felt weird all of a sudden.

Nigel grabbed my hand and whispered, "C'mon now, you don't want to be late. No dilly-dallying." A strange smile was on his face as he rushed me out of the vehicle.

"You two are up to something and I don't need the added stress. What is going on?" I demanded.

They looked at each other, then at me, then both looked toward the door of the midwife's office. My eyes followed the direction of their glance and there stood Harrison, smiling at me.

CHAPTER 15

"Oh my God!" I ran toward him, arms outstretched, desperate for his embrace. "You're here!"

"Of course, I'm here, darling. I couldn't miss this."

When I reached him, I took his face in my hands and kissed him. His arms wrapped around me and gave me a gentle squeeze as my fingers moved through the back of his hair, then landed behind his shoulders. I stopped, stepped back, and looked at him to make sure he was real, then kissed his chin and each of his cheeks, then the tip of his nose before pausing briefly to kiss his top then his bottom lip.

"I'm so glad to see you." Nearly in tears, I nuzzled my face against the softness of his shirt, breathing him in while I savored the way his arms felt around me.

"I made sure I could be here and *then* I made the appointment for you."

"And everyone was in on it. That's why Nigel drove and Lawrence was nowhere to be found this morning?" I asked.

"Exactly. He was picking me up at the airport." He took me by the hand

and looked into my eyes as he spoke.

"I love you for taking the time to be here with me."

"There's nowhere else I'd rather be. You ready?"

I looked around to find Shelby, Lawrence, and Nigel standing back near the vehicles chatting, then looked back at Harrison. "I'm ready."

Then, hand in hand, we went inside.

Della's office was warm and comforting, with quiet classical music coming from hidden speakers and cozy-looking furniture against the walls, large peace lilies under each window, and information pamphlets organized by trimester in various spots around the waiting room. Not surprisingly, we were alone here. I'm sure Harrison had arranged it that way. Della herself greeted us when we walked in and took us directly into a private room.

A tall woman with long graying hair tied half up with a thin lace ribbon, she had a welcoming demeanor and a calming voice. She introduced herself, and then the focus fell entirely on me, my history, and what my hopes and expectations for this pregnancy were. It never felt like a doctor's appointment; it felt like a chat with a new friend, and she listened to understand, not just to respond, which made me feel like she was truly there to help. It was a very different experience from any doctor I'd ever seen in the States. I wasn't just a faceless paycheck that had to fit into predetermined parameters. I felt like I mattered.

While we waited for the in-office hCG urine test to process, Della listened as I described my fears and explained in detail what my past experience looked like. She understood my concerns about my age, and how a failed previous pregnancy had affected me, and somehow, she made me feel capable again. She provided answers that helped me feel secure, and asked questions to divert my attention, reassuring me as I laid my trembling outstretched arm toward her, Harrison's hand in mine, and drew my blood.

Ugh, just get it over with, please.

This pregnancy was still in the very early stages, but after my blood had been dealt with, we were fortunate to hear the baby's heartbeat, which I knew Harrison was hoping for. I watched as his entire face lit up before he broke down completely in tears. Joyous tears, but still. I'd worried it would be too early to hear it, but what did I know? Our little one was strong, and thriving, and made sure we knew it. Maybe by some divine intervention, they knew I needed this win today.

Once Harrison collected himself, Della explained the lab tests she was running today were considered a prenatal panel and would determine a whole array of things while ruling out others. She'd be in touch once she got all the lab results, probably a week from now, and we would make further plans thereafter depending on the results.

"How big is the baby right now? Can we compare it to a...cherry?" Harrison asked, his eyes full of curiosity.

Della's head tilted to the side a bit as she thought of something to accurately convey the size of our child. "Well, you're ahead of yourself a bit. Right now, this little one is just that, little. Maybe about the size of a sesame seed."

"Really?" He seemed astonished.

"You've come in very early, which is good. Given Alice's history, her age, and some of the anxieties she's expressed here today, I'm glad we're starting this journey together so early. It will allow me to quell any fears as they arise, and keep a keen eye on progress as it happens."

Della went on to explain I'd be due for more blood tests and my first scan in mid-December. But we would learn the sex of our child, if we chose, in mid-February. I watched Harrison as she said it, and the grip he had on my hand tightened. As if fireworks were going off in his brain, I could nearly feel him buzzing, he was so excited. The way she explained and described everything made it all feel so easy. She even helped me install an app on my phone to track all sorts of different milestones.

Toward the end of the appointment, she shifted her attention to focus more on Harrison.

"So, Daddy, now that we've covered all of Mum's concerns, share with me how you're feeling about everything."

The inappropriate voice in my head giggled as I heard her call him 'Daddy.' I now had two reasons to call him that and it took all I had in me to stifle a smirk.

His eyes lit up in response to her question though, and he adjusted his posture, his shoulders dropping slightly as he straightened his back and joy spread across his face. "Oh, Della, I'm so excited to be a father I can hardly stand it, and to know that I'm going to share this child with Alice means everything to me." He was beaming.

"I think the two of you are going to be just fine, and I'll be here whenever you need me. Please know that if you have any questions or concerns, no matter the size, both of you can reach out to me anytime. I'm going to give you my direct line. Please don't hesitate." She turned her back to us and began scribbling her information on a business card, and I glanced at Harrison, an impressed look on my face.

I was fascinated. I don't think this is how it happens back home; physicians don't just hand out their personal contact info. Maybe this is normal in the UK, I don't know. Or maybe it's just because of who he is.

Don't question it, Alice. Just roll with it.

We wrapped up our appointment and Harrison scheduled the next one before we left. We'd be back the week before Christmas to see Della again and find out even more about our little one.

CHAPTER
16

Harrison couldn't stay; he left right from where I'd found him only two hours earlier, with Lawrence at the wheel. Shelby and I settled into the back of the SUV and Nigel drove us home. Leaving Harrison was always emotional, but this time, there would be no more appointments or special days to bring him back home even temporarily. He'd be gone now for another month to finish his film. I kept telling myself I could get through the next four weeks as a means to have him back for a lifetime. Hell, I'd lived forty years without him. What was four more weeks? But no matter how many times I said it in my head, my heart just wasn't convinced.

I was quiet most of the ride home, inside my head, thinking about what Della had said. Anxious for the results to come back so there'd be a few less worries on my mind. I pictured Harrison on the jet alone. And then I pictured myself there with him. Things at home were settled. Should I have gone with him? I didn't want to cancel on Emma, but I craved that man. I'd ached for the feel of his arms around me, and it had been so fleeting.

"Hello, anyone in there?" Shelby's voice interrupted my thoughts.

"I'm sorry, I wasn't paying attention. What did you say?"

"I wondered if you had anything fun planned while your friend is here?"

"Oh, yes, I'm going to have Nigel take us a few places around the city and probably take some time to just hang out around the house as well. I don't want to overwhelm her."

"I think the two of you would really enjoy Camden Market, and the Natural History Museum isn't the snooze-fest it sounds like. It's actually quite interesting. Those two things could fill a whole day and you'd be exhausted by the time you got home."

"I'll look into that when we get back to the house. I planned to sit down and try to work out a rough itinerary for us this afternoon. I thought maybe the zoo and Buckingham Palace, Windsor Castle and probably Kew Gardens because I loved it when I was here before. I do want to take her to Sky Garden for lunch. Have you been?"

"I've been in the past, but it's been a while. Do you want me to make that reservation for you?"

"Oh gosh no, I can do it. I've got to sit and map everything out. I actually quite enjoy doing that kind of thing. And it will take my mind off missing him." I sighed as the car slowed and we turned into the driveway.

"How long is she staying?" Shelby asked.

"Truthfully, I have no idea. I didn't ask. I assume a week or so?"

"Oh, you can easily fill a week. Let me know if you want any help with more sights. I'm glad to help or secure your tickets for you."

"I appreciate you; you know you're welcome to come along with us to any or all of these places. The more the merrier."

"You'll have to show me your final list and I may just take you up on that."

Nigel opened the back door and helped us out of the SUV. "What kind of trouble are the two of you finding this afternoon?" he asked.

Shelby spoke up first. "I'm heading to my place. I've got things there that need tending to.”

“Thank you for coming with me today.” I hugged her before she adjusted her purse on her shoulder and started walking toward home.

“I’m planning my time with Emma, cooking myself an early dinner, and crawling into bed before the sun sets. Maybe spend a little time in the yard first.”

“Boring! The both of you!” He waved his hand at me dismissively and laughed. “Well, if I’m not needed, I’ll be off then.”

“I’m all set for today Nigel, thank you. But prepare yourself, the next week or so we are going to be busy.” I shot him a cautionary look before I turned and set off toward the front door.

Inside, I slipped off my shoes and put them into the closet along with my purse as the automatic lock engaged. The sound triggered the memory of Harrison’s breath against my neck; flashbacks of the way his hands felt against my body, the way he kissed me and then picked me up and carried me to the shower flashed inside my head. *Stop it, Alice. It won’t make the time pass any quicker and will only bring unneeded sadness.*

Down the steps and into the living room, I cozied myself onto the leather couch, grabbing the cashmere blanket that was draped across its arm. It was cloudy out and would be a good day for a fire, but I didn’t want to go through the hassle of it just for myself. In another flashback, random bunches of embers burned a faint orange in an otherwise empty fireplace. Harrison’s breathing was rhythmic, and I felt his chest behind me as he slept, thick fog pressing against the windows like voyeurs looking for a free show.

I said stop it, Alice.

I pulled the blanket over my legs and realized how quiet the house was. No outside birdsong, Robin must be asleep in the treetops or shuffling around down by the stream. There was no humming from appliances, not even the ticking of a clock to break up the solitude. I pulled out my phone in an attempt to get my mind off of Harrison and typed out a text to Emma.

Can't wait to see you. I'm planning some fun stuff for us. Bring some comfy shoes because we'll be doing a lot of walking. Had my first appointment today. Harrison showed up and surprised me at the midwife's office. I miss him so much already.

I hit send and sat there, staring into space as I pictured him, wet, naked, standing in the Blakes' pool, every inch of him glistening. He was perfection in my imagination, and in reality, he had blown every detail of that dream out of the water.

My phone buzzed.

I've done all my packing, sign me up for everything. I'm ready, I can't wait to see you. I'm so glad he was able to be there with you. Seems every time he's faced with a challenge or a hurdle, he finds new ways to exceed your expectations. You deserve the best, and it seems like you've found it.

I responded immediately.

He really does, I don't know how I got so lucky. Anything you absolutely must see while you're here? What's at the top of the bucket list?

I got up and poured myself a glass of water, sipping it as I stared out at the backyard from the kitchen sink. Soon, the sounds of a baby would fill this house along with the joyous laughter of its parents. I was terrified and excited and exhausted, and somehow exhilarated all at the same time. *Am I ready for this? Can I handle it all? I've never done this before. But Harrison will be here with me, and I can do anything with him by my side, right? Everything will be fine. We'll be alright. …right?*

My phone buzzed again and I returned to the living room to grab it from the coffee table.

I definitely want to see Buckingham Palace, but mostly I just want to wander, and relax, and share some quality time with you. Don't plan too much. I wanna loaf around for a few days too. I re-sent the flight info, and I'll text if there are any last-minute changes. Love you!

My response was quick and short.

It's on the list, Buckingham Palace and loafing. Check, Check! Love you!

Dinner could wait; a nap was just what I needed. I pulled my legs up onto the couch and with the blanket still warm, curled up to drift off.

CHAPTER
17

Shelby and I spent two days finalizing all the details of the guest room for Emma, whose flight was due an hour from now. We'd transformed it from an unused, minimal, masculine-inspired space to something softer, more luxurious and cozier. I'd filled a large basket with all the comforts of home, products I love, and keepsakes to act as reminders of her trip. The linens were fresh, the pillows fluffed and the cozy blankets plentiful. She'd have bedroom views of the forest, and ensuite bubble baths would welcome her with candles and good books, eye level with the canopy, while the hillside sloped dramatically out of view below.

As I readied myself for the ride to the airport I wondered, *why am I so nervous?* For months, Emma and I had talked at length about everything. She knew more about me than almost anyone. The only difference was, we'd never met in person. *Everything is going to be fine, Alice. If anyone understands you, it's Emma.* I repeatedly assured myself there was nothing to be nervous about as I gathered my cell phone and lip gloss and dropped them into my bag. *You're going to have the best time together.* I threw my tote onto my shoulder and slipped my shoes on at the top of the landing before looking down onto the main living space, making sure everything was in its place. I blew out a nervous sigh, then headed for the SUV waiting in the driveway.

Nigel was his chipper self, as expected. He babbled on about this and that as I nodded and smiled. With one eye out the window, the other barely looking up to see him in the rearview mirror, I heard almost nothing he was saying. I was too busy thinking about Harrison. I wanted it to be him coming home so I could wrap myself around him, feel the strength of his body against mine, and lose myself in listening to him say my name. I wanted to plan our future and talk about the baby and everything that came along with it. And of course, as soon as Nigel pulled up to the gate at Heathrow, the memories flooded my mind of the last time I was here, leaving London and walking away from Harrison to go back to New England and James. I shook the thought from my head as Nigel opened the door to the backseat. I stepped out just as Emma walked out onto the sidewalk, pulling two large suitcases behind her.

She was taller than I expected and had the most beautiful jet-black hair I'd ever seen pulled back into a high ponytail, careless curls flowing downward behind her. Her cheeks were flushed pink, I assumed from the long flight and the bustle of the airport, her false lashes shielding dark eyes, her complexion flawless. Emma's figure appeared to be a lot like mine; busty with coke bottle curves on the thicker side, made more noticeable by the way the strap of her crossbody bag lay against her chest. A distressed tear in her jeans revealed part of a tattoo, as did the folded sleeve of her red plaid flannel button-down.

"You're finally here!" I shouted as I ran to her and hugged her. "C'mon, let's get out of this commotion." I grabbed the handle of one of her suitcases and ushered her back toward the SUV.

"I'm so glad to see you! This place is chaos!" She exaggerated an overwhelmed face and shook her head, then her eyes landed on Nigel. "You must be the illustrious Nigel I've heard so much about." She gave him an inquisitive side-eye as she approached him.

"And don't you forget it, love!" He leaned into her, shoving air kisses toward both cheeks. "Oh, you're a doll. Are there any more bags?"

"This is enough, don't you think?" she joked.

"Whatever you don't have we can always get; don't worry about a thing," I offered.

"You two climb in." He took the two suitcase handles and strode to the back of the SUV.

"So, are you hungry? Tired? Do you want to go get some food or just head back to the house?" I asked as Emma settled in beside me.

"Get in there you bloody thing. What have you packed Emma? Bags of stones?" Nigel's voice boomed in from behind us before the hatch slammed shut.

"Oh my God, I love him." Emma sounded surprised at her own admission.

"Nigel certainly is exceptional in all the best ways possible."

"That's why I love you, Alice." He batted his eyes as he plopped himself into the driver's seat. "Someone tell me where we're off to?"

I looked at Emma, and gorgeous as she was, she did look tired. "You probably want to rest, don't you? I know I did the first time I was here. It's okay. Besides, I want you rested and ready to see all the sights tomorrow."

"I'd actually love to lay down for a bit. The time change is so weird and the flight was...not comfortable."

"Let's just head back to the house, Nigel, please."

"Say no more!" He raised the partition and moments later, we were pulling away from the curb.

"I've got your room all ready for you, comfy and cozy. If there's anything you need or want, either we can go out and get it or I can have Shelby grab it for us."

"How's that all going?"

"What? Shelby?"

"Yeah."

"It's good. She's been a good friend to me, incredibly helpful, and we've found a good balance being in the house together."

"Well, that's good. I know at one point you were kind of nervous."

"Now that I've gotten to know her and her history with Harrison and all that, I think it just showed me how genuine she is, and what a truly good guy *he* is. It's not my story to tell, and if she wants to share, she will, but he really helped her out. They're like siblings, so, no funny business. Nothing like that."

"Well, that *is* good. And no one knows about you two yet, right?"

"Correct. We haven't really mapped that out yet. Probably when he's back from Brazil we'll figure it out. Until then, no one cares who I am. I'm just some random American woman with a chauffeur. No one even pays attention."

"Does it feel weird? That you have to 'figure it out?'"

"I haven't met all of his team yet. I don't know his manager or his publicist. And probably when we sit down to have the first meetings it will feel weird. I mean, the way we're supposed to publicly love one another being predetermined, our relationship governed by outsiders and all that, but for now, he's just Harrison to me."

"That's good. It seems like you're happy. Have you been feeling okay?"

"Yeah, really no complaints. The morning sickness is random and the midwife, Della, told me all is well. My bloodwork all came back normal, thank goodness. I was certainly paranoid about it while I waited for those results. It's still so early, but I feel good for the most part."

"Well, that's good too. Gosh, I can't wait to see London with you." She squeezed my hand in hers as she said it.

"We're going to have the best time! Some things I've seen before, but other things will be a first for me too. And we can relax some days at the house, go out shopping or whatever you like. After all, it's your vacation."

Emma smiled at me, one of those subdued, polite, nervous smiles, like there was more to be said, but for some reason, she wasn't saying it. As she turned her face away toward the window, I wondered if she could see through my cheerful exterior or sense that my feelings of inadequacy had started bubbling up, that the grip of loneliness had started twining its miserable fingers around my oxygen supply since the last time I'd seen Harrison. Maybe she regretted coming here. I had no idea, but something felt weird and I just couldn't put my finger on it.

CHAPTER 18

As we ascended the driveway, Emma commented that Harrison's house was quite understated compared to what her imagination would have had her believe. It wasn't the giant glass-clad mansion she expected, but something more normal, cozy. Beyond that, she hadn't said much in the time it took me to give her a quick tour of the first floor. She just nodded and smiled. Nigel strode past, carrying her suitcases to the guest room as I poured her a glass of water, and for the rest of the day, she was behind a closed door, resting. Nigel only stuck around for a few minutes after she vanished into the confines of the bedroom, then Shelby came with some groceries and did a few things around the house as usual before leaving in the early afternoon. It was as if Emma wasn't here at all until the scent of my cooking dinner hours later finally drew her out of the bedroom. She emerged, her hair a mess and residual creases left behind from the pillowcase still on one side of her face.

"Jesus, I was exhausted." She rubbed at her face, then her hair, realizing her curls were a scattered mess. "Oh shit, I must look like hell."

"You're fine." I tossed a hand sideways, dismissing her concern. "Are you hungry?"

"I mean, I could eat. Smells delicious. What's on the menu?" She smoothed her hair back and twisted it into a low knot with an elastic she'd pulled from her wrist.

"I've got lasagna fresh out of the oven, a tossed salad, and some garlic bread. Well, almost some garlic bread, I think it's got a few minutes left."

She hovered a moment over the bubbling pan of food, then grabbed one of the two plates and a fork that I'd set out and started scooping a large piece of lasagna from the pan. "It's like you know the way to my heart."

"I know the way to my own, and I don't think we're that different." I laughed and reached for the spatula she was still holding.

Emma set her plate on the table and returned to the kitchen to get a glass of water. "So, what's the plan for tomorrow?"

"Tomorrow I booked us tickets to the Natural History Museum. Rumor has it, it's fascinating, and if it sucks, we can leave." I shrugged. "After that, maybe a late lunch and then shopping at Camden Market? Or Borough Market, whichever you prefer. How's that sound?"

"Sounds perfect, actually."

The oven timer beeped, and I pulled the garlic bread out to cool on a trivet.

"Oh yum, I could eat this entire loaf myself," she said and started looking around the kitchen before pulling open a drawer. "Where do you keep the knives?"

I pulled a serrated knife from the drawer to my left and handed it to her.

"After dinner can we just hang out in our fat pants and watch a movie? I'm not sure I'm caught up on sleep yet if you can believe it." She sliced the bread, careful not to burn her fingers.

"That was my plan, and I can believe it, trust me. I've been there. It definitely takes some getting used to." I piled salad onto my plate and then headed toward the dining room. "As for tomorrow, I think Nigel plans to pick us up around nine a.m., but he could be here earlier if I ask him to. I figured that will give you time to sleep and then you can meet Shelby at breakfast before we head out." I set my plate down on the table and got comfortable. Emma followed suit, carefully positioning her water and the tray of garlic bread before taking a seat to my right.

"Yeah, sounds good to me." She shoveled a fork full of food into her mouth. "Oh, Shit! Hot!" Emma's mouth fell open and steam rolled out from the lasagna she was desperate to keep off of her tongue.

"You God damn fool, I just took that out of the oven!" I couldn't help but laugh at her.

When she finally got it swallowed, she asked, "Do you think I'll like her?"

"Shelby? I don't know. I hope so. She's funny. Pretty unassuming and she's easy to get along with, I think. She helped book a few of the tickets for the places we're going, so she might come along with us to some, but I'm not sure which ones."

"Sounds like fun." She took another steaming bite of lasagna and chewed quickly.

"No one's going to take that from you, you know," I laughed again. "Let it cool off, otherwise you won't be able to taste lunch tomorrow."

"I feel like it's been days since I've had anything to eat, and that flight felt like it took a week to get here. Not to mention I was jammed into the middle seat for it; an old snoring man with a hairy ear staring back at me on one side, and to my left, some guy who was legit full-on watching porn on his laptop. Just out in the open! Who does that?"

"What a creep. I would have asked to change seats."

"The flight seemed very full, and there were multiple crying babies scattered all over the place..." She shook her head, the corners of her mouth dramatically downturned. "Ugh. There was no escaping any of it." She rolled her eyes and then quickly changed her expression. "No offense."

"None taken; mine currently doesn't make any noise at all, which I'm thankful for. Hopefully you won't have to deal with any of that on your flight back."

She shrugged and avoided my eyes just like she did earlier today in the car, her face ruminative as if she had something to hide. Emma took another large bite of food and pushed pieces of her meal around her plate, giving her something else to focus her attention on. Several minutes passed in silence before she spoke again, clearly and deliberately changing the subject. "What movie do you want to watch?"

I looked up confused, wanting to flat-out ask, *why are you being so weird?* but unwilling to rock the boat so soon into our visit. "It's up to you. Your choice." I forced a smile before I returned my attention to my plate.

CHAPTER 19

Emma and Shelby's laughter rattled me from sleep the next morning. *Guess I don't have to worry about these two getting along*, I thought as I pulled myself from beneath the covers and shuffled into the closet, grabbing an ankle-length cotton skirt and my usual v-neck t-shirt along with an oversized cardigan on my way to the bathroom to get ready for the day.

Half an hour later they were still bantering back and forth when I found the two of them just sitting down to eat at the dining room table, Emma already dressed and ready for the day.

"Mornin', friends! Glad to see you two so comfortable with one another." I grabbed a muffin from the counter and sat down with them.

"We found out very quickly that we've got a lot in common." Shelby was buttering her toast.

"Yeah, what feels like a lifetime of being single, for one," Emma chimed in, then chuckled.

"You say that like it's a bad thing!" Shelby pointed her butter knife at Emma as she spoke.

Why are they getting on so well now, but Emma was so weird to me yesterday? I thought.

"I'm just saying I like having a hot body to put my cold feet on at night. You know what I mean?" Emma shot me a knowing look across the table.

I raised my eyebrows and gave her a nod of agreement, but in my head, I was thinking, *Oh, so today you're normal again? Maybe she was just tired yesterday; that much travel sucks. Give her a pass, Alice. Let it go.*

"I've got an electric blanket to keep me warm and the best part, it doesn't rattle on interrupting during my tele programs or leave the toilet seat up." Shelby rolled her eyes at me. "You know. You lived with one of those for too long."

"I did, but James wasn't all bad. Hell, in the beginning, he was amazing. But then again, aren't they all?"

"Oh, I don't know about that, now. Some of them are shit right from day one!" Emma pointed out.

"All I know is, I'm thankful for what I've got in my life now, and thankful for what I don't." I nodded as I spoke. Then my phone buzzed from my back pocket, a text from Nigel.

I'm in no shape to take you 'round today, love. I'm feeling quite poorly and will be staying under these covers. I've let Lawrence know and he'll be around to get you shortly. Don't be cross with me, please.

"I guess Nigel is staying home today." I looked at Emma. "But this gives you the opportunity to meet Lawrence. Speaking of, he'll be here soon. Are you almost finished?"

"Yup." She stuffed a piece of bacon into her mouth and washed it down with the last bit of her apple juice. "Bring it on, London!"

"Shelby are you coming with us today?" I asked.

"Not today. I'm going to tidy up the house and then I've got errands to run. I'll see you tomorrow morning. Same place, same time."

"Oh, okay, but you will come out with us sometime this week?" Emma questioned.

"Yes, I'm going to go with you lot to the zoo and lunch at The Spaniards Inn," Shelby explained.

"Sweet deal." Emma got up from the table and set her dishes in the sink. "I'm just going to grab my things, and I'll be ready."

"Okay, sounds good," I said.

When Emma was out of earshot I leaned in toward Shelby. "Every time I ask her about going home or her return flight, or how long she's staying, she changes the subject. Has she said anything to you?"

"You trying to get rid of her already?" Shelby asked jokingly, her accent thick.

"Not at all, I love having her here, just seems odd, that's all."

"I wouldn't worry too much about it. The conversation will surely come up again and you'll get your answer. Just enjoy your time."

Emma emerged from the guest room clad in faded and distressed blue jeans and a red-hooded sweatshirt, only now her crossbody bag lay draped to one side, and black sunglasses sat atop her head. "Let's see what this Natural History Museum is all about, wanna?" she asked, a smile spread across her face.

"I'm ready if you are!" I stood as Shelby headed toward the sink, tucking my chair back into its resting place.

"Do you think there's a woolly mammoth there?" Emma asked as I slipped my shoes on at the top of the landing.

"Ooh, that would be fun to see, but who knows." I shrugged. "See ya, Shelby. Thank you!"

"Enjoy!" She waved at us without turning around as she loaded the dishwasher.

Lawrence was waiting as expected, the back door of the SUV open, dark suit, dark glasses, hands resting clasped in front of him when we stepped out of the house and into the drive.

"Good morning, Lawrence." It was nice to see him again.

"Ma'am." He nodded but barely.

"Lawrence this is Emma, my friend visiting from Oregon." She stepped out from behind me and paused when she saw him, giving Lawrence his first full-length view of her.

The once straight-faced professional's stance softened and I watched as his eyebrows shot up above the upper rim of his sunglasses. Promptly pulling them away, he revealed a new excitement I'd never seen in his eyes before; he was on the verge of beaming, leaning in toward Emma, extending his hand toward her as she once again began to approach him.

"Hi," she said bashfully, pink rushing to the apples of her cheeks, her eyes fixed upward on his.

"Good morning, Emma." A strange combination of a half-smile, nod of acknowledgment, quick exhale, and nervous laugh all escaped him at once. For the first time ever, I think I was watching Lawrence awkwardly try to flirt as he left his first impression on my friend.

As soon as her hand touched his, a flush of crimson covered his face. Moments passed as they stared at each other, hands together but unmoving, smiling but saying nothing, and I stood watching them like an evil mastermind whose plan had come together without a hitch. Only, I'd never had a plan, and this certainly wasn't on my 'Emma's vacation' bingo card.

Just wait 'til Harrison catches wind of this, I thought, a slow devilish grin appearing on my face.

CHAPTER 20

Our time at the museum was short-lived. The exhibits were incredible of course, but my interest in them was irrelevant, because Emma seemed more intent on getting back to the SUV, more specifically, back to Lawrence, than enjoying what the museum had to offer. After all, budding love was more exciting than natural history, and I understood that. I'd been there not too long ago myself.

Shelby had somehow booked our tickets at the Tring location, nearly an hour away from home, giving Emma and Lawrence plenty of time to chat on the way there and back. While she took every opportunity to giggle at his jokes, bat those beautiful long eyelashes at him in the rearview mirror, and flirtatiously touch his shoulder from behind as he drove, I spent my time taking in the scenery to and from the museum. I only looked away long enough to secretly snap a candid photo of her leaned forward, her hand on Lawrence's shoulder through the open partition, the apples of her cheeks still pink against the white of her smile. I sent it to Harrison with the caption, *Apparently this is happening* followed by a shrugging emoji and my typical *xxx*. His lack of response told me he was busy on set. With my phone back in my pocket and my eyes back on the scenery, I drifted into my own world. In my head, I was back on a New Orleans balcony with Harrison's hands roaming my body, memories of his tongue against my thighs illuminated by city lights in the darkness, his face between my legs.

Not here, Alice, not now.

I looked back at the rearview mirror, watching the connection grow between Emma and Lawrence. I recognized those looks, full of wonder and anticipation of what might happen next. It wasn't that long ago I'd shared the same ones with Harrison. Hell, I'd be sharing them with him now if he were here. Instead, while Emma fell in love from the backseat, I sat there feeling like a voyeur. Like some sort of uninvited third wheel on a first date. Don't get me wrong, I was happy for them both. Love is such a hard thing to find in this world, I just didn't want to see either of them get hurt when she inevitably went back to the States. Maybe this was just lust, but only time would tell.

We arrived at Camden Market midday and enjoyed a cloudy afternoon shopping for souvenirs and trinkets among the hustle and bustle of London at lunchtime. We walked for what felt like miles and stopped so many places I quickly lost count. Our conversation ranged from currency exchange and weather to music, art, and books, with a good smattering of Lawrence-related questions, many of which I didn't know the answers to.

We grabbed a quick lunch to go at Emma's request, and headed back to find Lawrence waiting, a goofy grin spread across his face as soon as Emma came into view.

"What's next, ladies?" he asked as he helped her into the vehicle, his thumb rubbing against the top of her fingers, her hand lingering for longer than needed as she positioned herself into the backseat. A normal person may not have noticed that soft little swipe of the thumb, but I did.

"I think we're just headed back to the house, Lawrence, thank you." To verify I glanced at Emma, and she nodded.

"May I have a private moment?" Lawrence asked me under his breath when it was my turn to get into the vehicle.

"Certainly. I'll just be a second, Emma." I closed the car door to give Lawrence the privacy he requested. "Is everything okay?"

He sighed, composed himself, and then removed his sunglasses to look me in the eye. Then in almost a whisper he began, "Ma'am, I'm wondering how you'd, well, would it be okay if I..." He stopped and bit his bottom lip, eyebrows pinched together as he tried to find the right combination of words. "I'd like to..." He sighed. "This is probably inappropriate."

"Lawrence." I looked up at him stern but playful, one eyebrow raised. "I'm your friend, right?"

"Uh, yes? Ma'am?" He looked confused as he answered my question with a question.

"Stop this *ma'am* nonsense. My name is Alice, and I *AM* your friend. Now spit it out." I purposely laughed to try to calm him.

"I'd really like to ask Emma out for the evening, for dinner, you know, like a date. And you have Nigel, if you need to go out and I understand if you'd feel awkward about it. Maybe it's weird. I probably shouldn't even be thinking about this. It's okay if you say no, I was just—"

"Lawrence," I cut him off. He was rambling and avoiding making eye contact and I found it hilarious considering how serious and straight-faced and self-confident he usually was.

"Ma'...Alice?" He stumbled over what to call me.

"One condition." I raised my index finger in front of him.

"Name it." His response was lightning-fast.

"There will be no breaking of hearts. And you know, while I'm thinking of it, if dinner turns into dessert, and then drinks, and then an invite inside for a nightcap," I gave him a maternal look of warning, "don't be bringing her back to Harrison's for all that. Take her to your own house."

I winked at him and watched as his entire face turned a deep crimson. It was obvious how hard he tried to suppress his delight at the idea.

"We're all adults here, Lawrence. Have fun."

He nodded and reached for the door handle, then paused.

"Ma'am—" His chin wrenched to the left as he stopped himself, "I mean, Alice."

I looked up to meet his eyes.

"Thank you, Alice. Nothing gets broken, I promise." He smiled before pulling the door open for me.

I winked at him again as he helped me into the backseat with a still-smiling Emma, her face giving away how eager she was to know what we were just talking about.

"What was that about?" she asked after the door was closed.

"You'll know soon enough."

"TELL ME!" She grabbed at my hand and went silent just as Lawrence slid into the driver's seat, now well within earshot.

I squeezed her hand in mine as I shook my head then watched as her eyes rose slowly to find Lawrence's again in the rearview mirror, the pink in her cheeks appearing again just as quickly as her smitten smile.

CHAPTER 21

The ride home was short and quiet. Emma and Lawrence flirted silently in the rearview mirror, while I sat by watching and stifling giggles. As soon as I was out of the car, Lawrence helped Emma by taking her hand, as usual, but the lingering touch and the quick look she shot me when she stepped out into the driveway told me I better get into the house and let them be.

I had time to get inside and get comfortable on the couch before she burst through the front door, then slammed it shut, falling back against it dramatically.

"ALICE! MY GOD, THAT MAN!" Her voice echoed across the tile floors as she lay her head back, mouth open to the ceiling.

I looked up at her, smirking.

"He makes me pulsate in places that haven't seen excitement in a very, *VERY* long time."

I burst into laughter.

She dropped her palm against her chest and exhaled, eyes shut, then slipped her shoes off before making her way down the steps toward me. She spun herself in a quick twirl before collapsing beside me on the couch. Silent, she shook her head in apparent disbelief as she stared straight ahead, her bottom lip pulled in, her nostrils flaring in a deep inhale. She turned suddenly and shot me a wide-eyed look. "Dinner. Drinks." She paused, her face full of mischief, "What do I wear?" She scrunched up her nose as she shrugged.

It reminded me of Harrison.

"Did he say where he was taking you?" I asked.

"No. He just said to dress comfortable and he'd see me at six."

"Well, that gives you," I glanced at my watch, "just shy of two hours to figure it out and make it happen. Feel free to raid my closet if you want, but you may need to adjust your expectations."

"Thank you!" She leapt off the couch and spun to face me. "I hope you're not upset this is happening?" She clenched her teeth together, a nervous look on her face.

"Of course not. Go have fun. Lawrence is a good guy, and I made him promise not to break your heart."

"I mean I just got here to see you, and now I'm going out without you."

"You're gonna be like two peas in a pod, I can just tell. So, stop worrying about me and enjoy yourselves."

"I love you!" She squealed as she took off in the direction of the guest room.

"Love you!" I hollered back, then grabbed my phone from the coffee table.

Still no message from Harrison. I was disappointed, but he was working. I knew there'd be days like this while I waited for him to get back. I sighed then glanced up from my phone, my eyes landing on the lifeless fireplace in front of me. I decided to start a fire and watch a movie tonight until Emma got back. Assuming she actually came back. The corner of my mouth twisted into a dirty-thought-laden smirk.

Maybe when Emma heads back to Oregon, I'll fly out to see Harrison and spend some time on set, I thought. *Or would I be too much of a distraction? Would he be frustrated that I'd be taking up too much of his time, ruining his creativity? He always wants me to feel like the center of his attention.* I sighed again. *Certainly not feeling that way now, are ya, Alice?* My thoughts were desperate to pull in happy visuals but just as quickly they yanked me back to sadness, like waves in an angry ocean, churning my headspace into a jumbled muddy mess.

I got up, started a fire, and sent a quick text to Shelby.

Busy tonight? Emma has a date so I'm on my own.

As the fire grew, her response popped up.

Sorry, can't tonight. A date? With who?

I tapped in, *Lawrence. Wouldja believe it? No big deal, just thought I'd ask. See you for breakfast?* I hit send and leaned back into the comfort of the warm leather behind me.

Closing my eyes, I pictured Harrison again. He was always my go-to for comfort, hell even before I knew him, he eased the pain of loneliness for me. But since I'd touched him, loved him in real time, experienced him in real life, that comfort now came tinged with longing. I let my mind take me back into the garden of The Spaniards Inn, the mumble of people in the background, the tiny flecks of golden twinkle lights above us like a million tiny angels bringing us together. The inquisitive look on his face when I realized he was actually speaking to me, and the way the corners of his eyes crinkled as he smiled for the first time. I remembered the feeling that washed over me, because it was real life, not some fantasy daydream I'd configured with my imagination. God, his smile was magic.

My heart started to beat a little harder just thinking about the smell of his cologne that night; the way he'd actually listened to me when I spoke. Looking back, I think I fell in love with him the instant he was in front of me and knew he was really, actually real. It wasn't a conscious decision, it was entirely out of my control, and I was helpless against it.

A pop from the logs in the fireplace jolted me from my thoughts, and as I stood there making sure the hot little spark hadn't caused any damage anywhere, I realized the universe was trying to hand me a life lesson. Patience. Something I'd never had much of, and something I really wasn't interested in learning. Which is probably exactly why it was staring me in the face. I settled back onto the couch, annoyed that for weeks to come I'd be away from the man I so desperately wanted to feel close to again, when I was interrupted by the buzzing of Shelby's response.

Yes, breakfast. Should be an interesting convo. See you then.

She wasn't wrong. The date hadn't even happened yet and I was fascinated to see if Emma would spill the details or keep it all hidden away from us. I didn't know her well enough yet to know if she was the kind to make first moves, or if she was like me, more reserved until someone set the scene and initiated forward movement. I also couldn't remember a time since I'd known her that she had even been on a date. She struck me as more of a friends-with-benefits, when-the-occasion-arose kind of girl. At least I'd have a little entertainment while I suffered through another month without Harrison.

CHAPTER

22

Lawrence arrived promptly at six and rang the doorbell like the gentleman I knew him to be. I answered the door and found him dressed in faded blue jeans and a black button-down shirt, the sleeves rolled to the middle of his forearms, the top button of his collar undone. He looked surprisingly relaxed except for the nervous tension in his forehead.

"Hi, Lawrence. C'mon in." I held the door open, gesturing for him to come inside.

"Hi...Alice," the professional side in him hesitating to be so candid.

"Have a seat." I started down the foyer steps. "Emma should be out in a second. I've barely seen her since we got back earlier." He was silent as he followed behind me. "You smell good, but you look nervous," I added, trying to get him to loosen up.

"Oh thanks, I—" His voice stopped short as Emma emerged from the guest room.

She'd chosen one of my long cotton skirts in a deep shade of coral, pairing it with a cream-colored camisole and a matching off-the-shoulder v-neck sweater. A leather cross-body bag different from her usual one accentuated a healthy view of her cleavage and matched a well-worn pair of brown cowboy boots, which dangled from her right hand as she smoothed at her curls with her left.

"Hi." The blush of her cheeks rose to meet the eyelashes I was so jealous of.

Lawrence stood there a moment on the bottom step, a sweet look of awe on his face. "Emma, you're...beautiful." He appeared shy as he exhaled, seemingly thankful he was able to string a sentence together.

She tipped her head down to shield the embarrassment that was overtaking her. "You're so sweet, thank you." Then she looked up again to lock eyes with him.

I looked from one to the other and back again while they stared at each other in silence, waiting for someone to make the next move. *Awkward.*

"Okay, well, you kids have fun, and Lawrence, you have a key, so I'll lock up as usual." Still, no one spoke, they just stood there, looking at each other and smiling, googly-eyed like teenagers.

My God, what's it gonna take? I thought to myself, then coughed loudly. "Okay then." I moved toward Emma. "Do you need help with those boots?" I put my hand on her shoulder, which seemed to have a small impact.

"Um, no." She shook her head but barely, her doe-eyed stare locked on Lawrence.

Okay, let's try something different. "What time is your reservation, Lawrence?"

At the sound of his name, he turned and faced me. *Thank goodness, finally! At least that worked.*

"Reservation is at half six but not too far from here." He nodded slightly as if reassuring himself that was the correct information and I tipped my head twice quickly toward the door, indicating he needed to get it together and get moving.

He shot me a quick look of realization before straightening his back. "Emma, if you're ready, we'll be off." He held out his hand toward her, and she blushed again. Stepping toward him, she placed her left hand in his, slipped on her boots, smoothed at her skirt, and adjusted her bag, never letting go of his hand.

They walked together up the stairs as I found my way back to the couch. As Lawrence held open the door for her, Emma turned to me and waved. "I'll see you later." The look of pure mischief plastered across her face made me laugh out loud.

I bet you won't, I thought.

"Have fun!" I called out to them as the door shut, leaving me home alone once again. A familiar feeling I absolutely hated.

In the silence, I fixed myself dinner then ate and cleaned up the dishes, and as the hot water washed away what remained on my plate, I wished it would wash away the sadness I couldn't shake off. I dried my hands and wiped down the faucet and counter, reminded of the life I used to live and how this one had started to feel the same. I hated cooking just for myself. Hated eating alone. Hated the feeling that I wasn't important enough for anyone to seek me out and spend time with me or that I was no one's priority. Mostly I hated that I felt these things at all because I knew Harrison would be here if he didn't have a previous commitment. I didn't want him to be any less of a stand-up guy. I wanted him to honor his word and follow through with his dreams, but I also selfishly wanted him here with me, right now. I blinked back tears as I folded the kitchen towel and left it beside the sink.

tap tap tap.

I looked up, and though blurry, the kitchen lights illuminated a small, round, saffron-chested friend just outside my window. I couldn't help but be grateful. Robin seemed to be able to tell when I needed a little lift in spirits. I touched my index finger to the window as if to tell him I'd be with him shortly, then reached into the fridge for the blueberries I now kept on hand all the time. He didn't need many, just three or four, and that would keep him happy. With snacks in hand, I went outside to find him.

"Robin? Where are you, buddy?" I kept my voice soft and held out the palm of my hand.

He dropped down from the gutter above me and landed softly in my hand, his black eyes fixed on me, disregarding the sweet little friendship bribes I was offering.

"Aww, I'll be okay. Just a sad night. I'm missing Harrison, just feeling lonesome I guess."

Robin hopped up onto my shoulder as I sat down in a patio chair, my hand once again offering fruit as it rested against the chair's cold arm. Uninterested, he sang to me. A rambling warble at first followed by a few short *tic-tic-tic* sounds. Then he rounded out his ode to loneliness with another soft *fizz* sound. When he was finished, he wiped his beak on my shoulder, back and forth, almost as if he was trying to comfort me, a wild bird's version of, *there, there, I'm here with you.*

"That was beautiful. And much needed. Thank you. I hope you didn't journey out here after dark just because of me."

Another twittering *tic-tic-tic* and a swiping of the beak.

Is this bird actually trying to communicate with me? Am I full-on losing my marbles? I thought.

He hopped down to my hand, landing on the thick base of my thumb, his nails poking into my flesh but not enough to hurt. He looked up again, cocked his tail and his head at the same time, and then poked at the blueberries to determine which one he might be interested in.

"It's funny isn't it, how you can't speak English and I can't sing to you in your language either, but we both seem to feel comfort from one another. Maybe your soul is the one I lost so many years ago, huh? My guardian angel come to save me every time I slip into this loneliness?

Who's to say? But I'm thankful for you." For the first time, I gently reached out to stroke the brown-green feathers that covered his body with the back of my index finger, unsure if he would allow it.

He didn't move, and we sat there in silence while I stroked his feathers, and he picked at his fruit, staining my hand various shades of blue and aubergine. I didn't mind, I appreciated the trust he showed me and the sincerity of his friendship. Tonight, he'd sought me out, seen me upset and alone through the kitchen window, and gotten my attention. I had human friends that weren't that tuned in to the way I felt. Robin was just the little bit of magic I needed while Harrison was away. When he was finished with his berries he hopped back up on my shoulder and shook his head again, sending bits of blueberry to land against my ear and neck.

"Geez, thanks a lot, buddy," I joked. "And after all I've given you!"

I felt him bite at my earlobe, not to hurt me but presumably to clear a piece of fruit from its surface, followed by another warbling murmured song. Then he wiped his beak on my shoulder again.

tic tic tic.

"Oh Robin, you are an animated one. Thank you for sharing your evening with me and being such a lovely friend, but you better get off to bed now. You know what they say about the early bird," I cautioned.

Another warbled song and off he flew into the darkness.

I chuckled to myself as I wiped the remaining fruit bits from my neck, and washed my hands at the kitchen sink, the stains remaining no matter how I scrubbed. *Who would have imagined that I'd have a newfound friend in a bird?* I scribbled the word *mealworms* on the grocery list beside the fridge before shuffling back into the living room. *Shelby will think I've lost my God damned mind.*

I welcomed the comfort of the couch and the familiarity of 'You've Got Mail' in the background. *It could be worse, Alice. It could be so much worse,*

I thought, picturing my life if I'd never known who Harrison Edwards was. If I'd never seen him or heard of him a day in my life. If I'd never dreamed about him, if I'd never come to London. If he'd never appeared at The Spaniards Inn and changed my life forever.

The jarring sound of my phone vibrating on the coffee table pulled me out of the spiral happening inside my head, and as my eyes adjusted to the light on the screen, I saw it was Harrison calling.

"Finally!" I said out loud and slid the green icon to the right. "Hi, babe!"

"My love! I miss you!" His voice was low and raspy, which, let's be honest...it just does things to me.

"You okay? You sound like you're catching a cold," I asked, trying to veer my impure thoughts into something a bit more decent.

"I've had a hell of a day on set. There were so many scenes where I was yelling, I've nearly lost my voice. But we got them done, so hopefully that's the end of that. How are you, love?"

"I'm okay, I guess. Just watching a movie, waiting for Emma to come back." I pulled the phone away from my ear and glanced at the time. 9:45 p.m. "I should probably give up and go to bed."

"So ol' Lawrence, mister prim and proper, pulled the trigger and made a move today, huh?" I could tell by his voice he was smiling.

"Yeah, they both stopped dead in their tracks when they saw one another, like something out of a movie, and then it was a full day of flirtation without words in the rearview mirror, as I sat there—"

He interrupted me, "So, no Nigel today?"

"No, he wasn't feeling well so Lawrence took us around."

"I hope he's not feeling poorly too long. Send him my best."

"I will. I'll hear from him tomorrow as planned I'm sure. Enough about other people, tell me about you. You really doing okay?" I asked.

"I'm alright, love. I'm missing you though, and it's heavy on me that we're apart. I wish I could just commute to this set and be home in bed with you every night. I'd do anything to feel the warmth of you against my fingertips. I never want to be away from you, Alice."

"I wish you were here too. Everything is fine, but my heart misses your smile, and my lips miss your kisses, and well, my lots of things miss *ALL* your things." I sighed loud enough so he could hear.

"My things are desperate for your things too, darling, trust me. They make it known all the time." He laughed and I could see his dimples in my mind.

"You sure it's going to still be four more weeks?"

"Right now, they're telling me I should be home around first December. So, block off your social calendar, because I plan to kiss every inch of your body as many times as you can stand it."

"Don't make promises you can't keep now," I warned.

"You're going to be absolutely sick of me, I promise."

"Never. It's not possible."

There was a rustling of the phone and muffled discussion as if he'd had to cover the speaker with his hand.

"Okay, sorry about that, darling. They are calling us back for night scenes, so I'm going to have to go for now. I love you; I love you; I love you, Alice."

"I love you too, babe."

"Call you tomorrow." Then I heard a kissing sound in my ear.

This man, honestly. I closed my eyes and felt my cheeks warm.

I kissed my phone and put it back to my ear just as the line went dead.

I sat there a moment feeling sorry for myself, imagining what he was doing, who was around him, how they were able to enjoy the warmth of his personality, hear him laugh, and just be a party to the joy he exudes.

I couldn't help but miss him. In the moments that passed, I felt myself getting more frustrated, wanting to kiss him, feel his hands on my skin, to see that notorious dark curl fall forward, and watch as his fingers instinctively sink into his hair to pull and twist it away from his eyes.

But then I looked around me and realized, *Alice, you idiot. You're sitting on the man's couch, in his home, about to crawl into his bed. He chose you, you fool. What on earth do you have to be sad about? Just because he's working and not at home? To provide a life for you and the child you created together no less. Get a grip, lady. Your life is exponentially better than it has ever been. Stop sulking and go crawl into Harrison Edwards' bed, the bed he's decided he wants to share with you, out of all the people on the planet, forever!*

That voice in my head was right. I needed to get my shit together because another month of this kind of internal dialogue was going to drive me crazy. The fire was dead. I got up and made sure for the third time since Lawrence and Emma left that the door was securely locked even though I knew the lock was automatic, turned off the lights, and made my way upstairs to bed. With Harrison's pillow clutched tightly to my chest, its corner against my cheek, I thought, *tomorrow is a new day. I just need to get some sleep.*

And then I started wondering what Emma was doing.

CHAPTER 23

Since I'd been in London, I'd actually been getting some decent rest, a welcome change from years of restless nights. I assumed it was because this pregnancy, albeit early, was exhausting me. My dreams had become nearly non-existent and on the rare occasion they did happen, the images never stuck with me. There were people, but no faces, and places but no identifying markers. Until tonight.

Tonight, I was back in New England, alone in the driveway looking up at the old white farmhouse. It was summer because the grass was lush and green, and the cloudless sky was a deep royal blue. The gravel of the driveway crunched beneath my sneakers as I approached the porch, accompanied by the rhythmic sounds of chickadees echoing out from the nearby lilacs. From the crook of my right arm, a large tray-like antique basket hung, today's mail hidden below enough daisies to fill two large vases, picked fresh from the lower field before I'd walked the half-mile dirt driveway back home.

James was in the kitchen at the table when I entered, the screen door creaking and then slamming behind me. But he wasn't the James I expected. He was the James I'd met twenty-two years ago. Young and tan, quick to please, and always eager to touch me, he stood to greet me as soon as I walked in.

"Hi, baby, those daisies are almost as pretty as you are." He reached for me, one hand pulling the basket gently from my arm and placing it on the counter before returning to my hip, his mouth like a magnet landing on the skin left exposed by the neckline of my cotton summer sundress. His other hand was warm against my waist, then my ribs, then landed to squeeze my breast.

My head fell to the side as his mouth climbed my neck, his tongue at my earlobe as he whispered, "This dress would look better on the floor," before gently biting and pulling it into his mouth.

I could feel the strength in his hand as it moved from my breast to the back of my head. Sections of my auburn curls fell between his fingers before he grasped a handful and gently tightened his grip, pulling my head back slightly.

"James..." He felt amazing, but I didn't want this.

His free hand fell to the tie at my hip, releasing it from its bow, allowing my dress to fall open in the front, exposing more of my body to the humid summer air of the kitchen. He stood back and looked at me, at my body, and when his eyes met mine again, he said nothing, only flared his nostrils like a wild animal in rut and drew his bottom lip into his mouth.

"James," I said again, this time raising my hands in front of me, motioning for him to stay where he was, despite the pulse I'd developed between my legs.

He ignored me, yanking his white t-shirt from the waist of his jeans to expose his abdomen. His somehow twenty-seven-year-old abdomen, tan and taut and chiseled like I remembered it from the first time I'd seen it so many years ago. I was still forty, but James was exactly the way I'd found him two decades ago.

He stripped the shirt up over his head and slung it backward without regard to where it landed. Then, with a hand on each of my hips, he pressed me back against the kitchen counter, knocking the daisies and the mail to the floor. He stared at me as he pressed his body into me and I could feel the length of his erection throbbing through his jeans. He dragged his fingertips slowly from my knee to my hip, then traced forward along the edge of the leg of my panties, slipping two fingers beneath the trim and pulling them to the side before sinking the same two fingers inside of me.

"I don't think we should..." I began again, but before I could finish my sentence those same two fingers were against my mouth, silencing me.

His gaze burned hot as he held eye contact, moving his mouth closer, then closer still, to mine. His fingers slipped easily from my lips to my chin before he drew them both into his mouth and pulled them slowly back out again, a lust-filled grin spread across his face as his taste buds recognized me.

"Let me have you, Alice," he whispered before he kissed me, his tongue teasing at mine.

Then it occurred to me that Harrison had said those same words to me before.

My face twisted with frustration and annoyance, and I pulled away from him sharply.

"James, NO! I can't do this. I don't *want* to do this." I protested, my palms against his chest, pushing him, trying to unpin myself from the edge of the counter.

"Alice." He was stern, his face angry.

"No, James. Stop." I shoved him from me now, hard enough that the back of him hit a chair at the table.

"Alice." My name was drawn out as it left his mouth. His face morphed in real-time in front of me, from twenty-seven-year-old James to forty-nine-year-old James, the salt and pepper of his hair amplified, the sag of age in his skin, the weight of loss in the lines of his face, and the destruction of time all suddenly present in front of me.

"I have to go, James." I grabbed at the edges of my dress, trying to tie it back together and get out of the kitchen at the same time, struggling with no free hands.

"No, Alice," he barked at me, his footsteps heavy as he pursued me toward the door. "You're not leaving me." His breathing was labored as his body morphed from muscular to gaunt.

I needed to run, to get away from him but I couldn't believe my eyes. This happy, lighthearted man was changing to an angry hellish darkness right in front of me.

My dress secured, I flung the screen door open and began to run, James reaching the threshold just as the door snapped back, the hook and eye latch catching him in the eye socket.

"FUCK!" he bellowed, grabbing at his eye with one hand while shoving the screen door open again with the other. "Come back here, you bitch!"

I reached the car, but why were all the doors locked? Where were the keys? I glanced up and saw James, his right eye mostly closed, his face grimaced in pain, and his right cheek covered in bright red blood. He grabbed a hatchet that was leaning against the house and set off across the porch in my direction.

Get to the barn, Alice. Get the four-wheeler. Get away from him any way you can, I thought, the voice in my head racing faster than my legs would carry me.

I could hear him behind me, his footsteps getting closer as I wrenched open the barn door, old flaking paint slicing at the skin under my fingernails as I lost my grip. *My God, the smell of gasoline is overwhelming.* I gagged, unable to control it. My heartbeat pounded in my ears and I couldn't catch my breath, but as James approached, I could smell him, a stench of sweat and alcohol so pungent I could almost taste it. I threw myself up onto the four-wheeler, straddling it, desperate for it to start. *C'mon, C'mon, C'monnnn...* but with every turn of the key, James got closer and the engine only gasped out a continuous slow wheeze.

Suddenly James' bloody hand was in my hair, ripping me from the seat of the four-wheeler and onto the ground. "You're right where you deserve to be, you know that?" he sneered in my face. His facial features were even more deteriorated. His right eye socket was hollow and had already turned gangrenous at the edges, while what was left of the skin on his face was pocked and pitted as if it had been melted in a fire. His bottom jaw bone and lower teeth were exposed on the right side, and bits of his scalp peeled off and fell away, landing in the hay on the floor as he hovered only inches from me.

My gaze dropped down to where it landed. *Why is the hay wet?* I rubbed my fingers against it. *It's cold but doesn't feel like water. It's got a menthol after-burn.* I followed the path of wet hay as it trailed away from me and back toward the ATV. *Drip.* It was gasoline, and a steady flow of pale yellow droplets continued to fall from the belly of the four-wheeler, pooling wider and wider beneath it. *It's got to be almost empty,* I thought.

"It doesn't have to be like this, James," I pleaded.

"You made it this way." He twisted the length of my hair around his fist securing a tighter grip, yanking my face closer to him in the process.

"No. You don't have to hurt me." I coughed, unable to catch my breath while trying to suppress a constant gag from the combination of overwhelming smells. Tears streamed down my cheeks as full-blown terror set in.

"You chose this." His face was so close to mine that he was nearly touching me, his skin slipping from his cheeks.

"No, James, please. I'm sorry."

"No, you aren't. You're a fucking liar." His breath was hot against my face as I watched his flesh continue to rot away. Sections of his fingers pulled away from the bones in his hands and became tangled in my hair as he struggled to keep a grip on me. "A cheating whore is what you are."

It was as if I were experiencing this firsthand, and somehow also watching it happen from a different angle all at the same time. I knew he was holding me to the floor of the barn by my hair because I felt the pain, I could taste his stench, I could hear his skin melting and rotting as he held me captive, but I could also watch our every move from multiple vantage points.

I closed my eyes, disgusted by the corpse he was disintegrating into in front of my very eyes. His clothing was now torn and dirty, the majority of his body nothing more than bones while his innards were barely held intact by what was left of his rotting skin. *Think Alice, think...* Knowing his anger stemmed from Harrison, I tried one last-ditch effort to keep him from killing me.

"James, I'm pregnant." I sobbed openly, terrified of what would happen next. "Please, please don't hurt me."

Silence.

I blinked hard, trying to clear the tears from my eyes without the use of my hands. I didn't hear him breathe, I couldn't hear any movement in the barn at all, and then I felt him slowly release my hair, his hands dropping to his sides. I carefully straightened my neck then scrambled to sit upright and scoot myself backward and away from him, watching him. James blankly sat back without a word, his remaining eye focused on me, hopeless. His hands hung lifeless at his sides, and he came to rest on his haunches.

The light from the driveway spilled through the barn door opening and illuminated one last drop of gasoline as it fell from the underside of the four-wheeler, and in the same moment, James threw his rotting head back and exhaled a terrifying guttural scream. The lower portion of his jaw fell away and bounced off his decomposing chest, rattling as it hit the floor, sending dislodged teeth scattering around him. His entire body burst into a tower of flames in front of me, scorching the bales of hay in the rafters, causing the trail of gasoline in front of me to ignite and chase me across the floor.

CHAPTER 24

I gasped as I regained consciousness and sat straight up in the bed. Expecting it to still be the middle of the night, I squinted against the sunlight that poured in through the windows.

"Jesus Christ." I rubbed at my eyes and blinked hard, then let my hand rest against my chest, waiting for my heart rate to return to normal. "What the fuck, Alice." As the nightmare replayed in my head, my eyebrows lifted from a scowl to a look of shock, picturing James in flames in front of me.

I chuckled. *James in flames. Good one.*

I threw back the covers and headed for the bathroom to shower and get ready for the day. *Maybe he really did burn the house to the ground*, I thought. Either way, I needed to get these visuals out of my head.

Downstairs, Shelby was cleaning up the breakfast dishes.

"Morning. I made muffins, scrambled eggs, toast. Bacon. You hungry?"

"Morning, yeah, thanks. Where's Emma? I expected to see her down here with you already." I glanced toward the door. No cowboy boots.

"Not here." Shelby stayed busy at the sink but shot me a knowing glance with raised eyebrows.

"Hmph, guess it was a good date then, huh?" I poured a glass of juice.

"Something was good, I'd bet that much." Her head remained focused on the dishes she was putting in the dishwasher, but I could see the satisfied smirk on her face.

I fixed myself a plate and sat at the table.

"Well, I guess it's a good thing I didn't have anything planned for us today. What was the plan for tomorrow?" I asked as I smeared butter across half of my blueberry muffin.

"We were all going to the zoo, remember? And then I'd made a late lunch reservation at the Aqua Shard Restaurant for the two of you."

"Okay, well, I'm sure she'll be back soon. You busy today?"

"I'm just keeping to my schedule of stuff here and at home while Harrison is still away. Nothing too exciting, you know." She closed the dishwasher. "When you're done, just plop those things in there and set it running, okay?"

"Yeah, no problem. I'll probably do a load of laundry today, maybe catch up on some reading until she gets back."

Shelby had just pulled out a chair at the table when I heard voices approach the front door. As I stood to go open it, I heard a key slide into the lock and then click before it swung open. There on the landing stood Lawrence, in plain clothes but not the ones he had on last night, and Emma, in last night's now wrinkled clothes and sunglasses that shielded her eyes from mine.

"Good morning," I called out as I sat back down and took a bite of my eggs.

"I'll bet it was..." Shelby mumbled quietly in my direction.

"Hi, sorry I missed breakfast." Emma scurried down the stairs and back toward the guest room so quickly that I barely saw her whiz past me.

I looked at Shelby, who was chuckling to herself but looking smugly at Lawrence, whose cheeks were now a blushing crimson.

"Morning to you lot," he said, shaking his head.

"Mm-hmm." Shelby continued laughing as she sipped her tea.

From the guest room, a breathless Emma hollered, "We didn't have plans today, did we?"

"No, all clear," I yelled back toward her.

"We were hoping to see some sights together, if that's okay ma'-I mean, Alice," Lawrence caught himself.

"You're grown adults, like I said last night. You two do whatever you like. As a matter of fact, tomorrow there are tickets reserved for two, to the zoo and the Aqua Shard for lunch. Take Emma, surprise her. I'm sure she'll love it."

"Oh wow, are you sure? Didn't you want to do those things with her? I don't want to interfere." He held up a hand in protest.

"I've been to the zoo already and the Aqua Shard is a bit romantic for the two of us, no matter how good the view is. Just go enjoy it."

Shelby chimed in, "The lunch reservation is for half two and is under my name. The zoo tickets are good any time of day. I'll email you the confirmations later so you'll have what you need."

"Thank you both." He smiled at each of us.

"So, things went well?" I asked. "Where did you two go last night?"

"I took her round to The Spaniards Inn. I like it there, and the atmosphere is cozy and cheerful. Well, I don't have to tell you, do I?" He tipped his head toward me knowingly. "I figured it's full-on London to be fair, and seems like the place usually sets the tone for successful relationships, so, yeah, we had dinner and some drinks and..." He looked away to shield me from seeing his face.

Just then Emma shuffled out in a change of clothes, carrying a large over-the-shoulder bag stuffed to the gills with what I assumed were the majority of her clothing and toiletries. Her face, a mixture of hopeful nervousness, reminded me of my first morning after with Harrison. It only took one night with him for me to want to pack a bag as well.

"When will I see you again?" I half-joked.

"It's probably just for tonight?" she said nervously, then looked at Lawrence seeking confirmation before returning her attention to me. *That's a considerable sized bag for just one night.*

"No worries. Don't even think twice about it, okay? I know all too well what you're feeling. Now, give me a hug before you head out." I stood up and held my arms out to my friend.

"You sure you're okay?" she asked again, faking a frown as she stepped toward me.

"I'm fine! Shelby and I have things to do anyhow. Don't you worry about me. C'mere!"

When she embraced me, I whispered quietly in her ear, "If he really matters to you, don't let anything stop you," then I gave her an extra little squeeze, and she nodded against my shoulder before stepping back toward Lawrence, their hands connecting as if drawn together by magnets.

"Lawrence, you guard her with your life, capeesh?" I gave him a stern look.

"You know I will, Alice." He nodded happily, clearly proud he hadn't stumbled over what to call me, then looked to Emma, confirming she was ready to go.

In an instant, they were gone.

"So much for having a friend come to visit, eh?" Shelby prodded as I sat back down at the table beside her.

"Yeah. I guess so."

<h1 style="text-align:center">CHAPTER
25</h1>

I didn't see Emma again for six days. Sure, she sent texts and told me all about the fun she was having with Lawrence. About all the sweet things he was doing for her and how she adored the little cottage where he lived. She raved about the food and the view at the Aqua Shard and told me they'd been back to The Spaniards Inn at least twice since their first visit. She gushed about their compatibility and their wildly different upbringings and how they were literally finishing each other's sentences. Occasionally, she'd send me a photo of the two of them together, each one showing them holding hands in some scenic spot or his arm around her waist or shoulder at the pub, but the last one she'd sent me was of them kissing and the message read, *I never want to leave.*

I understood exactly how she felt. One night led to a week, and then suddenly you wanted to throw away your entire life to be here and stay close to these British men, consequences be damned. If anyone got it, I got it.

So, don't. I'd responded half joking. Thinking there was no way she'd drop her entire life to stay in London. But boy was I wrong. She'd texted me back, *Confession: I never had a return ticket. Lawrence or no Lawrence,*

I had planned to stay. To figure it out, to find work. I'd hoped we could start something together, a business, a charity, something to keep us both busy. You never said anything, but I know you noticed how I'd avoid the topic of leaving when you brought it up. When I said I was coming to visit in two weeks, it was because I had to give work my notice. I quit my job fully intending to never come back to the States.

Was I surprised? Kinda. We'd never discussed these things or planned for them. We never talked about ideas for a shared passion project, but also, no, because the traits I admired in Emma were reflective of the traits I'd been rediscovering in myself. Tenacity. Fearlessness. Taking control, asking for forgiveness instead of permission. I couldn't blame her for making bold choices for her life, for wanting a way out of everything she was familiar with to start something new with people she felt valued by.

How's Lawrence feeling about this? I'd asked.

He's the one that mentioned me staying. Last night after dinner, then wine in front of the fire followed by absolutely mind-blowing sex (sorry, TMI?) we ended up in bed. After about an hour of us laying together in the dark, out of nowhere he said, "I'd really like to give us a fair go, Emma. Stay here with me, permanently." And I get it now, the way the accent just makes everything seem more romantic. I felt like I was living a fairytale. I might sound crazy because it's only been a few days, but I could easily fall in love with this man, maybe I already have.

Nothing you just said sounds remotely crazy to me. Remember who you're talking to? We'll figure out the work stuff later. For now, bask in the happiness.

I sent the text yesterday, but she never responded. I wondered how long it would actually be before I saw her again. I mean, she still had stuff here, so she'd have to come back at some point, right? In the last six days, I hadn't gone anywhere so I'd had no need for Nigel. Shelby had brought in whatever I'd asked for or run out of, and any plans I'd made to see sights with Emma had all been handed over to Lawrence. Texts and calls with Harrison were scattered and infrequent due to a grueling schedule he was trying to keep up with, and I'd been holed up in this house, either cooking, sleeping, or spending time with Robin in the garden. I'd fashioned him a little birdbath and a small tray for his snacks. His palette changed as the days grew colder and it seemed mealworms and peanuts were a top choice, likely for their fat and protein content I expected. Which got me wondering if I should try live crickets. But surely Shelby would start asking questions if I asked for live crickets. I'd managed to wave her off from confusion about mealworms by saying I was trying to draw in bluebirds to the garden, a bird the UK has probably never laid eyes on. I guess Robin would just have to find fat little live crickets on his own in the spring.

I'd also been poring over books in my new favorite hangout, Harrison's closet. Being there made me feel closer to him, immersed in his scent, surrounded by his clothes, wearing his hoodies, reading the books I knew he loved while his chunky gold H ring was securely wrapped around my thumb. I painted my nails with his polish. I used his hair products. Every day that passed made me want to get on a plane and just go to him. Find him. Be with him. Knowing it would only sidetrack him and hinder his work were the only things that kept me from doing it.

Three weeks to go.

CHAPTER
26

Nearly another week had passed and all I cared about was finding new ways to get the days and weeks behind me. Every moment that passed was another one checked off the list. Shelby was in and out, and I'd brushed off multiple suggestions from Nigel to get out and enjoy London before the winter weather arrived. I still had my phone calls with Harrison of course, and the Monday morning text from him updating me on what fruit our baby was being compared to, but all I was really doing was counting down the days until he was back here with me. I found that the more I slept, the faster the time seemed to pass, and that was all that mattered to me.

Two nights ago, at my very nervous request, we'd resorted to attempting phone sex for the first time. What a mess that turned out to be. I'd tried to set the tone, said all the right things, and made all the tongue-in-cheek innuendos I could think of. I even made sure Harrison was alone before he called me, but with each attempt to get serious, one of us broke into laughter, or someone knocked on his trailer door. The second time we tried, we were interrupted by a call back from his director.

"Now I've got to find a way to get back on set without this thing leading the way," he'd joked and in my head, all I could picture was the way he'd scrambled to cover himself with a blanket on the private jet that day as we made our way back from the Dales. *If his jeans had been any more worn, he'd have burst right through the front of them. The perks of being with a younger man were indeed plentiful.*

Just as I let myself drift back into that day, reliving the way I'd climbed on top of him and straddled him to get him aroused, a violent pounding at the front door scared the hell out of me. I was alone and certainly not expecting anyone.

Who the... I hesitated, debating whether or not to answer the door or if I should just act like I wasn't here. *Maybe I should tell Harrison to send Victor or Hank back here to stay with me until he gets home.*

"Alice! Open the bloody door!" It was Nigel and he sounded frantic.

I rushed to the entry to let him in, all the while the pounding and shouting continued. "Open this door this instant! I know you're in there!"

I swung the door open, narrowly avoiding him knocking on my forehead with a closed fist. "What *is* the matter, Nigel? Come in here and stop yelling." I turned and headed back toward the couch.

"I've asked you and asked you to come out and get some fresh air with me, give me something, *anything* to do with my time, and you've brushed me off for nearly two weeks. I'm about to go stir-crazy!" He threw himself down beside me on the couch, clearly annoyed. "Don't you know I have a job to do? I'm supposed to show you around, take you places, get you acquainted with this city, even if your friend is off on a wild romp with her new beau."

"Okay, and?" I rolled my eyes.

"And?" His face was blank as he looked back at me, a sunken twist of his neck for effect. "Darling, soon you're going to be strapped to this house with a crying infant. Sitting here wallowing because the man of the house is off at work is a waste of perfectly good vitality." He stood abruptly and held his hands out to me. "Come on then. Get up."

I looked up at him, my face twisted into a disgusted scowl.

"Oh, honey, no. That's not what we're going to do at all. Absolutely dreadful," he scoffed.

He wiggled his fingertips at me, gesturing for me to stand up, and when I didn't, he stomped his foot. "You think he'd be happy, you behaving like this? Just because he's not here?" He sucked at his teeth. "My darling, no." An eye roll and another wiggle of the fingers.

"Nigel, I'm perfectly content right here."

"You certainly don't look it; you look a fright. How long have you been wearing this jumper?" The corners of his mouth turned down as he looked me head to toe and back.

I glanced down at myself. Chip crumbs sat atop the shelf my already large but ever-growing boobs provided. Brushing them away, I shook my head, dismissing their existence. "Who's here to care? No one."

"You remember that midwife appointment not so long ago where he just popped up on you?" Nigel's hand landed on his hip, while the other swung up into a circle motion. "Surprise! Who's to say he wouldn't do that again? And you're in here looking like some ragamuffin off the street."

"Well, Jesus Christ, Nigel, I'm clean. I just keep throwing this on because it reminds me of him."

"Honey, this old thing no longer smells like that man, okay? Put that in the wash, throw something presentable on, and come with me. Let's go somewhere. A walk in the park maybe, fresh air, birds and all that, hmm?"

He was so flamboyantly condescending, but the pretentious sneer in his voice was enough to make me soften.

"Fine." I took his outstretched hand and let him pull me up off the couch. "I'll be right back." I dragged my feet in protest as I made my way upstairs.

"A proper cardigan, darling, or at least a jumper. Not a"—he paused—"hood-ie." His attempt at an American accent was smothered by his sass.

"Yes, dear!" I hollered backward from the bedroom closet. Peeling the sweatshirt off, I tossed it into the basket of dirty laundry before yanking a v-neck shirt from its hanger. I threw an oversized mustard yellow cardigan over it and went back downstairs to find Nigel admiring the photos on the mantle.

"Now that's much better, wouldn't you agree? And look at you smiling! See, I knew it would change your whole mood," he said, patronizing me.

I approached him with a snarky look on my face.

"You know I've only been here like twice, right? And that was strictly professional. I can't believe you aren't even going to offer me a tour."

"You're the one who wants to get me out of the house, so we should go while I'm still willing. I'll show you around when we get back, promise. And I'm going to drive."

"Absolutely not! I've just been hired and you want me to be fired already?"

"Just let me give it a shot."

"And get us all killed? That's not happening." He put both his hands up in protest.

"Such a party pooper." Crossing my arms, I exaggerated a frown.

"So moody. Must be the hormones." He winked at me and threw his arm around my shoulder, prompting my smile to appear once again. "Well, c'mon then, let's be off."

We spent the remainder of the afternoon in the park, wandering the paved pathways, pausing to sit on a bench or take in the view when needed. We got caught up on all that I'd been doing around the house in the last few weeks, how I'd been feeling, and how I was really handling

Harrison being away. Nigel knew. He knew the first time Emma was off with Lawrence and I shooed him away from a day out. He knew how I handled loneliness, which is exactly why he was ready to break my door down today. He also knew that being part of the Edwards "family" meant looking out for each other, always, first and foremost. Kindness and love for one another was the top priority. I was thankful for his friendship and for his persistence, and I promised I'd do better than I had been.

"So did things get better, between you and your partner? Nigel, you never did tell me his name." I questioned gently. I knew the subject was still tender. His posture told me he didn't really want to discuss it, but what kind of friend would I be if I didn't give him an outlet? He glanced away from me, rubbing his hand across his mouth, dragging his fingertips down to his chin, and pushing them up to rest against his lips. A move I'd seen before. A move of trying to buy yourself time to steady your emotions and hide your response. My hand fell to his knee reassuringly when I saw him draw in a deep breath and hold it.

"We don't have to—" I started, my backpedaling interrupted by his emotional exhale.

"I'm sorry." He wiped at his face, then shook his head as he took a few deep breaths. "It's all fallen apart, Alice. All of it." Another sigh.

"Oh, Nigel, honey, I'm sorry." I scooted closer to him on the bench and put my arm around his shoulders.

His gaze fell to the ground, watching his feet intently as he pushed the toes of his shoes nervously against the pavement. "His name is William." His voice was no more than a whisper.

I squeezed my arm tight around his shoulders.

"If I'm being honest, I've actually been thankful for this time to myself. The day I took off and said I was feeling poorly, was the morning after he told me he'd taken on a serious beau," he turned his face away from me again, "and what we had couldn't continue any longer."

"I wish you'd told me sooner, Nigel. I would have been there for you.

We could have kept each other out of the depths of all these emotions. That's what friends—hell, *family* is for."

He turned his face to me, the whites of his eyes now bloodshot pink, and mustered a tight-lipped smile, tears on the verge of overflowing from his bottom lids.

"Thank you, Alice." His hand patted my knee.

"I love you. You don't have to hide any part of yourself away from me. Okay? The good or the bad. I'm always just a call away, and I don't want you to ever feel alone, Nigel. Ever. Forget this professional bullshit. That's secondary to you being someone I care about."

The tight-lipped smile came again, followed by a long hug. He rubbed at his cheek with his palm, trying to gather himself, looking around nervously to make sure no one was watching him.

"This was supposed to be about you!" He laughed. "Not me!" He swatted at my knee.

"We're just a hot mess, aren't we?"

"You're not wrong about that, my dear, to be fair."

"We should all get together soon, have dinner, take our minds off this stuff. I've barely seen Emma since she got here, and back home it's almost time for Thanksgiving." I paused, my wheels turning. "That's it! That's what we should do! We should have a Friendsgiving!" I said excitedly, trying to stuff away the feelings of loss that had hung like black clouds over my Thanksgivings. The visual of James crumpling into a tear-streaked mess after being told I'd miscarried while I lay in an emergency room bed flooded my mind. Nigel knew I'd lost a child, and knew that's what shifted the dynamic in my relationship with James, but he didn't know that it happened on Thanksgiving morning, and I didn't want to get into those details.

"That might be nice, actually. I've never had an American Thanksgiving. Do I wear a costume?"

"Yes, you can be the turkey." I laughed at myself. "No, just casual comfortable because we're going to be filling our bellies with all sorts of good food. I'll make everything that we normally have back home. Turkey, mashed potatoes, gravy, some veggies, and stuffing, and, Nigel, have you ever had a deviled egg?" I asked, my eyes wide with anticipation.

"I've had scotch eggs. Are they sort of the same?"

"Oh no, not at all. A deviled egg is," I gestured a chef's kiss with my hand, "so good!"

"We should all bring something to go with it!" he offered. Finally, excitement had returned to his voice.

"I'll probably enlist Emma to help me with my portion of the responsibility because if we all make food, we'll never eat it all." I laughed.

"I can make a Bakewell tart!" he exclaimed.

"I have no idea what that is, but okay. Maybe I can get Lawrence to make a dessert as well. I wonder if he cooks. Has he ever said anything to you?" I asked.

"Absolutely not. We haven't touched on cooking in our conversations, and frankly, you know him better than I do."

"I'll ask Shelby to make an appetizer. You have dessert and Lawrence has dessert, whether he likes it or is capable or not. This is going to be amazing. Except, Harrison won't be here to enjoy it with us." Half of my face scrunched up, disappointed.

"Next year he will, and so will the newest Edwards addition to the family. It will be a tradition!" The light in Nigel's eyes returned, and I was glad I'd been able to veer the discussion away from William.

"Do we decorate?" he asked excitedly.

"I mean, we can. I normally don't. For me, it's about gathering close to the people you love, sharing good food, and spending time together."

"Damn the decorations then! I'll find my loosest fitting trousers and bring a tart! This is excellent Alice! My first…what did you call it?"

I laughed out loud. "Friends-giving."

"Friendsgiving! Yes!"

"We can plan for next weekend. That gives me the week to find the ingredients and brine my turkey. How about Saturday? That way you can spend Sunday laying around bloated," I offered.

"Don't send Shelby after these things. Let's get them together; it will be good for us both to get out of the house."

"You're right, and while I'm thinking of it, feel free to bring an overnight bag and stay the weekend if you like. I'm sure Emma will be with Lawrence, and we can just hang out and spend the time together. Because listen, one week later, Harrison will be home again, and sorry, but I'm not going to want to see you or anyone else when I get him back home with me. DO NOT come knocking, you hear me?" I shot him a look of serious warning.

"That's a deal, darling. Oh, this is going to be proper fun! But now I'm hungry; let's go get something to eat!" Nigel took me by the hand and we were off in search of a late-day snack.

CHAPTER 27

The week flew by with Nigel at my side. By day we wandered London, in and out of specialty shops, securing all the necessary ingredients and planning our Friendsgiving dishes. I even taught him how to dry-brine a turkey. And when time allowed, I'd sneak out early in the day to lay out snacks for Robin. Even though I couldn't really spend any time with him, I didn't want him to be hungry or wonder where I was. Though I knew he kept an eye on me regardless. On Thursday, the real Thanksgiving back in the States, I spent the majority of the day thinking about Thanksgivings of the past as I lived, and grew to love, this new life of mine in London. My thoughts repeatedly dipped backward into the horror of the loss I'd suffered. I couldn't help it. The more I tried not to, the harder they pushed their way in, and I was so thankful not to be alone. Thanksgiving, the holiday, triggered the memories, but the actual date of the loss wasn't today. It would haunt me again Saturday. That's the trouble with holidays with fluctuating dates, they kick you down, then kick you again when you're in the depths of it. The chokehold squeezing tighter and tighter until you find yourself gasping for air. I was happy to let Nigel sidetrack me to keep me from getting completely lost in it; he had no idea just how much he was saving me from myself, and I felt indebted to him because of it. If I'd been here alone for this, I'm not sure how I would have handled it.

Midweek, Shelby brought the mail in, and to my surprise and delight, there was a large envelope addressed to me from America—paperwork from my lawyer. I'd been so busy wishing away the days, desperate to see Harrison again, I totally forgot that my divorce proceedings were still happening. I tore open the envelope to find a quarter-inch thick stack of paperwork adorned with a very formal-looking letter.

It began, *Dear Alice, I'm pleased to let you know that your divorce is complete. Included in this packet are copies of all rulings...* My mouth fell open and I threw the entire handful of paper back down onto the counter. I didn't care what the rest of it said, I'd read it later. I was FREE. A squeal escaped me so loud it surely would have terrified the neighbors if there had been any around to hear me, and Nigel nearly levitated off the couch, his feet never touching the floor as he spun around in terror.

"Bloody fucking hell, Alice!" His eyes were as wide as dinner plates.

I danced toward him. "I'm free, I'm free, I'm FUCKING FREEEEE!!!" I twirled around as I repeated myself over and over, landing against him. He hugged me and we danced together, chanting in unison.

"Congrats, darling! Long overdue!" He lifted my hand in the air and spun me around.

"I haven't been single since I was eighteen!" I laughed as the room spun around me.

"Babes, you technically aren't single now either!" he reminded me, and we laughed again until my cheeks ached and my sides hurt.

It occurred to me mid-twirl that James must have gotten his copies as well and the idea of it stopped me in my tracks. His likely arrived before mine, given the typical delay in the mail here. Unless he still had no mailbox or hadn't been to the post office. No matter how I tried, it was hard for me to imagine him or his reaction, wherever he was, because he certainly wasn't sitting on the porch or at the kitchen table. I doubted he was standing around in a pile of burnt ash. How poetic was that? His entire life reduced to a pile of soot, at the soles of those fucking boots he used to track dirt through that no-longer-existent house with.

Sympathy? Nah. Not here. Not from me. Those days were gone. Empathy? Eh. Maybe, but fleeting. I'd carried too much frustration for too long to let myself feel anything anymore for a situation that ran me into the ground and made me feel *less than* all the time.

Nigel stood there looking at me like I'd lost my mind for suddenly being so still.

"Sorry. I just realized if I got mine, surely he got his."

"Oh, he got his alright. Can you even imagine what his reaction will be when news breaks all over the world that you're linked to a movie star?" His hands formed imaginary explosives at his temples.

"Jesus, I actually hadn't thought of that." I sat down on the couch, suddenly feeling guilty. "Should I tell him ahead of time? Soften the blow?" I wondered if I should text him. He hadn't texted me since I'd been here, and then *Leave it alone, Alice,* echoed through my head.

"You don't owe that man a God damned thing, Alice. No! Let him find out like everyone else."

Tornadoes of thoughts were whipping circles inside my head, wondering how my relationship with Harrison would be presented to the world and how James would find out. Would it be hearsay or would he see it on a magazine cover while he stood in line at the grocery store surrounded by people who had known him his entire life? Oh God, and then the pregnancy news would break.

My forehead landed in my right palm. James would be mortified that I'd literally run off with someone and almost immediately gotten pregnant, and then I'd kept it from him. I was overwhelmed with shame. Should I have told him when I got back from London? Should I have been more honest? James had been difficult to live with and dismissive of me, but he'd never lied to me. He'd never cheated and lied, and that's exactly what I did, to a man who loved me in his own way and built his entire life around me. I did it all while I was still married.

I was sweating.

"Alice? Love, are you okay?" Nigel's hand was rubbing my back.

I blinked hard, a blank stare on my face. "I don't know if I am, honestly. I'm a liar, Nigel. And a cheat. Harrison will be disgraced by me. If anyone looks into my history, and I know they will, they'll see when I was divorced. They'll put two and two together on my pregnancy and he'll be ridiculed for it. His reputation will suffer, his work will suffer. He'll be ashamed of me. He'll leave me. What have I done?" I stood from the couch, my hand wiping at the perspiration on my forehead, and began to pace back and forth.

"Alice. He won't leave you. That man is completely enamored with you. And might I add, he was right there with you through it. He knew what he was getting into. You being married isn't news to him, love. He will defend you and whatever actions were necessary, I'm sure of it. Don't let this spin you out." Once again Nigel was at my side, hand on my shoulder, trying to save me from myself.

"I need to speak to him. I need to call him." I rushed to the kitchen to get my phone and dialed his number. Multiple rings later his voicemail picked up. After several deep breaths, I heard the beep and began my message. "Harrison. I really need to talk to you. Please call me as soon as possible. Everything is okay with the baby, but I need to speak with you. I love you so much." My voice had noticeably faltered toward the end, and I pressed three to re-record my message in an attempt to hide the fear in my voice. As the prompt began again, I panicked and hung up.

"I can't bother him with this nonsense. He's going to think I'm a lunatic." I wiped at my forehead again.

"Come sit down. Let's get our minds on something else for a while, okay? You might be overthinking this a bit." Nigel's hand once again rubbed at my back as he ushered me back down onto the couch.

"Sorry you had to see me like this." I felt awful.

"Think nothing of it. Here, let's try to redirect our thoughts, want to?"

Nigel started a movie on Netflix while I tapped in a text to Harrison. *I love you so much, but I worry what my divorce (now finalized, hooray) and this baby will do to your reputation. Call me when you can. I think we should talk. xx* I hit send and left the phone on the coffee table in front of me while I let myself sink back into the couch.

By bedtime, Nigel had gone above and beyond to try to keep me busy. We'd cooked and watched a few movies on the couch and shared stories by the fire, but in my mind I silently and anxiously waited for Harrison's call. Just when I'd crawled into bed, my phone finally lit up.

"Hi," I said softly.

"Hey, love. Why has this got you so worried?"

The sound of his voice so calm, so intent on making me feel better, so willing to listen and discuss and not shut down or retreat, brought tears to my eyes. "I cheated, Harrison. I cheated, and I lied about it, and I got divorced while I was pregnant. And now that the divorce is final, it's all going to become public knowledge and ruin everything you've worked so hard for."

There was silence on the other end of the line and I knew he knew I was crying.

"Alice. I need to make sure you can hear me, okay? Can you hear me?"

"Mm-hmm."

"Are you sure?"

"Yes."

"Then when I say this, please, don't ever forget it, and don't ever, ever question it. I love you. I've loved you from the moment I laid eyes on you, and there was no way I could outrun it. I didn't want to. You had me from the very first second, before you even knew I was there. Your smile, the light in your eyes that night, was electric. It was magic, Alice. And we talked about your situation multiple times. As a grown man with a place in the public eye, I was fully aware of what I was getting involved with when I asked for your number and if I could see you again, and when I kissed you in the Dales, and later when we took it a step further. I knew exactly what strings there were, and what obstacles we would face, and I knew that despite it all, I was forever a changed man because of the happiness you bring to my life, because of the joy you bring me every single day. Now, if this job and everything that goes along with it disappears tomorrow because of my love for you, then so be it. Let someone else have it. Take it from me and do whatever you will with it, because I've got you to love me and support me for the rest of my life, and I believe in my heart, Alice, that you love me more than all those people around the world combined. You're all I've searched for my entire life, and now that I've found you, darling, nothing else matters to me. Do you understand? I'm proud to have you by my side, and I'm proud of how we got here. In a world where everything is fleeting and fake and for headlines, Alice, you are the realest love I've ever known."

"Harrison, I don't know what to—"

"There is nothing to say, love. We're a team, now and forever. A united front with our joy on display, and to hell with anyone who doesn't support us." His voice was tender as he reassured me.

"I'd never let you throw this all away for me."

"If it's meant to go, it will leave and what's for me will never pass me by. I don't think it will be as big a scandal as you think."

"I still feel like a terrible person; I cheated and lied to James. Doing it to begin with was bad enough, but then keeping it a secret. I know that's not your problem, but it's still weirdly affecting me. It didn't even hit me until the papers arrived today, but now I can't stop thinking about it."

"James is a big boy. Had he not defaulted on his promises and made you feel inadequate, none of this would have happened. So, I don't think you should spend much time worrying about how James feels when James never spent any time worrying about how you felt all those years. And I'm sorry to be so blunt, but those are facts."

"No, I know. I know you're right. I just needed some reassurance, that's all."

"I will spend the rest of my life reassuring you that you are absolutely everything to me, Alice. You and our child and this life we're building together. My promises will never fall hollow, and I'll always make sure you know that you're my entire world. Without you, Alice, this family we're building wouldn't exist."

"I love you so much. God, I wish you were here with me."

"I wish I was too. Soon. I promise. And for what it's worth, congratulations on the end of that previous chapter. Hell, that previous book. Now we can write our own love story, and I know it will be one for the ages."

I exhaled a silent laugh through my nose. "You always know how to set me right when I'm lost. Thank you, Harrison."

"Get some rest, okay? Your stress only upsets my little raspberry-sized baby and until I'm there to talk to—" He stopped short. "You know what? Put the phone to your belly. Put it on speaker. I need to have a word with them."

I laughed. "Harrison!"

"No, no, Alice, come on. I need to speak with our child. Put it on speaker." I could hear his smile on the other end of the line.

I tapped the speaker button and held the phone to my belly. "Okay, go ahead."

"Is it on speaker?"

"Yes," I laughed. I couldn't help myself.

"Are you sure?"

"Yes, I know how to use a phone! This is not my first rodeo, my friend."

"Okay, you ready? Hi, baby, it's Daddy. I know I might sound muffled, but soon enough you'll be here and be sick of my voice completely. For now, while you're a captive audience, I need you to know that Mummy gets a little worried sometimes, but it's just because Daddy isn't home right now. I'm away, working. Soon I'll be home to talk to you every day, but until then, keep growing big and strong and don't take on any of Mummy's stress, and know that I love you so, so much."

In tears all over again, I tapped the speaker button and returned the phone to my ear. "You are the sweetest man."

"I love you, darling. I'll call you tomorrow. Don't worry about anything, okay?"

His accent never allowed the 'g' to be heard at the end of a word and the sound of him saying 'anythin' rippled through my mind. "I love you too, Harrison."

And then just like that, he was gone again.

Quick calls and texts with him had dotted my days and nights, but they were nothing in comparison to the comfort of his physical presence, and as I hugged my pillow wishing it was him, I told myself, *one more week, Alice, you just have to get through one more week.*

As if orchestrated by the devil himself, the next morning started with me in a cold sweat, rattled from a nightmare so real I thought for sure I was in the terrifying midst of losing my first child all over again. I woke clutching my abdomen with one hand, the other throwing back the covers then landing between my legs in search of blood. Untarnished, trembling fingers hovered in front of my face, serving as proof that it was just my imagination. I blinked hard to make sure I wasn't crazy before letting my head fall back against the pillow, seconds morphing into minutes as I tried to steady my breathing. A heavy sigh. Fear and anxiety always do this to me.

Calm down, Alice. It's not real. Everything is fine. You're okay.

"We'll be alright," I whispered, my hand on my belly gently caressing, comforting both me and my unborn, yet still very alive baby. *We'll be alright,* I repeated in my head, *it's just a nightmare.*

I took another deep breath before I decided the only way to stop thinking about this was to get on with the day. I grabbed my phone from the nightstand beside me and replied to Harrison's *Good morning, I love you* text.

I love you so much more than you'll ever know and hit send.

Three minutes passed with no response, so I padded off to the bathroom for a shower.

Half an hour later and still no response to be had, I made my way downstairs to find Shelby and Emma in the kitchen.

"This is a nice surprise. You're here much earlier than I thought you'd be," I said as I approached Emma and gave her a hug.

"Well, Lawrence had some *man* thing to do, so I figured I'd come hang here with my girls and help with all the cooking."

"Well, I'm happier for it! Now, Shelby, I don't know why you made breakfast at all, we're going to stuff ourselves silly later on."

"You still need to feed that baby and Harrison wouldn't be pleased if I let you skip breakfast." She wagged her finger at me. "Now come sit, let's chat."

"Where's Nigel?" I asked as I poured apple juice into a glass and grabbed a muffin.

"Still sleeping, I guess." Shelby shrugged and took a sip of her tea.

As I bit into my muffin I glanced at the clock. "I need to tend to this turkey. There's a whole process to this. It needs to sit out for at least forty-five minutes before I put it in the oven."

"Good heavens, this is an all-day event you Americans put on, isn't it?"

"It's so worth it. You'll see." I held what was left of my breakfast in my mouth as I lifted the turkey out of the refrigerator and positioned it on the counter, closing the door with my foot.

"Don't be mad, but I told Lawrence to pick up dessert before he arrives. He told me he's not really a whiz in the kitchen and dessert is definitely not his thing." Emma picked at her muffin as she spoke.

"It's fine. Nigel's got his little tart thing, and we'll all probably be too full to eat dessert anyway." I peeled the wrapper from what was left of my breakfast and threw it away, before reaching for my juice.

"Bite your tongue!" Emma said. "There is *always* room for dessert! I keep a separate stomach just for that purpose," she laughed. "I probably shouldn't even be eating this." She set her muffin down on the plate in front of her.

"I think you'll be fine. You've likely been working off a lot of calories lately anyhow," Shelby joked.

I couldn't help but laugh.

Emma looked up with a smirk. "That man's body is..." She scratched at her temple, eyebrows raised for effect, "statuesque. Solid. Zero body fat. NONE." She shoved the plate away from her. "It's insanity."

"Well, I'm glad you were able to come up for a little oxygen today. You've been here how long now? And I've barely seen you. Don't get me wrong, I'm all for finding love. I'm absolutely ecstatic for you and for the fact that you'll be sticking around, but I'm selfish. I wanted my time with you as well."

"There will be plenty of time. Now, if you're done with your breakfast, let's get busy. And you know what—NIGEL!" Emma hollered. "NIGEL, GET YOUR ASS OUT HERE!" she bellowed again, throwing her voice toward the guest room. "IT'S TIME TO COOK! WAKE UP!" she yelled again.

The knob turned and out shuffled a disheveled Nigel, hair askew in every possible direction, his robe hanging open to expose his two-piece satin pajamas. "Bloody hell, look what the cat dragged in," he mumbled as he rubbed at the side of his head with his hand, lazily blinking at the sight of Emma.

"Holy hell," Shelby whispered under her breath.

"I could say the same!" Emma laughed at him as she spoke. "Now get yourself together and come help us cook!"

In true Nigel fashion, he comically threw a leg out to the side, one of his slippers flying off and hitting the wall, then tapped his heels tightly together, raised his hand and saluted her, then spun around to face the guest room door before shuffling back in the direction he came. The forgotten slipper remained abandoned in the hallway.

"Today is going to be so much fun," I said. "I can feel it."

But the smile on my face quickly faded as the visual of the ER doctor standing in front of me flashed through my mind; his lips moved in slow motion, his voice echoing, *"I'm so sorry,"* in my head.

CHAPTER 28

The majority of the day had been spurts of hectic kitchen work paired with cozy downtime in the living room. All the food was ready, the telltale scents of my childhood Thanksgivings with their thyme-infused aromatics hung in the air while the turkey sat roasted and resting again on the counter. We all hovered nearby like a pack of hungry wild animals ready to feast, and were just waiting for Lawrence to arrive before we sat down to eat.

"What on earth could Lawrence possibly have to do that took him this long?" I asked.

"He probably needed electrolytes and a good exfoliation," Nigel chimed in.

"Or maybe the poor bastard just needed some sleep?" Shelby prodded.

"Ha. HA. You're all just *so* hilarious," Emma sneered back at them. "Let me text him and see where he is." She picked up her phone and began swiping and tapping at the screen. She glanced up quickly and caught me still watching her, awaiting an answer, but all I got was a brief yet dismissive grin before she returned her attention to the screen in front of her and followed the others back to the living room couch, leaving me alone in the kitchen.

Without thinking, I pulled my phone from my pocket. Still no messages from Harrison. *Must be a busy day on set,* I thought and sighed, wishing he was here. I laid the phone on the windowsill above the sink, sure to be forgotten, while I began rinsing the dishes that had started to accumulate.

"He said it should only be a few more minutes; he's just getting in the car now from picking up dessert," Emma called out to me.

As the three of them chatted amongst themselves in the living room, I busied myself setting the table and laying out the fall-themed napkins Nigel had chosen, then made sure the wine was open to breathe. Everything was perfect. The holiday lights were strung around the room thanks to Nigel; that had been a comedy show in and of itself. The music was low and the kitchen was a full-blown mess, but the mashed potatoes were whipped and buttery, the vegetables warm in their respective pots, and the gravy was the most gorgeously silky shade of deep amber I'd ever seen. Maybe it was the pregnancy talking, but I could have drunk that gravy straight out of the bowl. The turkey had rested long enough, but I had planned to have Lawrence carve it because that was one thing I wasn't very good at. And the deviled egg platter looked perfect, except for the one that was missing.

Okay fine, I ate it. So what?

A low knocking came from the front door, prompting me to turn around, but Emma shot off the couch hollering, "I'll get it!" before anyone else could react. I turned back to the sink and continued rinsing the dishes, trying to keep up with the work I knew was ahead of me. I planned this event; there was no way I was going to let Shelby deal with any of the mess. At least if the majority of the dishes were fully rinsed, it wouldn't take long to load them into the dishwasher later.

From behind me, I felt a sudden warm embrace, scruff, and familiar lips landing against my neck.

"Dessert's here," he whispered in my ear.

The bowl in my hands dropped back into the sink, sending water and soap suds flying in every direction. I spun around to find Harrison so close I could hardly focus my eyes on him. Speechless, I threw my wet hands around his neck and held him as close to me as I could. I don't know how many times I kissed him, I just knew that everything I ever wanted was once again standing in front of me, and my lips landed wherever he let them.

"Okay, spill. Who knew about this?" I demanded playfully when I was finally able to stop myself from assailing him with kisses.

No one said a word as they looked around at one another and back to me, each with a different look of guilt on their faces.

"Shelby?" My question was met with a nervous smile and a nod.

"Nigel?"

"Guilty as charged." He had a twinkle in his eye.

I released my grip on Harrison long enough to point at Emma and Lawrence and narrowed my glare in their direction. "I know you two are in cahoots!"

"I knew what it meant to you to have everyone together today." Nigel's voice permeated the space. "To make happy memories and create a new tradition."

"And YOU!" I pulled Harrison into me. "You never said a thing!" My eyes locked on his, I shook my head, still lost somewhere between disbelief and full-blown enchantment.

"Tricky one, aren't I?" He winked at me and laughed before kissing my forehead, his palms warm against my waist. All I wanted in that moment was to tell them all to get out of my kitchen and strip my future husband naked right here.

Instead, I looked up at him in awe. "I love you so much." I scrunched my nose at him, leaned in, and laid my head against his chest before whispering, "It's so good to have you home."

"I did actually bring pies though, if it matters." Lawrence held up a pie in each hand and then set them down on the kitchen counter. "One's mixed fruit and one is a chocolate pudding of sorts."

"Who's in charge of carving this thing? I'm wasting away to bits over here!" Nigel threw his hands in the air, exasperated.

"Would you like to do the honors, love?" I looked up at Harrison.

"I've no clue what I'm doing, but let's give it a go." He jokingly punched at the air, his dimples on full parade.

As Harrison attempted to carve his first turkey, everyone made themselves a plate and found a spot around our table. And we ate, surrounded by friends who had quickly become family, and it became clear that what we thought would be a fun day together was actually the beginning of a tradition that would last us through the years. There were toasts and shared laughter and all sorts of stories between the brief silences that always accompany great food, all of which resulted in empty plates and full bellies.

Nigel and Shelby scarfed down all the deviled eggs, while Harrison indulged in my mashed potatoes, and I found happiness with that gorgeous gravy. Lawrence and Emma were never too far apart, holding hands even as they ate. And as the six of us spent the rest of the day enjoying each other's company, Harrison continuously found ways to speak to me without words. His hand warm on my thigh with a knowing gaze or his foot finding mine under the table; from the moment he walked in, we'd been connected by touch.

And as I sat back in my seat and looked at all the faces around our table, I was grateful. Newfound love for some while others relished in their contented solitude, there was hope for new future possibilities surrounding me. And yet, not a single one of them knew the grip that the riptide of rediscovered loneliness had recently had on me, not to its true extent at least, and none of them knew just how much I appreciated them all in their own ways.

"I love every single one of you. Thank you for today, for appeasing this idea of mine." I leaned over and kissed Harrison, his hand moving up to my belly under the table and resting softly against it. "And Harrison," I cocked my head in admiration, "thank you, for all of this."

"The thanks go to you, darling. You brought us all here today with this amazing idea. You filled our stomachs and our hearts, and you've filled my life with everything I've ever wanted." He stared into my eyes as if no one else were in the room.

"Oh God, enough already. You all make me absolutely sick," Nigel joked, sticking out his tongue as he faked a gag.

"Alright then, while everyone is in the same room," Harrison stood from his seat, "I do want to make a bit of an announcement."

I looked around at everyone nervously and then back at Harrison, unsure what he might say next.

"Well, first and foremost, Alice, I'm here. I'm home, love."

I looked up at him confused. I'd expected he was just here for the day and would have another week away.

"The film wrapped late last night, which is why I'm stood here right now. It's done, and any time apart is now behind us." He leaned down and kissed my forehead before he continued, "The coming week is likely going to be the last normal one before things go a little crazy. With me being home, Alice and I will surely be seen out in the city. And Lawrence, you know what that means."

Lawrence nodded as he sighed, his face stern.

"What's he mean?" Emma leaned in and asked him quietly.

"Paparazzi."

"It's important to remember that no one person is safe, and everyone's got a camera at their fingertips. You *will* be photographed; it's inevitable. Nigel, I'll probably have you ride with Lawrence when we're out together, so you can see how this all works, but there will also be times I'll want you alone in a copy."

"A copy?" Nigel asked.

"An identical vehicle to the one I'm usually in. I've got two more of the same SUV being delivered tomorrow; that way if we need to bait and switch, we can. A copy of a copy of a copy. You know how it goes."

Nigel nodded. "Oh, okay, and who will be in the third one?"

"Victor and Hank will be trailing at their usual distance in number three. Sounds like overkill, I know, but the chaos always amps up after I finish a film and promo begins, and now they'll trail us for Alice as well, and with her being pregnant, I'm taking zero chances."

"A solid plan. We'll all be moving as a unit. I like it," Lawrence added.

Emma and I looked at each other nervously.

"It will be fine; we'll all be surrounded by safety. I'll see to it," Harrison reassured us. "Now, who's ready for dessert?"

"The dessert you mentioned earlier, or actual food?" I asked, giving him a look that I knew would send his imagination into overdrive.

"Patience, darling, patience," he laughed. "Anyone? Actual dessert?"

A collective groan surrounded the table as our guests rubbed their full bellies and Harrison hurried off toward the kitchen with Shelby close behind. Chatter resumed all around me and I was happy to sit back, knowing that these people could all talk at once, all they wanted. All that mattered to me was the man I loved was home for good.

CHAPTER 29

Exhausted from the events of the day, I sat lifeless on the couch wanting to go to bed, but unwilling to make the effort to get there. My head comfortably tipped back, eyes closed, the rhythmic whish and whir of the dishwasher had been trying to lull me into hypnosis while Harrison, the ever-gracious host, had seen everyone out to their cars. As he stepped back inside, the sound of the automatic door lock was once again a welcome and now familiar reminder that the rest of the world was on the outside, and everything I needed was right here, inside our own little world.

Harrison picked my feet up from the coffee table and settled in next to me on the couch, laying my legs across his lap, ushering me back from the brink of what I was sure was a turkey coma. He said nothing as he sat beside me, just letting his thumbs mindlessly rub against the jeans that covered my legs.

"It's just us now?" I mumbled, turning my head toward him slightly but never opening my eyes.

"It's just us, darling." A moment of quiet passed, then he leaned in and softly kissed me. His fingertips slid down the side of my throat, raising goosebumps and he pulled the neckline of my shirt away to expose my collarbone. He nuzzled me with the side of his nose, breathing me in, and then pressed his lips to my skin once again. Softly, he lingered there and I pulled in a deep breath, feeling my lungs expand, enjoying the thought that he didn't have to leave again. *His mouth could bring me back from the dead*, I thought to myself. *Just take me upstairs, don't say a word, just have your way with me.* I took my time as I exhaled, imagining what we looked like on the couch together, picturing him with his mouth on my neck.

"I've missed this." His lips moved slowly against my skin as he said it, then he breathed me in.

"Admittedly," I extended my neck, tipping my head further back to allow him more access, "an American Thanksgiving does have a very seductive smell," eyes still closed I grinned, stifling a laugh. "Drink it in, baby." My voice was breathy and overtly seductive.

He laughed his loud, genuine laugh. I knew he would. The one that bursts forth without restraint, where he covers his mouth out of surprise and maybe a little embarrassment. I loved that laugh. It wasn't professional or refined; it was Harrison, stripped, raw, happy. This time he let his face fall into my neck to hide the sound instead of using his hand, and I felt his nose press into the top of my shoulder, his residual quiet giggles jiggling against me; I couldn't help but laugh along with him.

"Your laugh is everything." I raised my hand to cradle his face and stroke his cheek.

"*You're* everything, love."

I sighed and ran my fingers up into his hair . "I'm exhausted, that's what I am. Will you take a shower for me? I don't have the umph."

"The what?" His accent made it even funnier.

"The umph. You know, the get-up-and-go, the energy. The life. The umph."

My eyes were closed but I could somehow feel him raise his eyebrows in the silence that accompanied the pause in conversation.

"Don't you pick on me, I'm tired." I managed a short-lived laugh as he got up from the couch.

"C'mon then, darling." He took both my hands and pulled me upward against him. "Let's get you upstairs."

Up the stairs and into the bathroom I kept thinking, *Alice, he's just gotten home, get your shit together. Be tired tomorrow. You've waited for this moment for weeks. Don't be that woman. Don't squander this. There are thousands of people on this earth who would take your place in a heartbeat.* I tried to pep myself up, but this baby inside me must have been having a growth spurt because despite how well-intentioned I was to please this man, my body was not having it.

While I closed myself away in the loo, I could hear him moving around outside the door; footsteps and the sound of a lighter all while he hummed a familiar tune I couldn't put my finger on. When I came out the lights were off and he'd lit candles all around the room, the sound of the shower splattering water against the floor sent flashbacks through my mind of a previous shower we'd shared here; his mouth against my skin, the water that fell from his curls, the way I'd behaved when he called me a tease. Each mental image inviting me to relive it, right now.

I found him stripped to his boxer briefs leaning against the bathroom vanity waiting for me, the contrast of his thigh against the lion tattoo and the black of his underwear caught my eye before the definition of his abdominal muscles dancing with the flickering of the candles pulled my eyes upward. His arms crossed against his chest made his biceps look even larger than I knew them to be, until he extended his arms to me, inviting me toward him. Despite my exhaustion, I knew being wrapped in his arms was the best place for respite, and I happily stepped into his embrace.

"Gonna try something a little different tonight, okay?" His voice was low against my ear and the way his accent broke up the word 'little' made me rethink my need for sleep as the palm of his hand eased up against my jaw, his fingertips gliding into the back of my hair.

He tipped my chin up and kissed the tip of my nose softly. The endless pools of cerulean green reflected the bouncing candlelight behind me as he fixed his eyes on mine, awaiting my response. I offered a brief nod, my body and all of my senses now at full attention.

I was barely able to form a smile before he pressed his lips to mine and kissed me in a way I was still getting used to. Gentle and then voracious, the movement of his tongue slow against mine, almost calculated, incredibly sensual, then hungry, as if his ability to control his desire came in waves. The depth of how he'd missed me was palpable in the way he sucked my bottom lip between his and lingered there, savoring every moment.

His hands, large and strong against my arms, ran lovingly down their length then across my hips, and landed firmly against my ass. His palms full, pulling me into him, he moved his mouth to my ear.

"You ready?" he whispered. His hands gripped and clenched both sides of my t-shirt at my waist, pulling it taut against my body, as if weeks of sexual frustration were boiling in his fists, the neckline of my shirt dipping just enough from the pressure of his hands to expose the diamond necklace he'd given me and the rise of my cleavage.

The tiny hairs on the back of my neck stood at attention at the mere thought of what would happen next, and unable to find words, I nodded again, my eyes locked on his. He led me to the threshold of the shower and stopped, pulled my t-shirt off, and dropped it before pushing my pants to the floor. After not seeing him for a while, I couldn't help but feel self-conscious about the changes my body was going through, and my shoulder rose to meet my ear as my body tried to shield itself from his view. I clasped my hands in front of my belly and twisted myself to try to look smaller, thinner somehow. Yet all the while his eyes stayed locked on mine, giving me an unspoken reassurance that he was in love with the woman I am, not just the body I reside in.

"Don't hide yourself, love." He flashed me the smile I can never refuse and my hands fell to my sides as his mouth met mine again.

Guard down, I let my hands explore his bare skin. He was just as I remembered, only better, because he was here with me, not just in my imagination. And this time, he wasn't leaving. He'd been in the gym when he wasn't on set, and his body reflected it. His already perfect abdomen was even more chiseled, the deep v-cut into the front of his hips prominent as I slipped my fingers under the band of his boxer briefs and toyed with the idea of dropping them to his ankles.

"You like that?" he asked, curling the corner of his lip, knowing what those dimples did to me.

"Oh, I live for this..." I smirked.

His brows drew tight and his lips parted as my hand carefully gripped his now very full erection through his boxer briefs. I watched him lustfully as my hand ran the length of him, teasing him with my fingers. Just as I was about to strip him bare, he stepped back, stopping me. I looked up at him, searching for a reason why.

"You're not in control tonight. I am." He was expressionless aside from the flecks of gold candlelight that still flickered in his eyes.

With a twist of his fingers, one hand unclasped my bra, allowing the fullness of my breasts to drop from behind the confines of underwire, while his other hand slipped beneath the waistband of my panties, two fingers finding the source of my newfound pulse.

My knees went weak. *Jesus Christ*.

His mouth landed hot against my neck as he coaxed me backward into the shower, sucking gently at my skin; his fingers remained firmly planted, yet dipped further and further into me as we moved. His other hand pulled at my bra, dropping it to the floor, then he repeated, "I'm in control."

He slid his hand out of my panties and pulled them forcefully to the floor, then peeled his boxer briefs down over his legs, exposing just how hard he was. In one fluid movement, Harrison threw his arm around me and lifted me up onto him. My legs wrapped around his waist and when he sat us down on the teak shower bench, he plunged himself into me at the exact moment my mouth found his.

A loud groan accompanied his exhale and echoed against the shower tile. He let his head fall back as his breathing accelerated, his eyebrows still tight as I met his thrusts with the slightest twist of my hips. I'd been watching him, and when he opened his eyes and met my gaze, I could have exploded. *Fuck, I'd longed for this.*

"You feel so fucking good, Alice." His breathing was heavy and erratic, his mouth still open even after he'd stopped speaking.

Unable to find traction against the wet tile, I ran my fingers up into his hair as I continued to grind against him. His palms and fingers were outstretched against my ass, holding me firmly against him, and I grasped fistfuls of his dark curls, his head tipping back again as I steadied myself against him. I watched as he gave himself over to pleasure, eyes closed, nostrils flared. He bit at his bottom lip as his chest heaved in search of oxygen in the steam of the shower. Another moan, another heavy exhale, then his hands gripped my ass tighter. "Alice."

Another twist of my hips.

"Alice!" He sucked in a deep breath and held it.

I smirked, knowing he was on the edge.

Another twist and a little tightening of my own.

Remind me, who's in control here? I smirked at the thought.

"FUCK!" His voice reverberated off the glass surrounding us as his body tightened, then shuddered, ripples of release hitting him one after the other. Every exhale carried another deep vocalization that sent me closer and closer to the edge myself. But for me, that wasn't the goal tonight. What we'd shared was already enough for me.

I watched as his abs flexed with each slowing breath. This sweet man, with his eyes still closed, the wide toothy smile I loved so much spread across his beautiful face, sat silently beneath me. Unable to stop myself

I kissed each cheek, then his forehead, then his lips. I could have stayed and kissed him all night, but at some point, we would run out of hot water.

"I'm just gonna—" I started to shift from my position, causing the deposit he'd just made to shift as well.

"OH!" he blurted out.

I settled back in place. "Everything okay?" I laughed, causing even further movement to happen down between us.

"Oh God, Alice!" His face twisted into something between a grimace and a giggle.

"Baby…look what you've done." I gestured toward the fallout. "If I didn't need a shower before, I definitely need one now, dirty boy." I leaned in and kissed him again, toying with his bottom lip.

"I was supposed to be in control, Alice." He threw up his hands in defeat. "No control. None."

"Next time," I reassured him. "Now c'mon." I pulled him into the hot water with me, rubbing my hands across his shoulders and down over his abs as the water washed away the love we'd just made.

Over the next twenty minutes, Harrison pampered me in ways I'd never experienced. He lathered, washed, and rinsed my hair, taking the time to massage my scalp and rub my temples. All the while kissing me whenever the opportunity presented itself. It felt like he was celebrating me, my body, my capability to be growing his child. I never knew a man could be like this. I never knew that this was what real love looked like. He washed the majority of my body for me, his touch alternating between a soft caress and then somehow knowing exactly which muscles needed the extra attention with the strength of his hands. He did pause to kiss my belly and apologize for 'haphazardly bopping anyone in the head.' *Honestly, this man.*

When he was done, he'd washed himself, dried off, and thrown on his robe before leaving me to handle washing the parts of myself he hadn't.

As soon as I shut the water off, he was waiting at the shower door with a robe he'd warmed for me in the dryer.

"My lady." He held it open and after I slid my arms in, he wrapped it and tied it at my waist, rubbing my belly before adjusting the neck for me.

"That necklace looks better than I remember." With his hand at the small of my back, he walked me toward the bed, blowing out the candles as he passed them.

"Does it have anything to do with the fact that it's on my body and not in a box?" My fingers toyed with the diamond as I spoke.

"That might be it." He pulled back the covers and fluffed my pillow before sitting down beside me on the edge of the bed. "How's this? Crawl in then, get comfy."

I slid into my normal spot and did as he asked, expecting Harrison to follow suit but he remained sitting at my side, unmoved, staring down at his nervous hands, each one picking at the other mindlessly. He'd gone oddly quiet, so I took my phone from the nightstand and pretended to check my notifications, all the while peering over the screen to catch him still fidgeting with his hands. He'd picked at his right middle cuticle so much it was now bleeding. I recognized this behavior though, because I too, spent a lot of time inside my own head. I knew something was weighing heavy on him.

"Hey," I reached out and put my hand on his arm, "you okay?"

He looked up like I'd startled him. "Uh, yeah. I'm just..." He shrugged one shoulder and looked back down at his hands.

I waited, giving him time.

"I know it's not the right time to say this, but..."

CHAPTER
30

Harrison Edwards was one of the most quietly confident men I'd ever witnessed. He always appeared fearless, unwavering in his dedication to anything he put his mind to, and was someone that everyone could rely on. He just showed up for people, he stood by them; it was just who he was, the reliable guy. He wasn't boastful or overly cocky. His confidence was calm and cool, just like the rest of him. So, when he turned to face me, visibly shaking, I couldn't help but start to worry.

"Babe? What's changed so suddenly? I thought things were good?"

"Alice, forgive me for this. Okay? I'm sorry this isn't more...I don't know...just, more."

"Okay? Harrison, you're making me nervous."

"*I'm* nervous, Alice. Because this is all real. It's finally real. Have you ever had everything you've ever wanted? I don't mean a new car or a dream vacation or a new house paid in full. I'm talking, everything."

I looked at him with questioning eyes.

"Have you? Because I have, right now, in this moment. I've got everything I could ever want in life, right here in front of me, and I'm terrified." He wrung his hands together and then wiped his palms on the parts of his robe that covered his thighs.

My eyebrows pinched together. "Terrified? Babe? Why?"

"You've got no worldly idea how much I'm in love with you, Alice. You've got no clue at all how much this life with you, with our baby, means to me. This is unconventional, I know, and it's certainly not everything you deserve." He slid from the bed down onto one knee and faced me.

My hand covered my mouth. *This is it, this is really happening*, I thought.

Harrison fumbled around in his robe pocket and pulled out a small wooden box, not the same fancy packaging that the necklace had been in. This box looked antique as he set it on his knee and then took both my hands in his still clammy palms. He drew in a deep breath, cleared his throat, and looked up at me resolutely, his hands still shaking.

"Alice, you deserve more than me, and I know you deserve a grander proposal than this. And I know that this love we share is still fairly new, that my being away has put some stress on an already unusual situation. But while I was gone, I had time to think, time to really map out what I want my life to be. I had time to reflect on what it felt like to have you here with me one moment and for you to be out of reach the next, and it solidified something I already knew, to be fair. I never want to be without you, Alice. You appeared so unexpectedly. After seeing you, hearing your voice, I realized I'd been living my entire life in a shade of foggy London gray, and then here you are, a wildly vivid technicolor. You brought a sunshine I didn't even know was missing and, in that moment, everything changed. Everything I'd been working for, everything I thought I knew about love, you changed it all for the better. You changed *me* for the better. My whole life I felt a piece of me was missing, a permanence I could never really pin down; there was always a void I could never fill, and then you arrived. A vision. Genuine, caring. We love all the same things, and we laugh so much together. I've never known another creature like you in my entire life, and I know the universe sent you to me, Alice. I'd be a fool not to recognize that you complete every single part of me that was always lacking. Darling, we created an entire human being out of the love we share, and I just know there is so much more in store for us. It would be my absolute honor if, for the rest of my life, you would let me love you unconditionally, to depths you've never known possible, and share boundless happiness with you. Alice, will you do me the honor of being my wife?"

Now I was the one trembling with tear-soaked cheeks, trying to blink my way through to see him clearly. "Yes, Harrison. Absolutely, for a million lifetimes, yes!"

"I'm sorry this isn't a better-planned grand gesture. I know you deserve so much more than me on my knee in this bedroom. You deserve flowers and music and—"

I cut him off. "Babe, all I want is you. And it wouldn't matter if you were in the hallway on roller skates or in the back of a truck on a pogo stick. You could be yelling this to me from the bathroom. You're all I want, Harrison. You are all I need."

He kissed the back of my hand repeatedly. "I love you so much, darling." His movement caused the small box to tumble from his knee, disappearing somewhere under the bed.

"Damn it." He looked up at me, his eyes apologetic that this wasn't going as smoothly as he'd hoped. "One second, love." The upper half of his body disappeared beneath the side of the bed and I heard him mumble, "You clumsy bastard!" under his breath. I wasn't sure if he was talking to the box or himself for dropping it, but either way, I couldn't help but laugh as I wiped away the wetness from my cheeks.

He reappeared, box in hand, and awkwardly got back into a 'down on one knee' position, wobbling as he turned the box to face me.

Bashfully, he glanced up at me. "This was my nan's ring." The corners of his mouth wavered nervously as he pulled the top open to reveal a simple rose gold band curving up to cradle a magnificent diamond; at first glance it looked old in the best way possible, perfectly vintage. The box cradle it was set in was one of intricately sculpted flowers, a single daisy nestled above two tiny roses, glistening and gleaming with bevels and melee diamonds. "It belonged to my mum's mum. When I pulled it out of the safe and saw the flowers, I knew it was serendipitous."

"Oh my God, Harrison, this is beautiful." I almost didn't dare to touch it.

"It's not the same as it was, I had the center stone replaced with something a bit larger than what she had. Back then things were...different. Simpler. The smaller ones are original. I hope you like it. I chose what they call an Old European cut, to keep with the feel of the rest of the piece."

"I love it," I gushed, anxious to see it on my finger but still unwilling to reach for it.

"Old European is traditionally a little less sparkly than today's new diamonds. Back then they were hand-cut, and the facets were meant to dance with candlelight. With this, I asked for the best of both worlds. I want you to sparkle darling, even when you've got nothing on but this ring and candlelight."

I leaned over to hug him and he rose to meet my embrace. I pulled away smiling and held my hand out, silently urging him to place the ring on my finger.

As he slipped it on, his eyes stayed focused on mine. "I promise you all of me, for the rest of eternity, Alice. In this lifetime, and all the lifetimes to come, I commit my heart and soul to you." It fit perfectly on my finger, and as he hugged me, I ran my thumb along its edges; soft, worn, having withstood the test of time by women that I'd never met yet felt an instant connection to.

I ran my fingers up into the curls of his hair and kissed him. *I used to daydream about this, and look at me now*, I thought. *Look at me now*. It echoed in every corner of my mind and I smiled to myself. *He thinks I'm sunshine, but he has no idea how bright of a light he has been at the end of a very, very, long, dark tunnel.*

"I pulled this out the night I met you. I came straight home and immediately went to the safe, called my jeweler, and started the process."

"You can't be serious."

"Oh, darling, as a heart attack. I knew immediately that one day, maybe not this soon, but one day, we would be together for eternity."

"I can't wait to be your wife. I don't even care that I've only been divorced for, what's it been? A few days?" I laughed, burying my face in his chest, the strength of his pecs rigid beneath the softness of his robe. "People are going to think I've lost my mind."

"Fuck what people think, respectfully. This is our life and our love and I don't care what the public thinks."

"Speaking of, how does something like this play out? Do we need to sit down and plan this announcement?"

"I don't know, I've never announced that I'm getting married before, but I think we just go about our lives and once the public sees us together, they can either get on board or piss off." He shrugged adamantly. "It won't be long either; surely when we're out someone will photograph us and sell it to some trashy rag. The difference between you being out with me before and now, is not only a finalized divorce, but you've got no reason to hide your beautiful face. Not that you did before either, quite frankly."

"I don't want this to affect your reputation."

"If my fans are *real* fans, they'll love you as much as I do. Don't spend any time on it, darling. Now, come to bed and let me kiss you to sleep."

"If you start kissing me, sleep will be the furthest thing from my mind." I gripped the collar of his robe in my hands, curling my fists beneath it to expose more of his chest. The wisps of chest hair against his Brazilian tan and the top of his eagle tattoo peeking out of the space where the two sides of his robe connected sent my thoughts racing. Right then and there, I knew there would be no rest in sight for me tonight.

CHAPTER
31

Sunshine seeped through the windows as I lay warm under the covers, my naked extremities wrapped around my future husband, the smell of breakfast wafting up from the kitchen. It felt like he'd never been gone and the time we'd spent apart could have been just a figment of my imagination. I kissed his stubble-covered jaw and felt him stir against my body.

"Good morning, future husband," I whispered as I kissed his earlobe.

"Mm, I like that." He squeezed me closer to him. "And I like this." His lips pressed to my forehead then relaxed there while his fingertips made tiny figure eights on my hip.

"I'm so glad you're home. Wait, are you going to swim this morning?"

"Not today. If I can help it, I'd like to spend the entire day right here with you. I've got time to make up for."

The rise and fall of his breathing, feeling his ribs expand against my body warm and slow was nearly enough to put me back to sleep, but it was his hands that kept me awake. They slipped from my waist up to my breasts, all the while his lips stayed pressed to mine.

"Shelby's downstairs," I murmured against his mouth.

"Eh." His hand moved up and held my jaw as he continued kissing me.

"Not eh, she's cooked us breakfast." I kissed his cheek.

"But—" He exhaled heavily through his nose and bit at his lip.

"No buts. C'mon." I moved toward the edge of the bed, ready to reach for my robe when he pulled me back against him, his mouth warm against the top of my shoulder, then focused his attention on my neck.

One swift movement and I was on my back, his body between my open legs, his mouth just above my navel, working its way upward toward mine he paused between my breasts. "Just a quickie. She won't come up here." A quick open-mouthed kiss landed on my sternum then his mouth moved across one breast, his tongue grazing its way to my nipple, stopping only briefly to devote its full attention to making sure it was fully erect before moving to the other. Both of my wrists were pinned above me in the pillows by just one of his palms as I felt him pulsate against me. I knew he was only waiting for me to grant access. His mouth was soft against my neck now, his tongue warm as he gently sucked at my flesh, letting my hands fall loose while he devoted his full attention to my breasts. I pressed my palms against his ass cheeks and adjusted myself beneath him, raising my legs and interlocking my feet against the small of his back. He locked eyes with me and I invited him inside. I struggled to keep quiet as he thrust into me again and again, each one accompanied by a heavy exhale or a quiet whimper. His muscles tightened with every plunging movement, and in no time, my breaths came hard and quickly, just like Harrison.

"You weren't kidding," I said, gasping for air.

"Darling, you are...divine." He collapsed onto me, his body sweaty. "I promise, I'll make it up to you later." His breathing remained heavy.

"Make it up to me? What's to make up?" I asked, confused.

"This seemed a little...one-sided." His dimples just ached for me to kiss them.

"This was an unexpected pleasure," I sighed. "Now get off me before I suffocate." He laughed and I felt his body tense. "No really, I gotta pee." I pushed him and strategically rolled out from under him at the same time. Quickly slipping on my robe, I tiptoed off toward the bathroom.

I cleaned myself up, brushed my teeth, and then stepped into the shower just as Harrison came into the room.

"You care if I'm in here?" he asked.

"Of course not." I dipped my head beneath the hot stream of water and proceeded to wash my hair while he brushed his teeth. When I finally had the suds fully rinsed off my face, I noticed him staring at himself in the mirror.

"You okay?" I could see from where I stood that his eyes were laser-focused on his reflection.

"Just thinking." Eyes locked forward, he blinked and pushed his top lip up in a movement as if to scratch an itch on the underside of his nose.

"About?" I reached for the conditioner, but my attention remained on him.

He ran his hands up into his hair, pushing it all away from his face. "Maybe I should shave my head."

Jesus Christ, nobody move!

"What prompts those thoughts?" I asked calmly, trying to appear unaffected while my heart nearly stopped beating in my chest and my eyebrows rose in disbelief.

"I don't know. Something different. Unexpected." He was still pulling the curls I loved so much away from his face.

"If that's what makes you happy. Let's do it," I lied though my teeth.

He turned and looked at me, straight-faced, staring but said nothing. And I stared back, a questioning look on my face. Seconds passed that felt like an eternity before he returned to staring at himself in the mirror, naked, body rippled like some sort of ancient, tattooed statue, yanking on the hair I adored; every muscle in his arm flexed as he tugged at his locks.

I gave up waiting and rinsed the conditioner from my hair. When I opened my eyes again, he was leaning against the shower door watching me, a Cheshire cat grin spread across his face.

"You know I'm just fucking with you right?" he asked, laughing.

I rolled my eyes and threw any water in my hand in his direction. "You're such a shit!" The droplets rolled down his bare body and I couldn't help but let my eyes follow their path.

"I know you love this mop. It's gonna stick around for a while."

"Well, it's not the mop I love." I reached for his hand and pulled him into the hot water with me. "It's you." The water poured down over his chest, causing goosebumps to spread all over his body and his nipples hardened against the temperature change. "Hair or no hair." I ran my fingers up against the back of his head and he tipped it back, letting the rain head saturate him.

CHAPTER 32

The next two weeks felt like a fever dream. Harrison and I went about our daily lives just like any normal couple. We spent every moment together, though most of them admittedly were in the house or on the grounds. We'd been lucky, we hadn't been found out by the public yet and I think Harrison was content to have me all to himself for as long as possible before swarms of people inundated us with flashbulbs and opinions.

My pregnancy was moving along just fine, the morning sickness had resolved and I was feeling pretty good aside from the exhaustion. But I knew Harrison still worried because of my age, and because our pregnancy was still technically in its early stages, he was fearful of what could happen, especially given my history. I'd seen him reading about it one evening on his phone. 'The Downfalls of Geriatric Pregnancy.' What a shitty title for someone who just wanted to bring new life into the world with a devoted partner who loved them. Geriatric. I wasn't eighty for Christ's sake. But I couldn't fault him for it; I worried too.

We were happy cooking together, reading books together, showering, and sleeping together. Making love far more than I was ever used to, sometimes three or even four times a day. We were inseparable, even if that meant I watched him while he worked out or went for his early morning swims in frigid nearby swimming ponds. I was always right there, attentive, anticipating his needs. And as 'sappy romance novel' as it might seem, he went above and beyond for me as well. We worked together to plan out the baby's nursery, choosing furniture and accessories that could be neutral to either gender. We wouldn't have that info for a while, but the nesting had already begun. It was strange because I hadn't felt the urge to do any of it until he was back home with me.

I even talked Harrison into hanging up a new birdhouse and bird feeder close to the patio. I hadn't told him about Robin yet for fear he'd think I was insane, but he agreed without hesitation to hang what I can only describe as a luxury bird condo on a nearby fence. The wooden feeder was a little less glamorous and was shaped like a gazebo. My little friend didn't take to either of them immediately, as I'm sure he had a perfectly suitable home in a lovely tree somewhere out there in the backyard and plenty of food options elsewhere. But one day, while Harrison was on a work call in the library, I set off in search of my little feathered friend, as I felt I had some explaining to do.

"Robin? Where are you, sweetheart? I've got snacks." Almost immediately he was on my arm, hopping down toward my hand to see what I had to offer. A dozen or so mealworms, a few peanuts, and of course, some blueberries. His eyes intermittently scanned the sky, always on the lookout for some unannounced aerial attack.

"Hi, friend. I've missed you." I took my spot in the patio chair, resting my hand on its arm again, a position that Robin was used to.

He looked up at me, his black eyes reflecting the sky behind me, the faint curve to the opening of his beak almost smile-like as he picked up two, three, then four mealworms, packing them into his beak before dropping them all again back into my hand.

"It's okay, I know. We both have been quite busy. Me with growing a baby and my future husband—your landlord—coming home. And I'm sure you've been gathering up all the little snacks you can to keep you fluffy and warm this winter." He cocked his head and started in on a new blueberry.

"I had Harrison put up a new home for you. I even put some starter sticks in there for you to arrange a nest. I did a little reading. It said the nests are typically built by the ladies of your species. I hope you have a lady friend that you'll introduce me to one day, but in the meantime, don't feel obligated to stay in this new house. Just know that it's there whenever you're ready to start a family, and you'll have a nice safe home to raise them in."

He shook his head, sending bits of blueberry scattering, and sang me his familiar warbling melody with his signature *tic-tic-tic* at the end, then moved on to a peanut.

"I also have a food station for you in case we're off for any amount of time. I'll slip some good snacks in there for you." He looked at me and cocked his head as if he needed more of an explanation.

"And by the way, Harrison is a good guy. You'd like him if you gave him a chance. He's a safe space. Kind, loving. Gentle, always." I reached out and stroked his back, careful not to disturb his snacking. "I'm sure you've witnessed that yourself in your time here. One day when you're ready, come and say hello to us both. I'll be right there if you're nervous."

He hopped up onto my shoulder and with another quick *tic-tic-tic* he flew off, just as if he'd never been there, leaving me with a handful of his leftovers.

"We have an appointment to get to, love," Harrison's voice came from behind me.

I turned and saw him leaning out the patio door. "Be right there." I set the remaining treats on the arm of the chair and made my way back inside. We were due at Della's shortly for our twelve-week check-in.

Our three-month scan had gone just fine, and it was nice to see Della again. Everything pregnancy-related was moving along just as it was supposed to. The baby was measuring perfectly and all my vitals were where she wanted them to be. Harrison was full of questions despite his very thorough research of all things pregnancy, but most importantly, "When can we learn the gender?" and "Is Alice okay to fly?"

For the last week he and I had been discussing taking a quick weekend trip, and only last night did we decide where we wanted to go—back to the Dales—but this time we wanted to bring everyone along with us as a sort of appreciation trip for their friendship and all that they do for us both. Tonight would be the perfect time to let them all know, because for the first time since Friendsgiving, everyone would be together at our place for dinner.

In the late afternoon, Harrison and I started prepping for the meal we would cook our friends and discussed the details of our trip. While he was busy chopping vegetables, I was researching online for a hotel that could accommodate us all comfortably and thinking about transportation. We could all easily go on the jet but we'd have to rent a van to travel almost two hours from Manchester to our destination. Easily doable, and with all of us together, two hours would fly by.

"Should we ask Hank and Victor to go?" I asked.

"Because you feel you need them there to be working or for fun?" His eyes were watering when he looked up.

"Must be one heck of an onion. You okay?" I prodded.

"I'll make it," he joked. "I don't really want to ask them to work. I'd like to just bring everyone, as part of their Christmas gift."

"I mean eight-passenger vans exist, but if they bring their partners, we might need to get one of those buses. Don't you think?" I asked.

"I can easily get us set up with one of those. That's no problem. And they're more comfortable, to be fair. Let's see how it's received at dinner, then I'll reach out to Hank and Victor after to give them the details." Teary-eyed, he went back to chopping his onion.

"I'm excited. I think this will be a nice little adventure for us as a group of friends, don't you? And I hope it gives me an opportunity to spend some time with Emma. I've barely seen her since she discovered Lawrence."

Harrison looked up at me, his eyes mischievous. "Oh, I think it's going to be a perfect little getaway."

CHAPTER 33

By five o'clock, everyone had arrived except Nigel, who was running late, though not by much, and by six o'clock we were all seated around the table, eating dinner and chatting. In the last hour, I'd learned of all the ways our friends were flourishing. Emma and Lawrence had been off on their own, Lawrence of course showing her all that London had to offer, sometimes popping by to share a short visit, or to have dinner and watch a movie with us, but for the most part, they were busy creating their own love story. Nigel had been enjoying getting to know Shelby; the two of them, both single, were out on the town at least four nights a week together and most often could be found at any pub equipped with a karaoke machine. The stories they shared of belting out George Michael and Queen were absolutely hilarious, and the way they explained their escapades was nothing short of legendary. It was nice to see they'd developed such a tight bond with one another.

When everyone's plates were cleared, Harrison stood from his chair and cleared his throat. "I have a bit of an announcement."

Immediately, everyone looked up at him, pensive, unsure of what he would say next or if they should even take him seriously.

"Again with the announcements," Nigel moaned jokingly.

"Oh, I think you'll like this one," I chimed in.

"My *fiancée* and I have been chatting and it would be our pleasure to take everyone on a little weekend jaunt to the Dales. Just for fun." Excited faces peered back at him, except for Emma whose exuberant eyes were, as usual, focused on Lawrence. "It's a bit of a journey, we'll go first on the jet, then it's a two-hour bus ride, so I'll understand if you don't want to go, but I hope you'll all join us. I'll reserve a luxury coach, so it shouldn't be too rough of a go. Lawrence, unfortunately, I do ask that you man the coach to ensure we arrive alive and not toppled over on the side of some country road." Lawrence nodded his acceptance of the task and Harrison continued, "I will be asking Hank and Victor as well. We're a team, and each of you brings something to our lives that we are incredibly grateful for. We just want to show you that you are appreciated." He gave a quick dip of his chin, as if to signal he was done, and took his place once again in his chair.

A chorus of thank you's filled the room.

"When will we go?" Emma asked.

Harrison reached out and touched my shoulder, rubbing it gently as he spoke, "Alice is in charge of all those details. Darling?"

"I need to call the hotel and confirm availability, but I'm hoping for some time between Christmas and New Year's, if that works for everyone's schedules."

"Well, I'll need to ask my boss for the time off," Shelby chimed in. "Sometimes he can be a real pain in the ass."

"Ha. HA." Harrison rolled his eyes at her. "Leave granted. And for the record, I'll be putting that in your personnel file." He glared at her jokingly and she returned the same look, sticking her tongue out at him.

"I'll be back in touch with everyone to let you know the exact dates, but the plan is, we'll all meet at the airport and leave together. The hotel is called..." I bit my lip hesitating, trying to be sure I had the right name. I'd looked at so many accommodations in the last twenty-four hours. "Simonstone Hall, I believe is the name. If it's available, what are everyone's thoughts on taking off the day after Christmas and staying a whole week? Just to wind down a bit, start the new year off right."

"That's fine by me," Shelby nodded. "I've got nowhere to be."

"Same here," Emma replied.

"I wasn't sure if anyone had family obligations during that time?" I questioned.

Everyone shook their heads as they looked around at each other.

"Well, good then. A week it is. We'll share all the details when they're solidified. Now, who's ready for dessert? I made Whoopie Pies."

Emma was the only one who didn't look at me like I was speaking a foreign language.

"Are they meant to be sat on?" Nigel questioned.

"What? No. Just wait, I'll get them."

As I headed for the kitchen, Nigel continued, "What? The only whoopie I know of is a whoopie cushion, meant to fake passing gas or making whoopie, and I don't think any of you want group sex with me." Laughter erupted from around the table.

I came back with a half dozen of the saucer-sized snacks and everyone's eyes widened. "They're like ice cream sandwiches, only instead of ice cream there's a marshmallowy frosting-like filling and the cookies are actually small cakes."

"So, nothing at all like ice cream sandwiches?" Lawrence asked.

"Correct," I laughed. "Some of the icing is pink, and some is blue, just for fun because we have no idea what we're having yet and won't find out until mid-February."

"Christ, I suspect it's a baby you're having! Hell, maybe you'll have one of each!" Nigel shook his fist in the air excitedly. "Pink *and* blue!"

"No indication of that happening at this point, but could you imagine, darling?" Harrison asked with excitement in his eyes.

"I cannot imagine twins, no. I absolutely can*not*." I laughed as I handed out the desserts. "And for now, I think we're lucky to be having this one. So, let's just see how this goes before we sign up for more."

"Do you think this will be the first of many?" Lawrence asked.

"If I could fill this house with children for this man, surely I would. But you know, I'm old so...I guess we'll see what happens." I shrugged and turned to take the now empty tray back to the kitchen.

"Stop that." Emma swatted her hand as if she were shoving my age out of the way. "Alice these look delicious."

I thanked her and took my seat again beside Harrison. "Have the two of you discussed anything future-wise?" I looked from her to Lawrence with expectant curiosity. Simultaneously, their heads turned toward one another, each looking for reassurance I presume, their cheeks flushing pink at the same time. Emma shrugged as she looked at him completely enamored.

"Absolutely saccharine, the both of you." Harrison shook his head. "I'm happy for you both though. The world needs love, and it's not always easy to find."

Meanwhile, Shelby and Nigel rolled their eyes at each other at the opposite end of the table. "Alice, these are divine!" Nigel exclaimed when he noticed me looking at him, a gob of blue icing falling from the corner of his mouth and slopping onto the table.

All I could do was laugh. What a patchwork, piecemealed group of random humans we were, all sitting here together, sharing our lives. I found myself continually fascinated each time we were all together at how strangers could become family. Each of us unique, each of us with vastly different histories and upbringings, and from every corner of the earth. But somehow, Harrison Edwards had brought us all together, and because of that, I was surrounded by love, safety, friendship, and loyalty.

Six months ago, I would not have been convinced this would ever be possible.

CHAPTER
34

I'd spent the last two weeks securing the accommodations, the travel, and all the fun details for our group trip back to the Yorkshire Dales. Simonstone Hall, a gorgeous 15th-century country house estate, opulent in its amenities and abundant with its promise of relaxation, sat perched above the valley of Wensleydale. Ready to accommodate with eighteen period-decorated bedrooms, two restaurants, a bar, a large glass atrium housing an inside pool area, and a full staff, Simonstone Hall seemed absolutely perfect for our needs. I suspected we could stay right on site and be lost somewhere between perfectly happy and spoiled rotten, all without ever leaving the deliciously manicured grounds. Yes, even in December it promised gorgeous scenery and sweeping views in nearly every direction. Harrison had urged me to reserve it in its entirety for our group for a solid week. I'd only been able to find an airstrip in Manchester for the jet, and two rented vans would be our only option for getting us and our luggage to and from Simonstone Hall. Harrison had tried, but a luxury coach wasn't available for the dates we needed, and having two vehicles would give us options for when we wanted to get out and explore separately.

The onsite chef and I discussed my want for what I was calling 'Family

Dinner,' served nightly. We would transform the main restaurant into one large family-style dining table, that way we could all reconvene and share the stories of our day with one another. I'd written up a list of local places that were open in winter, as well as hiking paths close by if anyone wanted to get out and see the countryside. It would be a calm and quiet week; a serene little getaway to recharge before the new year began. And for Harrison and me, a chance to get away and start planning our wedding.

Harrison had spoken with the owner of the estate, who assured us we would be shown the utmost privacy, and that no one from their staff would disclose our location on social media, or otherwise give any indication we had ever been there. Somehow the very persistent UK press hadn't caught us together in public yet, so no major announcement of our relationship had shattered this bubble he and I had been so blissfully happy in. That was one piece of the puzzle I was not looking forward to facing.

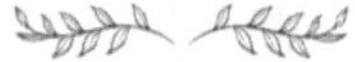

Just one week ago Harrison himself had driven us to a small Christmas tree farm outside of London. Seeing him in the driver's seat instead of Lawrence was definitely a turn-on, the way his hand held the steering wheel, the intensity in his eyes while navigating traffic. It reminded me of the road trip we took together in my dream and the visual of him singing along to Journey in my passenger seat with the windows down as he snaked his hand through the warm summer air, each visual pulling forth a reminiscent smile.

We wandered arm in arm, up and down well-worn footpaths in search of our very first Christmas tree. An eight-foot Norway Spruce, we decided, would be just perfect for us. Watching Harrison hoist it up onto the top of the SUV might have been my favorite part of our little adventure, and he made it look effortless, as if the tree were nothing more than a bundle of feathers. His extra workouts were certainly paying off, further defining a body I thought couldn't be improved on. Yet day after day, I saw his arms becoming bigger, more toned, his abdomen more cut, the definition in his back unlike anything I'd ever seen in real life before. All while my body felt like each new day blew another hot breath into my balloon of an abdomen. I had a long way to go still, but I was beginning to feel *and see* the changes happening to me.

I had never been a small woman to begin with. My belly wasn't remotely flat when he met me, and working out was never something I ever found any joy in, so I never did it. Gardening did plenty for my legs, my arms, and my back, and that had been good enough in my previous life because no one was paying any attention anyhow. Who I was then had been welcomed into this new life with open arms, but no matter the level of excitement or anticipation that Harrison exhibited for this pregnancy, and no matter that I knew he loved me and was attracted to me unconditionally, I still worried that at some point, he'd begin to look at me differently.

Decorating our tree once we got it home and into the house had been a true comedy of errors. We had no decorations, as Harrison had never bothered to have his own Christmas tree before now. No lights, no baubles, and no Christmas crackers, which he made abundantly clear was quite upsetting. He went on and on about them, telling me no Christmas at home would be complete without Christmas crackers, as I stood by fully clueless as to what they even were. A snack? What could possibly be so special about these crackers? Realizing this was quickly spiraling out of control, Harrison sent Shelby into the shops to get all the warm white lights she could find and no less than twelve boxes of multi-colored lights as well. "And don't forget the Christmas crackers, Shelby, Jesus!" He'd barked in her direction just as the front door was closing behind her, his accent dragging out the last syllable. I laughed without regard for how it made him feel; I couldn't help it. Even when he was annoyed, he was funny.

Shelby returned fully freighted with bags full of lights, baubles, and orbs of all shapes and sizes, and Harrison's beloved crackers, which as it turned out, weren't consumables at all. They were little brightly wrapped tubes resembling oversized candies that contained a paper hat, a joke, and some small gift. A UK tradition, Harrison said they were reserved especially for opening at Christmas dinner, and thus we would have to wait to see what fun prizes we would get.

It took hours to get the lights just the way we wanted, and any that remained after the tree was strung so heavily with them it could be seen from Mars, were draped all around the living room. I imagined there must have been rays of light shooting from the windows like lightsabers. I'd never used so many strings in one space in all my life, but he was happy, and therefore, so was I.

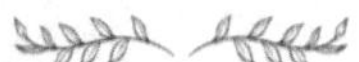

Christmas morning found London blanketed in snow and Harrison naked beside me. We hadn't gone to bed that way, so finding him like that was a pleasant surprise. There would be no Shelby, just us, alone, uninterrupted. I quickly but quietly padded off to the bathroom to relieve myself and freshen up before slipping out of my t-shirt and back into bed, my body bare. I teased him awake, my hands and mouth exploring his body, priming us both for what would turn into hours of feverish lovemaking.

By midday, we were slow dancing in the kitchen while we cooked, Harrison in nothing but his boxer briefs and me in my oversized t-shirt, my arms around his neck lifting the hem of my shirt to barely cover my backside. Harrison's voice was a gravelly whisper as his mouth lay against my ear, humming and singing along to the crackly kitchen radio; his breath causing every tiny hair on my body to stand at attention. His lips teased my neck as we swayed slowly in place, the palms of his hands warm against my lower back, he held me tenderly against him. We burned the food, but I didn't care.

Moments like these made me feel like I was young again, like I hadn't lived through so much misery. They reminded me that I never could have appreciated Harrison the way I did now if I'd never lived through my time with James.

We spent the rest of the afternoon lounging on the couch laughing at old movies, kissing like teenagers, and seeing who could land more pieces of popcorn in the other's mouth. Truth be told, my aim was shit and Harrison was quickly covered in rogue pieces of popcorn. Before sunset, we went for a walk out through the garden and down the pathway to the stream, pausing to sit a while on the bench and listen to the calmness of nature. Knowing we were leaving tomorrow for a week, I made sure there was plenty of food out for Robin, and we sat on the patio in silence and watched as the sun went down.

I'd begged him not to buy me anything for Christmas. Having him in my life was all I'd ever need, but no matter how I tried to explain it, he was Harrison, so his workaround had been to present me with a love letter. "I didn't spend any money on it, love," he'd said, looking up at me with puppy-dog eyes through his beautiful eyelashes, his left dimple accompanying his disarming half-smile. As if that made it alright. But who was I kidding? Everything *was* alright, just like he'd told me it would be months ago. And when I explained to him that I had nothing for him, that I'd had no time to get to the shops, or the forethought to send Shelby after something, he'd kissed me and laid his head in my lap, his cheek to my belly and said, "You've given me the best gift of my life, Alice." His eyes had closed as he paused. "This child we share is my life's greatest accomplishment, and I wouldn't have any of this without you." Then as if by some divine miracle, he and I shared the pleasure of feeling our baby kick for the first time. It was more of a flutter, but enough that Harrison felt it too. He looked up at me in amazement without a word, then quickly returned his cheek to my belly, hoping for more. Quietly, Harrison began to sing, "You are my sunshine, my only sunshine..." and as we sat there, still, hoping the flutters would continue, they did.

Our first Christmas had been, by my calculations, a success.

CHAPTER 35

Simonstone Hall had a way of sneaking up on you, especially in a dense cover of fog. The photos online showed it as a magnificent awe-inspiring structure, but its roadside entry was bland and dare I say, underwhelming. From the cobbled parking lot, it looked like any other row house with an aged stone facade, the fog making it appear damp and dreary with no character or charm whatsoever, aside from the five chimneys that stood tall behind various moss-covered rooflines in the grayness of the day. Despite having reserved the entire estate, there were no less than ten different footpaths and hiking trails surrounding the property, which would leave quite a few random people shuffling past at any given moment while we were here. Even in late December, I'd been told the Dales were an incredible sight to behold on a sunny day, drawing hikers from all over the world.

While the others gathered their luggage, I stood and took in my surroundings. The entry from the parking lot was quite the opposite of what I'd expected. The website had swept me off my feet with photos of four gorgeous stacked-stone gables, ornate stone-mullioned windows, and a multi-level sprawling patio overlooking miles and miles of valleys with stacked stone walls defining one man's paradise from his neighbors'. But this wasn't that. *Maybe when the fog lifts I'll get a chance to explore a bit and find that dreamy exterior.*

The interior though, was something to behold. Absolutely stunning, warm, and welcoming, the perfect mixture of historic and modern dotted with period pieces and dramatic artwork. All the walls were trimmed with deep picture-frame molding in a pale sage-beige color that reminded me of the grass in late April back in New England, clinging to the last of its chlorophyll, aching for spring sunshine. I imagined this room on a brighter day, soaked in sunlight, the gold accents of the lobby springing out from their surroundings to let you know they'd been polished to perfection, the various bouquets of flowers opening wide to welcome the sun's rays and guests alike.

I peered around. Off center from the main entry, there was what the lovely woman at the front desk deemed the *drawing room*. From where I stood, I could see what I assumed to be an original fireplace, its gaping mouth filled to the brim with flickering orange flames; what a welcome sight this time of year. The oak mantle was nothing short of massive and ornately detailed, while the moody, dark turquoise walls had a way of coaxing your eyes upward to land on a beautiful brass chandelier. Centered perfectly above three tufted velvet couches in a shade of dijon reminiscent of the 1970s, the chandelier cast an intricate pattern of shadows across the ceiling and walls. Perfect for a comfy fireside chat or a cozy spot to read, those couches would be seeing me soon, guaranteed. Cozy historic opulence, that was Simonstone, and I was eager to explore further.

We had all arrived together but quickly set off in different directions in search of our preferred rooms. Harrison told me he'd reserved the one he wanted for us ahead of time. I didn't know if it had a name or a number; I only knew he led me straight up a grand staircase in search of it. The walls of the first-floor landing were a kaleidoscope of delicate stained glass, arranged in tiny vibrantly colored squares depicting various flags and shields. I couldn't wait to see the sun shine through them. And as we wandered down the second-floor hallway, one side made almost fully of windows, we stopped to admire the miles of open countryside and noticed the peaked glass atrium off to one side below us. The bright blue of the indoor pool beneath it caused me to stop and look closer. A few lush potted palms stood tall behind chaise lounges on one side, and on the other side of the pool, there were two sets of chairs with small round tables between them. It wasn't a huge space, but I was looking forward to spending some time feeling weightless in the water.

Finally, inside our suite, Harrison closed the door behind us and fixed his eyes on me while I took a look around. For a place so prone to fog, I was surprised to find all the walls a rich dark green, with wood accents of aged oak. The main room housed a comfortable-looking living area with a balcony big enough for two, flanked by large windows overlooking the valley to the south. A nice spot for morning coffee, or maybe late-night nakedness. A flashback of New Orleans burst through my mind.

Off to the left was the bedroom in what I could only describe as a turret; round and tall with a spiked ceiling, I felt like a princess here in this ancient castle with my knight in shining armor. Half the room was stone, and the other half an olive green, the beige carpet plush beneath my feet, a TV situated off to one side. The large four-poster bed sat facing a set of wraparound windows overlooking the outstretched property below, perfect for watching the sun come up in the morning, Harrison's favorite. The headboard was covered in a deep green material with a gold laurel-leafed pattern, more of the same canopied over the top of the bed while soft sheers hung from every corner.

I ran my fingertips along the twisted gold rope holding them in place. "Well, this place is really something else. When we first arrived, I was a little nervous, not gonna lie." I made my way toward the bathroom. "Be right out, babe, I gotta pee."

Moments later while I stood at the sink, Harrison's voice permeated the door, "Shower big enough for two?" he asked.

"Everything looks pretty standard in here," I dried my hands and opened the door to find him leaning against its frame.

"We'll just have to squeeze in close then I guess." He took me by the hand, and pulled me into him, purposefully placing my palm against his back. His hand caressed my chin upward toward his and he kissed me slowly.

"I think it's the only way." I let my palms fall to the back pockets of his jeans as I kissed him again.

"Let's give it a shot, want to? We have a while before dinner, and I'd really like to feel you against me, but," he pinched part of my shirt and bra strap between his fingers, "not with these." His distaste for them was evident as he scrunched half his face and shook his head slightly.

I tucked my thumbs into his back pockets and tugged downward gently. "These are really problematic actually." I tried hard to keep a straight face.

"Are they now?" His dimples appeared and his nostrils flared.

I nodded and let my fingers drag gently across his waist to find the button of his jeans. I looked up and locked eyes with him, something I knew drove him wild. With a flick of my thumb and a deliberately slow release of his zipper, I slid my palm down the front of his boxer briefs to find him already hard.

"You come bearing gifts, I see." My hand moved lower against the soft cotton confining him, my fingers urging him to move his legs apart. He shifted to let me cup him fully in my palm as a fingertip teased even further backward.

"Jesus, Alice." The words fell from his mouth as he exhaled and leaned once again on the door frame for support.

I watched him with an innocent smile as he tried to maintain his composure.

"So many obstacles..." I shook my head with fake discouragement, and as I carefully withdrew my hand, making sure to let my fingers linger along the length of him as they passed, Harrison drew in a sharp breath from my touch.

His eyes looked from my shirt down to my pants and back up again. "You're one to talk."

I took a step backward. "Take what you want." I offered, the look on my face inviting him to take control.

In an instant, he'd pulled off my shirt and single-handedly popped the clasp of my bra, his mouth immediately drawn to my breasts as his hands made quick work of slipping off my jeans. I pulled away from him and turned to start the shower. As my hand reached for the knob, I felt Harrison's hand on my back, easing me to bend forward, the other at my hip pulling my backside against him. In no time, the hand on my back shifting to reach around and grasp at my breast.

I paused a moment, enjoying the feeling of him pressing into me from behind, his hand pulling me harder against him before his other hand slid from my breast, down my side, both of them landing at the waistband of my panties, two fingers on each side slipping beneath their edge, and pausing.

I turned my head and looked over my shoulder at him. "Find something you like?"

A mischievous grin crept across his face and he yanked them down over my hips, exposing me before pulling his shirt over his head and dropping it to the floor. I was still bent at the waist, my eyes teasing him over my shoulder when he drew his index finger into his mouth and then slid it between my legs to assess my readiness.

"Wait, wait, wait...the original problem is still a problem." I smirked at him and slowly pulled myself away from his hand to face him.

"Alice you're killin' me." His abdomen tightened as he exhaled, summoning my eyes downward.

"Anyone ever tell you how incredibly sexy you are?" I asked and pulled his jeans to the floor, lowering myself to the point of almost being on my knees.

"Well..." He paused and I looked up at him, smiling like a deviant. "I mean...I guess I'm...average," he said, the corners of his mouth twisting as he attempted to keep from smiling.

I reached up and slid the cotton boxer briefs down over his hips, then further still until they set free the impressive bulge they'd been concealing, laying the rest of his gorgeous body bare.

"Oh, you're well above average," I said, one hand wrapped around the back of his knee to steady myself as I kissed my way up his other thigh, working toward the ticklish crease at the front of his groin, tracing along its defined line with my tongue. "Well above..." I repeated once more, then gently ran my tongue up the length of his shaft and kissed just below the tip, parting my lips enough to let him feel the warmth of my tongue move against his skin. As I pulled away, I could see him visibly throbbing in my periphery, and as tempting as it was to want to send him over the edge right then and there, I stood and smiled over my shoulder as I stepped into the shower, leaving him there wearing nothing but the look of a man ready to devour me completely.

CHAPTER
36

Harrison took his time with me in the shower, there wasn't a single bit of my body that either his hands or his mouth didn't touch, and he delivered again when he bent me over the edge of the bed before we finally got dressed and headed downstairs to meet the group for dinner.

As we walked hand in hand toward the dining room, I thought back to a time last year. I saw myself at the kitchen counter in the farmhouse, my head in my hands over the sink. I remembered feeling hopeless, alone, and wondering how and why my husband could so easily disregard me. The night before had been one of the rare occasions I'd tried to catch his eye, desperate to feel wanted by the man who claimed to love me. I'd climbed the stairs and crawled into bed naked, taking my time not to immediately pull the covers up to my chin, making sure he had time to see that tonight, something far from the ordinary was being brought to the table. But just as I had laid down, James had turned off the light. I'd said nothing, but lay there staring at the ceiling, wondering if his hand might reach out in the darkness to touch me, reciprocate, or give me any indication that I could still arouse him. No touch came. I'd reached for his hand and set it to rest against the softness between my navel and the underside of my cleavage. He'd sighed and rolled over onto his side to face me. A flicker of hope buzzed through me, but his hand landed at my waist and gave a brief tap before falling lifeless again. A few moments later I'd pulled his hand up to cup my breast, my intentions blatant, but I was met with a haphazard squeeze, and then his snoring filled the room. Frustrated, I'd thrown his hand back in his direction and gotten up to put on my usual pajamas. He'd never even woken up. I'd lived that way for over two decades. Hopeful, rejected, disappointed. Hopeful, ignored, disappointed. Exhausted.

I didn't miss those days, and looking back on them now, I wasn't sure how I survived them with my sanity intact. I'd read books and articles and listened to podcasts about how to keep the spark alive in a marriage, and nothing I'd tried ever worked. A quote I'd heard replayed in my head: "When a woman no longer feels wanted, the lack of feeling desired becomes corrosive to a relationship." I couldn't remember who said it. I only knew I blamed myself, as most women did, when in fact it was a combined failure.

I looked up at Harrison, and his eyes, soft and kind, met my gaze. He was nothing like James. I didn't think he ever could be. He smiled at me sweetly, and my heart felt like it might explode. I squeezed his hand in mine. "I love you."

"And I you, darling." The instant he winked at me, I wanted to forget dinner altogether and take him back to our suite. The visual of his gold chain swinging in unison with each thrust made me hot just at the thought of it.

"I don't know if it's just the way you make me feel, or these pregnancy hormones, but I want round three. Like, right now." I shook my head, instantly embarrassed I'd said it out loud to him.

"Alright then." He turned back in the direction of the suite, spinning me with him.

"We can't be late for the dinner *we* are hosting, not on night one!"

"Dammit!" he joked.

"Don't you think they assume we've been up here christening the place?" he asked, eyebrows raised.

"Oh my God, Harrison. I hope not!" My cheeks flushed again.

We turned and began again toward the dining room. "You're crazy, you know that?" I smirked up at him.

He shrugged and smiled like a mischievous child as we headed down the main staircase and through the lobby in search of the dining room.

CHAPTER 37

Having reserved the entire estate for ourselves, there were no other patrons at the hotel and as predicted, Harrison and I were the last to arrive for dinner, our sincerest apologies plastered across our faces. Everyone was seated and chatting amongst themselves at the table, drinks in hand.

"Decided to join us, eh?" Lawrence joked and raised his glass in Harrison's direction as they traded a knowing look.

"So sorry, we…lost track of time." Harrison bowed his head briefly and looked up smiling like a devil.

"I'll bet you did," Nigel added as multiple sarcastic 'mm-hmms' teased us from every direction.

"Did everyone find a room they can be comfortable in?" I asked, trying to change the subject.

A chorus of voices and nods indicated everyone was happy as Harrison and I took our seats at the table. Then two men appeared in the large dining room entryway, the more petite of the two clearing his throat abruptly, seeking our undivided attention. Dressed in all black, his dark hair tightly slicked back in every direction, beady blue eyes, and pale skin, he wore his agitation in the lines of his forehead. I recognized him as one of the gentlemen who helped carry our luggage in earlier. The other man was considerably taller, easily over six feet, and tan with relaxed dark eyes and a shaggy haircut. I didn't know him, but he reminded me of the guys from the Jersey Shore television show. He clearly spent his free time in a gym or seeking out reflective surfaces to stare at himself.

"Ay, there he is!" Victor sprung from his chair and surged toward the doorway. "Mate, ya found us! Good to see you!" The two men leaned in for a bro-hug, slapping each other's backs roughly a few times before breaking loose. "Pull up a seat, settle in."

"What've ya got here for scran? I'm near a cob on, I've got to eat, mate."

I looked at Harrison, thoroughly puzzled. I didn't understand a damn thing he'd just said.

"I'll hold your things at the front until you're done with dinner; please retrieve them before finding your accommodations." The small man stepped back and ducked out of the room as his larger cohort bellowed toward him, "Alright then, I do fancy a bevvy!" But when no response came, the larger man simply shrugged and looked toward Victor for his next move.

"So, everyone, this is my mate, Julian. He's my old roommate from uni and will be my plus-one on this trip." Victor patted him hard on the shoulder. "Julian, this is...everyone."

Julian flashed a smile and a quick nod, raising his hand, and letting forth a mellow, "Alright," from time to time while Victor made individual introductions.

"What's that dialect?" I leaned in close and whispered to Harrison.

"Scouse, I'd say. Sounds like Liverpool to me," he whispered back.

Victor and Julian made their way toward the other end of the table while I glanced around and found Nigel eyeballing the newcomer like a piece of meat alongside his partner in crime Shelby, who was doing the same.

"You two behave," I cautioned, my finger pointed at one and then the other.

"Unlikely," Nigel mumbled under his breath toward Shelby while smiling at me as sweetly as he could manage.

Meanwhile, Shelby's eyes were planted on Julian as he took off his jacket and hung it over the back of his chair. I watched as she assessed every visible part of him. Her eyebrows rose as I watched her eyes scan from Julian's face down over his arms that presented like hostages in his tightly rolled-up sleeves. I'd never seen her like this before. The cool, aloof Shelby that couldn't care less about a man now appeared to be some new laser-focused version of herself.

"Shelb, you okay?" I half laughed as I said it. No response. "Shelby?" I repeated. She never turned her head, just kept a keen eye on the movement of Julian's hands as he discussed football with Victor.

I turned my attention back to Harrison, just as Hank said, "Bolton Castle is closed this time of year, mate."

"That's a bummer. That was on my list," I chimed in, inserting myself into their conversation.

"Maybe this time 'round we can get you two into Aysgarth Falls. Lawrence said you had to sort of bypass it the last time."

"Oh, that would be nice." I reached for Harrison's thigh under the table, my hand landing just one layer of denim away from the lion tattoo I so enjoyed. My body still ached from this afternoon, but just the thought of that tattoo had me wanting more. I squeezed his thigh and let my palm creep up, further and further still.

"We'd probably get *soaking* wet." My face serious, I looked at Harrison as I waited for his reaction to my double-entendre, my hand now flirting with his zipper under the table. His nostrils flared as he adjusted himself in his chair, trying, and mostly failing, to keep a straight face.

"Wet, yes," he cleared his throat. "The spray from the falls. The mist!" He squirmed in his seat and abruptly changed the subject. "Oh, look, the food's arrived!" His voice was loud, drawing everyone's attention to the doorway where a line of waiters were entering, each carrying two large oval trays covered in steaming plates of food. Harrison's hand landed on top of mine under the table, and he pressed my palm against the crotch of his jeans. *Mission accomplished,* I thought. While he held my hand firmly against him, I leaned over and kissed him slowly.

"Save me some of that for later," I whispered in his ear.

He smirked at me and shook his head. "Absolutely scandalous, Alice."

Dinner went off without a hitch; the food was beautifully plated and delicious; the drinks were plentiful and flowed endlessly, and our guests seemed void of concern for their effects. Shelby was able to pull her eyes from Julian long enough to enjoy her food, Nigel was drunk before dessert arrived, Hank and Victor planned to take Julian hiking tomorrow morning, and Lawrence and Emma were, as always, in their own little love-bird world. They'd barely made a peep the entire evening, just stuck close to one another and talked amongst themselves. Overall, our first *Family Dinner* of the week—plus Julian—had been a success, I thought.

Emma had been here for weeks now, and in many ways, she still felt like a stranger. She was always with Lawrence, rarely engaged with me, and I felt like I'd barely seen her, let alone been able to spend any time with her. We had been so close before she met him, and while I understood new love, I missed my friend. Tomorrow, I'd find a way to catch up with her. But tonight, oh, tonight I had a date with a lion tattoo and my future husband.

CHAPTER 38

Harrison and I spent the morning in bed, enjoying croissants and coffee, and each other, waiting for the morning fog to dissipate. Around noon we managed to drag ourselves from the comfort of one another's embrace in search of some way to enjoy the newly arrived sunshine. We found Emma and Lawrence headed through the lobby en route to check out a waterfall called Hardraw Force, and they invited us to tag along. *Maybe I won't have to beg for her attention after all*, I thought. It was an easy walk from Simonstone Hall, not more than a few minutes, and Emma and I chatted as we walked, leaving the men behind us as we meandered along.

"So, catch me up. I've barely seen you since you laid eyes on Lawrence. You got here and suddenly you were gone again."

"Oh, Alice, you have no idea." She grabbed my hand and squeezed it tightly in hers.

"You sure about that?" I asked, playfully leaning into her as we walked.

"Okay, maybe you do." She laughed. "But geez, these British men are next level compared to what I'm used to. Attentive, thoughtful, protective. Charming as hell."

"I think we both got lucky with this bunch. They've all got the same mindset it seems."

"And Lawrence can't seem to get enough of me! I'm exhausted, Alice. My God, he's insatiable!"

"Honey, that's the best part as far as I can tell," I joked. "That, and everything you just mentioned. It's like old-fashioned love in a brand-new world. Harrison doesn't want to just sit in front of a TV in silence. He wants to talk, all the time, about everything. He asks me questions and is genuinely interested in my answers. He actually listens when I speak and absorbs what I'm saying. He's helpful without me having to ask; he just *does* things. It's certainly a welcome change from the quicksand I'd been drowning in."

"I bet." She lowered her voice and continued, "Have you heard from James at all?"

"No, thankfully, and I hope it stays that way. I mean, nothing against the guy, I just...I want to leave that behind me and move forward."

"Understandable." She gave me a knowing look.

"I've got a wedding to plan, you know. Can you break away from Lawrence long enough to help, or are you just too smitten?"

"I've been wanting to spend some girl time with you, so let's plan a day when we get home to just deep dive into these wedding ideas. It'll be fun and what you don't use, maybe I will." She squeezed my hand again and pulled me closer, glancing at me like she had a secret to keep.

I gasped, "Emma!" My eyes wide, I stared at her, silently begging for more info.

"Shhh! Nothing has happened yet, but I really hope it does," she whispered.

"Everything alright up there?" Lawrence's voice came from behind us.

"Yup, all good here!" I hollered without turning around, then looked at Emma, who was nervously looking back at me. Both of us stifled laughter like a couple of schoolgirls.

Down through the spring-hungry valley, the walking trail pulled us into a section of forest, a small babbling stream running parallel beneath the leafless canopy ushering us to the parking lot for Hardraw Falls, which lay vacant except for one older model car. While Lawrence went to pay our admission, the three of us noticed several well-groomed gravel paths breaking off the main parking lot in various directions, but only one had a tall, carved sign giving details of the pathway that lay out behind it. It read: "Hardraw Force is England's largest unbroken single-drop above-ground waterfall, with a one-hundred-foot drop surrounded by fifteen acres of explorable grounds."

"There's also a natural cave nearby with an underground waterfall, but it's closed." Lawrence had reappeared from the coin machine that collected entry fees. "It's called Gaping Gill. I guess it's as deep as Saint Paul's Cathedral is tall and people get winched down into it. Sounded fascinating to me." He shrugged and looked at Emma. "Maybe we'll come back sometime when the weather is better."

"Sounds fun as long as the winch holds." Harrison gave Lawrence a playful push.

An older couple bundled in layers and scarves, their cheeks rosy, shuffled out of the path, their terrier dog pulling at its leash when it saw us. "Calm down!" the older man exclaimed. "Have you gone mad?" He pulled the dog's tether in an attempt to slow its pull, its front legs lifting off the ground in excitement.

"It's okay little one." Harrison dropped down to the dog's level. "Is it okay to pet her?" he asked.

"It's a he, and I think the old chap might be offended if you *didn't* make a fuss of him," the gentleman said.

As Harrison reached out a hand, the dog pressed itself against him and nuzzled against his legs, his little nub of a tail moving at lightning speed as Harrison's hands made quick work of rubbing behind his ears and down the length of his small body. "What a lovely gent you are!" The dog collapsed to the ground and rolled to expose his belly. "Yes, you are, such a good boy," Harrison cooed as he rubbed at the dog's chest.

"So, it's not just me? I see he's got this effect on everyone," I whispered to Emma and she chuckled.

"Come on then, off we go," the owner's voice prompted the dog to stand and make his way back toward his people. "Enjoy the falls," he called out as they walked to their car.

"Thank you! Have a good day," I shouted back.

"Alice, our baby is going to need a playmate." Harrison watched longingly as the dog jumped into the backseat, his head quickly popping up above the headrest to find us through the back window. "Look at him; he's adorable. His little tongue is sticking out."

"I think our hands will be full for a time with an infant, don't you? Let's pace ourselves." I patted his shoulder, kissed his cheek, and pulled him toward the path to the falls.

I stood before Hardraw Force in awe, the water like a freight train, gushing over the edge with a late-for-dinner urgency, crashing and dissipating into its own pool below. This magical place felt like elves or woodland creatures could pop out and approach us at any moment from the crags and outcroppings of rocks that lay dappled with dormant moss and the stains of last summer's algae all along the pool's edge. A long length of log lay toppled over on its side, coins of all colors and denominations protruding from its barkless skin, whispering silently to take a chance and make a wish of our own. I wanted to tell the log that all my wishes had already manifested themselves, that I had none left to wish, but I closed my eyes and bowed my head and secretly wished for a happy and healthy baby born of a full-term pregnancy.

"You know, they filmed Robin Hood here." Harrison slid his arm around my waist.

"I didn't. I can see why though; it's gorgeous. Imagine how lush it must be in summer."

"We'll be back again. We'll bring the baby, take a long holiday if you like when everything is brimming with new life."

"That sounds amazing." I tipped my head to rest against his chest.

A giggle from Emma in the distance caught my attention. They'd somehow found a way to get behind the rushing curtain of water and I could see her with Lawrence, his arms wrapped around her, holding her close, kissing her. He was different when he was alone with her; I could see it for myself now. He was relaxed. Happy. Jovial. Not the stiff, per-protocol professional I'd known him to be. The way he looked at her was beautiful to watch. I stepped out of Harrison's embrace and borrowed his phone to snap a few candid shots of them together. I turned to him as I placed the phone back into his pocket. "I bet you'll see them in the same position we are, sooner than you'd think."

"He's smitten with her for sure. I've never seen him like this, and I've known Lawrence for a good bit."

"I'm so happy for them," I added.

"How could anyone not be?" He wrapped his arms around me from behind.

"That feels nice, I'm getting a little chilly already."

"Maybe this will help." He turned me to face him and kissed me slowly. "Alice, your teeth are chattering! You should have said something sooner. Let's get you back and get you warmed up."

"I didn't want to drag everyone back so soon just because I didn't dress properly."

"Bollocks, they know the way back. Hey!" he hollered toward Emma and Lawrence, "we're headed back."

Startled, they broke from their embrace. Emma nodded and Lawrence gave a thumbs-up of understanding, then they went right back to kissing and paying us no mind.

We set off hand-in-hand toward the hotel, assuming we would see them later, but they caught up to us just as we climbed the stairs of the terrace. Inside, I could hear voices coming from the drawing room. Nigel, Victor, and Hank were settled in comfortably around the fire having afternoon tea and chatting when we all walked in and joined them.

"Where's Shelby?" I asked as I extended my arms closer to the fire to warm my hands.

Air burst from Nigel's nose as he rolled his eyes, unimpressed. "I saw her slink off with Liverpool a few hours ago."

Victor looked at me and shrugged, presumably as a means to release himself from any responsibility. I looked at Harrison suspiciously and back at Victor. "That's *your* friend. Is he normal or some sort of weirdo? Is she safe with him?" My voice was more forceful than I meant for it to be, but my concern was real.

"You've seen him, of course she's safe." Victor's flippant attitude rubbed me the wrong way. It reminded me of the way James used to speak to me, and I felt my ears flush red, searing with suppressed anger.

"Me seeing him is exactly why I'm asking!" I barked back.

"Alright. Everyone is safe and fine, and everything will be okay." Harrison laid his palm against the small of my back in an attempt to calm my nerves.

"You don't know that." My voice was now back at its normal volume.

"Shelby's an adult. She can handle herself. Trust me, she's no pushover." Harrison knew her better than any of us; he knew what she was capable of if necessary. He told me himself he'd taught her to fight when they were younger as a means of protecting herself.

Victor resumed his conversation with Hank while Nigel abandoned his tea and joined me and Harrison back in the lobby.

"I don't appreciate being left with these two today. Absolute knobs, the lot of 'em." He rolled his eyes again. "They're besties and I'm just the odd bloke left behind."

"Oh, I'm sure you held your own just fine." Harrison tried to be reassuring, but Nigel wasn't having it.

"I'm just not the gymnasium, protein powder, footballer type. I'm certain they weren't thrilled with my presence either."

Harrison reached out, his hand landing on Nigel's shoulder. "They're good guys; they're just used to spending a lot of time together is all. We can all find common ground if we look for it."

Nigel let out a sigh followed by a glance in my direction. "I found a spot that might be fun to visit if the weather's going to be clear. It's called..." He grabbed his phone from his pocket. "It's called...Bamford Edge." He held his phone toward me and showed me a screenshot of the view. "But it takes a few hours to get there. I thought maybe on our way back we could stop to look, then carry on to Manchester to the jet."

"What sort of place is it?" I asked.

"It's an overlook of sorts, with views in all directions. Most try to catch a sunset, but I'm rather interested in just seeing the view."

"Well, that sounds fun. We'll search for it tonight and figure out a plan. Thanks, Nigel." I patted his shoulder appreciatively. "Day after tomorrow we'll be venturing back to Aysgarth Falls, if you'd like to tag along. I'll propose it to the group tonight at dinner."

"I think we should make a point to get to know this...Julian." Nigel's snark made it known he wasn't a fan. "He's just breezed in here and taken my mate away and left me here to twiddle my thumbs alone, and if he plans to stick around, I think we ought to know a bit more."

"I think you may be right, to be fair," Harrison agreed. "Not that I have any reason to be suspicious, but Shelby's *family*, and we don't really know him."

I chimed in, "For the record, I don't like the way Victor just spoke to me. Just because we're on vacation and he's not on the clock, it doesn't mean he can be rude and dismissive."

"I know, darling." His hand rubbed my back. "I'll speak with him privately later. Just don't spend too much time worrying about—"

Through the doorway behind Harrison, I saw Shelby walk in, her eyes fixed upward, admiring Julian who was at her side. "Oh! Thank God!" I interrupted, grabbing her attention. I watched as her fingers reactively disentangled from Julian's and slipped into her pocket. "You're okay? Everything's alright?"

"Yes, love, everything's fine. Why wouldn't it be?" Shelby seemed confused by my concern.

"I was just worried about you is all." I hugged her and whispered into her ear, "I need details, asap," before pulling back to my spot beside Harrison and smiling as if I'd said nothing at all.

Shelby offered nothing more, while Julian split off and found Victor and Hank in the drawing room, causing a roar of garbled manly greetings to spill out into the lobby. Nigel wasted no time grabbing Shelby by the arm and nearly dragging her down the hall to one of their rooms, presumably to get those details I was eager to hear about. Part of me wanted to follow, but the urge to be with Harrison overrode my curiosity.

"Let's get you warm, darling." There was a sparkle in his eye as he wrapped his arm around me. "Come crawl under the covers and rest a bit with me. We've got plenty of time before dinner."

Who could say no to that?

CHAPTER 39

During dinner we solidified plans for the group to go back to Aysgarth Falls in a few days. While the conversation afterward varied amongst us, Nigel and I continued to steer the focus back on Julian, prodding him further about his upbringing, his interests, and his current occupation. Born and raised in the inner workings of Liverpool, Julian had grown up poor. He was the middle child of three with the oldest being a brother named Jacob, two years his senior, and a younger sister, Jacqueline, followed close behind. Bad enough being the middle child, even worse to feel forgotten for a darling baby girl who took away all the attention. Jacob had been brutal to Julian growing up, teasing and starting fights both at home and at school, leaving Julian to learn how to defend himself at a young age.

In college, he'd met Victor at a pub trivia game and they'd become fast friends. Spending most of their free time together at the gym or in the pubs, chasing women, and as he put it, "Laddy lads doing what lads do." The rest, he'd said, was history. It didn't take a rocket scientist to figure out that Shelby and Julian shared similar pasts and their innate need to fend off bullies and be loved while dealing with the atrocities of life was likely the glue that created their bond. Maybe now I'd be able to understand him a bit better. Maybe now, I wouldn't be such a skeptic.

Julian explained that these days he was a freelance boxing coach with hopes to one day open his own gym. *A noble enough dream, and certainly an attainable one. Maybe he's not a complete dolt afterall.* He'd focused his gaze on Shelby as he explained to me that being self-employed meant he could teach from anywhere, even London. I nodded as Julian continued to drop hints that he was taking this newfound love a little more seriously than any of us originally thought. And as Shelby's head dipped in an attempt to shield her cheeks when they blossomed pink, I watched as she avoided making eye contact with anyone but her dinner plate.

Another one bites the dust.

And then my thoughts shifted to Nigel. He was becoming the only one in our inner circle who didn't have a love interest. In time, I hoped that would change. He'd held on to his lover, William, for so long, hoping that one day it would turn into everything he ever wanted, only for it to fall apart. It was hard to start over from zero when you'd spent so many years trying to forge a relationship with someone. I knew that harsh truth all too well. Trouble was, Nigel had found himself building sandcastles far too close to the water in hopes the tide would never roll in and decimate what he'd poured so much love into. But the tide always came, just as the moon did, and the sun. It couldn't be stopped or wished away. And poor Nigel had to sit there and watch as the waves washed over the castle walls, leaving nothing behind but memories.

After dinner, as we all split off in different directions, I asked Nigel if he'd like to join Harrison and me at the pool. I knew what it felt like to see everyone around you paired off, happy and in love while all you felt was loneliness, and I wanted to offer him an alternative to sitting alone in his room. Shelby had left separately from Julian, but it had been clear he was going to be her evening entertainment. So, an hour later when Harrison and I walked into the atrium, we found Nigel reclined in a lounge chair, drink in one hand tilted to the verge of spilling, and scrolling on his phone with the other.

"There they are!" he bellowed, the unexpected volume of his voice startling me. A raise of his glass sent brown liquid sloshing over the side. "Shite…" he mumbled under his breath then drunkenly smiled at us again.

"Nigel," Harrison tipped his head in acknowledgment.

The glass panels of the atrium ceiling were fogged and sweating, leaving streaks of clear night sky to shine through like glittery black paint in the upper half while the rest of the windows were perfectly clear, allowing light to shine in from the string lights woven throughout the terrace outside. The interior pool lights gave it a vibrant neon blue glow as random wafts of steam rose from its heated water. I smiled nervously at Nigel then pulled off my sweater, revealing the top of my blue and white striped one-piece swimsuit underneath. It was the only one I'd brought with me in the move and with this bump of mine starting to show, it might not have been my best choice.

"Nice tattoo," Nigel slurred, referring to the permanent H. now exposed on my upper rib.

Strangely, his comment made me feel uneasy. Exposed. Vulnerable.

"Alice, darling, you must be careful of water temperatures." Harrison cautioned. "I don't want anything to happen to you two." He leaned in and kissed me, placing his hand on my stomach, then he held my hand to steady me as I hastily pulled my leggings off and set them aside in the chair next to Nigel. My hand instinctively landed at my lower belly, protecting its swollen shape, which for the first time felt quite obvious beneath the vertical stripes of my swimsuit. Harrison remained beside me, his right hand now against my abdomen, and kissed me again. The longer I stood there, the more anxious I was to get into the water.

"I'll just take a quick dip, then I think I'll sit at the edge and put my feet in," I reassured him. "You coming in, Nigel?" I asked.

"I'm content right where I am, thank you very much. Me and my friend here are getting quite close; I think you could say...it's getting pret-ty serious." He pointed to his glass, his speech slurred, revealing just how tipsy he really was; his tongue outstretched, darting from one side of his mouth to the other, searching the air in front of him to find the tip of his rogue straw.

"Well, that's quite a visual," I said, amused.

"No shit." Nigel's eyes grew wide as he looked past me and sat up straight, blinking hard at Harrison jumping into the deep end of the pool wearing nothing but a pair of skin-tight black swim shorts.

In an instant, he was under the water and my imagination flashed back to finding him in the Blakes' pool. The way I watched him that day as he cut through the shimmering blue water, his skin bronzed to a beautiful summer tan save for the shadows cast by the rise of his muscles and the ripples of the waves he created, his tattoos on full display like that of art in a museum. It was as if he were some sort of mirage. His clothes left in a heap somewhere off to the side, he'd emerged naked, every muscle in his body rigid, flexing as he moved.

"Hello?" Nigel sounded annoyed with me.

"I'm sorry, what?" I asked, still in something of a daze, my mind lingering in its own world.

"I said, I don't know how you do it."

"Oh. Right," I paused. "Yeah, me either most of the time." I stepped into the pool, the water warm as it enveloped my calves, then rose to my thighs.

Harrison's head broke the surface and he stood glistening in front of me, droplets of water dragging my attention from his shoulders to his abs. He shook the water from his hair, then raked it backward with his right hand, his signature twist of the fingers holding it in place. "I needed this," he said, then threw himself backward, the thrust of the water pulling at the front of his shorts, exposing the wispy dark hairs below his navel and his tightly toned lower abdomen before he sunk below the surface again.

Nigel's mouth fell open. "I think I'm gonna need another drink." His voice was loud enough to produce a staff member ready to heed his request.

CHAPTER 40

Yesterday Harrison and I spent the entire day in bed sharing daydreams about our future. His vision of our wedding was so charming; an intimate exchange of promises surrounded by flowers and beautiful views, with only our closest friends there to cheer us on. With no immediate family, we both wanted to somehow honor the people we'd lost. We talked about different ways we could celebrate them, bring their spirits into our aura. We didn't want to put on a huge production, and we didn't want to draw any more attention to ourselves than necessary. The decisions came easy with Harrison, and he didn't ask for much; simple things like love, truth, being one with nature. And a full moon. I was never sure which captivated him more, the feeling of waking to sunshine or his admiration for the moon. He said being married during a full moon signifies your relationship will be blessed with balance, unity, and a full, rich life together. But I didn't need a full moon to tell me that's what our future held. Harrison was a lover of the natural world as well as the cosmos, just like me. Further undeniable proof that Harrison and I were written in the stars.

Hours passed as we lost ourselves in conversation, and when the baby started kicking again, our conversation morphed into our shared hopes and dreams for our child. Harrison, of course, promised the entire world to be laid at their fingertips, always referring to our currently genderless child as "daddy's little girl" in hopes that he would spend the rest of his life loving a headstrong, intelligent little creature with curly pig tails tied up in tiny pink ribbons and a bright beaming smile. "She'll change the world, Alice, I just know it," he'd said.

"Not by having the world laid at her feet she won't," I'd lovingly responded.

We decided to reveal the baby's gender during our ceremony, Harrison's idea. He'd called it a 'welcome surprise among a day well planned.' Though we were still unsure how the actual reveal would happen. We'd covered nearly all the details as we watched the morning fade into a sunny afternoon and had only one last big decision to make: the location. We played with ideas like Bora Bora, the Maldives, and Greece. And then Harrison offered Italy in April. I'd be six months pregnant by then. It was hard for me to picture what my body would look like or how I'd feel in it. My belly would be hard to miss in a photograph, that's for sure, and my thoughts flashed back to the fears I'd had when I was eighteen; terrified to look pregnant in my wedding photos, I'd rushed into a marriage I'd never wanted in the first place.

Before I'd had time to think about or worry how a dress would fit, Harrison said, "What about non-traditional? Barefoot, if the weather allows. Comfortable, easy." It was as if he just innately knew the ways to comfort me, without me ever letting my fears be known.

His film career had taken Harrison around the world, but I'd never been to Italy and my only real knowledge of it had been from photographs of architecture that I'd admired and those "Picture it, Sicily," stories that Sophia shared on episodes of the Golden Girls. Harrison had mentioned Rome, Venice, and Tuscany as options, citing I'd love them for their architecture and the historic value, which of course was sweet of him, but never in my life had I imagined I would ever get to witness any part of it firsthand, so deciding on a specific location would take a little research on my part and a bit more time.

We'd had dinner that evening with the group, and then with mugs of hot chocolate, we'd cozied up with one another outside on the terrace, bundled in our warmest clothes, staring up at the night sky.

"We haven't been here that long, but this trip has been wonderful." I leaned toward him and sighed, my temple finding his shoulder. "Thank you for this."

"Oh, darling, I agree. We've only got a few short months before we become a party of three, and all I want is to focus on us as much as we can, do the things that make you happy, create memories we'll carry with us into old age. Make love in inappropriate places and build the life we thought was out of reach, together." He put his arm around me, drawing me in even closer to him.

"Would it be too indulgent to fly everyone home from the ceremony, then have the jet come back for us, and hop from Rome to Tuscany to Venice as a honeymoon?" I asked.

"Not at all. If that's what you want."

"It sounds ridiculous even saying it out loud."

"Why would you think that? Alice, we have the resources. That's what a jet is for. Flying, wherever we want to go."

"Where I'm from, it's the same as asking to fly a rocket ship to Mars. Makes me feel, I don't know, frivolous, I guess."

"I've worked hard for everything I've got, and what's mine is now also yours. If those are the places you'd like to go, that's what we'll do, darling, simple as that." He set his mug on the table in front of us, then ran his fingers through his hair waiting for my response.

"I don't know. I'm just thinking out loud." I looked up again at the sky. "Did you see that?" I pointed out toward the darkness. "A shooting star."

"Did you make a wish?" His voice was lower now, and without turning my head, I could tell he was still looking at me and not the sky.

I shook my head, eyes innocently fixed upward.

"Shooting stars need wishes," he whispered, his lips just below my ear against my neck, his free hand still hot from the mug slid up across the other side of my cheek, his fingertips in my hair as he positioned my mouth to meet his.

"This what you meant by inappropriate places?" I managed to say between kisses that were growing more passionate by the second. I felt his body move as he laughed through his nose.

"I mean...it could be." His lips continued to explore my neck, as he lowered my zipper and slipped his hand into the front of my jacket.

I indulged him for a moment, then shook my head. "I don't think this is it," I laughed.

"Damn." He sighed and withdrew his hand, then carefully pulled upward on my zipper, a discouraged look on his face.

"You sir, are insatiable."

"You say that like it's a bad thing." His eyes sparkled when he spoke.

"I'm glad to entertain this behavior upstairs, just not here." I set down my mug, then turned and kissed him deeply, my hands cradling his unshaven face. *God, I love facial hair on this man*, I thought, and gave a second thought to taking him right here on the terrace.

CHAPTER 41

The rest of our week moved at lightning speed. By day we explored caves and falls and forces. We took easy hikes and we biked and lay by the pool. We piled into the vehicles like school children on a field trip and followed the River Ure with its fields and farms surrounding us like something from a movie set, lush and laden with livestock, even at the tail end of winter, and we found Aysgarth Falls again. Though this time there was barely anyone around, and thankfully no one recognized Harrison. How could they when he'd grown out his facial hair as best he could, and pulled a knit cap down over his delicious curls? With the security of the entire group, we spent a full day armed with cameras to capture our adventures and had so much fun exploring. Each evening was shared around the table with our chosen family, indulging in some of the most delicious multi-course meals I'd ever had. Nigel had gotten used to Julian always being at Shelby's side and had seemingly given his unspoken permission for his friend to find the love that none of us had ever seen her in before. She did have a comfortable happiness emanating from her this week and I was happy for her. Emma and Lawrence were, of course, stuck to each other like velcro, but that had become normal before we ever arrived at Simonstone Hall, and Hank and Victor were perpetually on the brink of inebriation the entire week. My own experience had been more than I could have hoped for. By night, when we found ourselves alone, Harrison and I explored each other's bodies almost like we were strangers again. Lust-filled and lovestruck, this time away had awakened something new in each of us, something that allowed us to step out of the comfort zone we'd found at home and discover new ways to pleasure each other, and it took what we already had to fierce new heights. By the time we left the Dales, I'd never felt closer to him.

Despite everyone except for me being hungover from last night's New Year celebration, we all agreed that seeing the sun set from Bamford Edge in Derbyshire was absolutely paramount to end this trip, and luckily the weather cooperated long enough to afford us an awe-inspiring experience. It had been a meticulously planned two-hour drive from Simonstone Hall, with Victor and Hank taking their own van filled with everyone's luggage, while the rest of us rode together in the other. Happy chatter made the journey easy, with Nigel going on about how relaxing the trip had been, and Lawrence reliving the lifelong memories we'd created. Shelby did mention how unfortunate it was that Julian had gone back to Liverpool instead of experiencing the sunset with us, but seemed excited that she'd see him soon. He'd be coming to London to visit her and scout locations for his gym, so their separation wouldn't last long.

The steep thirty-minute walk to the top had been a welcome stretch for my legs and we reached the impressive overhang of stone just as the sun began its descent into Hope Valley. Only a few small groups were up there with us as we watched tufts of lazy clouds backlit by soft pinks and pastel oranges morph into shades of neon as golden hour washed the basin in amber hued light for as far as the eye could see. The smattering of patchwork fields and their stone boundaries draped in shades of warm honey and burning crimson were truly a sight to behold. The reflection off of Ladybower Reservoir was a vast mirror image splayed out below us. No one spoke, and only the intermittent sound of a phone's camera shutter drifted by on the breeze.

The sun disappeared quickly and left us cloaked in darkness. Ready to get back to the van, it became apparent I should've brought my phone with me on this vacation. We'd used Harrison's for photos and any navigation or necessary work calls that may have come through, but mine was powered off and sitting on my nightstand back in London, and here I was with no flashlight. *Brilliant, Alice, truly.* I'd figured anyone that mattered was here with me, so why would I need it? And after all the time Harrison and I spent using phones to connect to one another, I was ready to unplug from it for a while.

We managed to find our way down unscathed, but it took far longer to get back to the van in the dark than it had to reach the summit, and my legs, which were once happy to stretch, now ached to sit down. All I could think about was *just get me on that jet so I can cuddle up to Harrison and rest.*

CHAPTER
42

The air in London was crisp and the tarmac shimmered under streetlights as rain poured from the sky. After all our luggage was sorted, the group shared quick goodbyes and see-you-laters and we all scattered to our separate vehicles, bound for home. Harrison had driven us, and being the gentleman he was, he made sure to hold the car door for me despite getting drenched while doing so. I watched him as he drove, the headlights from the car behind us reflecting in the rearview mirror creating a mask of light across his gorgeous green eyes. Despite the unyielding glare, he remained laser focused on the road while his body sat relaxed in the driver's seat, his curls still damp from his act of chivalry, his left hand flexing as it gripped the steering wheel. I was so used to seeing Lawrence at the wheel that seeing Harrison there in his place, taking control of a vehicle, made me feel some kind of primal urge.

He glanced over at me, his barely-there beard managing to disguise the dimple his half-smile created. "You okay?" he asked and refocused on the road.

I paused, thinking, *no, I'm not. Pull this car over and take me right here on the side of the road,* then watched him until his eyes met mine again. "I just really wanna feel you inside me."

His eyebrows shot up in surprise, his eyes questioning if I'd really just said that out loud. He looked back at the road and bit his bottom lip, and without warning, the back of my head pulled tightly against the headrest from the car's sudden acceleration.

Our luggage remained in the car, forgotten while we were oblivious to anything but each other upstairs. Harrison ran his hands over my back, a trail of soapy lather left in their wake. His mouth eager to please against my skin, first at my neck, then shifting to my chin as I quickly washed and rinsed my hair. He massaged my thighs with his fingertips as the shampoo fell from my curls, and when the water ran clear again, his mouth was at my breasts. I washed away the day as quickly as I could, my want for him burning hotter with every touch of his mouth to my body, and thrust him into the water to do the same when I was done. There was no penetration, no satisfying gratification, only teasing, heightening of anticipation, edging each other closer and closer as mouths wandered over flesh and hands explored erogenous zones. I wrung the excess water from my curls as Harrison's mouth locked on mine, his tongue working its magic, his hands glued to me while we moved in unison, still wet, to the bed where he threw back the covers and laid me down against the coolness of the sheets. Between my legs, his hand slid to grip the back of my thigh, pulling my knee to rest against his ribs. One last kiss, then he stood straight, grinning like a deviant, and licked his lips, watching me. It was as if he wanted me to ask for it.

"Harrison." I tilted my head back and closed my eyes.

Nothing. Not a word from him.

I drew my other leg up, resting my foot on the edge of the bed just outside of his thigh. "Harrison..." I whispered, every part of me aching for him.

I drew in a deep expectant breath and as I let it out, he pushed my knees outward and slowly pressed himself into me. My back arched as he reached my full depth, and a not-so-subtle guttural groan escaped him. I opened my eyes to find his mouth open, his eyes shut and his nostrils flared. I'd have thought he was in pain if I didn't know he was trying his damnedest not to come.

Not wanting this to end yet, I pulled his face down toward me, giving him some time to calm himself, but instead of kissing him, I put my mouth against his ear, my hands gripping fists full of his wet hair. I sucked his earlobe into my mouth, snaking my tongue over it, biting at it playfully, then ran my hands down over his chest, stopping to firmly pinch both of his nipples and whispered into his ear, "Now fuck me like you mean it."

He exhaled forcefully, as if my words and his filthy thoughts had gotten the better of him. Then, without a sound he pulled himself back up to standing while he remained inside me, drawing back slowly, letting the tip tease its intent as I pulsated against it. A quick chuckle escaped through his nose, then a deep breath in before he plunged himself into me again. His brow furrowed and he grabbed both my legs from underneath, lifting my ass off the bed, his fingertips digging into the tops of my thighs as he positioned himself deeper and deeper into me. He held me there, the muscles in his arms bulging, the definition of his shoulders on display as he thrust into me over and over again, each forcing my breathy responses to climb louder and louder.

"That what you want?" he asked, a proud half-smile on his face as he looked down at me, flushed, panting, and sweaty.

I shook my head, looking up at him with lust in my eyes.

"No?" His expression was one of surprised curiosity.

"I said, like you mean it." I tried to keep a straight face.

I could see his wheels turning as he looked down at me and nodded slowly as if to say, *challenge accepted*, then released his grip on one of my legs. He licked his thumb as he locked eyes with me and placed it gently against my clit, the slightest bit of pressure taking my breath away. And as his thumb moved rhythmically, so did his pelvis, pulling me closer and closer to orgasm. Harrison moaned louder and louder with every thrust and I knew he was close. My breathing grew erratic as his thumb continued its quest. I could see galaxies as I closed my eyes tightly, my breasts bouncing in unison with his repeated indulgence.

"Alice..." His raspy voice tried hard to hide an urgency, and him saying my name turned me on even more.

"Mmm...that's what I like," I moaned, more seductively than needed for added effect, and lifted my hips into him, tightening my walls against him.

"Bloody...fuckin'...HELL!" he yelled as his body tightened up, drawing in sharp breaths as he released into me. His thumb slowed and then quickened until I too lost control. Soon Harrison dropped forward, his arms rigid holding himself above me. Slow kisses and soft cuddles followed before he moved half of his body off of me, his head against my shoulder and the weight of his arm now holding me captive against the bed. As the moments passed, we tried to get our breathing back to normal, our bodies randomly convulsing against one another in the silence of the afterglow.

I lay there thinking, *I have to get up and pee, but I just want to stay here with him.* And as the minutes passed, his breathing evened out and I could tell he was asleep. I remained still as long as my bladder could stand it, then realized in order for me to get up, he needed to move.

"Babe." I tried to gently jostle him awake. "Babe," I repeated louder, but still no response. So, I kissed what I could reach. Small little pecks across his fingers until he stirred, his eyes heavy as they opened.

"Hi," I whispered.

He smiled briefly then attempted to nuzzle his face into my neck, intent on finding sleep again.

"Babe, I need to pee, and you need to get yourself cleaned up. C'mon." As I started to slide out of the bed, parts of him collapsed beside me until he was nearly face down. "Can you even breathe?" I laughed. "Come on, lazy bones."

"I've got a lazy bone for you," his voice was muffled against the bed.

"Lazy is right, you can't even keep your eyes open," I snickered.

As I strode off to the bathroom to relieve myself, I heard him from behind me, "I hate for you to leave, darling, but I sure do love to watch you go." He let out a quick chuckle, proud of his joke.

"Oh, you'll get sick of me one day, I'm sure of it," I teased without looking back, the voice in my head saying, *it only took James two years.*

When I came out of the water closet, Harrison was at the sink. "Here you go, love." He handed me a warm wet cloth with one hand while the other grasped at his manhood with his own washcloth. *Jesus Christ, his body is stunning.* I kept thinking one day I'd get used to it, I'd stop my constant amazement, but that feeling hadn't arrived yet, and didn't seem to be anywhere in sight. He was nearly all muscle; there couldn't have been an ounce of fat on him. And no matter how well I knew him or how long I was around him, just looking at his tattoos still turned me on.

"Thanks." I took it from him and shifted positions so I was behind him. I cleaned myself while his stature blocked my reflection in the mirror.

He bent slightly to rinse his hands in the sink. "I'm a fan you know." He looked up and his eyes met mine in the mirror.

"Of?" I asked.

"The way you were talking to me. I like that." He licked his lips as he tried to hide his excitement, shifting his eyes to focus on his hands.

"Never underestimate the vocabulary of a mature, liberated woman." I winked at him and grabbed the pajamas that hung from my closet door knob on my way back to the bedroom.

"You really need those? 'Cause now that I think about it, I might have another round in me."

I shrugged, dropped the wet rag into the laundry basket and my pajamas to the floor, then looked at him seductively. "I'd rather that second round was in *me*..."

CHAPTER 43

When I woke the next morning, Harrison was still asleep. His stubbly cheek against my left breast, his usual morning drool on my skin. As I lay there bored, trying not to wake him, I realized my phone had been off for over a week. I fumbled through the sheets until my hand found it on the nightstand. Holding the power button until the screen lit up, I made sure the volume was off, then laid it face down and waited for any notifications to start rolling in. I closed my eyes and thoughts of an Italian wedding ran through my mind. I imagined sunshine and soft breezes, turquoise waters against white sand beaches. Harrison had mentioned bare feet and comfort, and I thought about flowy dresses, trees full of lemons canopied over tables with checkered cloths under candle-wax-covered bottles, and plates of gorgeous food. *Would it be warm there? Is it always warm? Could I be barefoot that time of year?* I could search for spots online to pass the time until he woke up, or maybe I could research Rome and Venice.

My phone started vibrating so frequently that it morphed into one long continuous buzz. I snatched it from its resting spot and tried to tuck it beneath me in the bed to avoid waking Harrison. *What on earth are all these notifications? Anyone who would have needed me was with me on that trip. This is absurd*! When the vibrations finally stopped, I pulled my phone from beneath the covers and unlocked the screen, only to reveal forty-six text messages, twenty-two missed calls, and countless emails.

"What the hell?" I whispered under my breath, clicking first on my call log. James. James. James. James. James. *What on earth could he possibly want? It's not as if the house were on fire or anything...*

Fifteen of the missed calls were James, the rest were various people from back home. Seventeen voicemails. I shook my head, unable to fathom what anyone would be calling me about, and opted to open my text inbox before getting involved with those voicemails.

The majority of the texts were also from James and they got more and more angry the further I sifted through them:

Alice, you need to call me. NOW.

Guess that 'text me when you need me' line was also a lie huh?

Pick up the phone ALICE! PICK. UP. THE. PHONE!!!!!

I can't believe you'd lie to me about this!

It's a good God damn thing I didn't know this when he was standing here in front of me. And you let me SHAKE HIS FUCKING HAND? WTF ALICE!

Name calling, vague accusations, and so much vitriol. I was baffled as to what had him suddenly so upset. I scrolled to the one message that had an attachment and opened it, reluctantly.

"Oh, MY GOD!" The words burst out of me as I sat up straight in the bed, sending Harrison's head flailing backward toward the mattress.

He propped himself up beside me with eyes barely open and stammered, "Are you okay? What's happened?" He swallowed hard and wiped at his cheek with the back of his hand, then at my chest as I tried to zoom in on the tiny photo on my phone screen.

It was an outsider's perspective of the night Harrison and I went to the pool with Nigel. There I stood, kissing him full on the mouth with his tattooed hand on my belly in that God-awful striped bathing suit. Definitely fucking pregnant, without a doubt. The photo was grainy and shadowy and had tiny bursts of light reflecting off the glass atrium from the twinkle lights strung around the terrace, but it was absolutely my profile, and anyone who knew Harrison would easily identify him by his tattoos. Nigel had been blocked by the way Harrison and I were standing, so it looked like just the two of us on some secret rendezvous. And to top it all off, the headline read, "*And Baby Makes Three! Harrison Edwards & Mystery Woman Share Secret Love Child!*"

"LOOK!" I exclaimed, shoving the phone at him.

He blinked against the brightness of the screen, rubbed the sleep from his eyes, and then sighed. "Oh Alice, I didn't want it to happen this way. I'm sorry."

"I have dozens of texts and emails and missed calls and voicemails from James, and from people back home. DOZENS!" I yanked the phone back to face me. "This photo is horrible! Who the hell could have taken this? What am I even going to say to him?"

"You don't owe him any explanation, Alice." Harrison's voice was flat as he dropped back against the pillows. "And I don't think I'd say the photo is horrible. It's a man in love, happily kissing the woman he adores on vacation as she grows him a family." The irritation in his voice was enough to make me instantly ashamed of my outburst.

"I know I don't owe him anything," I continued, more calmly this time, "but if I'm being honest, I've carried guilt about keeping this secret since I decided to leave him. There was always this tiny piece of me that thought I should've told him about the pregnancy. But the devil on my shoulder kept saying, *he'll never find out, it's not worth the argument.* What an idiot I am." I zoomed in again on the photo and leaned closer to the screen, trying to see any other definitive details.

"You're not an idiot first of all, and frankly, I really don't care how James feels. He's the one who wasted your love. He had years to nurture the marriage he had, to grab hold of the kind of love we've found in mere months. He had it and he pissed it away. I've got no sympathy for him."

"You're right. I know you're right. But I do feel like I should talk to him, then be done with it once and for all."

"You know I trust your judgment, but don't let him make you feel bad about what we share, Alice."

I sighed, and lay back against the comfort of my pillow, dropping the phone to my side. "I'm sorry I barked at you. It just caught me off guard. You see people announce babies or relationships in these nice photoshoots by People Magazine, and while that's not necessarily what I want either, I just didn't think we'd be thrown to the wolves in blurry candids by some creep. I don't know how you're not more upset about this."

"Well, this is normal for me, Alice. I've lived with this kind of treatment, these constant invasions of privacy, blatant disregard for the fact that I'm a human being just trying to live my life in peace, for a lot of years now. I just assume my every move is going to be splattered all over front pages tomorrow, because it could be. I told you this wasn't going to be easy, that you'd be fair game. This is the part you're going to have to form a thick skin against, because there will, especially now, always be someone taking your photo or recording you without you knowing. They don't ask until they've already done it half the time, and of course it gets splashed all over the place online within minutes because they had an exclusive and got a quick pay day. I've gotten pretty good at finding them in crowds and at restaurants over the years. They'll be hunting us for sport now that this news has broken." He sighed, visibly frustrated. "Maybe we should reach out and give someone an actual exclusive."

My face twisted into a deeper grimace with each situation he described. "I'm sorry this has become normal for you. People can be so self-serving and cruel." I laid my head against his shoulder and ran my fingers gently through his chest hair, his gold cross falling against them as they moved. "I love you. I won't let this get to me; I promise." I kissed his neck. "Any chance you're ready for breakfast? Smells like Shelby's back in the groove down there."

"Grab a shower with me first? No funny business, I promise." A sly grin appeared on his face.

"Bullshit. I know you better than that." I hesitated a moment, locking eyes with him, smirking. "Race ya!" I sprang from the bed toward the bathroom with Harrison in hot pursuit. His right palm landed firmly against my ass cheek, and with his other arm, he grabbed me and pulled me into his embrace.

"You little minx!" He scrunched up his nose, the tip resting against mine. Then, with no regard to morning breath, he kissed me all the way to the shower.

CHAPTER

44

While Harrison caught up on emails, I spent some much-needed time in nature in an attempt to straighten out my thoughts. While I filled the feeder for Robin and scattered a handful of mealworms around the ground at its base, I tried to figure out the best way to approach this situation with James. But there was no best way. There was only truth.

I settled into my patio chair to search the image, read the articles, and familiarize myself with everything I'm sure James had been over-analyzing for days. It wasn't hard to find. The story was everywhere, sporting various headlines ranging from joy and excitement to outright nasty lies; the only thing they had in common was the same grainy photo staring back at me. I bounced from site to site, disgusted and discouraged, picking through all the fictional stories they'd concocted.

The only remotely believable article stated the "exclusive" had come from a hiker passing through. It quoted, "I'd poorly planned my hike and stopped to seek a room, only to be turned away. I'd found nothing of a 'No Vacancy' sign posted anywhere, but there was no availability as the estate had been privately rented in its entirety. You've got to be quite posh to manage that. Of course, had I planned my hike a bit better, I wouldn't have found myself in this predicament at all, and I did eventually find respite. I do plan to sort my hikes better in the future." The article continued on, veering off the circumstance and landing hard on the visual details with the man describing the woman in the photo as *"quite obviously with child."*

Quite obviously? Real nice, buddy. It's not THAT obvious. What a dick.

At the end of the article, the gentleman circled back to the estate, adding, "I find no fault with Simonstone Hall. The place certainly is grand and looks magnificent. I've heard nothing but positive things about their dining experience, and I do intend to return with a reservation of my own in the future but only for one room. There's no need to be piggish."

My mouth fell open. Piggish? I wanted to scream. Harrison had taken us all on a vacation out of the goodness of his heart and covered every expense to show his appreciation for the friends he thinks of as family. But this was the drivel that made a headline news story.

Piggish. Ridiculous.

So, this guy had continued down one of the many trails that surround the property and snapped the photo on his way through. The atrium certainly affords someone a perfect view of its inhabitants, especially at night. If I'd known something like that was even a possibility, that random hikers might be caught out on the trail, I'd have told the front desk to allow them to stay. There were plenty of unused rooms and I'm certain Harrison would have agreed. Besides, that's what a non-disclosure agreement is for. No one should be turned away while out hiking after dark, and at the tail end of December no less. Even if it were due to their own terrible planning. Poor thing must have been freezing, exhausted, and pissed off. I almost couldn't blame him for selling the photos. The idea of only two people reserving an entire eighteen-bedroom country house probably presented as quite pretentious.

I set my phone in my lap and rubbed my temples. So now the world knew Harrison Edwards had a 'baby mama.' *Great.* Harrison's words echoed in my head, *"There will always be someone photographing or recording you without permission.*" Maybe I needed to find myself a stylist to help me present better to the public. That didn't feel right though; that just wasn't me. From now on, I'd be more mindful of my behavior and my wardrobe; it was all I could do. I certainly didn't want to be an embarrassment to Harrison. *Hell, maybe I already am.*

I flicked one of the untouched blueberries that sat on the arm of the chair. So far there had been no Robin. *I hope he doesn't think I've abandoned him. I wasn't gone that long.*

"Robin?" I said softly, not wanting to alert Harrison in the library.

I searched the large oak tree that sat toward the far-right side of the property. No movement amongst its branches, no birdsong. It was eerily quiet. I noticed the lawn was finally starting to bounce back from its slumber with sprigs of thin green grass protruding from the beige that winter had left behind. There were faint signs of life in the flower beds; the long emerald leaves of daffodils would soon drape themselves in perfect arches and the wavy leaves of tulips would unfurl from the earth.

"Robin?" I repeated and glanced up above me to the gutter. No Robin on his usual perch. *Hmph, I wonder where he is. I could have used his advice about this phone call.*

I wasn't sure how to approach the call I knew I needed to make. I wasn't doing it to appease James, or to set a story straight; I just wanted to get the guilt off my heart and set this secret free. I'd always hated talking to him when he was angry, and right now he was probably livid. My chest started to ache with anxiety. I had to get this over with.

A deep breath in and a long sigh later, I hit the round green circle on the most recent of James' missed calls.

One ring and I felt my pulse start to race along with my thoughts. Another ring and I picked up one of the remaining blueberries and began nervously rolling it back and forth between my fingers. Back and forth, back and forth.

Some anxious habits never die, I guess. I closed my eyes, another ring, a hard swallow. Back and forth, back and forth, the blueberry became softer with each roll. Then I heard him clear his throat on the other end of the line.

"Nice of you to finally respond." His voice was harsh and sarcastic, but remained a strangely familiar comfort.

"I was away without my phone; I didn't mean for you to think I was ignoring you."

"Doesn't matter. I probably shouldn't have sent those messages or called. The internet's told me all I need to know."

"I'm sorry you couldn't reach me. I'm sure your mind's been reeling." I tried hard to choose my words carefully. "Mine has been too—"

"Save it, Alice." He cut me off. "Don't bullshit me."

"I wasn't bullshitting you, James; I was trying to explain that I wasn't ignoring you." *Stay calm, Alice.* The blueberry was nearly liquid inside its paper-thin casing.

"It doesn't matter anyways, right? Because you're some celebrity side-piece now? You let him knock you up and drag you away with what? Promises of a fat bank account and shiny things?"

This asshole was really testing my ability to remain calm.

"Is that really what you think of me?" I set the blueberry back on the arm of the chair and flicked it with my middle finger, the purple liquid remaining while the bulk of the fruit shot across the lawn.

"Oh, I don't think of you at all." He chuckled to himself.

Was he drunk? It was seven o'clock in the morning where he was. *Stay calm, Alice. This is an opportunity. Take it.*

"Where have you been staying?" I asked in my nicest voice, pretending to give a shit.

"Remember, you gave up the right to know my whereabouts, didn't ya? When you ran out on me, as if twenty years never meant a fucking thing to you."

I took a deep breath and tried a different approach. "What happened to the house, James?"

"The same thing that happened to my marriage."

"And what does that mean exactly?"

"It means, I watched it burn down around me. That's what it means. You walked out the door, Alice, didn't give a shit about me or the house we built together, our LIFE." Any sarcasm was now gone, and was replaced entirely by anger. "You just left and never looked back. So, I did too. I went down to Eddie's and had a few beers. Sittin' there, everyone was looking at me, whispering about how my wife left me."

"I'm sorry, James, I never—"

"The only place I could get away from that bullshit was back home. So, in I walked to a silent, empty house that smelled like you'd just been standing in the kitchen. Like you were there a moment ago, like the ghost of you was suspended in the air, poking fun at me. Only you weren't there, Alice, and you never would be again. You were fucking gone. WITH HIM. So, I lit the candle in the living room thinking maybe I could erase you, even if it was only for a little while."

"James—"

"And then I went back to the kitchen to find something to eat, but there was nothing, Alice. There was nothing because there was no you. So, I sat down at the kitchen table alone, and guess what was staring me dead in the fuckin' face? That magazine with your little boy-toy on the front and whatta ya know, you were there too, gettin' on a fancy private jet with Mr. Moneybags."

"James—"

"So, I picked it up off the kitchen table and I slung the fuckin' thing across the room. I didn't want it in my sight. Next thing I know, I feel the heat off the living room. I look up and the flames are just everywhere. I never heard the candle shatter, I didn't see the fire start. I was just so God damn mad...okay, and maybe I was drunk. I remember trying to knock it down with the broom, but then the broom caught on fire, and that old house was like a tinder box. Nothing I tried worked. There was no stopping it once it started."

The magazine with Harrison and me on the cover, boarding the jet, had been the cause of the fire. The house burned down for the same reason his marriage did; he was right. It was my fault. So now, not one but two magazines had delivered news that broke his heart.

"I can't imagine how you're feeling, James. I'm so sorry."

"I don't give a shit anymore if you're sorry, Alice. 'Sorry' is fuckin' pointless when it's saddled up with 'pregnant with a celebrity's baby' after you ran away to a different country to cheat on me. 'Sorry' doesn't even matter. And frankly 'sorry' didn't do this, you did! You made a God damn joke out of me; do you realize that? You've moved on and I'm still in this town full of people we've known our whole lives. I'm still here, only now I'm nothing but the butt of the joke, everybody's funny punchline."

He didn't want another apology, and beyond that, I was speechless. I flicked another blueberry into the yard. Half of me *was* sorry. I did feel bad he was stuck there feeling like that, but the other half of me was indifferent to it. Was anyone holding him there? No. Surely he must have insurance money by now. He could go anywhere, see anyone, and do anything he chose. He could build himself a brand new life, but he was there, moping, wallowing in it. Typical.

What is it they say? "What's the difference between ignorance and apathy? I don't know, and I don't care." Well, I don't care. Me giving a shit is no longer a requirement hung over my head.

"So now you're silent. I pour my heart out to you and I still get nothing. Fucking classic."

"You said you don't want an apology, and there's nothing I can do to change any of this, James. It's not my responsibility anymore to change it. It's yours. You're a grown man. I know it's scary to have to take care of yourself, but people do it every day—"

"I never thought you of all people, would treat me this way." His voice had gone soft, and I heard his chin rub against the phone's microphone, or was that a sniffle?

Here come the theatrics. Cue the tears!

I took a deep breath and shook my head, the days of him manipulating me were over and I was sick of being pleasant. "Ya know what, James? I never thought you'd treat me the way *you* did for twenty-two sad, pathetic years. I guess unspoken expectations really fucked us both in the end, didn't they?"

There was a silence, then a strange sound I couldn't decipher before the line went dead. I held my phone out and looked at the screen. "Call Ended" blinked back at me.

"Well, that's the end of that," I mumbled to myself and flicked the last blueberry off the arm of the chair.

CHAPTER

45

I found Harrison still sitting at his desk, his brows drawn together as he stared at the laptop screen in front of him.

"Hey." I smiled as I leaned my body and the side of my head against the doorway.

"There's my girl." He pulled his glasses off and tossed them toward his keyboard. "How was your phone call?" He rubbed his eyes, and I fixated on the veins in his hands while he did it.

"It was pretty much what I anticipated it would be."

"Which was?" He looked tired.

"A bunch of bullshit. Blame. Fault. But I did find out how the house caught on fire," I said as I approached him. "What's got you concentrating so hard?" I asked, nudging him with my hip, my arm reaching across his broad shoulders to pull him against me. I hoped he wouldn't notice I was changing the subject.

"The contract for that directing gig." He sighed. "The detail is excruciating."

"Wanna take a break?" I leaned down and kissed the top of his head.

He backed his chair out slightly and slid his arm around my waist, inviting me to sit on his lap. "What I want is for you to tell me how you're feeling after that phone call."

"I feel...I don't know. Relieved, I guess." I shrugged. "He knows everything, and whether it came from me or a tabloid, who cares? He's mad. I suspect he threw the phone at the wall at the end of our conversation, which, for James, that tracks. I might have made a comment that sent his temper into overdrive."

"Oh? And that was?"

"I told him that unspoken expectations fucked us both in the end, but that was after he wanted to act pathetic in hopes I'd coddle him and appease his emotional manipulation. You know, for old time's sake, I guess." I rolled my eyes. "So, now he's got no wife, no home, and no phone. Idiot."

Harrison's eyebrows raised in unison as he blew out a laugh through his nose. "Okay then. As long as you're okay."

"I'm fine. Glad to have it done and dealt with, and now no more rearview mirror. Only windshield. Forward movement, no looking back." I kissed the tiny creases near the corner of his eye. "Let's finish the nursery this afternoon. Want to?"

"Sounds much better than reading contracts."

"Don't you have 'people' for this anyhow?" I stood from his lap and looked at him.

"I do." He nodded.

"Then let them do their job; let's nest together."

"Nest?" He looked up puzzled. "What's that?"

"Nesting. It's when you...I don't know, prepare your home for a new addition. You make things comfy and get ready for a baby. It's early, but it will be a nice distraction for us both. Nothing crazy, maybe just pick out a crib and a few little outfits." I shrugged.

He stood and closed his laptop. "And talk about wedding plans?" He looked down his nose at me. "The baby is coming regardless, darling, but all I want, is to marry you. Right now."

"This second?" I leaned into him, tipped my head back, and kissed him slowly.

His eyes remained closed as he barely nodded. "Mm-hmm." He wrapped his arms around me tighter, pulling me against him, kissing me with more passion than before. "Right." His lips paused, lingering against mine, then he kissed me again. "Now."

Jesus Christ.

"Like, *right* now?" I asked in nearly a whisper, our mouths still pressed together, my hands cupping his ass through the back pockets of his jeans.

He pulled back slightly, locking eyes with me. "I don't want to waste another second of my life not being your husband. The husband you've always deserved, loving you in ways you've only dreamed about." His hands slid up my back and into my hair, his thumb rubbing the space just in front of my ear as he kissed me again.

"Okay, so," I tried to compose myself before continuing, "maybe we deal with the crib another day." I laughed. "Let's plan this wedding!"

CHAPTER 46

By late January, Harrison and I had everything mapped out. All the wedding plans, a birth plan, we'd set up the crib in our bedroom, the honeymoon had been sorted for the most part, and we'd been thrust into the public eye by that hiker's story. The paparazzi had tried, and failed, to capture us together since then. But today, that would change.

We'd gone to the ponds early for Harrison's daily swim. It was nothing out of the ordinary. We'd been coming together since we got back from the Dales and thus far, we'd been relieved to only happen across a few very cold-hardy people on any given day. But this day, I sat on the bench, bundled warmly in non-descript cold-weather attire, including my knit hat and my sunglasses, as inconspicuous as any other random person would be. I watched as Harrison peeled off his clothes and dove into the pond, shuddering at the thought of him plunging into that icy water. I'd noticed every time he went below the surface, I'd reactively hold my breath until he reappeared. As he emerged, shaking his chestnut curls loose from the grip of the water, I resumed my normal breathing and heard a sound come from behind me. Not the crunch of leaves, or the approach of a squirrel. Something mechanical. A camera shutter.

Fuck.

My first instinct was to turn and see what we were up against, but my better judgment told me to sit still, eyes forward, and mind my own business, act like I wasn't here with a world-famous movie star and hope the paparazzi hadn't seen us arrive together. *He'll think you're no one if you just act the part.* Besides, we had protocols for this. Lawrence would arrive any minute and sit down beside me. I'd pretend I'd been waiting for him and then we'd leave together to get me back to the car safely. Harrison could handle himself if need be; he'd done it before. He'd made it clear the priority was to get me out of a situation and to safety first.

"Hell of a specimen, ay?" A man sat down beside me, but it wasn't Lawrence. It was the pap, camera in hand, focused fully on Harrison. His skin was dimpled, pocked, and scarred from old acne, and he had a wild, bushy beard.

My hair's pulled back out of my face, none of it is sticking out of my jacket, I thought. *Don't give yourself away, Alice. They're here for him.* My gloves hid my hands as I reached up and pulled the brim of my knit hat down closer to my eyes, my sunglasses shielding them from view. I pulled my scarf up over my mouth, despite it being just over forty degrees out, and shrugged, but the man wasn't looking at me, he was still clicking his shutter button at an increasingly rapid pace.

C'mon, Lawrence, where the fuck are you? I thought. *Just get up casually and leave, Alice. Just walk away like any woman would do if some creep sat beside her on a bench. Just act casual. Don't draw his attention.*

I stood to leave, forgetting my phone had been sitting in my lap, and watched as it fell to the ground, the screen illuminating a photo of Harrison and me kissing.

"Ay, you're her!" he exclaimed and started aiming his lens at me as I froze in position, dumbfounded. "C'mon, love, let's be friends, pose for me. Let me see that pretty face." His voice oozed a thick rasp like that of a heavy smoker. "What's your name, sweetheart?" I couldn't place his accent, but it was heavy. Maybe Scottish, I wasn't sure.

I reached for my phone, my sunglasses slipping down my nose in my haste, briefly exposing my eyes. *Click. Click. Click. Click. Click.* His shutter was working overtime. I snatched the phone from the ground and stuffed it into my pocket as I heard Harrison's voice in the distance behind me, "Get out of here! Get away from her, you miserable bastard!" I turned to see him gripping his clothes in one hand along with his towel and his shoes flopping back and forth angrily, as he shook his other fist toward the man. "Piss off! Piss off, I said!" He was running now, sopping wet in the cold air, still a good bit away from me, but the look on his face wasn't one I'd witnessed before, and one I wasn't eager to see again. He was angry, veins at his temples prominent, his chest a deep red, though I'm sure the cold water and the air temperature contributed to that.

I set off without a word toward the car, still wondering why no one had shown up to escort me away. Behind me, more clicking. I was familiar with cameras, but even I'd never heard a shutter speed so fast. He was capturing my every move. My heart was racing as the car came into view. Finally, safety was in sight. Then I felt a hand grasp my arm and spin me around. Thinking it was Harrison, I let out a sigh of relief, but it wasn't Harrison, he was still off in the distance sprinting toward me yelling, "Don't you fucking touch her!"

"C'mon, love, I just want to see your face." His grip tightened on my arm, "One clear shot and I'll go." He was my height, and his unkempt face twisted into a sneer. His teeth were yellowed to a shade of butterscotch behind a rust-colored wiry beard, his bloodshot eyes an icy blue, and he reeked of stale alcohol.

"Alice!" I looked up to see Lawrence coming toward me.

"Stop!" I grimaced as I yanked my arm from his grip and continued toward the car. "Get off!" I snarled louder as I felt him try to grab me again. Unrelenting, I could hear that God damn shutter clicking. "Oh, Alice, is it? Well, come here, Alice, let's have a good look at you..." Twenty years ago, the New England girl in me would have hauled off and punched him in the face, but as it turned out, the twenty-eight-year-old Brit who was in love with me had the same idea.

All I heard was, "You bastard!" and turned to see Harrison had one hand firmly wrapped across the front of the man's throat. "Never put your hands on my wife!" The paparazzi dropped to his knees, arms raised in defeat. Harrison let go of him and stood over the man, glaring down at him, his chest still heaving from the sprint, his muscles taut, the veins in the front of his shoulders, neck, and hands pronounced as he clenched his fists at his sides.

"Your wife, ay? Congrats, mate! You're a real mover and a shaker, don't waste any time, do ya?" A snarky nicotine-stained grin spread across the man's face. "Probably had no choice, what with the baby and all."

Harrison's hand, lightning-fast, landed once again at the man's throat.

"You put your filthy hands on her first, and therefore I expect you to get the fuck out of here without so much as a whisper of this ever happening. And for that matter," Harrison snatched the man's camera from him and wiped the memory card clean of any photos, then tossed the card to Lawrence. "There's my insurance."

"That's a whole month's income you've just pissed away!" the man blurted out, clearly horrified.

"Who bloody well cares? I suggest you move along while you still can." Harrison held the camera out toward the man, silently urging him to take it while he continued to stand over him in nothing but wet swim shorts.

"I could have you arrested for assault!" the pap snarled back at Harrison.

Harrison's nostrils flared, adrenaline surging through him as he turned to find his discarded pants lying in the parking lot where he'd dropped them. After pulling out his wallet, he threw a handful of hundred-pound notes at the man. "I'd recommend the contrary. Now take it and leave."

The pathetic pap scrambled to pick up the drifting notes now being blown around the lot by a gust of wind, stuffing them one by one into his pocket.

"And I'd suggest you don't show your face around me again if you value it in any way." Harrison's eyes narrowed in the pap's direction as he watched him scurry off to his vehicle, then immediately he shifted his focus to me. "Are you okay, darling? Did he hurt you?" The look in his eyes softened to genuine concern as he made sure I hadn't been injured.

I shrugged. "He grabbed my arm pretty hard, but it's nothing. Let's get in the car before you catch pneumonia. Here"—I pushed the rest of Harrison's clothes toward him—"At least put your shoes on. Lawrence, let's go."

"I'd like to know what the hell had you so bloody sidetracked, mate!?" Harrison barked at him.

Lawrence looked at him with obvious regret in his eyes. "I'm so sorry."

"If your relationship is going to take your attention away from your job, from Alice's safety, we may need to reevaluate your position." Harrison was stern in his delivery, and the rage in his eyes was frightening.

"C'mon, you're going to freeze to death." I pulled at Harrison's arm. "Let's please get in the car. I'm fine and we can talk about this later."

Lawrence held the door of the vehicle open as I got inside, then Harrison slid in and grabbed the interior handle, yanking it shut behind him, leaving Lawrence empty handed in the lot alone.

"I can't believe he would let this happen," Harrison said, clenching his fists as he spoke. "He's smarter than this." He opened his palm against his thigh, and his fingers reached toward his knee before curling back into a fist. Maybe it was the cold, or maybe it was adrenaline, but his hands were visibly shaking.

"Don't say anything now that you'll regret later. Wait until you've calmed down." I rubbed the top of his thigh and could feel how cold he was through my glove. "I'm sorry you had to come out of pocket for me. That guy was an asshole."

"The answer is usually money, one way or another, and I'd rather hand him cash and not have photos end up in the paper. I'm just glad you're okay. You're all that matters to me."

Lawrence got in, and without a word, we were en route home. The entire drive, the scene replayed in my head. It could have ended so much worse, and thankfully the people who'd been in the pond remained there instead of coming to see what the ruckus was about. No matter how hard I tried, I couldn't remember if anyone else had seen anything in the parking lot. One thing I knew for sure though, soon the entire world would know my name was Alice.

CHAPTER
47

The silence on the way home had been deafening. Lawrence and I traded glances in the rearview mirror, each of us acknowledging his lapse in judgment and how upset Harrison was without ever saying a word, while Harrison spent the ride chewing angrily at the inside of his cheek as he stared out the window. His wheels were turning as he picked mindlessly at his cuticles, but I knew by the look on his face that now was not the time to ask any questions.

Back at home, we'd barely come to a stop before Harrison flung open the car door and climbed out of the backseat. He reached for my hand and helped me out into the driveway just as Lawrence came around the back of the car. Without a word, Harrison slammed the door shut and headed directly toward the house, a tight grip on my hand.

"That's it for today." He dismissed Lawrence without so much as a glance.

Inside, I slipped my shoes off and followed Harrison upstairs to the shower. I could tell he was still fuming because he hadn't said a word to me since we first got in the car. I watched from the door frame while he undressed, saying nothing. His muscles flexed as he moved the handle to regulate the water temperature, and the heat of the spray hitting the cold tile caused clouds of steam to roll upward, disguising his body behind the fogging glass.

I turned to leave, figuring I'd let him shower and sort out his emotions, but before I made it to the bedroom I heard him yell, "ALICE!"

I stepped back into the bathroom, "Yes, babe?" I watched as he pushed his right hand into his wet curls and then dragged them away from his face, his other hand smearing across the glass so he could see me. He smiled, but he didn't speak, just leaned back under the stream of water, and I watched as it rolled from his eyelashes to his chin, down across his chest and his abdomen to his thighs. The water danced as it hit the floor, seemingly joyful just to have touched his body.

I spoke again. "Babe?" From where I stood at the shower opening, he turned and positioned himself in front of me.

"I'm sorry you saw me like that."

"There's no need to apologize. Your reaction was completely understandable."

"I just can't have anyone on this staff, friend or otherwise, that's going to be sidetracked. I couldn't live with myself if anything happened to you or, God forbid..." His voice trailed off as he shook his head and closed his eyes.

"Hey, we're okay." I pulled his wet hand from the shower and placed it on my belly. "Okay?"

"Can I make a request?" he asked.

"Of course."

"Will you close the curtains, and turn out the lights?"

I looked at him confused. "Okay..." I hesitated.

"Then join me. Let's let our senses guide us." His demeanor intrigued me.

I raised my eyebrows, my eyes questioning him.

He shook his head, unaccepting of my hesitation, then reached out with both hands and held my face as he kissed me. Warm water dripped down my neck and chest, coming to rest in my bra.

"Oh, look at that..." He ran the palms of his hands down the front of my shirt, leaving handprints on my breasts. "You're all wet. Oh, no." His exaggerated fake frown made me laugh. He smirked. "Well, that's rubbish then," and lifted my shirt up over my head, then dropped it on the floor at my feet.

"Mm-hmm. Real nice." I jokingly rolled my eyes at him.

"Real nice indeed." His eyes were focused on my chest as his index finger teased across the rise of my cleavage, leaving a glistening invitation his mouth seemed eager to accept.

"Seems like we're always in this shower together," I paused as he worked his way up to my neck.

"One of the few places Shelby will never walk in on us." He drew my earlobe into his mouth.

"True." I exhaled, eyes closed.

"The way your sounds echo in here, does something to me." His breath at my ear caused my breathing to deepen.

"And I love to get you wet." His mouth met mine and kissed me with intent.

His hands in my hair, gripping, pulling softly as his tongue toyed with mine. He waited until I started to unfasten my jeans then stopped me.

"The lights, Alice." He took a step back, and water rushed down over him from the showerhead.

I took a deep breath, trying to contain myself then turned away toward the window, pulling the curtains together tightly. With my back to him, I unzipped my jeans and bent at the waist, pulling them to the floor, and heard him suck air through his teeth in admiration.

His voice dropped an octave, "God damn."

I looked back and found him gripping the edge of the shower glass, his eyes unwilling to leave my ass long enough to look at my face.

Make it one for the books, I thought and stood up slowly, stepping out of the jeans that now lay around my ankles then kicking them to the side "See something you like?" I asked, my fingertips exploring my own waist, causing goosebumps to form. His eyes shifted, now locked on mine, and he nodded.

I made my way to the light switch in nothing but my underwear, then leaned back against the wall, wet bra clinging to my chest, and pulled my panties to the floor. I watched him, one eyebrow raised in excited anticipation as he continued to nod, his face growing more serious with every move I made. My hands slowly rose from my thighs up across my ribs, grasping at my own breasts as Harrison stood there transfixed by my every move. I leaned my head back and reached behind me, grabbing ahold of the clasp of my bra. "Is this what you want?" I asked seductively.

He nodded faster.

"Say it," I demanded, straight-faced.

"I want you." His breaths came faster as other parts of him made themselves known against the glass.

"How bad?" I asked, desperately trying not to laugh.

"Bad." He shook his head slightly, narrowing his eyes. "Real bad." He raked his hand through his hair again as his nostrils flared.

I let out my best seductive exhale, eyes closed, back arched, hand on the clasp of my bra and with a lustful gaze I asked, "You wanna watch?" I bit my bottom lip for added effect.

"Oh my God, yes."

As soon as I released the hooks, I flicked off the light switch which was also behind me, leaving us in complete darkness. Silence. Was the man too stunned to speak? I moaned into the darkness as I stood there motionless.

"Alice!" His voice echoed throughout the room.

I stifled my laughter, then moaned loudly again.

"You've *GOT* to be joking me! Come on!"

"Oh, Harrison..." I increased the urgency in my faked heavy breathing.

"TURN THE BLOODY LIGHTS ON, ALICE!"

I burst out laughing. "You're the one who wanted to be in the dark!"

"That's not what I meant at all!"

I moved back toward the curtains and pulled at one side, though barely. A thin stream of light sliced through the dark and landed against the black marble floor, while everything else in the room remained a mystery.

"There, at least now we can find the floor." I laughed, but when I glanced toward the shower, I couldn't see his face or define any part of him; his entirety was nothing more than a shadow.

"This is perfect, Alice. Join me." His voice was once again serious.

I felt my way toward the shower slowly, careful not to embarrass myself. One foot over the threshold, then the other. The glass, cold against my hand, his body hot to the touch. One hand against his shoulder, the other against his abs, the heat of his palms made me shiver as they slid down my ribs, then behind me, landing on my ass. His mouth on my neck, his tongue warm. He lifted me off the floor, my legs wrapping around his body, my arms around his neck. A high-pitched gasp escaped me as the cold tile was suddenly against my back when he set me down onto the shower bench. Everything on my body tightened against the chill. His fingertips dragging from my jaw to my chest, stopping at my nipples, pinching, squeezing in the dark. His chin softly laying against my sternum, he drew my breasts up to cradle his cheeks. The heat of his mouth on each one before dragging his tongue down over my abdomen.

Then suddenly nothing.

"Harrison?"

I was met with silence, though I knew he hadn't left. Only the gentle splatter of water against the floor to my right.

"Harrison."

I felt his biceps rigid against the backs of my thighs, his hands gripping their tops, he lifted me off the bench slightly and eased me forward toward him. With my hands on the bench to steady myself, I felt the soft stubble on his cheek brush against each of my inner thighs as he moved them further apart, spreading me open with his jaw. The backs of my thighs now pressed against his shoulders, his breath hot against my inner thigh. "Can I?"

I laid my head back against the tile, running my fingers up through the back of his hair and pulling his face into me, positioning him right where I wanted him as his hands played with my breasts. His tongue danced and darted, his lips teasing, his entire mouth sucking, tantalizing, until my breath caught in my chest. He used his hands, his mouth, and the tip of his nose to bring me right to the very edge, then pulled himself away again.

The heaviness of the steam and the skill of Harrison's tongue left me feeling starved for oxygen. I wasn't sure why he'd stopped, but then suddenly I felt his breath at my jaw, his lips gently pressing against me, softly moving toward my ear. I imagined being able to see him do all these things, from an angle outside of myself, and let my imagination run wild as his mouth once again found mine.

"You're amazing, darling." The slow drawl of his accent made my body pulsate even harder and I smiled, loving that my body's responses were no longer under my control.

"*You're* amazing," I whispered breathlessly, my mouth landing at his ear lobe, sucking it into my mouth while my fingertips followed the indentations of the muscles of his hips forward, tracing indistinguishable shapes below his waist.

He kissed me hard, his tongue against mine fervently, slowing only to mumble, "I need to feel you, Alice." He slid his middle and his ring finger between my legs, as his thumb danced across every nerve ending that mattered, his fingertips curling in a slow *come hither* motion against my g-spot. Once, twice, three times, and as I began to lose control, he slowly pulled his hand away.

"You're trying to kill me, I swear," I said, my breathing labored.

"Never, darling. I'm just loving you properly as you deserve."

Jesus Christ, that accent never gets old, and why does it sound even hotter in complete darkness?

"Let me love *you* properly then." I took his hand, stood, turned, and bent at the waist, then propped on my elbows I slid my ass up against his groin, knowing he could hear my smile as I spoke.

"Mmm..." he groaned happily. "Put me where you want me." His voice was low, and I pictured him looking down, his chestnut curls falling forward, his abdominal muscles tightening with each deep breath.

I reached between my legs and found him, throbbing, fully engorged, and tucked the length of him up against me. Savoring the moment, I paused briefly, still picturing him in my head, knowing his brows were pulled together, his nostrils flared. I moved slightly forward allowing him to push into me before slowly, gently pushing back onto him, feeling him sink fully into my depth. A low, deep moan escaped on his breath as he gripped my hips from behind. Then as he plunged himself into me, I felt his wet palm land with a crack against my ass cheek; the sting left in its wake unlocking a new understanding of what could send my future husband over the edge.

"I can't take it, Alice. My God." The urgency in his voice told me everything I needed to know.

"Oh, you can take it," I offered and arched my back as I braced myself against the wall.

His rhythm quickened and I imagined every muscle in his body rigid as he thrust himself into me over and over until he fully lost control of himself.

My forehead remained pressed against the cold tile of the shower wall while I waited for him to move, my arms beginning to tremble as they held me up off the teak bench. I was sure he'd stay there forever if I didn't initiate movement.

"I think you need an ice bath," I said into the darkness.

"That seems a little extreme." His hands rested on my hips as he spoke.

"Well, not right this second," I laughed, "but maybe you should have one here at home somewhere, as an alternative to wild swimming. Wouldn't it have the same desired effect?"

"I'd never considered that." He paused. "Cold water *is* cold water, after all, I suppose."

"It would certainly come with less…exposure. To both people and the paps."

"You might be onto something here." He smacked my ass again and I felt him pull away. Moments later the lights came on and he made his way back to me in the shower.

I hugged him, kissed him softly, and said, "I also think you need to go speak to Lawrence."

Harrison sighed heavily and nodded, then stepped under the hot water and let it wash down over him. We showered together in silence, and when we were dressed and ready for the day, Harrison grabbed his keys, kissed me goodbye, and set off in search of his friend.

CHAPTER
48

One ring. Two. Then I heard Nigel's voice on the other end of the line.

"Fancy hearing from you. Or anyone really." His voice was void of the regular Nigel flair.

"You alright?" I asked.

"I'm just mucking about in my own pathetic sorrows I suppose." I heard him sigh.

"What's got you so down? Talk to me."

"Well, as I'm sure you are aware, Shelby's been off in Liverpool for days with her new fixation, and that's left me alone, again. All loneliness and no play makes Nigel a dull boy," he whined.

"Yes, I certainly know that feeling. I think she'll be back though, tomorrow or maybe the next day?"

"Yes, but he'll be with her. Staying with her, you know. So, there goes the fun in that. He's found himself a location for his," he paused to accentuate his distaste, "gymnasium."

"Well, I'm glad for her. She's overdue for something to spark her joy."

"Yeah, yeah. Except now I'm the only one in the group who's always alone. It's rubbish. I don't even have a, what do you Americans call that...a wingman? I've got no one to go out with. At this rate, I'll be alone for the rest of my life."

"Oh, Nigel, why don't you come over and pick me up? Let's have a day out and about together."

"Darling, where has your lover run off to that's freed up any of your day?" His voice was thick with sarcasm.

"He's gone to try to patch things up with Lawrence. I'll tell you about that incident later. Come get me, take me somewhere where people don't read gossip rags."

"Oh, sweetheart, I don't think such places exist around here."

"You must have heard about the photo getting leaked?"

"I get all those trashy rags, so of course! And thank GOD I was out of view! My God, can you imagine?"

I could picture Nigel, his fingertips splayed at the base of his neck aghast at the thought. "Uh, yeah, actually I can imagine," I said flatly, annoyed at his insensitivity.

"Oh, I'm sorry. I didn't mean to be rude, but...you know me." He chuckled, seemingly unconcerned about my feelings.

"I'm going to text Hank and have him come here so we can go out with protection. Come over. Text when you're here. I'll be out in the garden."

I hung up the phone, sent a quick text to Hank, grabbed a sweater from the closet, then pulled a handful of blueberries from the fridge and went out on the patio to find Robin.

From my usual spot outside, I could hear Robin in the yard singing his happy little song off in the distance. Truth be told, every robin was Robin until the real Robin proved himself by plucking a blueberry from my hand. While I waited for him to arrive, I laid my head back and closed my eyes, drew in a deep breath of cool air, and slowly exhaled. I wondered how things were going with Harrison and Lawrence; they'd been close friends for such a long time, I'm sure the rift was resolved by now. And then my mind drifted to Emma. We had been so close before she got here, and since then Lawrence had taken my place. Was that bond lost for good, or would she circle back when the newness wore off? There was no way to know. I'd just have to wait and see. And then, like I often did, I got lost in my daydreams.

I was in Rome under sun-drenched skies, wandering the streets admiring the architecture and the history. There were no clouds in sight as I eavesdropped on passing conversations that made no sense to me, yet were some of the most beautiful sounds I'd ever heard. Harrison was to my right, my arm linked around his as we rounded the corner from a gelato shop. I stopped and stared in bewilderment at the Trevi Fountain and felt him admire me from behind his designer sunglasses, his white linen shirt unbuttoned to the halfway mark exposing the upper half of the eagle tattoo and leaving what lay below to my imagination, the breeze lifting not only the wisps of curls at his temples but the edges of his collar to expose the tattoos above his tanned collarbones. I'd never felt happier in my entire life. His smile was magnetic, and my beaming reflection in his glasses was proof this was what heaven must feel like.

Robin landing on my hand startled me back to reality. "Hi, friend." I opened my palm to expose the blueberries. "Here ya go. How've you been? I've missed you." The bird looked up at me like I was crazy, made an almost mechanical-sounding chirp, and then snatched a berry and flitted up onto his gutter perch to pick it apart. "Not going to stay and chat today? I was hoping to get your opinion on something. C'mon. Robin?" He didn't move from his spot, just continued to rip and peck at the skin of the blueberry to expose the sweetness it held captive. "I suppose we can talk from here while you snack." I turned to face him. "They've found out who I am. Well, they know my name is Alice. They've seen photos of me in a horrible bathing suit. They know I'm pregnant." I sighed. "The paparazzi have connected me to Harrison. One of them grabbed me, it was a whole thing. What a way to be introduced to the public eye, huh?" Robin released his grip on the hollowed berry, wiped his tiny beak on the gutter's edge, and came down for another, only this time, he decided the arm of the chair was a sufficient enough location for his needs. "It was bound to happen. I don't know why I imagined it would be a bit more refined than this. Part of me feels bad for Harrison to have this personal information exposed in such a way, but he seems secure in it. Says it happens all the time to him, which makes me feel horrible for him. I guess I shouldn't worry as much as I do." I reached my index finger outward toward the bird to see if he would allow me to pet him today, but he hopped to the side, grabbed another berry, and rose again to perch on the gutter. "Sorry, Robin, I didn't mean to spook you. Do you think I'm overthinking this? Part of me feels like I should just ignore the world and live happily in this little bubble we've created. I've got Harrison, of course, but I've also got wonderful support in Shelby and Nigel and Emma, and I've got you. You keep all my secrets." I smiled up at him as Robin continued to pick at the fruit.

Just then my phone buzzed inside my pocket. I pulled it out to find Nigel's text waiting to be opened and managed to scare Robin from his spot at the edge of the roof. "I'll see you later love. Here's some more snacks." I let the remaining blueberries spill from my hand onto the arm of the chair and set off to the front door to find Nigel.

The day turned out to be a much-needed escape from the confines of my own mind. Hank, Nigel, and I spent the afternoon in the garden of The Spaniards Inn, my favorite local spot. Knowing Harrison felt safe there alone, I was confident I wouldn't be overrun with flashbulbs or camera shutters. We noshed on plates of French fries and got caught up on the latest news, passing group gossip around like a game of Telephone. Hank confessed he'd been seeing a woman he met two weeks ago, describing her as "the unicorn that had always alluded him." You could tell he was smitten just by the way he spoke of her. Hell, I didn't know Hank even knew words like *alluded* but whether this was love or lust was yet to be seen. Apparently, Emma had baby fever but felt terrified to say anything to Lawrence for fear it was too soon. Victor had signed on as an investor in Julian's gym and was pretty excited about it—at least that's what he told Hank. Even better, the gym location wasn't too far from our house, and that allowed Julian to stay with Shelby until he found a flat in the city. Not surprisingly, Nigel's main focus of discussion today had been Shelby. She'd been his partner in crime since Nigel signed on to work for Harrison, and in the last few months, they spent a lot of their free time together. Now, she was fully sidelined by Julian. Speaking from more personal knowledge than I liked to admit, loneliness could be a constant nagging ache, one that settled into a person like arthritis, so I understood how Nigel was feeling. Cast off, unimportant, forgettable. In an attempt to put him into a brighter headspace, I waited until Hank went to the bathroom to share a secret.

I leaned in and spoke in a whisper, "Don't tell a soul, until I tell you it's okay, okay?"

His eyes lit up. "Oh my God, it's twins isn't it? Spill. I swear. Is it twins?"

"God no, it's not twins. This is about the wedding. It isn't far off now, and we have to get the location nailed down. Nearly everything else is decided."

"Okay, AND?" His eyes grew wider, silently prodding me.

"Italy."

He gasped. "Spring in Italy." He shook his head slowly and looked toward the sky. "When do we leave?"

"Maybe April. I think it would be a perfect time and I can't wait for you to see where I've chosen." I had a smug grin on my face as I searched for the screenshot I had on my phone.

"C'mon, before he comes back!" he urged.

I pushed my screen toward him, showing him the location, but gave no explanation.

"Oh. My. GOD, Alice. That is stunning. What does Harrison think?"

"I haven't told him yet. I just decided this morning while he was out." My phone buzzed in my hand and I turned the screen back to face me. "One sec, he's calling me."

"Hi, babe," I couldn't stop myself from smiling and turned away from Nigel as he made overly dramatic kissing faces at me.

"Hi, love. I'm at home. Where are you?"

"I'm at The Spaniards with Nigel and Hank. You should join us."

"I'll pop down. Are you inside?" he asked.

"We're out in the garden. See you soon. I love you."

"Love you, darling."

"Harrison's on his way," I said casually as I turned back to the table.

Hank was just sliding back into his seat. "Oh good, I've just ordered us another round." He tipped his glass back and in one mouthful finished his beer.

Nigel glanced at me and rolled his eyes; it was obvious he wished we were alone. I glanced around the garden amidst the awkward silence. Most of the booths and tables were full of people, the outdoor firepit surrounded by folks in comfortable-looking padded chairs, and even the little corgi at the table behind us that managed to lick my ankle every time he could find bare skin seemed quite content to sit in this cozy little garden.

And then with no warning, I felt chest-crushing anxiety begin to wash over me. I wondered how the people around us might react when Harrison walked in. Would they pull out phones when they realized I was Alice? *THE* Alice they've surely now read about in all the papers. Or would there be some uproar the moment they recognized him? Would anyone faint and fall from their chair? Okay fine, that's a little dramatic, but still. Maybe there would be no reaction at all. Who's to say? The night we met, no one approached him. There had been no outbursts or gathered crowds, no fainting ladies. No reaction at all really. Hell, even I hadn't seen him approach me. I hoped that would be the case today as well. His presence certainly could result in more public scrutiny. My heart began to beat faster and my breathing deepened. I poked my straw at the group of maraschino cherries collected at the bottom of my cup. "Old Alice" would have snacked on them without hesitation, especially in the middle of an anxiety attack, but now, I was "pregnant Alice" and that meant calming myself down, and avoiding the excess of the red dye I knew these cherries had been steeped in. My hand landed at the base of my cup and I glanced up again as I pulled in a breath and caught Nigel staring at me. Had he watched this internal spiral of mine?

"You okay, love?" He reached his hand across the table and found mine cold against my iceless glass.

I nodded straight-faced, staring back at him between nervous blinks. He knew me well enough now that I didn't have to say it out loud; he just knew.

"Do we need to go?" His eyes were so kind.

I shook my head and let out a sigh. He squeezed my fingers and then sat back in his chair, his eyes locked on mine, watching me, holding my hand waiting for me to drop my shoulders or relax my posture. I was embarrassed, though from the outside no one could have known what was going on in my head. Hank was completely oblivious to it all, relaxed back against his chair, his fingers clasped behind the back of his head, people watching as his muscular arms looked like giant oversized elf ears protruding from either side of his head.

"Ooh, yes! Thank you, mate." His eyes lit up as the waiter arrived and started handing out our drinks.

"May I also have a glass of water, please? Oh, could you make that two actually, my other half should be joining us any moment." I swallowed hard, wishing Harrison would just magically appear out of thin air.

The waiter nodded and gave an accommodating smile, then disappeared back into the restaurant.

Hank drew a long swig from his glass. This was his fourth beer, and he was supposed to be on the job. At least Nigel knew when to restrain himself, apparently Hank did not.

"Looks like you're going to drive Hank back, Nigel, and I'll be riding with Harrison." To show I wasn't being snarky, I shot him a smug but pleasant smile, even though in my head I was less than impressed.

"I'm fine." Hank brushed off my concern without any idea how much being dismissed like that pissed me off.

Would Harrison agree with you though? Would your boss think you were fine to drive his future wife and unborn child around London after four beers? Doubtful.

My frustration with Hank had overtaken my anxiety, but that was a conversation for later with Harrison alone, not here. Not now. Right now, the baby was kicking.

"Nigel come here, want to feel the baby? He's kicking."

"HE? When did you find that out?" He rushed around the edge of the table and slid in beside me.

"Well, I refer to them as he or him because I just think there would be nothing greater on this earth than a miniature Harrison running around, but we won't know for sure for a few more weeks yet." I pulled Nigel's hand to my lower abdomen and held it gently in place.

A few moments passed and the baby remained still.

"Seems the lad just doesn't like old Uncle Nigel, I guess." He screwed his face into a deep, sour frown.

"Just be patient." We sat still a few moments more, waiting.

Just as Nigel shifted in his seat, presumably intent to move back to his side of the table, the baby kicked again and landed firmly against his palm. He yanked his hand back and his eyes sprung open wide in amazement.

"Oh no, absolutely not. Doesn't that feel peculiar to you? I don't think I'd like that one bit!" He shook his head and grimaced as he moved back to his original position across from me.

"Heey!" Harrison appeared, leaned down and kissed the top of my head, then got comfortable in the seat beside me.

"Mate." Hank dipped his chin in acknowledgment.

Harrison reached out and shook his hand, then offered his hand to Nigel.

"Oh, you know I'm a hugger." Nigel stood and held out his arms.

Harrison gave me a look as if to say, *since when?* then got up and hugged Nigel. Back in his chair beside me he asked, "So what have I barged in on?"

"Well, your child just full-on kicked me in the hand. That one's gonna be a footballer for sure!"

"I think she'll be whatever she wants to be, but yes, those kicks really are something aren't they?" Harrison looked down at my belly proudly.

"She?" Nigel asked.

"She." Harrison said matter-of-factly.

"Your soon-to-be wife just referred to the child as a boy. You'll have the poor babe confused in no time!" Nigel chuckled, apparently finding himself hilarious.

Hank leaned forward and rested on his forearms. "Alice, have you had any weird cravings for food? I know my sister made some bizarre choices when she was pregnant."

"Well, it's funny you mention it." I bit at the corner of my bottom lip, trying not to smile.

Harrison interrupted, "Mate, I catch her at least three times a week eating tuna fish straight from the can! Like some sort of vagabond." His eyebrows were raised in amazement.

"Oh stop! It's not that bad." I felt my cheeks flush.

"Canned tuna?" Nigel seemed shocked. "Oh, Alice!"

"I drain the liquid out first; stop picking on me!"

"Beyond that, she's keeping the blueberry industry afloat." Harrison shook his head. "Truly, I don't know how she hasn't begun to turn blue yet."

I shook my head, embarrassed, and looked down at my lap. Those blueberries were mostly for Robin. Harrison just didn't know about him yet.

"What else? Let's see, there's watermelon, eggs," his thumb and his index finger unfurled in succession, "there's peas and bananas." His middle and ring finger followed as he counted off my preferred grocery items.

"It's all healthy and all of them play a vital role in the baby's development." I made a face at Harrison and stuck out my tongue, feeling disheartened.

"The child is going to emerge with fins, and have an affinity for homesteading." He wrinkled his nose and stuck his tongue out back at me.

"Well, you look amazing, and who cares what you're eating. You're growing a human being for Christ's sake!"

"Thank you, Nigel." I smiled sweetly in his direction.

"Oh, darling, I think you're just perfect." Harrison kissed my cheek. "Even if you do eat tuna fish like a homeless cat."

I smacked his shoulder as all three of the guys laughed loudly. I looked around, expecting everyone to be staring in our direction. But no one was. No one cared that Harrison was here, and no one cared that he was here with me. They were all minding their own business, enjoying all that The Spaniards Inn had to offer. The food, the drinks, and the ambiance unmatched, this place had always been a welcoming haven for us. It was a special place, with special neighborhood regulars; it was where this real-life love story began, and where it would continue for years to come.

CHAPTER 49

That night at home, tucked warmly beneath the covers, I looked over at Harrison and made a confession. "Babe, I want red onions and lemon trees."

"You and these cravings, Alice, honestly. The whole tree now?" He laughed.

"No, no..." I sat up and faced him. "I would love for our celebration dinner to be under a canopy of lemon trees, with the girls in dresses and the guys in nice shirts, the center of the table lined with candles and twinkle lights above us, delicious food."

"It sounds wonderful, but don't you mean rehearsal dinner?"

"I don't think with so few of us there, and how informal it is, that we need a full-blown rehearsal, do you? I'd much rather live in the moment when it comes to the ceremony, but I do want a celebration dinner beforehand with everyone. It's all the same, but just no rehearsal necessary."

"Whatever you want, my darling, you shall have," he said with a look of love on his face.

"Do you have a vision for what *you* want?" I asked.

"I just want you. I don't need anything else."

"There's nothing you specifically want? Location? View? Time of day?"

"You, Alice. I just want you."

I leaned in and kissed him. "I love you."

"I love *you,* darling. Now, tell me more."

"This morning I found a place in Italy called Tropea. It's in Calabria. And there's this church on top of a giant beautiful rock formation surrounded by the most gorgeous ocean view. And I think we could have a small ceremony out on the cliff of The Sanctuary of Santa Maria dell'Isola overlooking the Tyrrhenian Sea." I rolled my tongue to make crazy sounds. "I'm sorry, I've probably butchered that."

"You can have it all, my love." The edge of his thumb stroked my jaw. "But I've got to know, what role do the red onions play?" The sincerity in his eyes reminded me again why I found him so endearing.

"Tropea is famous for its sweet red onions. Sorry, I should have mentioned that sooner. My brains are scrambled." I sighed.

"If you want it, it's yours." He pulled me close and kissed me again.

"Do you want to write your own vows?" I asked as I lay back against the pillows beside him.

"I've got half of them in my head already."

"You do?" I looked at him, surprised.

"Mm-hmm." He nodded proudly.

"I'm nervous to." Movement at the foot of the bed caught my attention. Harrison had a habit of rubbing his feet and toes together when he was in bed, and it still caught me off guard sometimes. "Don't get me wrong, I want to. I'm just nervous I'll fall short of expressing myself the way I really want to."

"Don't be worried about that, love. I know the way your heart feels for me. I've read the way you write about things that matter to you. I'm sure whatever you decide to say will be beautiful."

"Oh, I've found a place for us to stay also. It's not peak season yet, so I hope we can reserve the entire place for our group again, that way we're all together. There are seven rooms, so there should be one for everyone even if we have to bring an officiant with us," I rambled excitedly. "It overlooks the beach and the sanctuary, but we'll still need to find someone qualified to conduct the ceremony. Maybe we can interview a few people, unless you know someone? Speaking for myself, religion really doesn't play into this, so..."

"I'm not sure how that works. If we can bring someone or what's required. I'll research that and figure out the marriage license stuff tomorrow after we meet with Della. Are you excited for the scan?" Harrison's eyes lit up when he mentioned it.

"I am. Part of me really wants to know the gender though, not gonna lie. Waiting is going to be so hard for me." I felt bad making him wait.

"I know, me too, but I really like that we're going to make it part of the ceremony. That way she gets to be a part of our special day too." He grinned mischievously.

"I think you meant he."

"I don't think I did." His eyes sparkled as he continued. "I don't care what they are, Alice. I just want them to have your kind eyes, and your sweet smile, and I hope they love as genuinely as you love. As long as our child is as sweet as their mum, that's all that matters to me." He patted the top of my leg.

"I want him to have his daddy's dimples and long eyelashes and his daddy's beautiful heart. I want him to admire the moon and appreciate the sunshine and love poetry. Seems I want a miniature you and you want a miniature me." I laughed.

"Nothing wrong with that. You never know. This could be our first of many."

I sat up and looked at him. "Oh, you think so, huh?"

He winked at me then flashed a sweet smile.

"Hey, you never did tell me how things went with Lawrence this morning," I said in an attempt to change the subject completely.

"When he came to the door and saw it was me, his first words were, 'I'm sorry mate,' before he'd even said hello. And I could tell he was genuinely apologetic. I didn't ask what had sidetracked him, though I'm sure he was either texting or chatting with Emma. I did however say to him, if it were my actual job to keep watch on Emma, and this happened to her, he'd be just as terrified and angry as I was in the moment. He agreed, and we shook hands, hugged, and moved on. Water under the bridge. He's been my mate forever; he knows me better than most. He understood where I was coming from."

"Well, I'm glad you went over. I'm sure he was nervous to make the first move."

"We've had a good row or two in our time, and I'm sure there'll be more before it's all said and done, but we always work it out."

My eyes were getting heavy, and Harrison's hand beneath the covers rubbing my thigh was enough to lull me toward sleep. "Babe, I'm exhausted. Be the big spoon?"

"Absolutely." Harrison reached over and shut off the bedside lamp, then rolled toward me and kissed my cheek before inching down, pressing his body against me, the palm of his hand coming to rest at the front of my hip.

I snuggled my cheek against my pillow and into the dark said, "I love you so much," then laid my hand on top of his.

"I love you too, darling. Have the sweetest dreams." He rubbed my lower abdomen. "Love you too, little one."

CHAPTER 50

Today was the day. Harrison and I would be seeing our midwife Della to finally get our anatomy scan done. I'd been back here several times for short monthly appointments as required, but now that I'd hit the twenty week mark, this appointment meant we'd be learning so much more about the state of our baby's health, and of course we were both excited about getting to hear the heartbeat again. I was proud to be halfway through this pregnancy and still feeling good, but to say I wasn't worried about my age affecting the health of my child would be a lie. For the last two weeks my sleeping pattern had morphed into what my grandmother would have called "fits and starts." That meant I was lucky to get a few hours of rest at a time, but sleeping through the night, uninterrupted, was a thing of the past despite my complete exhaustion by mid-afternoon most days. Harrison bought me special pillows to try to help, and he massaged my feet, legs, and back every evening while we watched TV before bed. Of course, it was relaxing and I loved every second of it, but none of it could lull me into dreamland for any normal amount of time. I also had near constant heartburn, which I guessed was to be expected at this point, but as a believer in old wives' tales, I envisioned this child with a full head of chestnut curls just like his father. Hell, at this rate he might have a beard too.

Della's office was just as cheerful and welcoming as always, and today we were met with bunches of sunshiny daffodils propped in a vase at the front desk, their brilliant orange centers like that of fresh egg yolks. Once we were in a private room we settled in quickly and updated Della on what had been happening since we saw her last. I let her know I'd been keeping up with the pregnancy app on my phone, and reading the milestones book she'd recommended, and I told her about the sleep issues I'd been having. Once all our questions were answered and I was in position on the table, Della dimmed the lights.

"Okay, so—" she began.

"WAIT! We don't want to know the gender yet!" Harrison blurted out.

She laughed and said calmly, "That's perfectly fine, I can turn the screen away so you can't see."

"I didn't mean to shout. I just wasn't sure how quickly you'd be able to tell."

"Babe, she hasn't even done anything yet." I chuckled and took him by the hand in an attempt to redirect his nervous energy.

"I'll take measurements today, snap a few photos for you, you can hear your baby's heartbeat, and we'll count fingers and toes, just to make sure everything is developing as it should be. We'll also check your cervix and update your due date depending on measurements." Della's voice was soothing against Harrison's panic.

"We'd love to have the photos and gender put into an envelope so we can open it together when we're ready," I said, squeezing Harrison's hand in mine as Della turned the screen from our view and I fixed my attention to the ceiling.

"That's no problem at all. I'm just applying a little warm jelly, and we'll get started."

Harrison drew in a deep breath and steadied himself in his chair while I tried to control my thoughts, and my breathing. The wand moved back and forth, pressing into my abdomen in search of sound while Della concentrated on the screen in front of her. I looked to Harrison, searching his face for reassurance as the room remained silent. My anxiety was creeping in and almost certainly raising my blood pressure. I'd been feeling flutters and strong kicks, and was excited to be hearing a heartbeat today. I didn't know if it would sound the same as before or different. I wasn't sure what to expect honestly, but I was beginning to feel overwhelmed. This was a real human. Not a speck the size of a sesame seed or just some imaginary fruit-sized reason not to eat deli meat, but a healthy, growing, actual human inside of me. More importantly, a child created from the love I shared with Harrison. I'd never made it this far in my first pregnancy so this was all new to me, and it was absolutely exhilarating, and…terrifying.

The wand continued to search and still, no heartbeat. Harrison's face had lightened to an unbecoming shade of pale and stared back at me with no expression at all to help me figure out what he was thinking while my mind was reeling. *Why can't she find it? Is something wrong? Is there no heartbeat to find? Is our baby…No! Don't even think about that, Alice.* Harrison and I stared at each other, waiting, hoping, anxious. I closed my eyes to try to calm myself. One deep breath, a long exhale. And another, then…

Whoosh, whoosh, whoosh, whoosh, whoosh.

My eyes flew open and locked on Harrison's excitedly.

"There we are. Nice and strong." Della's voice was like a warm blanket being wrapped around me.

Our little one's heartbeat was rapid, much faster than I imagined it would be. Harrison squeezed my hand and let out a sigh of relief as he stared back at me. I could see the tears ready to spill over onto his cheeks.

"We did that," I said.

He stood from the chair at my bedside and leaned in to kiss me. "Yes we did." He had such a proud look on his face.

"I'll just be a moment taking some measurements. You'll hear me clicking my mouse. So far everything looks on par with what we expect at this stage. I think your due date will still fall in early July. But I'll include the actual date in your envelope if you wish?"

"That's perfect! Thank you, Della," I said.

Harrison was still staring at me. His eyes would fall to my belly in amazement, and then back to meet my gaze lovingly. He looked astonished, and I guess I was too. It was crazy how this soul came to be ours, how the stars aligned and brought Harrison to me, how we were sitting here now, in love. Had the universe always known this was my fate? Had I been working toward this my entire life? Had my silly little daydreams been some weird déjà vu moments giving me insight to my future? Who could ever say for sure? All I knew was I'd never been happier in my entire life than I was in this moment.

When the scan was done and we were ready to go, Della handed us our envelope and wished us well. We'd see her again in a month.

CHAPTER 51

Harrison and I both managed to keep ourselves quite busy in the days following our scan. We'd sneak off early to museums or waste hours at the cinema, have picnics in the park, or spend afternoons on long walks or puttering together in our garden. But no matter what I did, or how I occupied my mind, all I could think about was that envelope.

Last night I dreamed I was part of a runway fashion show, showcasing wedding gowns for pregnant women. I was making my way down the runway, just about to stop at the end of the catwalk, when my water broke. But instead of amniotic fluid, it was green and yellow pastel confetti that scattered at my feet in front of everyone. Embarrassed, I'd looked into the crowd and found everyone in matching clown masks; hard white plastic with outrageous eyebrows, giant mouths and bulbous red noses. A contraction hit me out of nowhere, and when I bent at the waist in pain, there was the envelope, laying face up on the floor covered in sparkly purple glitter. As I reached for it, it leapt from the floor as if a gust of wind had lifted it from its resting spot, grew wings and flew away. I stood there confused as a crowd of clowns laughed at me in unison.

When I woke, I lay there wondering, was this some sort of sign that we were going to lose the envelope? Or the baby? Green, yellow, and purple. None of which were typical run-of-the-mill gender defining colors. No hints there. They were the colors of Mardi Gras though. Fat Tuesday was next week. *Mmm...beignets would be so good right now. Focus, Alice!*

I could hear the brass band in my head, and remembered the feeling of stepping out of the car into the sticky humidity of New Orleans back when I'd dreamed of Harrison and I taking that road trip. Part of me wished we could've taken that trip in real life before pregnancy put restrictions on us, but there was a wedding to think of, and besides, the temperature, the heaviness of the air, and the crowds of New Orleans in reality would surely stifle the freedom we'd had in that dream. And I didn't want to tempt fate and end up with Harrison leaving me at the zoo. But oh, the things that happened on that balcony...I'd gone back there in my mind so many times while he was in Brazil, I knew his every move like the back of my hand.

Today's plan involved Harrison heading out with the guys to figure out his wedding attire, and I'd be with my usual group to do the same. He'd have Lawrence, Victor, and Julian with him, while I'd have Nigel, Hank, Shelby, and Emma with me. If our wedding was really going to happen like we planned, there'd be stairs to climb to get to our ceremony and I wasn't interested in a heavy dress or layers of makeup. I just wanted to be comfortable. Something flowy, lightweight, and with a little give to the seams because this belly of mine wasn't going to be getting any smaller. Harrison preferred me not to wear a lot of makeup; mascara and some tinted lip balm was enough for me on a regular day, and it let the tiny freckles brought on by the sun that he loved so much shine through. My research told me the temperatures in Tropea had been hovering in the mid 70s, making it unseasonably warm in the last few weeks, so I needed to prepare myself for that as well.

Harrison left before me, and while I waited for my friends to arrive, I sat in the garden and chatted with Robin. It seemed I no longer had to call to him, as he arrived within seconds of me opening the patio door. During a recent shopping trip, I'd found a small ring dish, its dainty gold edges scalloped and hollowed, a perfect foothold for a small bird, its depth enough to hold a few medium-sized blueberries and just enough mealworms to fill his tiny belly. He'd grab a few from his dish, then flit about the yard in search of a good spot to snack and chatter back at my constant rambling. Spring in London was upon us, and I knew Robin would soon take a mate. I wondered to myself if that would change the way we spent time together, if he might shy away from me, or if he'd bring her to meet me. Time would tell. When he left, he was still flying out toward the tree line, and so far, I hadn't seen any activity around the birdhouse we hung for him. Back in the kitchen, I washed his dish and placed it near the sink just as a knock came at the door.

Nigel drove us around London, where we popped into various boutiques and shops looking for something more than casual but less than formal, each one falling short of what I wanted in one way or another. Despite winding up empty handed, I was glad for Emma and Shelby to both find something they loved and even Hank found himself a casual suit to wear in spite of his grumpiness at being stuck with mostly women today. Back in the car we had only two shops left to explore when I got a text from Harrison.

Hey love, missing you but guess what? I've found the perfect look. Bag secured. xxx

I responded: *Not me, striking out everywhere. *sad face* Wanna tell me what you got?*

His response was immediate. *If you don't find what you want, we can always have it made. Knowing you, you're not asking for anything over the top. Don't waste your worry on that, love, okay? And I'll show you tonight. There's no rule against seeing a groom before the wedding is there? It's sick, Alice, I can tell you that. It's definitely got the flavor. Are you having any fun? xxx*

We are having a lovely time, aside from Hank wishing he were with your group. Sick and flavorful, huh? Should be interesting. Is there purple glitter by chance? Hope you guys are having a good time too. See you back at home in a few hours? What time is the officiant supposed to be there again? I hit send and waited for his reply.

Moments later, my phone vibrated.

Purple glitter? No. Haha, dare I ask? He's set to arrive around 4 p.m. xxx

Okay. I'll tell you about the glitter when you show me what you got today. I love you, babe, see you soon. xxx I hit send and put my phone back in my purse.

"How's Harrison doing?" Nigel asked, making eye contact with me in the rearview mirror.

"He's found his outfit. He's described it as 'sick' so this should be interesting." I raised my eyebrows doubtfully.

"Oh lord." Shelby rolled her eyes.

"Is this going to be a fiasco?" I asked.

Hank chuckled. "No. To be fair, one thing I can safely say about Harrison, his style is spot on. Unconventional? Yes, sometimes, but always incredible."

"I wish I knew what he got so I could be on the same level of...sickness," I scoffed as I heard it come out of my mouth. "I feel weird even saying that out loud. Maybe he was right. Maybe I should just get something made. I'm certainly not having much luck today; maybe it's a sign."

"We'll get you sorted; don't you worry." Shelby patted my shoulder. "I had my suspicions an occasion like this wasn't going to be an 'off the rack' moment. But everything will be just fine, you'll see." She smiled, but I had no idea what she was getting at.

CHAPTER
52

Promptly at 4 p.m. I opened the door to find a gentleman smiling back at me. He was easily six-foot-three, with dark trusting eyes and flawless cinnamon skin, the hair at his temples just beginning to ease toward gray.

"Hi there, nice to meet you." He held out his hand. "I'm Rupert. You must be Alice." His voice was much deeper than I would have expected. I shook his hand and welcomed him inside.

"It's so nice to meet you, Rupert. Please, let me introduce you to Harrison." I led the way down into the dining room where Harrison sat smiling eagerly at our potential officiant before standing to greet him. "Nice to meet you, mate." Harrison shook his hand. "Have a seat."

"Thank you. Lovely to make your acquaintance as well. I've seen many of your films and I must say, I'm a fan."

"Thank you." Harrison nodded and smiled politely.

"Would you like something to drink?" I asked.

"Oh no, I've brought water with me. Thank you though." He settled into his chair and glanced down at the packet Harrison casually slid in front of him. "Oh, so Italy? Lovely choice. Have you chosen a city?"

"Italy is okay, right? You're able to travel with us and handle the ceremony for us in Tropea? Well, Calabria." Harrison raked his fingers back nervously through his curls as he spoke.

"Absolutely, and Tropea is gorgeous! On a clear day you can see Mount Stromboli, one of Italy's active volcanoes, and the food there is…" He made a chef's kiss gesture with his hand. "Have you decided what sort of ceremony you prefer?"

"Well, neither of us are religious, but certainly spiritual, in ways. We'd like to write our own vows, exchange rings, but there's one thing we want to do that might be a bit unusual." Harrison couldn't stop himself from smiling, and I watched as he glanced down at his hands; his thumb nervously picking at his right middle finger.

"Certainly, this is your ceremony. Every human is different; we cannot expect all ceremonies to be the same. I am purely a means to make sure you get what you want, a facilitator you might say."

I reached out and took Harrison's hand in mine to stop him from anxiously picking his cuticles. "We'd like to take a few moments to reveal the gender of our unborn child during our ceremony. We have the information tucked away in a sealed envelope. We'll have you open it and announce it in front of our small group."

"Yes, by all means we can do absolutely anything you choose. So, this is also a reveal for the two of you, not just for your guests?" Rupert asked.

"The only thing we currently know is that there's a healthy baby in there," Harrison gushed and placed his hand on my belly.

"How wonderful! Congratulations to you both. This will be a first for me. Now in Tropea, will you be on the beach?" Rupert asked as he flipped through the packet of information Harrison had created for him.

"Well, this is where things might be strange," I hesitated. "We want to be married outside overlooking the ocean at the Santa Maria dell'Isola sanctuary. So not inside, but out in the garden."

"The view over the Tyrrhenian Sea from the sanctuary is unmatched. I've been there but it's been about ten years ago now. Being that you're with child, you know there are a number of stairs you'll need to ascend to reach the summit?"

"Oh yes, I'm fully aware and I'm prepared. This won't be a big to-do. A short ceremony late in the afternoon, and we'll make sure to pay the fees and rent the entire space for the time we need; there won't be any non-guests present. Just our very small group of about ten people. We'll be staying locally, where we'll also rent out the entire hotel. Do you have any issue flying with us on a private plane and staying in the same accommodations as our group? We would of course cover any costs for you," I offered.

"Not at all. I can be as present or hidden as you like."

"I also think I'd like to be the last to arrive. Again, a change from the norm, but it would give Alice and our group a chance to get up to the sanctuary and get settled, then I could arrive and we could begin the ceremony," Harrison offered.

"I actually really like that idea. I can take my time, and you're one of the most fit of the bunch, so it will be a breeze for you to climb those stairs." I laughed. "Then once you get there, and walk down the path to me, we can welcome people, make our promises to one another"—I felt my cheeks get warm—"and then we can exchange rings, and save the best for last."

"The big reveal." Harrison's eyes widened and a toothy grin took over his face.

"Yeah." I looked at him adoringly.

"Oh, you two are *absolutely* made for one another," Rupert interjected, breaking the steadfast gaze Harrison and I were locked in.

We chatted a while longer, finalizing details of payment and discussing dates, modes of travel, and making sure expectations were vocalized. The longer we talked, the more Rupert seemed perfect for us. He was intelligent, well-spoken—and spoke fluent Italian just like Harrison—he was relaxed and seemed to know many parts of Italy quite well. Harrison and I gave each other the nod of approval, and while Rupert was in the bathroom, we signed the contract he'd given us to look over. Sure, he was the first person we met with, but why continue searching when he checked all our boxes?

With everything signed and settled, Rupert packed our contract and the packet Harrison had made for him into his briefcase, then mentioned he needed to call an Uber.

"No need, let me have one of my guys take you. They can be here quickly and take you wherever you need to go."

"That's so kind, thank you."

"Of course." Harrison turned to face me with mischief written all over his face. "Alice, darling, why don't you give *Nigel* a quick text, have him take care of Rupert." The intent in his eyes left nothing to the imagination.

"Yes, Nigel! Excellent idea." I tried to sneak a glance at Rupert's ring finger before heading to the kitchen to grab my phone, but his hands were in his pockets.

"Are you married, Rupert?" Harrison asked.

Way to play it cool, H.

"I'm not." He sighed and looked down at the floor bashfully. "I just do the marrying."

I typed so quickly into my phone it was barely understandable.

Nigel, quck, need yu to giv somne a rid.

Only after I hit send did I notice what a mess I'd sent.

Oh shit! Our officiant needs a ride. Please, put on some cologne and hurry up.

I hit send again and set my phone down. Realizing I'd left out one other important factor I hurriedly typed one more message.

Tall dark and handsome! and hit send again.

"Okay, he should be on his way shortly." I rejoined the men in the dining room. "Won't take long, Rupert. He's on call for these types of things all the time."

"Thank you. I'm very much looking forward to joining you on this adventure, and of course, I'll be at your beck and call for anything you may need in the time leading up to the ceremony. I moonlight with planning, so I'm sort of a one-stop shop, if you will."

"We appreciate that. I think the hardest part is going to be climbing all those stairs. The execution of everything else should be a breeze with so few of us to worry about," I added just as there was a knock at the door. "You boys talk amongst yourselves. I'll get that." I set off toward the front door, and to my surprise, there was Nigel standing proudly on the welcome mat.

"Christ, that was fast!" I whispered to him.

"I was only at Shelby's, now let me see what I'm up against." He craned his neck to get a better view of Rupert in the dining room. "Fuckin' hell, Alice, you weren't kidding," he whispered excitedly.

"Would I joke about tall dark and handsome? I think not." Then with a bit more exuberant volume in my voice, I said, "Hi, Nigel, come on in."

Seconds later, Nigel stood before Rupert in my living room, a dip of his chin in acknowledgment, a bashful look on his face, his cheeks tinged crimson.

"At your service, mate. Where might I deliver you?" Nigel offered smugly, noticeably clinging, though barely, to what was left of his professionalism.

Rupert, seemingly unaccustomed to this type of attention, smiled back shyly, his eyes remaining focused on Nigel's. "I've got a place in the city, not too far out."

Nigel sized him up, his eyes taking in and assessing every inch of him.

"Oh?" he asked.

Rupert smirked and stood taller, suddenly cocky. "SoHo." He tipped his head to the side slightly and blinked as he remained focused on Nigel.

"Oh." Nigel's fingertips landed at his sternum, his signature pearl-clutching move while his eyebrows raised, impressed. "Well, then, allow me." Nigel extended his arm toward the front door.

"Thank you both. We'll touch base soon. Call me with any questions." Then Rupert set off toward the front door while Nigel glanced back at us and winked as he followed close behind.

CHAPTER
53

It had been a hectic but wonderful day. Harrison and I were both exhausted, and while we got ready for bed, I was finally able to ask him about his suit.

"I've waited as patiently as I could all afternoon. Please, I'm begging you, show me what you picked out today." I tapped my fingertips together in anticipation while I stared at his reflection in the bathroom mirror.

"I'm not sure I want you to see it until ceremony time. That's only fair, right? And it's being tailored, so it's not here anyhow." He laughed and applied moisturizer under his eyes. "I'll tell you this, though, it's made from the finest Italian linen and has trousers and waistcoat to match. Notch lapel, two-button jacket, Alice it's so posh in the most relaxed way. It's not white though, it's more of a beige, sandy color, you know, beachy, and has embroidery embellishments." He gave me his cheekiest glance as he rubbed the remaining moisturizer into his hands. "And I'm pretty sure when you see it, you're going to want to marry me." His eyebrows danced repeatedly as he gave me the worst rendition of a flirtatious look I'd ever seen.

I shook my head, a look of concern on my face. "You sure about that?"

"Heeeyyy!" A look of rejection replacing the flirty expression.

"I'm only joking, but I do have a question." I followed him back to the bedroom.

"What's that?" he asked.

"What do you call an illegally parked frog?"

"What?" He spun around to look at me, confused.

"Yes, what. That's the question," I said and crawled into bed.

He slid beneath the covers beside me as he thought long and hard, then looked at me, still confused. "What do I call an illegally parked frog? I've no idea." He rubbed the knuckle of his index finger against the underside of his chin, perplexed.

"Toad." I looked at him straight-faced.

"Oh my God, Alice!" He nodded. "You're right, I'll give you that one."

I pulled my laptop out of my bedside table and adjusted myself to sit comfortably beneath the covers while it booted up. "I'm gonna write a bit before bed. Okay?" I asked.

"I was going to work on my vows, as long as you can keep yourself from peeking." He pulled his journal from his own bedside drawer.

"I'll be good, I promise." I leaned over and pushed my cheek toward him, inviting a kiss.

As we sat snugly propped into bed, Harrison beside me bare chested with a notebook in front of him, wearing the reading glasses that made me want to ride him like some sort of bucking bronco—*if only I had the energy*—and me with my laptop, I kept looking over at him, unable to stay focused on the task at hand.

"I can't concentrate while you've got those glasses on," I said, mildly frustrated.

"Oh, that must be just dreadful for you," he joked, slowly pushing the covers down to expose more of his abs.

I turned my head sharply in the opposite direction. "No," I placed my palm over my face briefly, then peered out between my fingers, "I won't fall victim to…to…"

"To what, Alice?" He pushed his glasses tight to the bridge of his nose, and blinked at me, knowing those glasses drove me wild.

"Are you trying to seduce me? I'm going to get to this ceremony and my vows will read, *Sorry, I couldn't resist you when I was supposed to be writing my vows, and now all I'm left with is a blank page and a scandalous memory*. Is that what you want?" I yanked the covers up and covered as much of his bare skin as I could. "I've got to focus."

"I'm just messing with you, love." His chestnut curls dropped forward as he returned his attention to his notebook, and I sat watching him, mesmerized.

Truth is, I couldn't concentrate, glasses on and bare skin or not. I couldn't pour myself out with him sitting there beside me. I needed to be alone. I needed to dig into the depth of my emotions. And knowing myself the way I did, I'd probably cry and wanted to spare him witnessing that. I'd also intermittently been working on my first novel. I'd jot down ideas and thoughts as they came to me; nothing was cohesive and certainly didn't make any sense. Just random scenes in succession on a page, disjointed gibberish for now, but it had been a nice outlet for me. I opened the file and began typing. The soft clicking of the keys stood out against the sounds of Harrison's pen pressed to the pages of his notebook. A flickering candle on the nightstand beside me, we worked in unison, each of us creatives in our own right. Me, constructing an escape through fiction while Harrison laid out his truth in vows. The sound of his pen constant, I paused to watch him. His brow tight, writing came easy for him. He nodded as he found his rhythm, words pouring from his right hand across the page as the invisible weight of his emotions lifted from his shoulders. *This man loves me*, I thought. The ease with which his promises were laid bare on parchment, the way he smiled to himself as he wrote, oblivious to me staring at him.

I never once breached his trust by looking at his words, I focused solely on Harrison himself. The way his curls lay against his temples in tiny duck-tail wisps above his barely-there sideburns, the sharp angle of his jaw and the way it clenched when he was searching for the right words. The small remnant scar above his left eyelid reminding me that even beautiful things had imperfections. The tiny beauty mark sitting vigilant, guarding the dimple in his left cheek I loved so much. His masculine nose. The fine lines like starbursts that formed at the outer corners of his eyes when he smiled, and his expressive forehead when he surprised himself with his thoughts. His earlobes, and the small vein that ran the length of his neck. My eyes dropped to the tattoos that lay against the fronts of his shoulders, his skin like bronze velvet thanks to Brazil and good genes. *My God, I didn't deserve this beautiful man.*

When he finished, he pulled in a deep breath through his nose and smiled contentedly as he released it, obviously proud of himself. He pinched his bottom lip between his finger and thumb and pulled slightly, glancing over his masterpiece until he realized I was watching him. "Heeyy, no peeking." He quickly flipped his notebook closed, scowling.

"I wasn't looking at your writing, babe, I was just watching *you* as you loved me on paper."

He tossed his notebook onto the floor while his adoring eyes stayed fixed on me. "I'd like to love you right here on these sheets."

"It comes easy for you, writing these," I glanced down at my keyboard in front of me, my right ring finger lightly running across the raised lettering on the backspace button. "I'm not sure I can fully put into words how much you mean to me and all the promises I want to make to you. You're everything I've ever dreamed of, Harrison."

"The right words will come."

I shrugged.

He took my hands in his. "Alice, I don't want to wait. I know you're barely divorced, and you were married a long time, and this is new still, kind of. Not really. I know you're worried what people will think or what they'll say and all that. But I don't want to watch days pass by when I could be your husband, right now."

"I feel the same way, and I don't care what the people think or say or what they write about us. I just don't care anymore. I love you. I was meant to find you and we were meant to have this family, and if that means I had to let go of things to make room for what feels right," I paused, "what *is* right, then I just can't make space for how other people feel. How *you* feel is all that matters now."

He studied my eyes a moment, and in his I found a yearning, maybe for reassurance, or truth or confirmation, then he grabbed me and kissed me; one of those breathless, messy, off-kilter crooked kisses that happen when someone just can't hold themselves back anymore.

"Let's just go. Let's settle all the accommodations and book the spot, and let's. Just. Go," he managed to say between a flood of kisses all over my face.

"We can call them in the morning. Tonight, I want nothing but you and those glasses to show me just how badly you wanna call me your wife."

CHAPTER
54

The calls had been made, the accommodations booked, the sanctuary put on hold for our private ceremony, and our next appointment with Della had been converted to a video call. In less than two weeks, I'd be the wife of Harrison Edwards, and I could barely contain my excitement. Harrison was at his desk in the library making sure our marriage license and travel documentation were secured and legal, while in the dining room I blurted out all the details to Shelby at the breakfast table.

"Can you even believe it? I need to find a dress! You said you knew someone? Do you think I can see them soon? Are they usually booked pretty far out? How quickly do they work? Will this be done in time? We leave for Italy in nine days!" I wasn't stopping to give her time to answer me.

"There will be plenty of time. I'll set up the dress appointment for today or tomorrow, and all will be just fine." She was so calm.

"Harrison said his suit is a shade of sand, with embroidery and…I don't even know. I guess a cream color would be fine for me. Off-white." I was rambling, and I could feel myself doing it, I just couldn't stop. Poor Shelby. "Harrison said his was Italian linen. He called it 'posh.' I just want to be comfortable."

"Alice."

"I've got to figure out flowers."

"Alice," Shelby repeated.

"Where am I going to find flowers? I don't speak Italian. How am I going to pull this off?"

"ALICE!" Shelby took me by my shoulders and made me look at her. "I'll get the flowers dealt with. And you have...what's his name? Reginald? He can help. He speaks Italian."

"Rupert." His name fell from my lips in almost a whisper as I sat there doe-eyed, breathing heavy, feeling terrible for being so anxious.

"Right, Rupert. I'll never remember it. Although, Nigel called me in the middle of the night last night and was in nearly the same state you are about how delicious this *Rupert* is." She rolled her eyes. "The two of you are a perfect pair; you're both a knotted-up mess of nerves all the time. You've got to calm down. Write down what you want; I promise we'll get it all sorted. Alright?" She stood from her chair and wrapped her arms around my shoulders while I sat, overwhelmed, and let her. After a few moments Shelby sat back in her seat.

"Thank you." I sighed. "None of this should have me going crazy. I just need *him* there. If there are no flowers, no photos—oh shit, I need a photographer." Elbows propped on the table, I let my forehead drop to my palms. "Harrison must know someone he actually trusts?" I asked.

"We will work it all out. Knowing him, I'm sure he's already thought of that, and has probably already called someone while he's been back there this morning." She tipped her head toward the library. "Now, you finish your breakfast and I'm going to get my friend on the phone and see when we can get this dress sorted for you." Her hand touched my shoulder for only a moment, and then I was alone. A cold plate of food in front of me, my head was all over the place as I stared blankly out the window. I had a million things to do, and each individual task was somehow immobilizing me.

I noticed a flash of orange, and there was Robin in the yard. Normally he'd be hopping around the lawn, stopping at random to take an insect hostage before gulping it down, but today he was plucking fine strands of grass, bunching them together until his tiny beak was laden with green sprigs, then flitting toward the house Harrison had hung for him. Over and over he did this, and each time he approached the round entrance of his new home, a small face would appear inside to receive Robin's offerings. I was only able to catch quick glimpses of his new mate, but their appearance was nearly identical, her orange facial feathers a smidge drabber than Robin's vibrant hues. *I'll need to give her a name*, I thought, *something beautiful. Reminiscent of the garden, meaningful.* I watched in silence from the dining room as she arranged the bundles of grass Robin delivered to her. She was nesting, an urge all too familiar to me.

I think I'll call her Sunshine, Sunny for short, or maybe short for Sunflower. A nod to happiness, bright, and cheerful, and a most welcome addition to our garden.

Shelby's voice grew louder as she approached from the guest room down the hall. "All set, we'll meet up with my friend this afternoon and get your dress all taken care of."

"Shelby you're a lifesaver!" I said, relieved.

"I'll call Nigel and make sure he knows when to pick us up, but in the meantime, make a list of flowers and details you don't want forgotten. We can work on those today before we leave." She set a small notepad in front of me, then busied herself cleaning up the kitchen while my mind went completely blank.

I could have sat here for hours watching Robin and Sunny, mindlessly staring out the window, wasting time, but that wouldn't do anyone any good. Just as I began to jot down a few notes, Harrison kissed the top of my head and sat down beside me at the table.

"Alright, darling, I've got it all finalized. We'll be legal in the UK and in

Italy. Rupert's all set with the change in date and he's helping to secure the venue for dinner just as you asked. It will take a little travel, but we've got that covered. Rupert is on the case! He'll take care of it all."

"You've been busy in there, huh?" I rubbed the back of my neck and noticed my eyelids felt suddenly heavy.

"It's all about delegating, love. You doing okay?"

"I'm just tired. This 'growing a human' stuff isn't for the weak," I lied—well, sort of. It wasn't easy and was getting harder by the day, but I hadn't been sleeping well for a while and it was catching up to me. I sighed and searched again for Robin through the window.

"No offense, you do look a little worn out. Maybe you should lie down for a bit?" The warmth of his palm against my shoulder was a comfort.

I shrugged and shook my head. "I've got my…dress stuff this afternoon with Shelby and Nigel," I said, discouraged. "But I think maybe you're right. It can't hurt to rest for a bit. Wake me around noon if I'm not already down here, and we can have lunch together before I go?" I asked.

"Of course. I've got a few more calls to make anyhow."

"Harrison? Do we *need* a photographer?" I squinted through tired eyes.

"Well, that's up to you. Certainly I'd like to capture our day."

"I think I want to go old-school. Maybe have Nigel run a video camera or something. We can give everyone disposable film cameras and see ourselves through our friends' eyes. Thoughts?"

"I love that. Now, enough thinking, go get some rest, love." He kissed me, then as he made his way back to the library, I climbed the stairs ready to feel the coolness of my pillow and the weight of our blankets engulf me.

My eyes were barely closed when my subconscious led me straight back to the farmhouse. Relaxed in the shade of the porch, I sipped iced tea while tiny bits from a lemon slice floated like lost sailboats across its surface. The line of trees at the edge of the property stood tall, their leaves various shades of green against a deep blue, cloudless sky. A gentle breeze sent wafts of freshly mowed lawn through the porch, carrying with it the lazy summer coo of a mourning dove. In the distance, just out of sight, the sound of children's giggles could be heard. I lifted the glass of iced tea to my temple, its sweat mingling with my own, and closed my eyes as I welcomed its coolness.

The stretch of the old rusty coil spring let me know the screen door had opened. Accustomed to its familiar intrusion of peace, I braced myself for the slam I knew would follow, but it never came. I opened my eyes and found Harrison there with his own glass of iced tea. His green eyes sparkled and his easy smile was as bright as the sun. Behind him, a shaggy little white dog was at his heels, following his every move.

I watched as Harrison quietly leaned against a porch pillar and looked out over the acres of green grass and swaying fields beyond. He was barefoot, his calves lean and tan, his thighs covered by loose fitting black Bermuda-length shorts, a faded white t-shirt so worn the concert dates on the back were completely obscured, the familiar Rolling Stones tongue logo still legible across his broad shoulders. His close-cropped hair was a disheveled mess and lay sweaty against his neck, save for the mass of curls secured tightly in a claw clip atop his head. He was relaxed, sipping his tea when three children rounded the corner of the house, their exuberant laughter contagious. I watched as he glanced over his shoulder at me and smiled proudly. A boy about six—tan from spending his days outside, the crown of his curls bleached by the summer sun—was followed closely by two younger girls who looked to be around four years old, both identical, their chestnut ringlets tied up in ponytails, the only defining characteristic between them the color of their tiny hair ties. All of them were barefoot just like their daddy, the soles of their feet stained green, the twins in hot pursuit of their older brother. He'd let them catch up, then turn and raise his arms above his head and roar at them before taking off in another direction, their squeals of excitement enough to make me want another one.

Life was easy with Harrison. It was calm and he was always there. If not his own physical being, the embodiment of him in our children guaranteed I'd never be lonesome for the rest of my life. Flashbacks of births and birthday parties, Christmases, and anniversaries scrolled through my mind as I sat quietly and watched the children run themselves ragged, my husband keeping a keen eye in case he was needed to tend to a scraped knee or a stubbed toe. Harrison had been present for everything, fully hands-on, committed, and ready at a moment's notice for anything. He'd delivered our son, who'd made his entrance to this world far too quickly, an impatient soul just like his mama. He'd been by my side through IVF, handling the injections and mood swings and our firstborn while cramps kept me in bed for days on end. He never left my side when the girls arrived. We spent a month at home without them while they found their strength in the NICU, though you'd never know it looking at them today, raucous balls of unlimited energy. Every moment of our life together, Harrison had been a devoted husband, a loving and playful father, and my life raft when the current wanted to pull me under.

"Come play with us, Daddy!" a squeaky little voice called out, followed by an outburst of giggles.

Harrison set down his iced tea in front of me on the table, and leaned in for a kiss, his palm soft against my cheek. "Pray for me, darling," and in a flash, he was down the steps, arms waving above his head like a mad man, a long, loud, drawn out, "Ahhhh…" sending the kids scattering and enticing the dog from the shaded comfort of the porch out into the blazing New England summer sun.

A kiss on my cheek roused me back to reality. How was it noon already? I felt like I'd just laid my head against the pillow a second ago. I blinked hard before I turned to face Harrison.

"Was it a good one? Must have been." He smiled at me from the edge of the bed.

"What makes you ask that?" I rubbed my eyes as I tried to orient myself.

"You were smiling in your sleep. I suspect you must have been dreaming about something good." He smoothed my hair away from my face while I lay there thinking about what I'd just seen.

"You ever have déjà vu?" I asked. "Like had it actually come true? That happens to me sometimes."

"I don't know, not that I can think of off the top of my head."

I pictured the girls' ponytails bouncing along as they chased their brother. "I could tell you every single detail, but I don't want to jinx it."

"That good then?" He seemed surprised.

"Everything we've ever wanted and more." I stared up at the ceiling, replaying the images in my head, smiling to myself.

"Well, let's hope it all comes to fruition." His thumb gently grazed back and forth across my cheekbone. "Are you hungry? I've got some sandwiches made downstairs. Nigel arrived a few minutes ago and hasn't stopped talking about Rupert since he walked in the door." He rolled his eyes and smiled. "Seems all of the people we introduce around here fall in love."

"I suppose that's a good problem to have." I sat up and swung myself around to the edge of the bed beside Harrison; I knew better than to stand up too quickly these days. After a moment, he stood, reached for both of my hands, and pulled me up into a hug.

"I'm glad you got some rest; you'll need it if you plan to spend the afternoon with Nigel," he joked, his arms still wrapped tightly around me.

"Jesus, yes, I'm going to need strength. Point me in the direction of these sandwiches." I kissed his neck and we headed downstairs.

CHAPTER
55

The afternoon wasn't as hectic as I expected. Shelby's friend was a delight and worked quickly through my fitting. To my surprise, I ended up choosing a lightweight gown with an A-line empire waist and delicate, flowy petal cap sleeves. The front and the back each had respective v-cuts and a romantic sweeping train that morphed from the cream color of the dress down to faint glimpses of pale mauve along the edges, a special nod toward Harrison's gender of choice. The gown was dreamy and the lace appliqué across the bodice gave it the sense of whimsy I'd been searching for but hadn't yet found until today.

Everything was coming together; with finding the dress behind me now, somehow it all felt a lot less overwhelming. Fluffy white peonies and white ranunculus would be all I had in my bouquet. They were simple and understated but elegant and smelled heavenly. And frankly, I didn't want to fuss with details anymore. I just wanted to focus on Harrison and my vows. They were the last piece of the puzzle.

Nigel, however, had plenty of fussing to do. He couldn't wait to spill the details of his previous evening. Apparently, he and Rupert made a detour on the way to SoHo and wound up in a gelato shop for an hour swapping stories and getting to know one another, then people-watched in Chalcot Square before landing at Primrose Hill for the duration of the evening, until security kicked them out at closing time. His yammering on about Rupert was a welcome distraction from all the static in my head, and seeing him excited about someone made my heart smile. Nigel was a little high-strung and maybe some would consider him a lot to handle, but he was a sweetheart underneath all those insecurities that sometimes made him seem a little crazy.

I didn't know Rupert well enough to have any kind of opinion, other than if Nigel was happy, then I was happy. And he certainly seemed pleased, especially when they'd made plans to see each other again tonight.

Harrison met me at the door when I got home, a look of utter amazement on his face.

"Thank God you're back. You've got to come see this!" He took my hand and nearly dragged me behind him toward the patio door.

"Okay, hi, hello, I missed you too," I said sarcastically as I tried to keep pace with him.

He turned around and kissed my cheek. "Hi." He paused briefly and with a tight-lipped smile he batted his eyelashes at me, then spun back to look out the patio windows again.

"Hi." I laughed. "What am I looking at exactly? Oh, and yes, I did find a dress, thanks for asking."

"I'm sorry, love. I want to talk about your afternoon, I do, but you've missed so much while you were out. I'm just...where did it go?" He looked down his nose out across the backyard in various directions.

"Where did what go?" I asked.

"Earlier I was out here and, Alice, you won't believe it, there was a bird and it came down and sang to me."

"It *sang* to you? What did it sing? Something by the Beatles or…" I joked. "Better yet, does it take requests?" I knew exactly who he was talking about, and I knew what I was about to do was going to blow his mind.

"Fine, you make your jokes, but this was incredible. I'd never had anything like this happen to me. I felt like…like…" he searched for the words, "like a Disney princess!" His eyes were wide with wonderment.

I went back to the fridge, grabbed a few blueberries, and proceeded to the sink.

"Wait, don't go, let me see if I can find it again," he begged, his eyes glued to the windows.

I rinsed the berries under the cold water and placed them into Robin's tiny ring dish, then opened the patio door. "C'mon. Let me introduce you," I said nonchalantly. Stepping out onto the patio I sat in my usual chair with Harrison close behind me. "Take a seat."

"Robin? Where are you, friend?" I said in a sing-song voice, looking around the yard.

Harrison sat to my right, visibly confused. "Wait, what?" he asked.

"C'mon Robin, it's okay. He's safe, he won't hurt you." I set the tiny dish on the arm of the chair, exposing the blueberries. "I've got snacks," I continued to look across the yard, out toward the trees, searching the branches for him, but couldn't see him anywhere.

Then a faint rustling sound alerted me to my left, where Robin hopped out through the tiny circular door and landed on the foothold of the birdhouse Harrison had hung for him.

"There you are. Are you enjoying your new home? C'mon, Robin," I cooed.

He took flight in my direction, wings outstretched, his blaze orange breast headed straight for my hand. I could see Sunny still inside, her little head poking out of the birdhouse door, surely wondering where Robin had gone off to.

"Hey, buddy, I've missed you. You got inquisitive while I was away, huh?" Robin landed on the meat of my thumb, his tiny claws grasping hold of my skin as I used my other hand to gently stroke the feathers down the back of his head.

"What on earth?" Harrison's voice caused Robin to lift into the air, and land again, this time on the mound of berries. He clutched a large one in his foot, almost immediately tore open its skin, and began munching on the sweet fruit inside.

"Nest building is tough work and now you've got an appetite, I see." I glanced toward the birdhouse and found Sunny's little black eyes still inquisitively staring back at me. "Did you tell Sunny it was okay to come have some snacks too?"

"There's two?" Harrison blurted out, once again scaring Robin off his snacks and up onto the gutter.

"Yes. Robin and I have been friends now for quite some time. Sunny, on the other hand, just arrived recently to start a family with Robin in the house we hung for them. She seems a bit timid still. Or maybe there's already eggs in there, I'm not sure."

Harrison was dumbfounded, blinking back at me in silence.

"Robin and I have shared secrets and lots of snacks." The tiny bird once again landed on the dish beside me and started in on another berry. "Just talk slow and quietly if you must. He's not used to you yet, and I want Sunny to learn we're safe."

Harrison nodded at me slowly, apprehensively, seemingly terrified to speak.

"How have you been, Robin? Have you got babies in that house yet?"

He shook his head and bits of blueberry skin went flying. A quick little *tic tic tic* and he was back to eating, the back of my finger once again stroking his head.

"Please tell Sunny she can join us anytime. She seems lovely. I'm so happy for you both."

With that, Robin took another small berry in his grip, and off he went toward the birdhouse, delivering the small token to his lady love.

"I thought I was lucky when I saw him, but Alice, this is tremendous. And here I thought you were the one eating all the blueberries!" He shook his head, realizing his mistake. "Not only are you Cinderella, you're Snow White, too!"

Robin landed again, this time on my forearm, and looked up at me, cocking his olive-brown crown to the side, his orange chest on full display.

"Aww, I love you." I reached out to pet him again, but as all birds do from time to time, Robin shook his tiny body in a half-circle motion, ruffling his feathers and nearly doubling in size, his sudden movement causing me to pull back my hand. "You're just so adorable." I smiled down at him and then glanced at Harrison, who was still watching in amazement.

Another sideways glance and a quick *tic tic tic, tic tic tic*, then Robin hopped down to the gold embellished snack dish, took one last berry in his grip, and disappeared back into the birdhouse.

The sun had begun to set, leaving Harrison and me in the cool shadows cast by the house. I stood from my chair and reached for his hand. "Ready to go in?"

He looked up at me from his seat as if I'd just performed magic.

"What's wrong?" I asked smugly, wiggling my fingers as a means for him to hurry up.

He took my hands and stood. "You've been keeping this from me."

"Robin was my little secret, yes. It started out in such a strange way. He pecked the window whenever I was alone, and when I finally came and sat with him, we became fast friends. When you were in Brazil, we spent a lot of time together out here chatting. It was like he wanted to be sure I wasn't lonesome." I turned back toward the birdhouse. "Have a good night, Robin. G'night, Sunny." Then, hand-in-hand, Harrison and I headed back inside.

"Were you lonesome while I was away? I thought Shelby and Nigel would have kept that at bay."

I spoke over my shoulder while I washed my hands, "Well, when Shelby had gone home for the day a lot of the time she and Nigel were off together, or Nigel was handling his own form of loneliness, and I certainly wasn't going to project my issues on anyone else. I did a lot of reading, escaping in books, and you know, talking to birds." I shrugged, embarrassed.

"I'm sorry, love. You won't be faced with that ever again." He wrapped his arms around me from behind, his chin resting on my shoulder. "Where I go, you go. I promise. I know what you went through before, thinking you could count on someone and they let you down in the worst way. You won't have that with me. I honor my words." He held me a moment, breathing me in, then turned me to face him.

"How about a date night? It's still early."

"That sounds nice. Where are you thinking?"

"Oh, you leave that to me. Go find a dress that makes you feel beautiful, and let me handle the rest." He kissed me, innocently at first, then held his ground and opted for something deeper, dancing on the edge of erotic.

"You keep that up and I'm not leaving this house." My eyes flirted with his.

"Foreplay starts hours before the actual act, so, prepare yourself, love." He winked at me, the edge of his index finger holding my chin upward, he kissed me slowly, his mouth and his intentions setting my imagination ablaze.

CHAPTER
56

Two hours later when we arrived in Westminster, I emerged from the SUV in the only black dress that still fit me, heels I knew I'd regret later, a few swipes of mascara, barely there blush, and a fierce red lip, with one side of my loose waves pinned up behind my ear. Nothing remotely glamorous, but I felt beautiful, and that was the only parameter set forth for me to achieve. Harrison, on the other hand, was in a full-blown black-on-black-on-black tux, a single red calla lily pinned to his lapel, coincidentally the same shade of red as my lips. My God, he was stunning. He'd slicked his hair back at his temples and left his curls tousled up top, sparse little duck-tail curls were left peeking out from behind the bottom of his ears. He looked like a new-age James Bond, and all I could think was, *I get to go home with him tonight, and every night.*

We stepped into the Harben Room at The Pem, a privately-reserved, behind-closed-doors, intimate dining experience that promised to arouse each of the senses and take us on a journey of flavors. The place screamed of opulence, with a dining table lengthy enough to seat twenty. A red velvet runner trailed from one end of the table to the other, though nearly hidden under a succession of crimson, burgundy, and vibrant green flowers of varying heights. Flanking that stood multiple wine glasses per table setting, the sheen of their reflection enhanced by the candlelight that danced beneath them. They were right, visually, they had already aroused me.

Harrison pulled out my chair, and like the gentleman he was, waited behind me as I sat. A metallic gold feather perched on a folded cloth napkin greeted me as he helped push my chair in. He leaned down and kissed my cheek before taking his place at the end of the table to my left.

Our waiter was a slender chap bent slightly at the waist with white tufts of hair protruding straight out from the sides of his mostly bald head.

"Good evening," he drawled, two words that seemed to last a lifetime, as he filled our water glasses, white cloth over the wrist, posh as could be. Harrison's eyes met mine and he winked, then quickly scrunched his nose. I knew that move; he was thinking about peeling this dress off of me. I felt my cheeks flush as the thought crossed my mind, and fingered the diamond necklace he'd left me when I'd arrived in London, knowing it would draw his attention to my chest. I watched as he tried to keep his composure in front of our waiter, and let my ring finger trace along the rise of my cleavage, barely contained by my off-the-shoulder dress.

"The gentleman"—his accent droned monotone as he shook his head slightly upward—"has already chosen"—he raised his eyebrows and puckered his lips as his chin fell back down—"your courses for this evening." He looked up at us from under his droopy lids, his short rectangular glasses nearly falling off of his beak-like nose as he spoke. If I didn't know better, I would think he was drunk, but here in England, I knew he was just eccentric.

"Yes, on second thought, I'd like to have all the courses come at once if possible." Harrison shifted his eyes past our waiter to meet mine. "And I'd like for us not to be disturbed unless absolutely necessary." Harrison's eyes sparkled as he spoke, his jaw clenching as he anticipated the waiter's response.

"Yes, sir."

"I'd also like two Shirley Temples," Harrison added, his right eyebrow lifting as he smiled. "Tall glasses please."

"Yes, sir," he repeated slowly. "All at once." He dipped his head in acknowledgment.

"That will be all, thank you." Harrison remained focused on me until the man was gone and the door was closed fully behind him.

"What a character, huh?" he asked me.

"He reminded me of the food critic on Ratatouille, only…ancient," I whispered, fearful the man might still be within earshot.

For the first time since we sat down, Harrison smiled down toward his lap, then looked up at me again, his face serious. "Do you have any earthly idea how breathtaking you are in that dress?" he asked.

Unable to control my face, I looked at him as if waiting for a punchline, a self-deprecating habit I really needed to work on. "I guess not," I finally said.

"I couldn't have handcrafted a more perfect human to dedicate my life to. To have my child, *children* if I'm lucky." His face was smug, but I knew he was only trying to make me feel good, and my cheeks burned hot at his compliments; my heart started to race in my chest just from the way he was looking at me.

"Alice, I—"

A soft knock on the door interrupted him and sent his eyebrows into a tight pinch, his face clearly suspicious our meal might already be arriving, but only our waiter appeared, carrying a large glass carafe of water and the two Shirley Temples as requested. The open door ushered in a mingling of various scents. Savory, sweet, spicy, each one eliciting a craving without ever having been introduced to my actual tongue. Once again, The Pem had checked another of my senses off their arousal list with what seemed like very little effort, and I was eager to see what Harrison had chosen for entrées.

Our waiter shuffled toward the table at a glacial pace and unloaded the tray without a word. When he had finished, he tucked the tray under his arm and hovered a moment, then drawled, "Will there be anything else?"

"I don't mean to speak out of place, mate, but please *only* come back with our full meal, and not before. We don't want to be disturbed, even at the cost of propriety." Harrison's face was stern.

"Yes, as you wish," the older man replied and shuffled back out of the room.

I shot him a questioning look as I took a sip of the bubbly pink concoction in front of me.

"What?" he asked bluntly.

I shrugged, poking the cherries down to the bottom of the glass with my straw.

"You think I was rude." It wasn't a question.

"I think he was just trying to be accommodating to us. He's just a little old man doing his job. Probably working for tips."

"I'd given him a tip, and that was not to come back until he had everything, all at once. Or maybe you also didn't hear me when I said it?" He was scowling at me and coupled with his tone, I was triggered.

"So, an unassuming waiter made you angry and now you're going to lump me into it as well? I can go and you can really be undisturbed if you like?" I stood and pushed my chair out from behind me.

"That's a bit rash, don't you think?" He reached out in an attempt to persuade me to sit back down.

I pulled my arm away reactively. "What's rash is suddenly your knickers are in a twist because a waiter brought us drinks that you specifically requested. You're angry at him for doing his job, and on top of that you think you're going to speak to me the way you just did?" I shook my head, angry and disappointed.

"I think you might be overreacting a bit. Sit back down, please." His eyes were pleading with me far more than his words were.

Not inclined to create a scene in the restaurant, I sat down discouraged, and took another sip of my drink. Minutes passed as we sat in silence, neither of us wanting to speak first. I spent them admiring the candy apple red walls and the intricacies of the matching velvet damask pattern that swirled across them, chewing the inside of my cheek—a nervous habit when I was trying not to speak my mind, and doing almost anything not to look in Harrison's direction. It felt like he was staring at me, but I wasn't about to turn toward him to find out.

Who did he think he was? He wasn't going to speak to me like that. I lived that life already and I wasn't about to live it again. James sucked all the tolerance for that bullshit out of me completely. The more I thought, the more I chewed my cheek, and I felt myself slowly shaking my head out of frustration. *Now wait a minute, calm down. He's not James, and this isn't normal for Harrison. What must be weighing on him to make him act so out of character?* I sighed heavily, growing more irritated with my own thoughts, my face tensing more with every new question I was asking myself. *Take a drink, Alice, and chill out.* I could hear my grandmother's voice in my head. *Your face will stick like that if you keep it up.*

I looked down at the gold feather that lay against my napkin and realized she always came to me in feathers, reminding me when I needed to stop, slow down, and think things through. If she were here, she'd be saying, *don't be so quick to anger; the world's not ending, this is just a misunderstanding. Don't be rash, you love this man for good reason.*

The silence was becoming awkward, but my stubbornness wasn't going to allow me to break first. I knew if I looked at him, I'd melt like I always did, so my eyes remained focused on the flowers in front of me, the snake-like dance of the candle's flame, their reflections on the empty wine glasses, anything but Harrison.

Another knock at the door and I braced myself for Harrison to come undone, but as the door opened, I looked beyond him and saw our older gentleman had been replaced with three women of various ages pushing carts covered in plates, and as they placed them gently on our table, each one looked more divine than the last. Asparagus tart with spring greens, roast lamb and mash with a silken gravy, stuffed artichokes, poached fish. The dessert array was just as enticing. Lemon meringue accompanied by sorbet and hazelnuts, slices of chocolate torte with raspberries standing proud atop them, vibrant sprigs of mint erupting from their hollowed tops and raspberry sauce draped over the torte's edges, chocolate cake with vanilla bean cream and cherries. There was no way we could eat all this, but damn if I wasn't going to try.

"Good evening, Mr. Edwards. As the executive chef here, I'd like to personally welcome you and Alice to The Pem. We hope your experience here is extraordinary, and one that not only invigorates your senses but remains exciting in your mind long after you've gone home. Your choices tonight are excellent, and we look forward to seeing you again soon." Her smile was one of confidence, as she stood proudly at the edge of our table.

"Thank you, this all looks incredible. I've looked forward to dining here for some time, and appreciate the care you put into your craft. I see that you also support the Young Women's Trust. We will certainly be making a donation before we leave this evening." He nodded.

"Thank you, Mr. Edwards. Please enjoy and let me know if there is anything else we can take care of for you this evening."

Harrison's eyes scanned across each of the plates and finally landed on the carafe of water. "I think we are set up to have a perfect evening, but thank you. We would, however, like to remain undisturbed for the remainder of our meal."

"Absolutely, Mr. Edwards. Enjoy." She turned and, flanked by the other two women, headed back toward the main dining room. The door closing behind them returned us once again to awkward silence.

CHAPTER 57

We ate without a word. I'd take what I wanted while avoiding his glances and he'd finish what remained. Silverware against fine china was all that could be heard until I reached for the chocolate torte. He took the plate from my hand, tenderly setting it back down on the table. I still didn't look at him. I just let him take it and focused on the table in front of me as he took my left hand in his. I knew this was an unspoken white flag, a peace offering. A truce. I didn't want to be mad at him, I just wanted him to know I wasn't going to be spoken to like a child being reprimanded or like one of his employees. I was no less than he was, and in my heart, I knew he knew that. I swallowed hard and nervously straightened my fork beside my empty plate.

"I love you," he said quietly and squeezed my hand. "This isn't how I wanted this night to go. I wanted to talk about the wedding and our future. I didn't want us to sit here in silence. This was meant to be Mum and Dad's fancy night out on the town."

Reluctantly I shifted my eyes to meet his, never turning my head.

"I'm sorry. I shouldn't have spoken to you like that, Alice. Of all people, I know what you've endured, and you don't deserve anyone, especially me, talking to you in that way. Can you forgive me?"

I turned to him, his apology making my willfulness suddenly dissipate. "I'm sorry too. I shouldn't have barked at you either. I'm sorry I ruined dinner."

"Nothing is ruined. We're bound to have disagreements; we are only human after all, and certainly not perfect. What matters is that we talk through things and find compromises. Treat each other with kindness and love."

"So, you don't think I'm perfect?" I joked, trying to make things feel less heavy.

He smiled. "I mean…" He glanced down, then shifted his eyes back up to mine, licking his lips.

"Baby, I'm perfect for you. And you know it." I stared back at him flirtatiously with a quick one-sided nose scrunch to try and make him laugh.

"The only thing stopping me from clearing this table, and making love to you right here, right now, is the fact that there's about a hundred courses worth of plates covering it."

I shrugged. "I guess that's your choice."

"Is that so?" He seemed shocked. "So, what if I…" He let go of my hand and his fingertips grazed the side of my exposed thigh under the table, the slit in my dress allowing for easy access.

I pulled in a quick deep breath at the warmth of his touch and held it while his fingertips breached the boundaries of my gown. His palm hot against my upper thigh, I closed my eyes, letting that same deep breath escape through my nose, I tried to maintain a straight face as his palm slid further and further up.

"Should I stop?" he asked.

I shook my head. "No." I swallowed hard. I wasn't sure if it was his accent, the bass in his voice, or the look in his eyes, but I wanted this man, and I wanted him now.

"Hmm, what about if I…" His hand moved toward my inner thigh.

I uncrossed my legs and shifted my posture, allowing him better access, then watched as a surprised yet satisfied look spread across his face.

"Is that an invitation, Mrs. Edwards?" His nostrils flared and the familiar Cheshire cat grin appeared.

"Maybe it is if you're going to call me that," I teased, and let my legs fall open a bit more.

Harrison looked at me a moment as if trying to gauge my level of seriousness, his eyes narrowing, unsure if I was truly willing to do such a thing in a restaurant. Then as if some steadfast decision had been made in his head, he stood from his chair and walked toward the door. He stood for a moment with his back to me and I imagined the devilish look that must be on his face. His shoulders rose and his back straightened as he took a deep breath, then with a twist of his fingers, I heard the door lock, ensuring we wouldn't be interrupted.

He turned to face me and smiled, his lustful eyes locked on mine as he walked back to the table. Then, one by one, he carefully began stacking plates, one on top of the other, with no regard for the remaining food he was smashing between them. He continued in silence until two neat piles stood before him, silverware jumbled together at their tops; the only remaining plate held the torte and the raspberry sauce, placed intentionally just beyond my reach. He was in no rush, just building the anticipation in his mind I was sure, while I was turned on simply by watching my future husband take care of the dishes. He pushed the two stacks back, clearing the entire end of the table where he'd been sitting all evening, the muscles in his jaw clenching while he did it, a sure sign he was seeing this play out in his mind. He wiped his hands on his napkin, let his tux jacket slip backward off his shoulders, and neatly draped it over the back of his chair as I sat there fixated on his every move. Then he shifted his focus to me.

Harrison stepped to the side of the table where I'd been sitting. All six feet of him stood over me looking absolutely delicious as he grabbed at his bowtie with his right hand and pulled it loose, leaving its untied edges to lay against the clearly defined muscles beneath his shirt. He unfastened the top two buttons and pulled at his collar, exposing the tattoos at the top of his chest. He reached down, placed his hands on my knees, and gently spun me in my chair to face him. I looked up and smirked knowing it would send his thoughts into overdrive. He expected me to be timid in this setting, and I was determined to show him I wasn't. He extended his palms to me, inviting me to stand in front of him and when I did, he softly kissed the top of each of my hands and placed them on his shoulders. The king of the smoldering stare held me captivated and smiled just enough to produce the dimple I loved, knowing that's all it took to bring me to my knees. We always did more talking with our eyes than we ever did with our mouths when we were intimate. He had eight inches on me and there was never a time that didn't play to his advantage.

With my hands on his shoulders, he kissed me deeply, his palms at my jaw, his fingertips in my hair. As his tongue explored mine, his hands fell to my hips, pulling me back toward the space he'd been sitting for dinner. He moved the chair out of the way with his foot, leaned my butt back against the table's edge, then leaned himself up against me. His mouth on my exposed neck, his hand gliding up my back and into my hair again, he continued to kiss me as our breathing deepened. Then suddenly he stopped. He stood a moment, slipped a thumb beneath each of his suspenders and pulled them down over his shoulders, letting them fall to his sides while looking me up and down. He took a seat in front of me, positioning my legs between his thighs.

He looked up grinning, his green eyes electric against the dark frame of lashes. It was as if he was telling me he craved me without saying a word, then let his forehead fall softly against my belly, pausing as my fingers ran through his curls. He looked up at me again but still said nothing, only smiled mischievously before kissing my abdomen. I tried to read his thoughts as he stared up at me and I stroked his cheek with my thumb. Was he nervous? Was he trying to work up the courage to make love to me in public? Or was he just trying to make this last? I couldn't tell, but I had no intention of turning back now.

He kissed me hard, his hand falling from my cheek to my bare shoulder, the tip of his middle finger tracing down the length of my left arm. He pulled his mouth from mine long enough to watch his own hands as they moved, his left settling around my waist, pulling my body against his, while his right reached for the zipper of my gown running the length of my side. Inch by inch the zipper lowered, and my dress fell further open to expose the black lace bra and satin panties hidden beneath it. Soon, the heat of his hand against the bare skin of my abdomen was all I felt as he let my dress fall fully to the floor.

He stood back to admire my body and once again unleashed the left dimple I was so God damned fond of, then wrapped one arm around my back and lifted me up to rest on the table's edge in front of him. He sat back down, and as his eyes remained locked on mine, he took each of my shoes off then let them fall to the floor, intentionally resting my feet on the outside of his thighs. He gently kissed each of my knees, then pushed each one outward before looking up at me again. I watched him, trusting him, hopeful but unsure of what his next move would be. He watched me while his tongue alternated between my inner thighs, accompanied by kisses on the left then the right, higher and higher, until his lips grazed my satin-covered center. He paused and smiled, licking his lips as his nostrils flared in anticipation. Was he looking for permission? Reassurance I was still willing? Maybe he expected me to tell him to stop? Maybe he just wanted to know I was watching him pleasure me. I didn't know, but every time he looked at me, I just wanted to scream for more.

I could tell he was trying to savor this experience. With his palms at the back of each of my knees, he pulled me closer to the edge of the table, closer still against his ever-hardening, throbbing body. His hands slid upward over my ribs, up over my breasts, his index fingers slowing to tuck themselves inside the lace edging of my bra then tracing outward, teasing their release. He leaned in, his breath against my skin as his right hand slipped behind me to release the hooks that held me captive. His fingers tickled my spine, his touch hot against the cold air in the restaurant that aided in keeping parts of my body at attention.

We didn't speak, just remained fixed on each other's gaze while his hands roamed my body and mine undid the remaining buttons on his shirt exposing his tanned, tattooed abdomen. I ran my fingers up into the back of his hair, gripping fistfuls I pulled his face closer to me, then kissed him with a feverish passion. His right hand landed playfully against my throat, and I tipped my head back as he squeezed carefully, while his mouth explored my breasts, one then the other and back again. He was making this about my pleasure more than his own.

My body was eager as his hands squeezed at both sides of my waist, then slid backward reaching for my ass cheeks, his hands positioning me right where he wanted me, pressing my knees further outward. His open mouth at my cleavage, I watched him start to lose control then slow himself down again by nuzzling his cheeks against the skin of my chest. A deep breath later, he cradled my thigh against his ribs while his other hand eased me backward on the table, his caress assisting in the arching of my back. Soon his index finger fell to my lips, the raspberry sauce from the torte dripping toward his first knuckle begging to be tasted. I took his finger into my mouth, twisting my tongue around it, licking and sucking until it was clean. He teased it down the center of my body from my chin to between my breasts and then landed exactly where I wanted him the most. A quick burst of air through his nose let me know he was satisfied that everything leading up to this point had adequately prepared me to handle everything he had to give.

I listened as he unfastened his pants, and let my hands roam over my own body while he did it, knowing he was watching. Then he grabbed my hips and pulled me just beyond the table's edge, his fingertips parting me as he raked my panties to the side. I felt him slide into me slowly, a little at a time then pull out, over and over again until he was as deep as he could get. Then he paused and I watched as his head bowed in satisfaction exhaling through his nose. One hand back on my hip, the other holding my panties, he pulled back and thrust fully into me. Wine glasses fell and rolled off the table as he continued. Candles were knocked over, their flames dispelled by their own hot liquids, and with every earth-shattering plunge, the stacks of plates rattled, threatening to topple over and alert an entire dining room of our scandalous behavior. No matter how I tried, I couldn't get a firm grip on the edge of the table, and no matter how laden with full vases it was, that table runner was getting pushed further and further toward the other end with each of Harrison's herculean efforts. And just when I thought he'd start slowing down, he worked even harder. He swiped his finger through the raspberry sauce again and painted a heart around each of my nipples, making sure each was sucked thoroughly clean as he rhythmically pushed himself into me. His thumb lightly circled my clit in unison with his thrusts, causing my body to tighten uncontrollably. My back arched and I clawed at the table as I closed my eyes and fell into the space of darkness where the stars shined and everything felt warm. I lost control of myself against him, and lay there unable to catch my breath, my body pulsating, and shortly thereafter so did he.

CHAPTER 58

Harrison lurched forward, his hands flat against the table on either side of my head, bracing himself while he caught his breath, leaving my panties to snap back into their intended position, forcing an unexpected gasp out of me and causing a new wave of arousal in an already sensitive spot.

"I can't believe we just did that," he said between heavy breaths. His head was bowed and I couldn't see his face.

"Second round in the main dining room?" I joked and watched his head pop up in shock.

"Alice!" he exclaimed, his voice apparently louder than intended. He quickly covered his mouth with his hand.

"Your cheeks are pink," I teased.

"Well, that's your fault." He huffed, still trying to regulate his breathing. "We've got to clean this up and get out of here." He shook his head and then let it fall forward again, kissing my belly while he was down there.

"You're going to have to help me up," I laughed as I tried to lift myself onto my elbows at least.

"Okay." He looked up at me. "On the count of three. Ready? One…two…" He sucked in a deep breath, then let his head fall forward again as he blew it out, his curls tumbling forward in the process. "Darling, you've exhausted me. Think they'll notice if we just sleep here?"

"C'mon," I struggled to lift my back off the table. "I'm too old to be splayed out on a dining room table that's not in the privacy of my own home." I wiggled my fingers at him, begging for assistance.

He stood and pulled me by both hands into a sitting position, and when I was finally able to see the extent of the mess we created on the table behind me, my mouth fell open. "Harrison, we're going to be in trouble."

He scurried past me as he tucked himself back into his boxer briefs and pulled his pants back up over his ass, leaving them unfastened. I watched as he grabbed the carafe of water, much of it already spilled over its edge, then lifted it to his mouth and swallowed down what was left.

"Let me get my clothes back on and I'll help you." I reached for my bra and once everything was back in place, I slipped my dress and my shoes back on and smoothed my hair.

Behind me, Harrison was using a credit card to scrape the hardened wax off the tabletop, but I knew from years of keeping house, it had the potential to leave a permanent mark. Fingers crossed we hadn't ruined something important. I quickly straightened the flower arrangements and the table runner, and tried to move the broken wine glasses into a more cohesive pile with my foot. Once we'd done all we could to get the place back to the way we found it, Harrison fastened his pants and got his shirt and bowtie put back in place and threw his jacket on while I texted Lawrence to meet us out front.

"You think anyone's out there?" I asked, growing increasingly concerned. "Do you think anyone heard us?" I was terrified to open the door and find someone on the other side ready to throw us out in some giant spectacle or publicly reprimand us at the very least.

Harrison cracked the door open and peered out. "I think…" he whispered, "*this* is incredibly obvious." He turned to me and laughed then fully opened the door. "The coast is clear. Let's go. You head for the car, I'll handle the bill." He kissed my cheek and off I went toward the door in search of Lawrence.

Headed for home, we chatted behind the closed partition about the excellent food, the attention to detail of the entire experience, and the service. Harrison explained how he left our gentleman waiter a nice tip along with a short note of apology for being so abrupt with him, which pleased me. Harrison Edwards was a lot of things, but rude wasn't one of them. I didn't entirely know what got into him, and honestly, I didn't want to bring it up. I just wanted it behind us. He also said he'd left tips for the three women who'd delivered our delicious meal and what he described as a "healthy" donation for the Young Women's Trust as promised. Part of me wondered if we'd get an invoice for ruining their table or for the broken wine glasses, but Harrison assured me he told them we'd knocked over a candle, and in the panic of trying to contain it, a couple of wine glasses had toppled over and hit the floor. *Such a bullshitter*, I thought. *You should have told them you were railing me to death on their dining room table. Bet that would have gotten you a few interesting looks, and probably a nice spot on their blacklist.*

We also chatted about last-minute wedding plans, and I caught Harrison up on the flowers I'd chosen, as well as odds and ends for the celebration dinner. I mentioned the hotel room configurations and how if things kept moving at lightning speed with Nigel and Rupert, we might have an extra room available to use as my bridal suite.

And then as we pulled into the driveway, Harrison reminded me just how incredibly close it all was to being real, and that soon, I really would be Mrs. Edwards. Saying it out loud wouldn't just be some playful nickname.

But the voice in my head just kept repeating, *you'll be Mrs. No One if you don't get your vows written, Alice.*

CHAPTER
59

The last five days were busy with details, and I'd recount all the things I accomplished if only I could remember them. I knew Harrison and I spent one day at Kew Gardens because that just happened yesterday. He'd watched me become so tightly wound over writing vows and worrying my dress wouldn't fit that he'd whisked me away for a day of flowers and fun to try to calm my nerves. The Orchid Festival was on, as well as an exhibit called "When Flowers Dream" which was an absolutely stunning mix of artwork to witness. We'd gone unnoticed despite the festival happening, and even though the walking was good for me, honestly, I think Harrison was trying to tire me out. There had been late nights, shower times, early mornings, afternoons, and I spent every waking moment thinking about the things I wanted him to know, about the ways I adored him, the ways he changed my life, made me feel safe, the way I never wanted to live another moment without him by my side. But wasn't that what every bride feels and says? Wasn't that expected? No one showed up to their own wedding and said, 'Well, you make a decent sandwich and I appreciate you consistently putting the toilet seat down. Here's to forever.' Would I fret so much over these vows if he wasn't who he was? His celebrity didn't factor into my feelings for him at all, but it did play a role in the fact that one day, these vows of mine could leak to the public somehow. I was well aware now, that everything could always potentially leak, and would I be scrutinized for not being eloquent enough? Or being too sentimental? Of course, I couldn't win; I'd always be too much or not enough in the public's eyes. Or was my need to make this such a memorable admission of devotion because I didn't get to do all of this the first time around? My first wedding had been held in a local park, with a barbeque in my mother's backyard afterward purely to appease the family. It was nothing I wanted, and that included the marriage itself, in the very beginning, but I'd made the best of it. Needless to say, last night I was asleep as soon as my head hit the pillow, a welcome change from the more recent norm.

The previous four days were a lot fuzzier in my memory; I know we picked out wedding bands together, Harrison opting for a gorgeous hammered black tungsten with a rose gold interior and thin rose gold inlay. The shine of the gold against the depth of black reminded me of the first time I saw Harrison's bathroom with its glossy black marble floors, the hammered copper tub, and the way the light hit its finish and cast glimmers across Harrison's wet abdomen as he made love to me in the shower. And now, watching as he tried on his wedding band, the matte black of the ring against the tattoo on his hand and the shine of the gold was stunning. I opted for the much thinner, daintier, matching diamond-encrusted rose gold band, its sparkle would be a permanent reminder of those glimmers.

I know there was time outside spent with Robin and Sunny, though she was still far too afraid of me to venture out and say a proper hello. Maybe it was because she was on the verge of laying eggs? Or it could be she just wasn't used to humans the way Robin seemed to be. Either way, Robin kept her supplied with plenty of snacks; as soon as I doled them out, he shared half with her. Then there was time spent in our own home gardens, out in nature, hands in the dirt in an attempt to quiet my mind, but that didn't work. It only left me alone with my thoughts, undisturbed, aside from Robin perching on my shoulder, waiting for me to unearth a good worm or two for him.

There were very early mornings when I lay in bed and watched Harrison as he slept, dissecting every move we'd made together in the last five months, remembering moments and scribbling bits here and there on post-it notes of things I wanted to remember for my vows, all of their various vibrant colors left clinging to the screen of my closed laptop, awaiting their final sequencing.

There'd been a dress fitting in there somewhere as well. Shelby and I had gone together, and how I managed to get out without Nigel or security was beyond me. The dress shop tailored a bit more, let out the bosom a smidge, and hemmed up the train a little after I explained the number of stairs I'd need to climb to reach the sanctuary. And after seeing it on again, I'd requested they add the tiniest bit of sparkle detail to the bodice in amongst the lace, just for a little something extra. The dress wasn't what I'd originally pictured when I thought of a wedding to Harrison Edwards. It seemed too casual, too plain, but for early spring in Italy overlooking a gorgeous sandy beach and turquoise water for as far as the eye could see, I knew it would be perfect.

After breakfast this morning, Shelby waited until Harrison was back in the library on the phone with Rupert, then pulled me into the guest room, and to my surprise, there was my dress hanging in its travel bag, finished and ready to carry me into my future. I lowered the zipper and found the detailing I'd asked for had been beautifully hand-stitched. It wasn't overly shimmery, it wasn't too ornate, it was just perfectly eye-catching. I stood there a moment and stared at it, wondering if Harrison would like it and how it would look against his suit. Then I felt Shelby's arm around my shoulder.

"You're going to stop him in his tracks." She leaned her head against mine and squeezed me tighter. It was almost as if she could read my mind.

"You think so?"

"Oh, I know so. That man is so taken with you. There are two things I know about Harrison. One, when he loves someone, he makes sure they feel it. And two, when he knows something is right, he shows no hesitation. And he's done that with you. Look at all that's happened in such a short time. You said yourself, he saw you smile at The Spaniards Inn that night and he approached you. He found out you were married and didn't shy away; he sought an explanation. He's never wavered, never second-guessed. Alice, he messaged me the night he met you."

"He did?" I turned to face her, inquisitive for more.

"He couldn't wait to tell me about you. He said, 'I think I've found the one, Shelb, she's unlike anyone I've ever known.' He knew the moment he laid eyes on you."

I was flattered, not only by what he'd said to her, but by the fact that he couldn't contain it, didn't want to. Harrison made me feel like a priority in his life every second of the day, as if I was all that mattered, and though he showed me how he felt about me, the reassurance of hearing it from someone else drove home just how much he really did love me.

"I can't wait for Sunday," I said quietly.

"Four more days." Shelby smiled as she pulled the zipper closed on the travel bag.

"Think you can keep him occupied a while today? I've got to sit down and focus on organizing my thoughts. I've got to get these vows finished."

"Of course. He's got Lawrence taking him somewhere today anyhow, and had asked me to keep *you* occupied. Sneaky little devil. I wonder what he's up to." She puckered her lips and looked at the ceiling as she tapped her chin with her finger suspiciously.

"What do you know?" I demanded.

"I could be completely wrong, but I think he's going to get your wedding gift," she whispered begrudgingly.

"SHIT!" I exclaimed, frustrated with myself for forgetting about wedding gifts. "Shelby I'd forget my own head somewhere if it wasn't attached."

"Take your time today. When you're done, we'll go out and take care of his gift. Everything will be fine."

"I don't know what I'd do without you. You welcomed me in here and became my friend. Hell, you're like a sister to me. You keep my frazzled head on straight most days. I hope you know just how much I appreciate you." I wrapped my arms around her.

"Ah, well," she hugged me back, "Harrison doesn't invite just anyone home with him. He keeps a well-curated select few in his tight little circle." She patted my back before pulling away to face me. "I'm thankful for it, and I'm thankful for you. I've come to love you and all your frazzles." She smiled sweetly. "Now go, get your writing done. Find me when you're finished."

Three hours later, my vows were finally, perfectly complete, and my head was still spinning as Shelby and I circled the round-about on our way into the city with Nigel at the wheel and Hank riding shotgun. I'd had an epiphany while writing my vows, giving me the perfect idea for Harrison's gift. I just needed to get back to the jewelry shop. I didn't feel like I needed to bring the entire crew with me to do it, but this time I couldn't sneak away. Shelby, Hank and Nigel chatted while I stared out the window feeling like I never left the house without an entourage anymore, questioning whether or not having them around me called more attention to the group as opposed to me just going out alone. It wasn't safe anymore, especially pregnant, but to aimlessly wander a bookstore or waste hours admiring architecture while inside my own head had been one of my favorite pastimes, and now, that sadly seemed to be a thing of the past.

While the jeweler engraved Harrison's gift and Shelby took a call outside, I sat quietly watching Hank admire himself in the mirror, not at all an uncommon thing for him, as he tried on different chains. On the other side of the gallery, Nigel sat at a counter, experimenting with pinky rings, each one larger and more gaudy than the last. We were a sometimes odd and definitely eclectic bunch, but I was sure glad *these* people had become *my* people. Hank would protect me at absolutely any cost, and Nigel and Shelby would fight to the death for me, and I for each of them. And as much as I grumbled about never being alone, the despair I used to live with, drown in from constant loneliness would never be an issue again now that I had them around me. There had been days I begged the stars to save me from always feeling so alone, and now I was surrounded by love and care all the time. I had Harrison to thank for that, or maybe it was fate.

"Okay that's sorted. One less thing to think about," Shelby announced as she walked back through the door toward me, her voice rattling me from my inner thoughts.

"What's that?" I asked.

"The venue for dinner wasn't sure about any food allergies, and they wanted to finalize the way the place settings were laid out. All sorted, not to worry." She slipped her phone back into her purse and sighed as she sat down beside me. "Where were you?" she asked. "You looked a million miles away."

"I'm exhausted. How do you think Harrison will take it when I tell him I want a month honeymoon?" I rubbed my temples with my fingertips.

"I think you could tell him you wanted a holiday on the moon and he'd find a way to make it happen." She gave me a knowing look and I chuckled because she was absolutely right.

The jeweler appeared from the back room and presented me with Harrison's gift tucked nicely into a small polished walnut box. It was perfect, just as I'd envisioned it would be, and I knew Harrison was going to love it. I thanked the gentleman for his attention to detail and his willingness to drop everything to help me ensure this wedding gift was memorable. I paid the bill, and we were off again, headed for home.

Shelby was right, everything was sorted. It was time to catch a flight.

CHAPTER 60

After a short two-and-a-half-hour flight, we arrived in Naples, Italy. Mount Vesuvius greeted us as we made our descent and beyond that, from the air, Naples appeared like an abstract Claude Monét version of Waterlilies II or Flower Beds at Vétheuil; the deep blue of the ocean, its white surf lapping against a landscape dappled in vibrant dots of pinks, yellows, and oranges broken up by the verdant green of the treetops. Italy was going to change my life; I felt it before my feet even touched the ground.

Thanks to Rupert we'd secured not only private ground transportation to the port required to get to Capri, but also a private ferry service, and as we shuffled through the airport in search of the bus, I found I was overwhelmed by beautiful people quick to smile and offer a welcoming *"Buongiorno"* as we passed by. Most of our group spoke fluent Italian, Harrison and Rupert especially, but Emma and I were lucky to understand even the most common words. Harrison told me he'd spent time in Italy throughout his life, a summer here, a winter there. He'd filmed here and he'd vacationed, and I quickly noticed an obvious ease about him. He didn't seem tense and he wasn't scanning the people around him like he did in London or New England, like I now felt myself doing. No one seemed to bother him, no phones were out to sneak photos, no commotion ensued, no crowds gathered. There was no screaming or grabbing or paparazzi stopping us or slowing us down. Maybe this was why he was so agreeable to spending such a long honeymoon here. And listening to Harrison speak full conversations to people in Italian, well that just made me want to rip his clothes off, and it took every ounce of decorum I had in me to resist.

Soon we were on the ferry, bouncing and bobbing along in the very active Tyrrhenian Sea, my gills turning greener with every wave that splashed over the bow. In my wildest imagination I never would have thought I'd be seasick on a ferry boat on my way to Capri to have dinner before my wedding to Harrison Edwards, but here we were, head hung between my knees as I sat at the back of the boat, Harrison by my side.

Tonight we would dine beneath the lemon trees at Da Paolino, but today we would settle into our villa and relax a while. The temperatures here were warmer than London, but this year they'd been unseasonably so, hovering around 70 Fahrenheit at the height of the afternoon for the past three days. Up until now, I'd been eager to sit out and enjoy the sun, but the way this boat was rocking, I just wanted to lay down and be still.

"It won't be much longer now, love. Sometimes it helps if you can see land, and I can see the island coming into view. Do you want to pick your head up and maybe that will help?" Harrison rubbed my back as he tried to console me.

"I think I'm okay right where I am, as long as I don't think about it or, you know, move, I think I'll be alright." I could feel myself swaying with the movement of the boat, and thinking about it made me want to vomit. I shifted my body, pulling my knees up into the fetal position on the bench, my head in Harrison's lap.

"Try to be still." He stroked my hair. "We'll be there soon. Just hold on as best you can."

I closed my eyes and tried to focus on my breathing, counting in, two, three, and out, two, three, over and over, and pictured myself lying comfortably on our couch in London. Still, solid, unmoving. Harrison's hand rhythmically brushing over my temple, smoothing my hair back, lulled me straight into unconsciousness. Forty-five minutes later the ferry was docked, and I was upright again without incident, walking down the gangway that led to the private entrance of our villa.

Perched up on a hill, the home stood three stories high, each upper-level room with its own balcony, a terrace flanked with gardens and citrus trees, and the expansive lawn that sprawled down toward the ocean had been perfectly manicured, showcasing fancy crisscrossing stripes left behind by the landscaper.

As an ornate stone pathway ushered us upward, Rupert rattled off the property amenities, but I was only half-listening. I heard, "Nine bedrooms all with private baths," and "An outdoor kitchen and bocce ball court," while the string of plush chaise lounges that sat in ankle-deep water on the sun shelf of the infinity pool held my attention.

"I'll be seeing *you* soon," I mumbled to them as I continued toward the house.

Stark white marble floors and a fully white interior made the villa seem hollow. The tiniest sound begged an echo to bounce off the walls, while the only colors to be found were the greenery of the garden and deep cerulean sea views from every window. There were a few random swipes of neon pink and orange strewn haphazardly across the designer pillows on the furniture, but that was it for interior color. This space was meant for a very upscale client, and while I knew Rupert was trying to make sure there was room for everyone and show us all a great time, I felt incredibly out of place, shushed almost, like whispers were the only appropriate way to communicate. There was no warmth, no coziness, just a museum-like feel that made me anxious to get back outside.

Everyone vanished in search of their preferred room, while I stood there, frozen by my nerves.

"You're not happy?" Harrison whispered to me.

"I'm okay. Overwhelmed I guess," I whispered back.

"Your face is saying otherwise." His eyes scanned me, concerned.

"I'm okay. Still just not feeling great. I think I'd like to rest a while out by the pool." I tried to appease him with a grin, an attempt to get my face to match my words.

"You're sure? Not getting cold feet on me, are you?" He held me by my shoulders, his eyes begging for reassurance.

"You can't be serious!" came out louder than I expected. Embarrassed from the echo, I glanced around to see if anyone was listening. "No," I whispered. "Never! I'd like to skip all of this quite frankly and just get straight to the ceremony."

"Then tell me what's bothering you."

"I just feel out of place here. I don't know how else to describe it. I'm sorry." I felt terrible saying it out loud, and I hoped he didn't think I was ungrateful, plus the disappointment in his expression didn't help. "The bright side is, I've got you here with me, and it's only one night. Come sit by the pool with me a while? Maybe after we can take a walk before we head off to dinner?" I asked, trying to perk him back up.

"We can do that, but I need to know what's making you feel out of place?" he questioned. "I don't understand."

"It's so empty feeling and quiet and, see, we're both whispering. I feel like I shouldn't touch anything and like I can't talk at a normal volume in here." I bit at the inside of my cheek, uneasy. "You probably think I'm crazy."

He looked at me a moment, mischief in his eyes, then yelled at the top of his lungs, "CRAZY?" his eyes wide, teasing. His voice bouncing off the walls, the floors, the ceiling. "NOT AT ALL!" he laughed.

I rubbed my forehead with my palm, further embarrassed and he pulled me into a hug.

"Scream all night long if you want, darling!" he reassured me.

"Or don't," Shelby muttered as she breezed back into the room looking like a brand-new woman in a wide-brimmed hat and a long, pastel yellow sundress, Julian on her arm, proud as a peacock.

"Where are you off to?" Harrison asked.

"We're all going to head into town, make sure everything is set for tonight. Thought you two might like a little alone time anyhow." She pushed her oversized sunglasses on. "Need anything while we're out? We're going to stop into a grocery and get some snacks and drinks before we head back."

Harrison glanced at me, then looked back at Shelby. "You know what we like, and thanks for being so thoughtful."

"No need to christen all the rooms while we're gone either," Emma chimed in jokingly as she appeared from another bedroom, hand-in-hand with Lawrence.

"Yeah, keep off the countertops too," Shelby said as everyone in our group made their way out the door together, laughing.

"Looks like we'll have the pool to ourselves then." Harrison winked at me. "C'mon, let's find a room and get changed."

CHAPTER

61

The afternoon had been delicious with Harrison, quietly lounging by the pool, soft touches and adoring looks, the sun warm on our skin, and the sounds of the seabirds down near the ocean as our soundtrack. We'd talked about the honeymoon and what spots we wanted to see the most in Rome, Venice, Sicily, Tuscany, and we even added Florence to the list. We spent a little time feeling the baby kick and discussed names. We decided to ask Shelby to be the godmother and Lawrence to be the godfather, the two most loyal and dependable options should anything ever happen to us. A huge consideration and responsibility, we opted to wait and breach that topic with them after we returned from the honeymoon. We also spent a little of our afternoon daydreaming together, eyes closed, speaking our future into existence. Harrison surprised me by saying he might like to buy a plot of land somewhere back in New England one day to keep me connected to the place I'd loved my entire life; the dream I'd had of him and the children running in the yard lit up my mind when he said it. He asked if I thought James would put the land up for sale now that the house was nothing more than a pile of ash, and I couldn't help but laugh knowing I'd never want to be back there again on that property. House or no house, the memories there were more plentiful than the leaves on the trees, invisible like pollen until you realized they were choking you to death. No thanks. I'd pass on that.

Soon the gang was back and it was time to head out for our celebration dinner. Everyone was dressed 'casually classy' as requested; the men wore suit pants and button-down shirts while the ladies wore long summery dresses. The evening remained warm as the early spring heatwave showed no signs of departure, the breezes slowed, and the ocean fell calm as the sun began to sink lower in the sky.

We arrived at Da Paolino promptly at 5 p.m. and I was met with the most beautiful scene I'd ever witnessed. Granted, I'd chosen all the details, but to see it in real life and not just in my imagination was enchanting. The long white table was set for twelve. Yellow chargers held mosaic blue and pink plates, a discreet nod to our thirteenth guests' unknown gender. White cloth napkins cradled gold silverware, each held in place by the weight of a single perfect lemon. Pristine wine glasses and champagne flutes stood tall behind clear water glasses accented with cobalt stripes, while textured turquoise glass vases overflowing with hot pink and buttery-yellow roses were arranged at either end of the table. A grouping of cream-colored votive and pillar candles sat nestled amongst dozens of whole and half-cut lemons in the center of the table. The visual was gorgeous and the scent in the space was invigorating. Lemon trees canopied the entire table, their trunks growing out of designated openings in the floor. Lush green leaves and bright yellow fruit illuminated by the under glow of the candles clung tight to the draping branches above us and emitted the most delicious smell.

In no time we were being catered to; the champagne flowed, the wine abundant, and everyone seemed to be enjoying themselves. For the first time in a long time, I noticed Lawrence was the one who couldn't take his eyes off Emma instead of the other way around, while Nigel and Rupert were in their own world at the other end of the table, sharing soft touches, sweet glances, and believe it or not, a few stolen kisses when they thought no one was looking. Shelby and Julian were always making each other laugh and tonight was no exception; they giggled and playfully touched one another all evening while Hank and his lady-friend and Victor and his plus-one congregated as their own sub-group just like always. The first and second courses came and went, followed by the third, and then the most luxurious assortment of desserts I'd ever seen in my life appeared. Tiramisu that at first glance was easily six layers deep in individual etched-glass goblets, raspberry Bomboloni—Italy's version of a jelly-filled donut hole—stacked in a pillow-soft pyramid and dusted with a combination of cinnamon and powdered sugar. And the star of the show, a triple-layer lemon blueberry cake. Luscious mascarpone and lemon curd filling spilled from each tier's circumference while purple orbs peeked from dense blankets of pale yellow cake, giving it a rustic appearance; the top of the cake offered a bit more pizzazz as tufts of sugared mascarpone stood tall, the entire top layer dusted with edible gold leaf and bits of lemon zest mingled amongst candied lemon twists and blueberries. A tangy lemon glaze drizzled from all its edges and pooled at its base on the cake stand. It was almost too beautiful to cut into…almost.

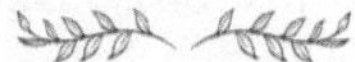

Indulgence seemed to be the only word that could describe tonight. The calming trickle of a nearby water fountain, the flavors of authentic Italian fare being served by a world-renowned chef, the scent of lemons and cinnamon, and Harrison's cologne beside me combined with the dancing candlelight and the laughter of the people I considered family…Capri had proven itself abundant in all things. My heart was full as I glanced around at everyone having the time of their lives, all of them here to celebrate the love that Harrison and I had found in one another, many of them in love themselves. Then I realized Harrison's eyes were locked on me.

He leaned toward me. "You look so beautiful tonight." His eyes were smiling before his mouth did.

I blushed and looked down at my lap. Everyone else in the room faded into muffled background noise; everything but Harrison blurred from my view. I felt an overwhelming gratitude. In my lifetime, I'd never known of a woman like me getting to experience these types of things, and what were the chances of the man I'd daydreamed about so vividly, for so long, turning out to be my actual soulmate? Slim to none, that's what. Or, so I'd thought.

He lifted my chin with the side of his index finger, making sure my eyes met his. "I hope all your dreams come true, Alice. It's my mission in life to see to it that they do."

"*You,* are every one of my dreams come true." I gently squeezed his hand in mine and settled them both beneath the table against my thigh.

He leaned in and kissed me, his finger still holding my chin, but barely, as he pressed his lips to mine and lingered there.

"Get a room, wouldja?!" Shelby bellowed from the other end of the table.

"They've got one, and we're stuck in the next room over!" Lawrence taunted while Harrison continued to kiss me, his intensity increasing with every remark.

"Am I getting hazard pay for this, boss? Ugh, my eyes!" Victor's voice joined the chorus.

"Save it for the honeymoon!" Nigel barked, causing Harrison to smile and almost laugh while he continued his unrelenting show of affection.

He kissed me until Shelby stood and tapped her water glass. "I'd like to propose a toast." She tapped her glass again and the muffled chatter around the table quieted. "To Harrison and his beautiful bride to be, Alice." She tipped her head lovingly as she spoke. "H, my big brother. You've always been the kind and caring chap I could rely on when no one else in this world thought I was worth caring about. You've watched out for me and made sure I knew I had a place in this world, and now, you've given me the kind of sister I always wanted. Alice, you've been the loveliest surprise. You arrived and integrated seamlessly into this little family unit of ours, and only amplified the joy and the love that surrounds us. You were probably terrified, as one would be when faced with this group"—she winked at me—"and I think I speak for everyone when I say, I hope you know just how much you are loved by us all. And this baby of yours is going to be spoiled to the core by the time we're through!" She raised her glass a bit higher in the air. "May you love as long as you live, and may that love live on long after. We love you both so much. To Alice and Harrison!"

A collective, "Hear, hear!" surrounded us, and everyone sipped their drinks.

"I'd also like to make a toast if that's alright." Lawrence stood and everyone turned in their seats to face him. "Boss, you've changed my life. Who knows where I would've ended up if not for you, mate, and I can't thank you enough for your unwavering belief in me, and your loyalty to me, and really, your incredible, constant, patience." Laughter poured from the group. "Mate, you truly are the best, one of a kind. And Alice, I could see it in his eyes he was mad about you the moment you two stepped out of The Spaniards Inn that first night. It was written all over his face. The most serendipitous part of it though, is through you, I've also found the love of *my* life in Emma. And without you, Alice, I don't know if our paths ever would have crossed. So, thank you both for changing my life for the better, each in your own ways. To Alice and Harrison!"

Applause, love, and a sense of belonging surrounded us. Our celebration dinner had been just what I'd needed to fully feel like I truly belonged in *this* life. What once was, was now packed away and stored in a locked vault, never to be unearthed or explored or experienced again.

Back at the villa, most of the guys hung out on the terrace and enjoyed cigars and bourbon. Nothing could pull the new girls away from Hank and Victor, and none of us were interested in trying. Meanwhile, Nigel, Shelby, Emma, and I sat around the pool staring up into the glittery blackness.

"Nigel, I saw those kisses tonight, you know. You aren't fooling anyone if you think you're slick." I closed my eyes, uninterested in his expression, one hand resting against my growing belly, the other hanging down at my side, my fingertips playfully swishing around in the pool.

"Darling, I wasn't trying to be slick. Rupert is a doll, and I don't have to tell you about 'when it's right, it's right,' now do I?"

I sighed happily. "You absolutely do not. I was just picking on you anyhow. If Rupert makes you happy, that's all that matters." I shifted slightly in my chaise lounge. "I might sleep out here tonight. That house is too…I don't know, barren for me."

"Barren?" Emma laughed. "What does that even mean?"

"I don't know. It's cold, and it gives me the heebie-jeebies."

"What, the hell, is a hee-bie-jee-bie?" Shelby asked, giggling, the champagne having gotten the better of her tonight.

"The willies. You know, it weirds me out. It's just…sketchy." I didn't know how else to explain it.

"You just wanna be able to do the deed with your man and not be heard," Emma added, also tipsy on tonight's libations.

"And that." I laughed. "I don't know if pregnancy is meant to increase my sex drive or if the exhaustion of it all is meant for the opposite, but I can't keep my hands off him, and seemingly he can't keep his hands…or mouth…or anything else…off of me either."

Nigel groaned. "Jesus, Alice, c'mon. Remember some of us aren't so lucky."

I looked over to find him fully relaxed on his chaise, eyes closed, a rare thing for him. "Yeah, well, the night is young, my boy. It might be that you're the one that needs to sleep in the yard to fend off the sex-echoes of that castle." I laughed. "I noticed you opted for water more often than champagne tonight too. Proud of you."

"Well, if he does make a move, I want to be coherent for it," he said flippantly.

"Remind me, why aren't *you* the one making the moves?" Emma asked.

"I don't know. That's never been my role in life. I feel more secure in being wanted, when someone else makes the first move."

I sat up and turned to face him. "Nigel, I love you, but I'm only going to say this once. If you always do what you've always done, you're gonna get what you've always gotten. Nothing will ever change. Take it from someone who finally did something different and got the most spectacular result. Rupert could be your soulmate, your dream come true, like Harrison is for me."

"I know…" He was subtly trying to get me to shut up, but I knew he knew I was right.

"That's the thing about dreams; if you don't chase 'em, you'll never catch 'em." I relaxed back into my lounge chair. "That's all I'm gonna say about it." I waved my hand in the air, brushing the topic free to float away on one of the evening's breezes.

CHAPTER 62

I didn't sleep outside in the lounge chair, and I never heard any crazy sounds coming from Nigel's room. Honestly, part of me was sad not to. I'd wanted him to throw caution to the wind, make a move, and get his groove back. Maybe it was as simple as Rupert hadn't stayed in Nigel's room. There were certainly enough bedrooms in the villa for everyone to sleep in their own bed. I'd find out today when we were back on the jet and on our way to Tropea.

As for me, last night was amazing. I'd had a nice long shower while Harrison was enjoying his time with the fellas, I'd meditated a bit, trying anything I could to get myself centered and prepared for the ceremony. I went over my vows again and tweaked a few lines. Then a while after I'd turned out the light, I heard Harrison slip into the bathroom, and I dozed from the calming sound of water splattering against the shower floor. I'd heard him pause at our bedside and take one last sip of his bourbon, then drop his towel to the floor. He slid in close behind me, his skin hot against mine, and kissed the back of my shoulder, then brushed my hair away and kissed my neck before turning me toward him and sharing the lingering taste of bourbon still on his tongue. He was tipsy, maybe more than tipsy, and that made him not only intently serious and laser-focused, but incredibly handsy, and the hottest part was he knew any sound we made would reverberate throughout the entire house, so silence was an absolute requirement. He'd explored my body with his mouth, slowing only to savor his favorite spots, before burying himself in me completely. It took all I had not to vocalize my appreciation for how intense and wildly erotic it was. Over an hour later, I was breathless and sweaty and had ripped the designer sheets from the mattress with one hand, while my other fist clenched the iron headboard, white-knuckled. I watched as Harrison panted above me, his curls falling downward along with the swaying gold cross he always wore around his neck. His ribs expanded beneath his tattoos as his mouth curled into a smug, satisfied grin, seemingly desperate for oxygen.

We'd packed everything and finally gotten back on the plane and were in the air on our way to Tropea when I cornered Nigel and asked him how his night went.

"All I heard, aside from the throbbing in my ears, was crickets from the direction of your room last night," I said quietly. "You didn't make the move?"

"When I went inside last night, he stopped me and pulled me aside on the terrace and asked if I'd like to share a nightcap with him. And of course I wanted to, so I said, 'Meet me in my room when you're done out here.' I didn't want to rush him or make him feel pressured." He glanced around to be sure no one else was listening to our conversation.

"And?!" I prodded.

"And about ten minutes later he knocked on my door with two drinks in his hands." My eyes grew wide with anticipation as I silently begged for more information. "So, I invited him in. He handed me a glass and I pretended to enjoy bourbon while we sat on the edge of the bed for a while, talking. We really do have a lot in common..." He looked in another direction.

"NIGEL!" I demanded in the loudest whisper possible.

"And then I basically downed the entire shot's worth of liquor, set my cup on the nightstand, and proceeded to kiss that beautiful man full on the mouth, all gas, no brakes." He wasn't trying to hide how pleased he was with himself at all.

"Jesus." My hand flew up to cover my open mouth while my eyes remained the size of dinner plates.

"Darling, even Jesus couldn't believe it." Nigel nodded, satisfied.

"Did you…" I stopped short.

"Oh, a lady never tells." He smirked at me and paused. "But no one's ever called *me* a lady…so yes, we absolutely did, and it was…mind blowing."

I put my arm around him and hugged him. "I'm proud of you! And also, for being able to keep quiet; I know what a struggle that is." I dipped my head and then looked up at him, grinning.

"You dirty little trollop!" He slapped my thigh.

"Guilty as charged, and not remorseful one single bit." I scrunched my nose at him quickly and shot him a look of cocky accomplishment.

"I wouldn't want to be in charge of laundry in that place today," he joked.

"So, wait, do you think this is just a 'for fun' thing, or is this the beginning of something more?" I asked.

Nigel raised his eyebrows. "He said he really wants to spend some good quality time together getting to know each other better and wants to see where this goes." He grew serious. "And, Alice, I really like him. He's so gentle and so tender and took my feelings into consideration. It felt different than other situations in the past. I really hope this goes somewhere." He took my hand in his. "You and Harrison are making love connections left and right. Think Lawrence will let us have a group wedding?" The humor reappeared in his voice.

"That's a discussion for Lawrence, not me. I've got my hands full already."

"Your marriage is going to be magic, Alice, I just know it. That man," his head tipped in Harrison's direction, "loves you in the ways we all search for."

"Oh, I know he does. I just need to get out of my head and stop worrying about things that probably will never happen." I bit at the inside of my cheek nervously.

"What are you worried about? Maybe I can help."

"Stupid things, really. What if my dress doesn't fit, what if it rips, what if I'm too sweaty after climbing those steps, or what if he gets cold feet? What if…he starts to think of me the same way James did?" I rolled my eyes in acknowledgment that my concerns were farfetched.

"You're right, those things are stupid." He laughed. "You know you could have on a dirty bin bag, wet with sweat, and nothing would turn him away from you. He's not going to get cold feet, and I don't think he's capable of being like your ex. He doesn't *need* any of this you know; he'd have married you on your front step if he could have, I'm certain of it. He just wants to make sure you're happy." He turned to face me directly. "I've lived a lot of life, and I've never seen anyone look at someone the way he looks at you, Alice. Every single time, you are his focus, his happiness, his passion. You're everything to him; we all see it. And really, I think you know that."

"I do." I nodded. "Sometimes it's just nice to hear it from someone else. Thank you, Nigel."

He shifted back in his seat beside me. "Now, what's the scene like at this hotel?"

CHAPTER 63

The rules in Tropea were either strict or non-existent, and their motto should have been, *live as you want, but drive as we tell you.* Some areas didn't even allow non-resident cars, and others had their parking spaces color-coded based on whether they were free to use or charged a fee. Oftentimes visitors were required to hire a service to transport them to their hotel, and that was our fate, but Rupert had it all under control; it took an hour and a caravan of four vehicles to deliver us and our luggage to our hotel from the private airstrip we'd landed on, but we finally made it Saturday around 10 a.m.

The weather was warmer than yesterday, and the air sweet. Small shops along the cobblestone streets had baskets piled high with lemons for sale, while strings of bright red Calabrian chiles or bushels of pungent—and world-famous—red onions hung abundant from the corners of shop awnings. Their intoxicating scents tantalizing your senses and teasing you to step inside. There were also a few of the more touristy shops selling beachwear, bars with music overflowing into the streets, and old-fashioned shop windows advertising gelato much too vibrant in color to be natural. Granted, it was still only early March, but there were far fewer people milling around than I expected in a beach town such as this, especially in a heat wave, but I was thankful for the calm; fewer people would now always equal more freedom.

It was said that Tropea boasted long, wide stretches of soft, white sand beaches; sand so soft it coerced people into jewel-like turquoise waters so clear it was hard to gauge their depths even when in it, and whoever said it, they were right. The view from the balcony of our fifth-floor penthouse suite—and the fact that this hotel had an elevator because many don't—was exactly why I wanted to book it. It wasn't the most luxurious; it didn't come with the most extravagant amenities, but it also didn't echo when you spoke. It felt comfortable and spacious and clean, and it was built atop the crown of a massive, towering cliff of tuff—a kind of volcanic ash compressed over centuries to form rock. The other six guestrooms were spread among floors two through four, while the lobby, bar, and small gym were all located on the first floor.

On our balcony, Harrison and I were hundreds of feet in the air, overlooking two beaches and the Santa Maria dell'Isola Sanctuary, which was the crown jewel and solitary structure on its own tower of tuff, and also where in just twenty-four hours' time, we would climb three-hundred stairs and Harrison would become my husband. Our room had a telescope, which was a thoughtful touch, and as soon as I saw it, I knew we'd spend time getting to know the stars from this vantage point while we were here. Off in the distance, I could even see the Aeolian Islands and the active volcano, Mount Stromboli, just like Rupert had mentioned the first night we met him.

Before our arrival here, I read as many articles and travel blogs as I could get my hands on to make sure Tropea was the kind of place I wanted to be married in. Each of them raved about the food—red onion gelato? *I think I'll pass*—the friendly locals, and how this was one of the more historically important, but lesser-known towns along what was known as *la Costa degli Dei*—The Coast of the Gods. Ancient legend suggested Hercules himself founded Tropea and originally named it *Tropeas*, meaning trophy, for the prize he had discovered. Today, I knew exactly what it must have felt like to be Hercules, because this place felt like I was living in the best kind of daydream, and the trophy was coming home with me.

As a group, we spilled out onto Spiaggia del Convento, one of the beaches below our hotel, but ended up wandering around separately. As a New Englander, it felt wrong to be barefoot in the sand in March, but the color of the Tyrrhenian Sea was persuasive, and its waves whispered, "It's fine," every time they hit the shore. Harrison and I found a spot at the far end of the beach and sat together, his arm around my shoulders, my hand on his knee. The sun was warm above us, and we listened to the gulls as we watched a yacht glide past on the horizon.

"I'm surprised you don't have a yacht," I said when it had become merely a dot in the distance.

"I'm far too impatient for that sort of travel. When I've made up my mind, I don't want to waste any time." Harrison's eyes sparkled when he spoke.

I picked up on his implied point and smiled. "You wouldn't want to see the flying fish, or a whale breach, or a pod of dolphins together out in the open ocean?" I asked.

"Oh sure, those things would be beautiful to experience, but I've just always fancied the air over the sea. A whale is a whale, but a cloud can be any shape you imagine it to be." He lay back on his elbows and looked up at the sky.

"I suppose that's true. And, well you know…seasickness."

He laughed. "Yes, seasickness. No one wants that." He drew in a deep breath and let it out slowly, his feet crossed, toes rubbing against his other foot. "Lay back, darling; watch the clouds with me."

I lay back and turned to my side, resting my cheek against his chest. I had no interest in the clouds, only Harrison. His cologne was ingrained in his clothes; vanilla, warm spice, and the slightest hint of tobacco took me back to the night he introduced himself to me at The Spaniards Inn, the first night I ever experienced him in real life. That night the notes of vanilla triggered reminders of the vanilla bath products that played a recurring role in my road trip dream about him, back when he was only a figment of my imagination. I closed my eyes and breathed him in. It didn't matter if we were in Italy, London, or some daydream version of New Orleans, Harrison was my home, no matter where on this earth we were.

"You guys fancy a bite? We're all going to go find some food." Hank's voice cut through my memories as his hulking shadow blocked the sun.

I sat up and blinked hard as my eyes adjusted to the brightness again. "I can always eat," I offered, rubbing my belly. "Harrison?"

"Sure." He stood and brushed the sand from his worn blue jeans, then offered me his hands to help me up.

We made our way across the beach, warm white sand beneath our feet so soft it felt like satin, and with shoes in hand, we joined the rest of the group in search of lunch.

CHAPTER

64

Bellies full, the afternoon was spent wandering the narrow cobblestoned streets, popping in and out of shops, and taking advantage of spots like *Montagna di Tropea* to grab photos of the expansive tuff cliffs and explore the grounds of the sanctuary before tomorrow's big event. Looking from the sanctuary back toward our hotel was just as impressive as the sanctuary itself. Hotel after hotel stood at the top of an incredible chiseled rock formation, the main street hugging its base, while the beach bellied up against the roadway. As the afternoon wore on, the sea calmed and we were able to skirt the towering rock that the sanctuary sat on, and kayak to *Grotta del Palombaro*, a natural cave located on the sea side of the tuff. It lay hidden from town, and was only accessible by water; the peaked opening of the cave kept a vigilant watch over the sapphire sky and the diamonds that danced across the sea. We were lucky to spend a little time there relaxing on the beach before making the journey back.

As a pregnant forty-year-old woman, who was never what anyone would consider "fit" to begin with, I was exhausted. After all that eating, walking, and kayaking—and let's not forget those three hundred stairs— my extremities were jello. A glutton for punishment? Maybe. But at least we hadn't been in any rush. We took our time, stopped and snapped group photos, and took in the views. No one would ever have imagined my wedding day was only hours away by looking at me; any nerves I'd felt before were gone. I could relax now. Harrison was undeniably my best friend, and I knew I had nothing to worry about. If the dress didn't fit, he'd still love me in shorts and a t-shirt. If I couldn't make it back up those three hundred stairs, he'd marry me on step number 132. If it all went wrong, it would still be alright.

It was funny, when I stopped to think about it. The spiraling I used to do so often, the worried voice in my head that used to rule my life, had all been calmed to a hush since Harrison came along. I never felt inadequate or invisible, I never felt like I was less than. He never dismissed my thoughts or my dreams. I was never overlooked or ignored. I was a part of his decisions, and we talked openly, all the time, about our feelings. Harrison was everything I never had, and all I'd ever wanted, and he never missed an opportunity to let me know he felt the exact same way about me.

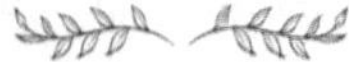

After showers and a much-needed nap, Harrison and I decided we would get takeaway from a nearby pizzeria and watch the sun set from our balcony.

"I know it's customary to spend the night before the wedding apart, but I really don't want to be away from you," he said as we walked back to our hotel.

"I was just thinking the same thing." I looped my arm through his, careful not to upset the pizza box in his hand.

"Do we run the risk of jinxing this whole thing just to be close tonight?" He smiled as he said it.

"I don't know. Do you think you could live without me?" I asked jokingly.

"I'm certain I couldn't, which is exactly why I don't want to be away from you tonight."

"Such a conundrum you've found yourself in." I shook my head. "It's a tragedy really. What ever will you do?" I said sarcastically and laid my palm to my cheek, an innocent look on my face.

"I think I'll bribe you with pizza and kisses under moonlight and maybe, just maybe, if you're lucky"—he tripped over a high cobblestone and nearly spilled the pizza from the flimsy box it was in but managed to keep himself upright.

"Oh my God," I couldn't help but laugh at him. "Are you okay?" I covered my mouth as a means to shield my laughter.

The apples of his cheeks bloomed crimson as his eyes darted around. "I hope no one saw that."

"That's what you get for trying to bribe a lady with moonlit kisses"—I couldn't stop laughing—"Mr. Debonair," I exaggerated.

"Maybe we shouldn't tempt the jinx Gods after all." His eyes widened and then he rolled them.

"We can decide after dinner. You know, that extra room is still open; Rupert decided to room with Nigel I guess."

"Did he?" Harrison seemed genuinely surprised.

"Nigel told me this morning on the flight they did the deed last night, and apparently are working toward a relationship."

"No way, well good for them." He smiled. "It was high time for Nigel to find someone."

"When we were out earlier today, he'd whispered in my ear they were sharing a room, and then later Rupert said my gown and everything for tomorrow was in the room that had had his name on it. So, that's that, I guess. Another love connection sorted." I dusted my hands together.

Harrison pulled open the lobby door and held it for me.

"Thank you, sir. You're much too kind." I batted my eyelashes at him.

"My utmost pleasure, my dear. Forgive me if I'm being presumptuous, but may I escort you to your room?" he asked, his accent thickening as he pretended to be a stranger.

With a look of surprise and a slight turn of my chin, I replied, "Why, what would my *fiancé* say?" loud enough for the woman at the front desk to hear.

"Leave him. He could never treat you like I can." He shook his head upward as he spoke and "never" came out as a boldly and dramatically accentuated "nevvah."

Fully aghast at his statement, I let my fingertips land at my bosom and said nothing.

"You see, I'm an incredible lover. And, I've got pizza." His face serious, he once again accentuated the word *lover*.

I caught a glimpse of the lady at the front desk in my periphery, her eyes wide, mouth hung open in shock at what she was witnessing.

"Well, when you put it that way…" I slowly dragged the back of my index finger from his abdomen up across his chest. "I'm certain I'd be a fool not to." Then I flirtatiously booped him on the end of his nose.

"By all means, lead the way." He held his hand out, ushering me to go ahead of him.

When the elevator doors opened, I looked over my shoulder at the horrified woman at the desk. "Don't wait up!" I called out, winked at her, then shoved Harrison inside.

Seconds later we were already headed toward the fifth floor, but I was certain she heard the salacious moan I let out just as the doors closed. When the laughing subsided and we stepped back into our suite, Harrison was still shaking his head at my shenanigans.

"What's life if you can't have a little fun?" I asked.

"True." He set the pizza box on the table and pulled me against him, holding me close.

"Say you'll stay with me tonight." He kissed me gently, his lips lingering, the tip of his nose rubbing gently against mine.

"We'll see." I looked up at him sweetly and kissed him again.

"Fine." He scowled playfully.

"Now come on, we'll miss the sunset." I smacked him on the ass, then grabbed two bottles of water from the fridge and headed toward the balcony.

It didn't matter which direction we looked, there were beaches spread out below us; groups and couples on blankets with bottles of wine all stared out at the sea awaiting the transformation of the canvas laid out above them. Barely-there tufts of white clouds lazily scrolled past in the distance, their edges silvery against a sky that had already started shifting to pink.

"This pizza is amazing," I mumbled, my mouth full.

"Too much sauce," Harrison said as he dabbed at his slice with a napkin.

I took another bite before I'd even finished chewing the last one, and realized he was watching me eat. "What?" I asked.

"Nothing." He smiled and restrained a laugh as he watched me chew.

"WHAT?" I repeated after I swallowed. "Tell me! Do I have grease on my face?" I wiped at my chin with the back of my hand and saw nothing every time I checked it.

"No, love, nothing is on your face. I just love to see you happy."

"Okay," I said sarcastically, took another bite and stared out at the sky.

"Can't I look at my wife? The mother of my child, and enjoy her while she enjoys life? You know, our child is the size of a coconut right now."

"Mm-hmm"—I nodded, my mouth full—"about to be the size of a basketball."

"Alice, you're glowing." He paused and watched me as I glanced at him suspiciously with my eyebrows raised and then returned my focus to the sky. "No really, the reflection of the sky on your face is orange." He leaned over and bumped my shoulder with his and smiled sweetly.

I puffed a soundless laugh through my nose, and looked at him, my face growing serious after a moment. "Tomorrow at this time you'll be my husband." I paused, watching his face. "Legally bound." I widened my cautious, questioning eyes at him quickly.

"Yes?" He spoke slower than usual, dragging the word out and looked at me like I was crazy.

"Are you ready for that?" I asked him, scanning his eyes for reassurance.

His expression shifted to something between defensive and surprised. "Are you not?" he asked.

"I am, a thousand percent, I am." But my attempt at reassurance seemed to fall flat.

I watched Harrison as the sun dipped lower, flirting with the horizon; its reflection on his tanned face deepened to a beautiful shade of coral, while his eyes softened from suspicion into worry. As we sat in silence, I thought about whether I should try to explain myself further or not. I only knew I didn't want to leave it as it was. He deserved to know why I asked him that, but I didn't want to make things worse. I'd clearly already upset him. "I don't want you to ever wonder how much you're loved, Harrison."

He turned to face me and took my hands in his. "I know you love me; you just caught me off guard with that question, that's all." He was trying to convince us both that he was fine.

"Neither of us like to think about it, but obviously I've been through this, and I've seen the shitty side of what 'legally bound' entails. I just needed to try to convey the weight of it to you is all."

His eyes narrowed. "I know the weight of it, Alice. I'm prepared for the weight. I thought that part was obvious." He was frustrated, and I could understand why.

I took a deep breath, worried I'd upset him even more. "People talk about how marriage is hard, and it can be draining, and it's so much work. And unfortunately for me, I found that to be true, but that was when I was married to the wrong person. Life with you has been different. It's been easy, fun. It's been comforting and enjoyable. It's been a completely different experience than I've ever had before. There's no reason why any of it should change after we sign a piece of paper. But there will undoubtedly be times when we disagree and argue. There will be times we differ on views of how to raise this baby for sure, and who knows what else. It's how we work together in those times that defines a marriage, at least that's my opinion. It's not always going to be kittens and rainbows; I just want you to be prepared for that. I want you to know that if we ever do disagree, or argue, or hell, we might even full-on fight, I'll never walk out on you; I'll never turn away in hopes you'll chase me. I'll never love you less or want to leave. No matter what happens at surface level, the undercurrent is always going to be fully committed, never give up, unconditional love."

"I'm ready, Alice. For anything life throws at us, I'm ready to take it all on *with* you. Not against you, not without you. Signing a piece of paper makes you my teammate. 'Legally bound' to me, means I'm finally no longer alone in this world. And marriage, to me, means holding on through the good, and holding on even tighter through the bad *and* the ugly. Sickness and health, I have you by my side to navigate it all. I'm sure we'll fight and all that at some point, but it's certainly not in my character to ignore you or make your life hard. I'd never not be there when you needed me, Alice. The rest of your life won't ever be like it was before, I promise you." His eyes pleaded with me to believe him.

"I know, babe." I gave him a knowing nod. "I know."

He leaned his shoulder against mine again, but this time stayed there and tilted his head toward me inviting me to do the same, and I did.

"Remember when I was in Brazil?" he asked quietly as he remained focused on the sky.

"Of course. I'm old, but I've not lost my memory yet, geez," I joked.

But Harrison was serious. "Remember how badly we wanted to be together?"

"All too well."

He turned and looked at me. "Then stay with me tonight. I don't ever want to waste a moment away from you again."

In the quiet of an Italian seaside town on a Saturday night, we watched as the sun dropped out of sight, sending a burnt-orange aura up into the heavens. The lights surrounding the Santa Maria dell'Isola eased their way through the increasing darkness and illuminated the church that'd been a beacon of refuge since it was a monastery in the 4th century. Beams of golden light from every possible angle highlighted the bluff, from its rocky base to the limestone staircase winding its way to the summit, to the grand church itself sitting proudly atop its tuff; it appeared like some sort of medieval fairytale lighthouse, and I found I was in awe of it after dark even more than I was in broad daylight.

I decided I'd stay with him tonight, and every night, because Harrison was right; I would have turned myself inside out just to be near him while he was in Brazil. Not to mention, I'd waited my whole life for a man to love me the right way, in all the ways that I loved him, and I wasn't inclined to squander a single second more, traditions be damned.

CHAPTER 65

A crisp ocean breeze sent the window sheers dancing and blanketed me in goosebumps, rousing me from an incredible sleep. We'd dozed off sweaty from what felt like hours of making love and left the windows open to listen to the waves. I pulled the covers up over my bare shoulders and cocooned myself while I remained the big spoon, my burgeoning belly pressed to Harrison's back. He was snoring, though barely, and I lay there quietly listening to him breathe, watching as the shadows of the gulls outside the window hovered briefly and then dropped out of sight.

What an absolute whirlwind this has been, I thought while my thumb mindlessly grazed the small indent of his sternum, ever so gently, back and forth. *Six months ago, I was angry. Depressed. I felt invisible. Today I'm lying in a hotel in Italy, pressed against a man who can't stand to be away from me for even a moment. In mere hours he'll be my husband. It's crazy how quickly life can change when you stop tolerating things that make you miserable and start actively searching for your own joy.* I smiled to myself for how far I'd come, then the muscles in his thighs flexed and his toes reached for the end of the bed as he woke.

"Good morning," I whispered against his neck and kissed his shoulder. I felt him draw in a deep breath when my lips touched his skin, the slightest hint of a moan slipping past as he exhaled.

"You were right, you know," I said.

"Was I?" The rasp in his voice lit my imagination on fire.

"Mm-hmm." My lips rested against his skin, the palm of my hand creeping up across his abdomen to his chest, and he rolled over to face me.

"You are, in fact, an incredible lover."

He smiled, his eyes still puffy from sleep, then laughed as he nestled his face against my bare chest. "You're crazy."

"You know, pretty soon, I gotta get outta here. Any last words as a single man?" I let my cheek rest against his reckless curls; the amber, white musk, and citrus that remained from his shampoo daring me to inhale them.

"Hmm…" He thought a moment and I felt his body move as he looked up at me and said, "I've never loved you more than I do right now, and if you ask me again a thousand times, from here to eternity, my answer will always be the same." He smiled as he looked for my approval. "How's that?" The lines around the corners of his eyes appeared in synchronicity with his dimples, his happiness nearly palpable, his excitement childlike.

"I love you so much." I leaned down and kissed him on his forehead.

"And I love you, darling."

"I got you something for today. You want it now? I know it's not really customary that I give it to you while I'm sitting right here, but when has anything we've done ever been customary?"

"Right, sure. Is it…possibly…an elephant?" His face was serious as he pulled himself up to sitting, adjusting the pillows behind him.

"Uh, nope." I got up and pulled a robe from the hanger in the closet and wrapped it around me, then grabbed the small box from the pocket inside my suitcase. "A bit smaller than an elephant." I got back into bed and held the box out for him in the palm of my hand.

"Ooh, much smaller than an elephant," he said, appearing dissatisfied.

"I can return it." I pulled my hand back. "I'm sure I can find you a nice pachyderm when we get back to London. It can be best buds with Robin in the backyard."

"Shelby's head would spin if we did that. Imagine me asking her to please walk the elly after breakfast." He made a shocked face then laughed.

I held my hand out toward him again. "Open it."

He pulled the end of the ribbon and the bow fell apart against the top of the box. "You know, you didn't have to do this."

"I wanted to. It's nothing extravagant. Just a little something special."

He opened the box to expose the silver cuff links laid delicately inside, and I watched as his eyes squinted at the fine engraving on the onyx inlay. "I can see the dates, but what else is this?" he asked, trying to make out exactly what he was looking at.

"Just coordinates. On one, it's the date we met with the coordinates of The Spaniards Inn below it. The other has today's date, and the coordinates of the church where we'll be married."

"Oh, Alice, this is…" He seemed at a loss for words.

"Just a way for you to wear your heart on your sleeve and look fancy while you're doing it. You like 'em?" I pulled the corner of my bottom lip into my mouth and waited nervously for his response.

"I love them." His gaze rose to meet mine. "This is so thoughtful."

"Better than some dumb old elephant?" I winced, waiting for him to tell me *no*.

"Well, I mean"—he shook his head—"Have you kept the receipt? Because…"

"Stop it!" I swatted at him playfully and then got serious. "I figured you can wear them to premieres, and you know, when you win the Oscar for Best Director, and…"

"Don't jinx me, love!" He pointed his finger at me and laughed. "I also got you something. Do you want your gift now, or do you want to wait?"

"So, you're over here telling me I don't need to get you a gift, but you got me one?" I shook my head with disapproval. "I'm not sure I can live with these double standards. It's just too much." I threw my hands up in front of me.

"If it makes you feel any better, I think you'll like it." He rolled to the opposite side of the bed and opened the nightstand.

"It's been here under my nose the whole time? What if I'd opened that drawer?" I asked, surprised.

"But you didn't, did you?" He stuck out his tongue and handed me a small gift bag.

"Is it a…new sombrero? No wait. Maybe it's a camel to go with your elephant. I know, it's a hula-hoop."

He chuckled. "Open the bag, Alice."

I reached in and pulled out a small scroll tied with a tiny gold string and a very small, lightproof, zippered bag. Confused, I looked from Harrison to the items in my hand and back again. He nodded, as if urging me to keep going.

"Is there an order to this?" I asked, unsure which to look at first.

He shrugged. "Either one, it's up to you." He gave the slightest nose scrunch and waited for me to choose.

I pulled the string loose from the scroll and unrolled it. In very fancy calligraphy it read, "This star is hereby and forever more yours, a gift from your husband on your wedding day. He has lovingly named it Alice." And below, as if our minds functioned as one cohesive unit, were the coordinates to find the star he'd bestowed my name upon. I looked up to find him staring at me.

"As much as I want to, I can't give you the sun or the moon, but I can give you a star. So that's what I did. You're the brightest glimmer in my universe."

"Promise me we'll find it tonight with the telescope?"

"Why do you think that thing is in here?" He shot me a sly look, and I knew then that he'd requested it special for this very reason.

"Okay, so what's this little bag?" I carefully pulled its top edges apart and found a damp cloth with a single seed centered inside. I looked at Harrison, once again hoping for more information.

"I requested a seed from the most prized lemon tree in Capri when we were there the other night. That way, when we get home, we can plant it in the yard as a reminder of our time under the lemon trees."

"Will an Italian lemon tree even grow in London?" I asked, terrified to kill the poor thing.

"Time will tell, but hopefully, with a little love, it will give us fruit for years to come, and maybe one day we can celebrate our anniversary under our very own lemon tree, right in our own backyard."

"These are the sweetest gifts, Harrison. Thank you. I can't wait to be your wife." I leaned in and he met me halfway, wrapping his arms around me tightly.

It was then that I noticed the time. "Babe, I've got to get down to the other room and start getting ready."

"I hate to say it, but the sooner you leave, the sooner I get to climb those stairs and see my wife waiting for me." He winked at me and then lay back against the pillows again.

"See you at the top of the rock in a few hours?" I asked.

"It's a date." I leaned in and kissed him softly, then got up, gathered my things and slipped my feet into the sandals by the door before turning back to look at him one last time. He was sitting propped against the pillows smiling as he watched my every move. His entire body was tan against the stark white sheet pulled up between his legs that draped backward over his hip, the lion tattoo on his thigh peeking out from under its edge, taunting me back into bed and begging me to put my mouth against it. The A. he'd permanently placed on his ribs reminded me of his devotion. He was perfectly adorned with ink, earth-shatteringly handsome, the most emotionally intelligent man I'd ever known, and he was all mine. Forever.

CHAPTER
66

I'll never get this moment back again.

Over and over, I heard it in my head while the hot water of the shower poured over me, and again as I carefully made sure every surface of my body was smooth. I heard it as I stood in the mirror, watching my reflection as I wound curls around my fingers to define them before leaving them to dry, and I heard it as I applied the scarcest amount of makeup to my eyes and lips.

Slow down, there's no rush.

I repeated as I sat alone in front of the open window of the third-floor room I was in, watching the beach awaken, people shuffling in with their beach chairs and blankets, striped umbrellas in every color of the rainbow being driven into the white sand. The breeze billowing through the curtains, swirling around me like a comforting hug had been sent directly to me from the heavens. I wished my grandmother were still alive; she wouldn't believe this even if I showed her proof, and for a moment, somewhere on that breeze, I swear I heard her voice, "I'm so proud of the woman you've grown into." She'd hug me and rock me back and forth while she did it, something she did for half my life, a sign she wanted to hold on just a little bit longer. It was like she'd burst through the window on that breeze just to let me know she was somehow here with me. I know she would have been, if she could have.

Remember these moments.

It echoed in my head as I put on a pair of my mother's earrings, my designated 'something old.' She'd worn them at her wedding and then given them to me when she celebrated her divorce. Maybe they were tainted, "jinxed" as Harrison would say, but they were one of the few things I had left of her, of days when she was happy.

I heard it again, when my grandmother's garter barely made it above my knee; the only thing that fragile 1950s garter didn't represent was *something new*. It was old, it was borrowed, and it was *something blue*. And my leg might be by the end of the day; my grandmother had been a petite woman, and I was anything but. We had no plans of a traditional garter removal, but it was important to her that I wear it. She'd said as much when she'd gifted it to me. I appreciated that the pastel blue, though faded, might be a sign that the gender in the envelope that Shelby held hostage could in fact be a little boy. Our baby would be my *something new*.

The girls would be here soon to help me get my dress on, finish my hair, and attend to any of the fine details I may have overlooked. Women I'd known for such a short time, had truly become my sisters. Unconditional in their love for me, I could count on them for anything. They'd hold my hand as we climbed those stairs again and stand by my side until Harrison arrived. I wasn't being fussy today; I couldn't be. I just wanted to be mindful. Today would stand out in my memories for the rest of my life and I wanted to look back and remember myself happy, calm. Not scattered and anxious. And Harrison wasn't a fan of perfect anyway.

A knock at the door shook me out of my thoughts. The girls had arrived.

We used the gold string from the scroll Harrison had given me this morning to tie my hair half up, while the rest of my auburn curls fell loose down my back. Shelby and Emma could barely wait to gift me a beautiful tennis bracelet which added the perfect bit of sparkle on my wrist, and when I stepped into it, my dress fit like a glove. A tight glove, but a glove nonetheless. The detail of the bodice would draw attention down to my baby bump, the bump I'd once been so afraid for people to see, the bump I was now so incredibly in love with, and the bump made a slight bit plumper by the undeniable temptress that was Italian food. A quick spritz of Harrison's favorite perfume to either side of my neck, a swipe or two of strawberry lipgloss, and a good long look at myself in the mirror.

I was ready to be his wife.

An hour later, when I had the last of those stairs behind me, I found myself on the stone terrace of Santa Maria dell'Isola. With its tall arched doorways and striped facade, it was an honor to be in the presence of such a historic and meaningful place. I stared up at it while I tried to catch my breath, welcoming any good juju I could, to infiltrate me via my lungs. Not only was I thankful I'd chosen flats with cushioned insoles, but I was also incredibly grateful for the two friends who knew me well enough to make me take my time getting up here. We smoothed each other's hair, shared a bottle of cool water, and most importantly made sure we were presentable and didn't look like we'd just climbed to the top of a towering rock at the edge of an ocean. I'd thanked them both for making sure my cheeks didn't turn too pink, and I didn't sweat off the eye makeup I'd been so careful to apply.

"Harrison didn't sign up to marry a raccoon," Emma had said halfway up the physically taxing climb. "Just take your time. The show doesn't go on without you."

The ocean breeze, though warm, was a bit more pronounced up here, but a welcome guest nonetheless as we meandered around the edge of the church and through the lush greenery of the gardens to find the spot we'd chosen for the ceremony. Rupert was there looking dapper, flashing me a supportive smile from beneath an arch of well-established hot pink Bougainvillea vines, his ceremony book in hand, the vast blue-green ocean sparkling behind him for as far as the eye could see. As we approached, I could see the rest of the group patiently mulling about waiting for me to appear, and erupting into loud cheers when they saw we had arrived.

I took my place near Rupert while Emma fanned out the small train of my gown and Shelby handed me my bouquet. Looking out across our group of friends, I felt their excitement, and their congratulatory smiles began to put my rapidly beating heart at ease. Any moment, Harrison would appear. I pulled in a deep breath, felt my dress get tight around my ribs and smiled to myself before letting it out. *Everything is going to be fine*, the little voice in my head consoled, only now, that voice was Harrison's.

"Three minutes!" Lawrence shouted. "And don't worry Alice, I've got your ring!" He patted his breast pocket and found it empty, a look of alarm stealing the color from his face. He shot out of his chair and started patting himself down, searching all of his pockets, desperate not to make eye contact with me. Then suddenly from his left front trouser pocket he pulled my wedding band, and a sigh of relief dropped his shoulders into a relaxed slump. "It's okay! Crisis averted!" he shouted, then smoothed his shirt and sat back down, his cheeks now fully inflamed.

"Shelby," I said calmly, "have you got Harrison's band?" I bit the inside of my cheek trying to remain calm.

"I do," she replied quietly. "Get it? I do. Because this is a *wedding*." She raised her eyebrows and gave me a look like she was waiting for me to laugh, but all I could do was shake my head. Shelby might have been more nervous than I was.

Another deep breath. Any minute he'd appear.

"Everyone, please take your seats," Rupert announced out of the blue, just loud enough to make me jump a little.

I turned and looked at him, his big toothy grin staring back at me. "You okay? You ready?" he asked quietly.

I nodded. "More than ready."

"Good," he whispered. "Alice, turn and see your man." He nodded quickly as he looked past me.

There he was, standing tall, broad-shouldered in his linen suit. Our eyes met and I smiled then watched as he drew both his hands up to cover his face, the cuff links I'd given him this morning catching the sunlight and glimmering as he tipped his covered face toward the sky, a move I'd gotten used to as a means of him attempting to regulate his emotions. Tears welled in my eyes as I watched him walk toward me, his chin noticeably quivering, his nostrils flared and his tight-lipped smile trying to hold back his tears.

I handed my bouquet to Shelby and reached out my hands for Harrison as he took his place beside me. He shook his head, swallowed hard, and then wiped at his face with the backs of his hands.

"He's gone!" he exclaimed, followed by a quieter, "I was doing so well…" He smiled again as he raked the fingers of his right hand through his curls, a flick of his wrist twisting them around before facing me and joining hands with me again.

"How on earth did you get up here so quickly?" I whispered.

"I've been inside the church for a while. I didn't want to chance seeing you in your dress before this very moment. You are"—he shook his head—"spellbinding, Alice. An absolute vision. I've got to be the luckiest man alive."

The urge to kiss him was stifled by Rupert's voice. "Friends who are family, I'd like to thank you for being here today, to share in this wonderful occasion. We're here together to unite Harrison and Alice in marriage, but before we begin, I'd like to extend the opportunity to anyone who feels this union is unjust to speak their mind—" But Rupert was interrupted.

Harrison turned quickly toward our audience. "None of you say a bloody word!" he cautioned jokingly, his index finger pointing violently at our group of friends, prompting laughter from the crowd.

"With no objections, we'll begin. Alice, Harrison, the two of you have not only discovered one another in a world of roughly eight *billion* people, you've chosen to make the conscious decision of commitment and consented to the sacred bond of marriage. If you're ready, we'll get down to the business of vows, those eternal beloved promises that will guide you in the years ahead. Alice, ladies first." Rupert dipped his chin at me.

I smiled nervously at him, and then at our friends, as I pulled a small script from the bosom of my dress. I inhaled nervously as I looked Harrison in the eye, and then let it out slowly.

You got this Alice, said the voice in my head.

"Harrison," I licked my lips and swallowed hard, my chest feeling like it had a stack of bricks on it, "you quite literally walked out of my dreams and into my life, and since that night, I've never been the same. I feel like a better person just being next to you. The way you *show* me you love me instead of just saying it, the ways you take care of me without me having to ask, and the unconditional devotion I feel from you..." I glanced up from my notes to find tears already streaming down his cheeks, and I squeezed his hand in mine. "These are just a few of the *infinite* reasons I love you. Your heart is kind, and your intentions are pure, always; you give without expectation and you make me smile every single day. No matter how wild or crazy my dreams may be, I know you'll always be my biggest cheerleader with words of support and encouragement. From the moment I met you, you've made me your priority. You welcomed me into this foreign world I knew nothing about, and by that, I mean...London and navigating rogue photographers." I looked around at the crowd as they chuckled. "With you, I never wonder if I'm loved, because I know the ways you love me eclipse all means of measure, and with you, I know I'll never feel invisible or alone. You represent safety and truth and everything that is good. For me, Harrison, you are 'Home.' I vow to you that I'll always listen without judgment and nurture your dreams without bounds, because I know that's what makes your soul shine. I vow to be comfort whenever and however you need it. I vow to be honest and transparent with you always, and be the soft place you land when days are hard. I vow to always stay committed to this union and defend you in rooms you aren't in. I vow to love you unconditionally, Harrison, recklessly and relentlessly, every single moment of your life, from now until the last breath leaves my body. I promise to fill our home with love, laughter, and happiness. And as many children as I can give you. I promise all of me, every day, to you. I love you." I folded the piece of paper and tucked it back inside my dress, then smiled up at him through tears of my own.

"You're a tough act to follow," he choked out as he wiped the tears from his cheeks; laughter once again resounded from our friends.

"Harrison, when you're ready, you may begin." Rupert's voice was soothing as I braced myself for Harrison's vows.

He cleared his throat and adjusted his stance. "Alice. My beautiful, darling, Alice." He stared into my eyes and spoke from his heart with no notes. "Like a shooting star, you appeared that night, unexpected, grabbing my attention simply by being. This magical cosmic soul, your light never faded from my mind. It only glowed brighter and brighter, burning hotter every time you smiled, every time I thought of you, it made me yearn to be near you. I'd never experienced such a gravitational pull; all that mattered was to be in your presence. Your time in London was limited, and I knew it, but somehow that compelled me to know you, to throw everything else to the side and focus my attention on this radiant woman who made me feel like a flower that had never gotten enough sun. My entire life I was nothing more than a closed bud, but your warmth and your spirit showed me what it felt like to blossom. To unfurl and accept life could be so much more than the solitude it had always been. I became something beautiful because of you." He started to tear up again and I watched as he swallowed hard, taking a moment to collect himself before he continued. "I always thought that real, true love was out of my reach, that I couldn't or would never find it because of who I am and the career I've chosen. Trust is something that has never come easy for me, but you changed that, Alice. You showed me truth and honesty, and that I could let down my walls. You've been who I needed my entire life and could never find. The first night I saw you, I knew you were the missing piece of me, the part that would make me feel whole. I know your life before me was treachery, but from now on, Alice, I'll see to it that you flourish, you stretch out into happiness and freedom of expression. You don't hesitate, you don't second guess. Whatever you want is available and yours for the taking." He waited, scanning my eyes until I nodded in agreement. "I want to thank you for loving me the way you do, Alice, and for letting me love you in return. These are my promises to you: I vow to hear the words you don't say, as well as the ones you do. And I promise to carry whatever burdens of life are bestowed upon us and make certain you never feel the weight of them in any way. I vow to always put you first and to never let you, or make you, feel alone. I promise to talk openly with you, share my thoughts and feelings with you always, to never keep a secret, or lie by omission, and I vow to make sure that you never question my intentions or my love for you. I promise and I vow to you that you will always, from this day forward, be the love of my life. No matter what this life throws at us, my heart and soul are fully committed to you. You can lean on me, and know that I've always got you. You're absolutely everything to me, Alice, and I've come to know that I simply never want to live without you. There is nothing we cannot face if we stand together, and though I cannot promise you perfection, I can promise you my willingness to seek it with you, forever, always by your side."

The sound of muffled sniffles could be heard amongst our group of friends, and all I wanted to do was kiss this perfect man standing in front of me, but instead, I stood there trying with all my might not to let anyone see that I was ready to openly sob.

"Brilliant," Rupert chimed in, "not a dry eye in the house, I'd say." He turned the page of his ceremony book and continued, "Harrison, do you take this woman to be your lawfully wedded wife, to live together in matrimony, to love her, comfort her, honor and keep her, in sickness and in health, in sorrow and in joy, to have and to hold, from this day forward, as long as you both shall live?"

"I do, I absolutely do." His smile could have lit up a dark room, his dimples teasing me to lose control of myself.

"And, Alice, do you take this man to be your lawfully wedded husband, to live together in matrimony, to love him, comfort him, honor and keep him, in sickness and in health, in sorrow and in joy, to have and to hold, from this day forward, as long as you both shall live?"

"I do." I smiled, anxious for what was next.

"And now we've come to one of the final rituals in a wedding ceremony, a gift of tangible commitment. May these rings represent the promises you have made to one another here today and remind you on tough days that your love is unending, just like the rings you've chosen for one another. Harrison, as you place this ring on Alice's finger, please repeat after me."

Lawrence stepped forward and handed Harrison my wedding band, who held it in such a way that the sun caught one of the diamond facets and nearly blinded me where I stood.

"With this ring, I thee wed, and pledge to you my love, now and forever." Rupert watched as Harrison repeated those words to me and then gently slid the band onto my finger.

Shelby slipped Harrison's band to me just as Rupert repeated, "Alice, as you place this ring on Harrison's finger, please repeat after me." And again, he watched as I repeated the words to Harrison, and slid the wide band over his knuckle.

Harrison was visibly elated, glancing from me to the ring and back to me again.

"By the authority vested in me by the United Kingdom as well as the Calabrian Government in the fine country of Italy, I now pronounce you husband and wife! Harrison, you may kiss your bride!"

His eyes sparkled, the crinkles at their edges deeply defined by the widest smile I'd ever seen on his face. He stepped forward, took my face in his hands, and then kissed me deeply, partially dipping me backward as he held me in his arms, whispering as he kissed me, "I love you so much, darling." Our friends stood and whistled and applauded until Rupert shushed them.

"Quiet, QUIET, we have more pressing business to attend to now! QUIET!" He hollered over their applause. "Shelby, the envelope, please." She pulled it out of nowhere and handed it to Rupert.

In my head I heard a silent drumroll as my thoughts swirled from pink to blue, girls' names and boys' scrolling through my mind like a news alert as the three familiar little ones came from around the corner of the house, running across the lawn, the image just as crisp now as it had been in my dream, the sound of their giggles echoing in my mind causing me to smile uncontrollably.

Harrison's eyes lit up as he held both of my hands, and I looked down nervously, the band on his left hand a reminder that no matter what, we'd be alright.

"Okay, now Alice and Harrison have no idea the gender of their child, but this envelope holds that very information. They wanted to share this news with you, their cherished loved ones, as part of their grand reveal, so with no further ado…" Rupert's hands were shaking as he tenderly tore open the flap on the envelope, then carefully unfolded the document, making sure not to let us see any of the details on the paper. He smiled to himself, then looked at us both. "Are you ready?"

Harrison nodded and I could barely muster a whispered, "Yes, please."

"Alice, in July, you and Harrison will be parents to a healthy…baby…" He paused for added effect, "GIRL!"

Harrison threw his head back and punched the air triumphantly while I couldn't stop myself from crying happy tears. "Daddy's little girl," I whispered into his ear as he hugged me, his excitement making him nearly vibrate.

"In one day, Alice, you've given me everything I've ever dreamed of. My God, I love you, I love you, I love you like never before." He stepped back and stooped to the level of my belly, cradling it with his hands. "Daddy loves you so much, darling. Now we must find a proper name for you, little one!" He kissed my abdomen countless times then stood and embraced me again before we turned to face our friends, all of whom were on their feet, yammering on about who'd guessed correctly and who hadn't. Rupert pulled the long trail of photos from the envelope and handed them to us, and as I stood there looking through them, I heard a champagne cork fly loose from its restraints in the background and the chatter of my friends increased in volume around it. Rupert hugged us both, followed by Nigel's arms around me and the more people hugged me, the more their voices faded to background noise while I blankly smiled and nodded, the thoughts in my head overtaking me.

A girl. Just what Harrison had hoped for. The mauve on the hem of my train played a more vital role in this day than I'd thought possible. And then my thoughts drifted further back. Back to the baby I'd lost all those years ago and I wondered if this soul could be theirs, a second chance at a life with me. *The oldest child in my dream had been a boy. Maybe it was his soul that was lost, and this was one of the two daughters...but they were twins. This baby definitely isn't twins. Maybe my subconscious was just toying with me. More importantly, what will we name this little girl?* I wondered what Harrison was thinking. I couldn't wait to get back to the hotel tonight and be alone with him again, but first these three hundred stairs had to be traversed yet again.

CHAPTER 67

We'd stayed in the garden long enough to watch the sunset and somehow it seemed everyone had secretly smuggled in their own small bottle of champagne, thus making the trip back down that winding staircase a bit more of an adventure for those who opted to partake. Harrison only had one celebratory glass with his mates after Lawrence bestowed a sash upon him that read "GIRL DAD" in bright pink letters and I'd giggled when Emma tucked the "Boy Dad" version into her tote bag and shot me a glance like, *maybe I'll be using this one*. Our very own life of the party, Nigel, played music from his phone as a means to get people dancing which made for a perfect little celebration.

It was well after sunset when we got back to the hotel and all I wanted was to shower, have dinner, and get off my feet. Harrison, of course, helped me out of my dress and released the golden string from my hair, then waited patiently while I let the warm water wash away all the sweat and exhaustion of the day. When I emerged from the bathroom in a robe with my hair tied up in a loose, messy bun, there was Harrison. His suit jacket lay over the back of a chair, his arms crossed, his collar opened wide, and his shirt sleeves rolled to the tops of his sculpted forearms. His bare feet were crossed out in front of him, as he leaned against the television console smiling.

"Hi, wife," he said, the bass in his voice making me want to drop my robe to the floor.

I smiled. "Hi, husband."

"Are you hungry?" he asked, stepping toward me.

"Insatiably." I reached out to him and he took my hand.

"Well, then come with me, Mrs. Edwards. I've got a surprise for you."

I smiled at him sweetly, laid my fingertips to his palm and he led me out to the balcony. Not only was the telescope set up, illuminated by the brightness of a gorgeous full moon, but a baby grand piano had been delivered and was sitting out in the open air of the night behind a table set for two, complete with candlelight, two Shirley Temples, and two plates of food.

"Harrison…" I blinked hard, thinking this surely must be a mirage. *A piano on a penthouse balcony?* Then I remembered exactly what he was capable of.

"The last six months with you have been a wonderful gift, and it's incredibly important to me to end yesterday's chapter of my life with you, here in a place that will now forever hold a special place in my heart. I promise you, Alice, I will give you one hundred percent of me for the rest of my life. And starting tomorrow, there will be plenty of time for us to rest before we welcome our little girl, but I wanted to share this evening celebrating you. So, I wrote this for you, just for tonight." He sat down at the piano, his bare feet flexing against the pedals, his fingers trembling as he tried to find the proper positioning. His nerves sent his right hand through his chestnut curls but they fell forward again as soon as he repositioned his hands on the keys.

His head remained down as he played a short intro followed by, at first, a lower, almost ominous sound, though beautiful. Then the dainty repetition of a slightly higher note morphed into a rhythmic ballad, the keys singing the only song of love they knew. The deeper notes offset when Harrison crossed his left hand over his right and began exploring higher notes. It was as if the breeze brought with it the harmonies of a trumpet and a flute, a musical love story snaking its way through the night like smoke in the air. I stood and listened, mesmerized, fascinated by my husband's endless talents, his devotion to me, and his ability to always surprise me with acts of incredible love. Behind him, a shooting star shot across the sky, reminding me of the words in his vows, and in that moment, he looked up at me. He didn't speak, only continued to play with a determined look on his face. The twinkling of the stars above us sparkled in unison to the tune he was releasing into the night. I could have listened to him play the piano forever, and parts of me wished it would never end, but just over ten minutes later, the crescendo had come and gone and he was left sitting there, biceps taut beneath his sleeves, his curls like a veil, his jaw flexing as he sought the right time to slow the melody and meet my gaze again.

In the distance, fireworks erupted somewhere out in the middle of the Tyrrhenian Sea, another of the surprises he had arranged for me. The timing of their release was perfect; reds and blues, greens and golden sparkles exploded against the blackness of the sky as his fingertips slowed their pace, but still kept time, until finally, the piano fell silent. His right hand reached for the newly placed wedding band on his left ring finger, adjusting it with admiration, and then he looked up at me and smiled.

SIX MONTHS LATER

Harrison and I puttered around the garden while the baby slept soundly upstairs, her monitor silent beside me on the patio table. Her nap time was nearly over, and we were expecting everyone to show up at any moment for a backyard barbeque to cap the summer and welcome fall, but looking back over the last few months, so much had changed around here.

Harrison and I had traveled alone to Rome and Venice, Sicily, Florence, and Tuscany, whiling away the days, enjoying the scenery and soaking up the culture. It had been magic. Carefree, and untethered we'd roamed through Italy like drifters never being bothered by anyone, being welcomed everywhere we stopped for respite. We even spent some time with one of Harrison's friends high atop the hill in *Civita di Bagnoregio*, a place I lovingly referred to as the forgotten city. With very few residents and no traffic, it was a peaceful land with absolutely no connection to the outside world. Harrison felt at home there, with zero worries about photographers or tabloids. He could be himself without fear of the world's judgment.

Robin's first four babies fledged quite a while ago, probably late March when we were gone and missed it, but he and Sunny were working hard to produce their third and final brood of the season. She had never really come around to being as friendly as Robin was and that was okay; he always made sure to deliver snacks to her while she looked after the nest. A devoted father, Robin had been vigilant with each of their broods, taking his role as the sole caregiver quite seriously. But in between, he'd made time for me, quickly forgiving me for having been away for a month on honeymoon.

In July, we welcomed our beautiful daughter, with her daddy's dimples, and her head full of curls and long eyelashes. Maybe that heartburn myth really was true. My labor was long and exhausting, twenty-eight hours to be exact, but to see her perfect face and to know she was healthy was all that mattered. Everything else was just details. Harrison had done well through it all, better than I expected really. He wanted to help deliver her, and I thought for sure he'd wind up passed out on the floor, but he didn't. He was such a doting father, up all hours of the night to check on her, changing diapers, and sitting with us while I fed her, but it was all the singing he did when he was rocking her that really made me ache for more children. It was still a little soon to think about seriously, but…more and more I found myself feeling unopposed to one more. Okay, maybe two. Three, tops.

Shelby and Julian officially moved in together shortly after they returned from our wedding back in March. We had, of course, left her in charge of the house, and asked her to look after Robin while we wandered the Italian countryside. Every time I asked, she swore she'd never get married, and was steadfast in her opinion that living together was enough, but I imagined one day, she'd give in. Julian worked hard at opening his gym in record time and thus far found pretty impressive success.

Now, Nigel and Rupert were another story. Rupert was completely unwilling to give up his place in SoHo and Nigel refused to give up the home he'd lived in for decades, despite it being in both their best interest, not only for growing their relationship but financially as well. Safe to say they'd found themselves at an impasse. And it was a point of contention every time we saw them. They'd argue about who should give up what, like an old married couple, badgering one another, then making up just as quickly. Sometimes I thought they fought just so they *could* make up and it was so obvious; the two of them were so madly in love it was almost too much to bear.

Sounds of the baby whimpering came through on the monitor. "Babe?" I called across the lawn to where Harrison was watering the potted seed from the lemon tree we'd planted, its tiny green sprout barely out of the dirt.

"Yes, love?" he'd called back.

"The baby is waking up; do you want to go up and check on her?" I asked, knowing he loved for her to see his face after a nap.

He made his way back toward me and leaned down to kiss me before setting the watering can beside my chair. "We're going to need to bring that pot in and put a dome on it before winter."

"I think you're right. It will do well on a windowsill if it's got some humidity."

"Love you." He headed toward the patio door just as the sounds of the baby rustling again grew louder. "I'm coming, darling!" Harrison exclaimed as he picked up his pace.

"Love you!" I called out in his direction.

Just as Harrison disappeared inside, Emma and Lawrence came through the gate into the side yard. They'd gotten engaged just last month, and soon after began discussing starting a family together. She'd been adamant that it would be best if our children were close in age, just an excuse I'm sure, but good on her nonetheless for going after what she wanted.

"We've got cold salad; I'll just pop it in the fridge," Lawrence said as he walked through toward the kitchen, while Emma plopped down in the chair beside me.

"What's new with ya?" she asked.

"Not too much. We spent the morning at the park and Harrison's just gone up to check on the baby."

Just then I heard his voice through the monitor as he entered her room, putting my finger to my lips to quiet Emma so I could listen in.

"Hi, my darling, how are you? Daddy's here," he cooed, then I heard him kiss her. "Are you ready to go downstairs and join the party? Mummy's waiting for you, yes she is." I heard him say, "Who's a big girl?" and assumed he must have lifted her from her crib. He kissed her again repeatedly, his smooching sounds barely loud enough to hear over her own cooing. "Oh, is that so? Do we need a new nappy?" he asked.

"He's so good with her," Emma said. "I hope when the time comes, Lawrence is that involved."

"He's really such a good father. I knew he would be, but he's exceeded every expectation I ever had."

More garbled baby sounds were followed once again by Harrison's soft slow accent. "Okay, we've got a clean nappy and a very happy girl, don't we? Come on then, darling, let's get you back to Mummy. I know she misses you. Yes, she does." His voice started to grow fainter as he must have picked her up and headed toward the door. "I just love you to bits, darling, yes I do. Little Miss Luna Emilia is *Daddy's* girl, isn't she? Did you know your mummy named you after the moon 'cause it's one of Daddy's favorite things?"

YOU BRING ME HOME.

Acknowledgements

First of all, I'd like to thank me. I'm proud of myself for sticking with this project through unimaginable grief and the loss of Oscar. Even when grief and being overwhelmed tried its hardest to get me to quit, I persevered. Without my unrelenting and tenacious pursuit of not only finishing Alice and Harrison's story, but of reaching a broader audience and chasing my goals every single day, the need for these acknowledgements wouldn't exist. I've learned that being an indie author is not for the weak, and I've shown myself in the last two years that focusing on the goal, chasing the dream, and never giving up is how some of the most rewarding things in life are achieved.

To my mother, I love you the absolute *most* of the most. There aren't words that could accurately convey how thankful I am for you. Hope this one doesn't make you blush too much. xo

Many thanks go to the family and friends who cheered for me after the release of *She Lives in Daydreams*. The love and support you show me fuels the fire for me to continue writing, and to continue on this path where my imagination leads, and I simply follow.

To my editors, my graphic designers, and my sounding boards, thank you for loving me through the worry, the revisions, the chaos, and the shenanigans. More importantly, thank you for believing in me. It's made all the difference.

My sincere and heartfelt thanks as always, go to H. For not only being my muse, a source of unbridled joy, and the catalyst for this little writing career of mine, but for being someone worth looking up to and a constant sunny day in a world running rampant with darkness. Merely thanking you seems so insufficient for the ways you inspire me every single day. You've changed my life, and the way I view myself, and I'm not sure my thanks will ever be enough.

To The Spaniards Inn, who've been a source of inspiration for me for such a long time, I appreciate you so much. You've been so supportive and have tolerated all my many comments of longing to be there on Instagram. One day, I'll spend an entire day in your garden basking in the sunshine of the Heath with a Shirley Temple in one hand and a good book in the other. And if I'm really lucky, H. just might stroll in and sit down with me.

The real hardcore ride or dies (in no particular order): Zeralda, Sarah, Kristen, Heather L, Janine, Amy, Cynthia, Ronja, Amanda, Morgan, Barbie, Niamh, Ashley, Coco, Dannii, Kelly, Lacey, Lesley, Kay, Carrie, Krissy, Debbi, Gina, Miranda, Sunny, Lori, Esther, Susan—my goodness there are so many of you. I know I'm forgetting someone. Forgive me, you all know I'm a scatterbrain. Most days it's you lot that keep me afloat. Your love, support, kind words, and encouragement have pushed me over hurdles, through roadblocks, and into my true potential. I love you all so much more than you know. Thank you.

Undying gratitude goes to all my Harries, old and new, who were there before *She Lives in Daydreams* existed, and those of you who have surrounded me in love since. You are always there around the clock when there's something new (or old) to be excited or commiserate about. We're spread far and wide across this planet, and come from every background imaginable, but are bound together by a single shared interest. Thank you for always welcoming me, laughing with me, and supporting me every step of the way. I can only hope that I've made you feel the same way.

I want to remind folks of two things and caution of a third. First, the word Fiction, as defined by Merriam-Webster states: Something invented by the imagination or feigned. And second, the word Daydream is defined as follows: A pleasant visionary usually wishful creation of the imagination.
These stories were never meant to be real or believable. They were meant to be an escape. In the future, I urge you not to take things so seriously.

For anyone I missed, and I'm sure there are a few, please know that your

support never ceases to amaze and delight me. I appreciate it, and you,
so much.

Potential Triggers

Please be advised, this book may contain other triggers for you that are not listed here.
These are the most blatant.

Abandonment
Miscarriage
Alcohol/Drug Abuse
Addiction
Anxiety
Betrayal
Cheating/Adulterous Behaviors
Criticism
Death/Dying
Depression
Divorce
Explicit Language/Swearing
Gaslighting
Grief
Loneliness
Loss
Pregnancy
Rejection
Same-sex Relationships
Sexual Encounters
Slurs
Teenage Pregnancy
Violence
Vomiting

Please, always put your mental and emotional health first.

Photo by Ann Marie Ford for amfordphotography.com

About the Author

Nakia Cramer is an American author born and raised on the coast of Maine. When she's not writing, Nakia enjoys music, photography, kayaking, and spending time in nature observing the wildlife that surrounds her Maine lakefront home, as well as traveling to the Gulf Coast and daydreaming of one day visiting the UK.

Follow along with Nakia on social media!
On Facebook at AuthorNakiaC
And on Instagram, X/Twitter, and TikTok at AuthorNakia
Nakia is also on Goodreads!